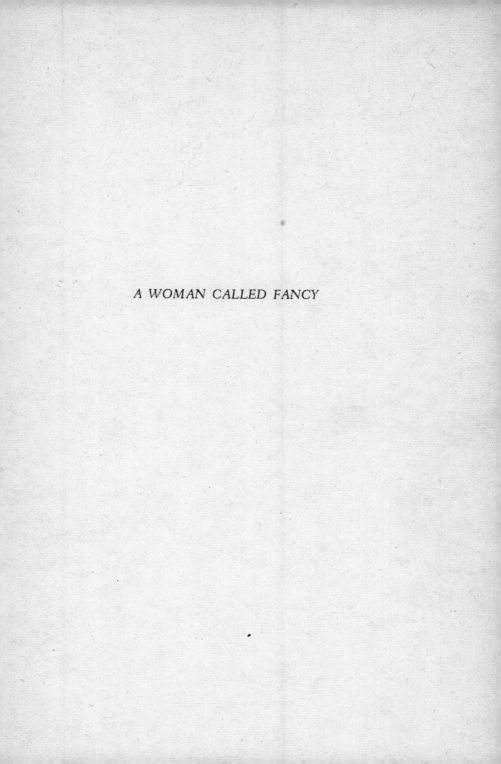

A WOMAN CALLED FANCY

FRANK YERBY

A WOMAN CALLED FANCY

THE DIAL PRESS  NEW YORK, N.Y.

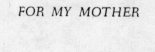

FOR MY MOTHER

A WOMAN CALLED FANCY

1

THE WILLIAMSONS' FARM lay on a hillside so that when it rained the water ran down and away from it. In fifty years it had worn out and starved out the three families who had tried to work it. The Williamsons were the fourth.

From where she lay, half hidden in the rank Johnson grass, Fancy could see the gaunt figure of her brother, Randy, bent tiredly over the handles of the plow. He moved along behind Mike, their lone mule, an animal so old that Pap, in his better moods was fond of swearing he'd bought the critter offen a man called Noah, who'd brung him to Carolina on the Ark; and after him came Maw Williamson, her gnarled hands busy with the cotton seed. She looked, Fancy thought bitterly, a mite older than the mule, and not half as human.

It was hot. That was bad, Fancy knew. It had just turned planting time and already it was hot. Above her the sky was yellow-white, every bit of the blue washed out by the sunglare, and nowhere was there any cloud. Fancy narrowed her deep blue eyes to a squint, and peered upward into the limitless depths of the sky. Up there,

I

tiny black dots moved in slow, lazy circles, so high up that only when she squinted could she see them.

"Damned old buzzards," Fancy muttered. "Circling up there a-waiting. Well, you won't get me. Rest of my folks can hang around here and rot; but not me. I'm going somewheres. Down to Augusta, maybe. Find myself a rich gentleman acquaintance and marry him —just you wait!"

She looked away from the all but invisible turkey buzzards, and picked up the ragged seventh-grade reader that lay upon her flat stomach. She had read it through so many times that she knew it by heart. And that, considered in its rightful place in the scale of things, was an accomplishment to be compared with the moving of a very small mountain. In seven generations of Williamsons, Fancy was the first ever to learn to read and write. She had done it herself, alone and unaided. If her pronunciation was often widely at variance with the actual sound of the words, the fact remained that Fancy could read a newspaper, on those rare occasions when anybody had a newspaper, and was always called upon to interpret the mysterious scrawls upon paper which occasionally came from the more adventurous sons and daughters of the hill people who had managed to escape.

But she put the book down after a moment and again stared up into the yellow-white sky. This time she did not squint, but looked upward with the opaque gaze of the dreamer. There were vague pictures moving in the light-flooded depths of space, and she was in each of them, striding lightly, gaily among handsome and beautifully dressed people, stopping now and again to exchange a word with some of the finest. Most of the people in these magic lantern pictures that Fancy's imagination cast upon the sky were young, handsome men. And they had one thing in common: they all adored Fancy.

This was the gulf that she had unwittingly opened between herself and her own: the wordless have not the materials for dreams.

The wind shifted, and jerked her back to reality. It came up the hillside from the hog pen below, and the smell of the razor-back hogs and the slops upon which they were fed tugged at her nostrils. Fancy brought a grimy palm up and covered them. Then the wind died down, and the only smells left were the scent of the rank grass, and the sweat in her ragged dress.

Do nice folks sweat? she wondered. Reckon they must. But most likely they bathe twice a week and change all their clothes and use powder and perfume and even paint. Maw says that it's wicked to paint, but if I had my druthers—I'd druther be wicked than ugly.

Fancy lay there a long time, until some of the yellow-white began to spill out of the sky, and the blue crept back in and deepened. Turning her head a little, she could see that Maw and Randy and the mule were beginning to lose color, to blacken against the rim of the sky, the edges of them sharpening. After a while they were like those figures that that crazy artist who had traveled through the hills with the medicine show had cut from black cardboard with his little scissors. Only they moved still, jerkily, and above them was the pale glimmer of a star.

Fancy sighed and sat up. Time to be getting along home. Time to wake up Pap—if she could wake him up by now, after a day of sitting on the porch pulling on his brown jug. That was all Pap ever did. Life had put a curse on him, so that nothing he ever did came out quite right, and he had many sorrows that required daily drowning. In the meantime Maw and Randy ran the farm, with a little help from Fancy when they could catch her long enough to make her do it—which wasn't often, for among the things that Fancy understood was that a person who didn't know when to give up was a fool.

She started downward toward the house, the Johnson grass rippling against her skirt, walking slowly with short, mincing little steps, which she told herself was the way a lady walked. She was, if anyone had been there to see her, a sight to see. But there was no one there—no one to see the slight, small girl, just turned nineteen, whose hair was blacker than the wing feathers of a rain crow, and whose eyes, oddly, were the exact color of the evening sky come harvest time. Not that there hadn't been plenty of hill men who hadn't remarked these features, together with the mouth that was a mite too big for her face, and was the dark red of wild cherries, and looked a little sullen in repose.

Fancy had had her share of suitors—and more than her share it

3

seemed to some of the other lonesome hill girls' way of thinking. They had come in droves: big, rangy boys with the knots of muscles jerking above their lean jaws, their eyes hot and honing; substantial farmers, already turned fifty and more, lean as the hills, with money in their pockets to buy Fancy aprons of crisp calico—even a preaching man or two. But Fancy would have none of them, much to Pap's outraged disgust. At nineteen, Fancy was already an old maid by hill standards. Maw, for instance, had borne her first stillborn infant before her sixteenth birthday, and continued to produce blue, strangled, pitiful little bundles of flesh, until finally, late in her thirties, Randy and later Fancy had miraculously survived. It was this long run of bad luck with children—valuable in the hills as hands—that had made a drinking man of Pap.

Now, in his old age, Pap had pinned all his hopes on Fancy. He had given her encouragement and help in shooing away the boys, but when she just as stubbornly refused to form a connection with some upright widower of sixty with money enough for Pap to borrow for seed and debts and whiskey, he had felt the sharpness of the serpent's tooth. Yet persuasion, threats, and even his big razor strop, availed him not. Fancy ran and hid, or stood and fought. At nineteen she was single still, and nary a prospect in sight.

The shadows lengthened out before her, blue on the path that led down to the house. Finally from a little rise she could see the house itself. She stood there looking at it. It had been built by the second of the three families who had preceded them, and it was old. To anybody else besides Fancy, that wouldn't have mattered much: most of the farmhouses were old. But Fancy dimly guessed that a house didn't have to be dilapidated or shabby; there must be houses with their shutters firmly attached, and whose roofs didn't leak. Ten years ago, when she was nine, the last porch step had rotted through, and Pap had been gittin' around to fixing it ever since. There were boards missing from the porch itself and the roof of it slanted down at a crazy angle, where two of the posts had been broken in a windstorm some four years before. Pap had just looked at that and picked up his jug. He hadn't even threatened to fix them.

Maw was too tired now to replace the oiled paper over the windows, so in the wintertime they froze and in the summer the bugs

4

feasted off their unprotected hides. The house had never been painted in all its long life, and wind and rain had scoured it to a weathered gray that fitted into the age-old, tired hills, and which in spring, the flowering wisteria vine softened almost into beauty.

It was spring now, and the wisteria blew pale violet up to the mossy shingles of the roof; but Fancy couldn't see that beauty. Her reaction to the house in which she had been born was very simple: she hated it with all her heart.

She stood there looking at it for long minutes, then she came on down the path. When she was close, she saw that Pap wasn't asleep after all. He was sitting on a cracker box behind the screen of the wisteria talking to old man Wilkins.

Fancy's breath stopped still. Of all her suitors, old man Wilkins was the most persistent. She could see him now, sitting on the porch rail, stooped over like a red, bald turkey buzzard, moving his store-bought teeth loosely around in his mouth as he talked. Because of those teeth, nothing he said ever came out clearly. He talked, Fancy thought, as though he had a mouthful of hot mush. His faded blue shirt was as clean and pressed as ever, and his jeans were shiny at the knees and in the seat. His remaining wisps of gray hair were slicked down as usual with grease, and he fanned himself with his straw hat.

Oh no! Fancy thought bitterly. Oh God, oh Jesus, not again!

But it wasn't one of those things that running away from would help. Better to make an end to it right now. Better to tell that old buzzard that no matter what kind of a bargain he and Pap had struck between them it wouldn't do any good because she would never marry him.

Don't want an old man like him, she thought. Want myself a young man with blood in his veins, and not one of those hillbillies neither. A man who's polite and talks fair, and who'll take off his hat to me and bow and say, "Howdy, Miss Fancy—deelighted to make your acquaintance."

Old man Wilkins was grinning at her now, his store-bought teeth clicking up and down with the effort.

"Howdy, child," he snickered. "My but you're a sight for sore eyes!"

5

Fancy didn't answer him. His voice, she decided, sounded exactly like the whinnying of a horse. She stared at him, the corners of her mouth drooping a little into a grimace of acute distaste.

"Fan!" Pap wheezed; "ain't I done learned you to speak when you're spoken to?"

"See nothing, say nothing," Fancy said tartly. "And I sure Lord don't see anything right now—leaseways not nothing much."

"Now look ahere—" Pap began; but old man Wilkins laid a restraining hand on his arm.

"Young gals is like fillies," he whispered; "lots of spirit. Pays to gentle 'em. Take your time and they can be broke. . . ."

"Not by you!" Fancy spat. "Not never by the likes of you!"

"Now look ahere, Fan," Pap said in his whiskery quaver. "Mister Wilkins just paid you a mighty high honor. He come way over here to ask me for your hand. That ain't to be treated lightly—Mister Wilkins is a fine, upstanding man—a pillar of the church, and mighty respected in the community. . . ."

"Mister Wilkins," Fancy said coldly, "is an old goat who don't remember that he's sixty-five years old and that I could be his granddaughter. He may be a pillar of the church, all right, 'cause he spends most of his time leaning up against one, pinching young girls as they come out of meeting. And if he didn't have a heap more nerve than he's got common sense, he'd know I wouldn't have him on a Christmas tree."

Pap stood up majestically, swaying like an oak in a high wind.

"It'll pay you to curb that tongue of yourn, young lady," he growled; " 'cause I already done give my consent."

Fancy stared at her father, her blue eyes widening.

"Pap—you didn't!"

"Yes I did," Pap said. "Time you stopped being so dadblamed ungrateful towards the folks what bore and raised you. Mister Wilkins already promised to take care of most of my heaviest burdens. . . ."

There was white fire in the blue eyes now, and seeing it, Pap quailed.

"Now Fan—" he quavered.

"Now nothing! So you aim to sell me like a horse to straighten

6

out the mess your drinking got you into! And I'm s'posed to be grateful. For what, Pap? Tell me that. I never owned a dress or a pair of shoes what you paid for. I ain't never had nothing that you give me, except a mighty heap o' lickings! I'm s'posed to be grateful for that? I'm s'posed to be proud of the fact that all over the hills I'm known as that no-'count Rand Williamson's daughter? Don't you reckon I get tired of folks pitying me 'cause I come from dirt and ain't never going nowheres—leaseways so they think. But I am going somewheres, and not with this horny old buzzard, neither! I'll see the both of you laid out with your big toes pinned together before I'll let this old fool lay a finger on me!"

She whirled then and fled into the house, leaving a trail of half strangled sobs behind her.

"I'm mightily sorry," Pap said. "But don't you worry none. Her maw'll be home in a little while, and she'll talk some sense into her."

"She better," old man Wilkins growled. "You already bled three hundred hard-earned dollars out of me with your promises, and I ain't waiting a day longer—not nary another day!"

"Now don't fret yourself," Pap said soothingly, "Fan'll marry you all right. Just you wait till her maw comes home. . . ."

Hearing these words from where she stood just inside the hall, Fancy knew for the first time in her life the real meaning of despair. Maw wouldn't side with her either—not with so much money involved. Maw was an honest woman who hated debt. She'd be sorry to see Fancy wed to this sickening old man, but not sorry enough to discount the advantages of the match. And Randy would be worse than hopeless. After years of struggling with the wornout washed away soil of their farm, he'd be willing to sell his sister for much less than that.

It would be dark in a little while—long before Maw and Randy came, Fancy reckoned. For a long time now, she had been telling herself that she was going to get away—that she was going down out of these red Carolina hills, down to where the Savannah River flowed slow and peaceful in the sun. Across the river on the Georgia side was Augusta—the biggest city that Fancy had ever heard tell of. There the rich, handsome young men she had dreamed of would be waiting. It had been a vague dream, more wished for than ever consciously planned. But old man Wilkins with his yellow false teeth clicking in his big, ugly mouth had put an end to that. The dream was a dream no longer. It was a plan.

It took her only a moment to gather her belongings into a bundle —her other dress, and the nice underthings that were not, like all her others, made of floursacking. Then she stole into the kitchen, and felt for the loose brick in the chimney. It gave under her fingers, and she drew out her treasure—the five dollars and sixty-two cents she had managed to save over a period of more than three years. She wrapped it in a bit of cloth and tucked it in her bosom. Then she went back into the hall and waited.

It wouldn't be fair to run away before Maw and Randy had had their say. Maybe she had misjudged them. Maybe they'd stick up for her after all. But if they didn't . . .

She saw them coming slowly, tiredly down the path just as she reached the doorway. Randy shuffled along, leading the ancient mule, and Maw walked with her head and shoulders bent, the perfect picture of the kind of weariness that has stopped hoping for rest or for anything better. Maw had stopped wishing, stopped dreaming so many years ago that the life had just about gone out of her. She didn't even talk much any more—as though even words cost her more effort than she could rightly afford.

Looking at her now, Fancy felt a wild surge of pity for this gaunt rack of bones and meager flesh that had given her life. Poor Maw, she mused, if I leave her, reckon she'll pretty nigh give up the ghost—sure Lord ain't nothing much left of her now.

I can't leave her, I can't! Fancy thought. But if she agrees with Paw she'll be sending me away anyhow—and the only thing I'll change will be the place where I'll be going. Old man Wilkins' place is nigh onto twenty miles from here anyhow, and Augusta ain't much further. Oh, Maw—it's up to you, now. You can lose me or keep me just by saying the word. . . .

"Sary—" Pap began.

"Yes?" Maw said tiredly, "yes, Rand?"

"Mister Wilkins is here on a mighty important errand," Paw said. "He's come to ask us for our little Fan. . . ."

Hypocrite! Fancy thought wildly. Mealy-mouthed hypocrite—why . . .

8

Maw turned her watery gray eyes upon the face of Fancy's ancient suitor.

"Well, now," she drawled, "I don't rightly know what to say. . . ."

"I'd be mighty good to your little girl," Wilkins put in quickly.

"Don't doubt that," Maw said; "only it 'pears to me that there's a mighty big difference 'twixt your ages."

"There was a big difference 'twixt ourn," Paw said.

"Twelve years," Maw said softly; "but Mister Wilkins got a much longer lead on Fan than that. 'Pears to me . . ."

" 'Pears to me he ought to be interested in a woman, not no girl," Randy put in hotly.

"Now wait a minute, you two," Paw growled. "There's a mite more to this than meets the eye. Mister Wilkins has agreed to take over our biggest debts, and it looks like to me that that ought to be thought about. . . ."

Fancy stared at her mother in the gathering darkness.

Oh, Maw, no! she prayed. Oh, Jesus, Maw—say no!

"Well now—" Maw began.

"There's another matter what ain't even been mentioned," old man Wilkins put in, "and what sure Lord ought to be. Right from the first Rand here entertained my suit right kindly—so much so that I let him have money from time to time. And that money up to today amounts to a mite more'n three hundred dollars—which ain't to be sneezed at, Miz Williamson."

Sarah Williamson turned and stared at her husband.

"Oh, Paw—no!" she breathed.

Pap squirmed upon his cracker box.

"It's a fact, Sary," he whispered.

"Of all the low down, ornery—" Randy began.

"Hush child," Maw said gently. She turned back to old man Wilkins. " 'Pears to me," she said, "that you done took unfair advantage of Paw's weakness. But be that as it may, a debt's a debt—and we ain't got a Chinaman's chance of paying it off. Mister Wilkins, I give you my consent—mighty unwillingly. When you want the hitching to take place?"

"Right now—tonight!" old man Wilkins said; "I already waited nigh onto three years and . . ."

9

Fancy didn't wait to hear any more. She went down the hall and out the back door. She made a wide circle out and away from the house until she came to the place where the pines made night shadows across the little hollow where the hog pen was, and went down into that running. From there on, it was downhill all the way. Going down made it get dark faster. She was going downward and away from the setting sun. By the time the slope had lessened into near-flatness, all the blue had gone out of the sky and the stars hung low over her head and blazed.

She kept going. Like all the hill people, she was accustomed to walking miles on the simplest errand. But this one, she knew, was far from simple. Without even thinking about it, Fancy realized that she had taken her life in her two hands.

Have to get myself a job, she thought. Don't rightly know what kind—ain't never been learned to do nothing useful. I can sew a little and clean and cook—but down there they've got colored help to do those things. Maybe I can get myself a job in one of the mills—they don't hire nothing but white folks for that. . . . But that won't be no good either. Never meet anybody big or important like that. If I did they wouldn't pay me no attention sitting in front of a machine. I'd be a lint head, mill trash. Nope, got to think of something else. . . .

But thinking about it didn't help. The world past the rim of her hills was beyond Fancy. The very people who inhabited it were a strange breed, who refused to take exact shape even in her dreams. Besides, this part of the trail was strange to her. She needed all her attention to stay on it. Here the signs were less definite—much of it was overgrown, forming one of the barriers that the hill people kept between themselves and the outside. Over trails like these change passed but slowly, so that much of the speech and most of the customs of Queen Elizabeth's time were still a part of Fancy's life. The journey she was making at night stretched over more than miles—it covered centuries, too.

By the time that the black had begun to gray out of the sky, and the stars were dimming a little, Fancy gave it up. She was beyond pursuit now. And the ache in her legs crawled upward until she hurt all over and the tiredness settled down like a weight upon her eyelids, so that several times she lost the trail. Finally she moved off it and lay down under an oak. The grass grew tall and sweet-smelling there, and before she got through the first line of her prayers, she was asleep.

When she woke up, the whole world was washed in sunlight. Looking out from under the shadow that the oak branches made was like staring into a haze of gold. Over the field of high, waving grass, insects danced, suspended like motes in the light, and the air droned with their humming. On the branches above her, a blue-jay scolded noisily, and a cardinal flashed from leaf shade to tree shadow tracing a trajectory like flame across the sunny places.

Fancy got up quickly and started to run out into all that excess of light. It seemed to be waiting for her, that wide, bright world, splashed with sun and dappled with shade. Even after she had no more breath left for running, she continued to walk very fast, until before she knew it, she was out of the hills altogether and there was the river before her, slow-flowing and muddy-golden in the midday sun.

Fancy stood quite still and gazed at the Savannah. It was the largest body of water she had ever seen in her life. From where she stood she could see the willows trailing their branches into the water on the Georgia side, and higher up, as the banks rose steeply along the Sandhill, the dogwood trees making spring snow, among the darker pines. She turned finally, and started downstream toward the bridges in the distance. She walked slowly, prolonging her moment, half out of fear, and half out of the unconscious desire to preserve it.

Then the bridge lay before her, arching up over the sluggish river, over the little fishing skiffs that drifted slowly downstream, toward where the spires of the churches and the tops of the taller buildings of Augusta showed above the dark green of the trees.

Fancy started up over the footwalk of the bridge. In the middle she stopped and gazed down curiously at one of the fishermen sleeping in a rowboat below. The man was black—inky-, sooty-black. Fancy stared at him with breath-gone fascination. In some of the lower hill towns there were signs: "Nigger, don't let the sun set on you in this town." Or: "Nigger—read and run; and if you can't read—run anyhow." But in the section of Carolina where Fancy lived, there was no need for such signs. Life was hard enough for white people; there was nothing for a black man to do. So it was that the black fisherman sleeping in his rowboat was the first Negro that Fancy had seen in all her life.

She came down into McKinney Street, and walked down it until the bustle of Broad Street attracted her attention. It was packed from one side to the other with the wagons of the countryfolk come to town, for it was Saturday, the day for marketing. Fancy moved among the throngs of calico-clad women, and men in shiny blue jeans, their straw hats pushed back from their foreheads, engaging in long, slow talk on the sidewalks. The talk, what she could catch of it, was the same as at home—the weather, crops—a run of bad luck with the stock.

It came to Fancy suddenly that she was hungry, so she stepped quickly into a little restaurant run by an enormous Irishwoman, and parted with a single nickel for a cup of coffee and a roll. Then she went on east toward the spire of the Confederate Monument, reaching it just as the Dinner Car of the horse-drawn railroad pulled out for its run up to the Sandhill. The car bore a red flag, and was drawn by horses laden with sleigh bells so that they jangled musically at every step. But it was the people on the car that caused Fancy to stop and stare in open-mouthed wonder. The ladies were dressed all in white for the most part, and bore the sauciest little frilled umbrellas in their hands. Their bonnets were lace-edged too, or, if they were straw, had stuffed birds or bunches of artificial fruit upon them. All the ladies wore bustles, and their waists were scarcely a hand's span in width. Most of the men wore tall silk hats, and Prince Albert frock coats; a few were wearing the newer sack coat; but to Fancy, the strangest thing about them was their mustaches. The men of her native hills were either clean-shaven or fully bearded; therefore, to Fancy, this array of handlebars, mutton chops, burnsides, and even an imperial or two was a sight to see.

The car passed on up the street, and Fancy walked over to the monument, crossing one half of the street that Augustians proudly boasted was the widest street in the world. She stood there a long time gazing at the figure of the Confederate private, resting upon his musket and gazing with sad dignity back over the lost years. Circling the monument she read the names of General Lee and Stonewall Jackson under the figures that pictured them, and stared

12

uncomprehendingly at the statues of Generals Cobb and Walker. She had heard about G'n'l Lee, and Stonewall Jackson, for Pap had fit somewhat ingloriously in that war; but the other two men meant nothing to her. She reckoned that they must have been great men, too, and turned away from the monument.

She had no aim in mind—no conscious plan. All she wanted to do now, today, was to see the city. Tomorrow was time enough for making plans. So she strolled slowly down Jackson Street until she came to Greene, and wandered eastward until she had passed all the lovely old houses, and had reached a place where the houses were shabbier and the speech of the people sounded foreign to her ear. She stared curiously at all the old Irishwomen, wearing quilted silk hoods of black, with "goffered" muslin ruffles around their faces, their stooped shoulders bent under their shawls despite the heat, and their work-worn fingers busy with rosaries, as they hurried to midday mass.

Fancy couldn't make them out, but she accepted them without too much wonder. This was her new world, and if such people lived in it they must be part of it.

Half an hour later, she had left "Canaan" and "Dublin," as the Irish sections were known, behind her, and was resting in the shadow of a house in the "Terry," watching the hordes of Negroes stream past, laughing, skylarking or simply walking. Fancy marveled at the black washerwomen who balanced huge bundles of snowy linen atop their heads, going by at a steady pace and sucking peacefully on their corncob pipes at the same time.

Then she straightened up, staring at the slant-eyed oriental, complete with a straw hat in the shape of a low cone, and a queue hanging down his back, moving with delicate little steps that scarcely stirred his bright-colored, baggy trousers. Behind him a mulatto girl walked at a respectful distance, and in her arms was a child whose hair curled more softly than her own tight kinks, but whose eyes had a definite slant.

Augusta sure is some place, Fancy thought. But before she could think any more, the roar of an angry bass voice sounded inside one of the houses, punctuated by high-pitched liquid tones. Then the door burst open, and a slim Chinese flew out of it, propelled by a massive boot, to sprawl in the street almost in front of the spot

13

where she stood. The Chinese picked himself up and set off down the street at great speed. A moment later the door opened wide, and a man strode out on the veranda.

He was quite the biggest man Fancy had ever seen—and the handsomest, she decided a second later. He was dressed in a linen sack coat, and had a broad-brimmed Panama on his head. His hair was long, and dark, and his mustache was simply terrifying. Fancy guessed that he stood well over six feet tall, and the anger in his eyes made them magnificent.

"Where'd that Chink bastard go?" he roared; then his gaze fell upon Fancy. She could see the anger leaving his eyes. They widened and light leaped into them. He looked her up and down slowly, and nodded his massive head.

"Where'd you come from, little gal?" he said.

Fancy pointed indecisively.

"Over there," she whispered.

"Where's over there?" the big man demanded.

"Ca'lina," Fancy said.

"You got any folks in Augusta?"

"Nosir. I'm all alone here," Fancy said.

The big man put his head back and laughed aloud. It was a tremendous sound. To Fancy it sounded like thunder. It made her shiver a little as if she was cold; but she couldn't be cold, not in the pleasant sunshine.

"Duke," the big one chuckled, "this sure Lord is your lucky day!"

"Duke?" Fancy said. "Who's Duke?"

"I'm Duke," the big man said. "Reckon I'd better introduce myself proper like. Duke Ellis, at your service, Ma'am. Now what might be your name?"

"I'm Fancy," Fancy murmured.

"Damned right you are, but what's your name?"

"That's it—Fancy. Fancy Williamson."

Duke stared at her.

"Honeychild," he breathed; "I ain't never heard tell of a name what was more fitting and proper. Come along now—take my arm."

Fancy hesitated then slipped her arm easily through his, and they started up Campbell Street away from the Terry.

"Ain't nobody ever told you," Duke teased, "that blue eyes don't go with black hair? Appears to me that your folks kind of mixed you up. But babydoll do I like the mixture!"

"Why'd you do it?" Fancy asked.

"Why'd I do what, Fancygal?"

"Kick that poor Chinaman."

"That blamed Chink ruined four of my best shirts. Got 'em all the way from Atlanta—ruffled fronts, too. So naturally he had it coming. Let's don't worry about him—we've got to attend to you—"

"To me?" Fancy echoed blankly.

"Yes, baby—to you. You're a mighty pretty little gal; but old Duke can't be seen round town with nobody dressed like you."

"What's wrong with my dress?" Fancy pouted.

"Everything," Duke said flatly. "Honeychild, you're as pretty as a speckled setter pup, but you just ain't got no style. And my lady friends got to have style."

"It's the only dress I got, except one," Fancy said sadly.

"That's all right, Fan," Duke said; "from now on you're going to have lots of dresses. We're going to stop by my house for a minute to pick up my buggy, then we're going straight up to J. B. White's Department Store. When we come out of there, ain't going to be a lady in Augusta finer than you—just you wait."

Fancy stared at him speculatively.

"You must be rich," she said.

"Now ain't you a smart one," Duke chuckled.

"Well—aren't you?"

"You're looking at the second richest man in Augusta, Georgia—right next to old man Phinizy himself. Four years ago wasn't nothing in my pockets except holes. Then a damyankee come down here and showed me how to get turpentine out of them trees on that nogood place of my paw's. Now they call me the Turpentine King. Folks what wouldn't spit on me before, bowing and scraping now, and siding up to offer me their hands. Damn them!" Duke added savagely. "Think I forget mighty damn easy!"

Fancy stared at him admiringly. In the back part of her mind there was just the ghost of a suspicion that it wasn't quite the proper thing for her to do to let this big man buy her dresses. But if she was going to be his wife, it wouldn't make much difference; besides whatever Maw and Pap considered proper didn't count any more.

It Lord hadn't been proper for them to sell her like a hog or a sheep to that filthy old man Wilkins.

His wife. Mrs. Duke Ellis. Mighty fine ring to that. Come to think of it, he hadn't said anything about getting hitched. But he must have it in mind, she decided, or else why was he buying her clothes?

Two hours later, she came out of White's Department Store in a happy daze. She wore a dress that equaled and surpassed the ones that she had seen on those fine ladies this morning. Fortunately, fitting her had been an easy matter. Of course, she could hardly breathe with that corset pinching her waist so; but anyone with half an eye could see that her waist was slimmer than any other girl's on Broad Street. In a store window, she caught a glimpse of her bustle. Lord but she looked fine! And that little yellow straw hat, with the brim bent down back and front and that bunch of artificial flowers waving on the top. She'd never even seen a hat like this one, let alone worn one.

Duke's big hands were filled with bundles. Inside those bundles were six other dresses, innumerable petticoats, and the very finest underwear, trimmed with the nicest lace. Course, she had blushed a little when he'd bought those things, but a man had a right to pick out the best things for his bride.

Duke strode along beside her, grinning, his big cigar clenched between his even, white teeth. When they came to the buggy, he put the bundles in the back and helped her up.

"We'll drive over to Doc Beale's drugstore and have a soda," he announced grandly, "then I'll take you around town to see the sights. Dinner at the Globe. That's the finest hotel in town. Can't nobody say that Duke Ellis don't treat his lady friends right."

Coming out of the drugstore, whose black marble soda fountain was still in that spring of 1880 one of the marvels of the city, always pointed out proudly to visitors, Fancy clung to Duke Ellis' arm and smiled up at him shyly.

"Reckon I'm fair about to bust," she said; "didn't reckon anything on earth could taste so good as that charcolate soda."

"Old Doc sure knows how to make 'em, and no mistake," Duke chuckled. "What you want to do now, little Fancygal?"

"Go riding," Fancy said without hesitation. "I'm plumb tuckered out from walking, and I'd sure admire to see more of Augusta."

"At your service, dollbaby," Duke said, and helped her up into the buggy.

He headed east, down Broad Street, pointing out the Monument that she had already seen, and the celebrated haunted pillar, with its black imprint of a human hand near the base.

"They say a nigger who was being sold down the river away from his folks left that print there in his own blood. Ever since then everybody who's tried to move it has died—leaseway that's what folks say. I don't hold with such talk myself; but it does seem kind of funny that when the hurricane blew down the old market that pillar was the only thing left. . . ."

"Poor fellow," Fancy said softly.

"He was only a nigger," Duke said complacently. "Can't work up much sympathy for them burr-headed bastards myself. But folks hereabouts is mightily superstitious. Take Wylly Barron, for instance. He runs that gambling house in the Atkinson Hotel down on Carmichael's Range. Well, old Wylly's got his mausoleum all waiting for him down in Magnolia Cemetery. Had it built fifteen years ago, when a poor devil what lost his last cent playing faro swore that Wylly wouldn't have a grave to lie in, then went home and blew out his brains. Shook Wylly up, that did. So he built that there fancy marble tomb of his, and made a will saying that after he's laid in it, the key is got to be thrown in the river. Looks like that tomb's going to have a long wait—Wylly's as healthy as a horse."

"You don't believe in luck and signs?" Fancy said.

"No, baby—just what's betwixt my ears, and underneath my right fist. That's all the luck a man needs."

"Reckon you're right," Fancy said.

Duke turned northward and pointed out the bales of cotton blocking the sidewalks on both side of Reynolds Street.

"Half the damned cotton in the world ends up right here, I reckon," he said. "Heck, it's getting late—and it's a long drive up to my cottage on the Hill."

Fancy stared at him. Then she shrugged. Well, if he wanted to show her his cottage, she'd be glad to look at it. Maybe he wanted her to stay there until arrangements could be made for the wedding. Sure would be a fine thing to be married to such a man as Duke— yes sir, it sure would. . . .

Duke swung the buggy in a wide semicircle that brought them through Telfair Street. As they passed the First Presbyterian Church, Fancy caught his arm.

"A wedding!" she said; "oh, Duke, honey, do let's wait and see it!"

Duke pulled the horse up, and stared at the people coming out of the church. Then he frowned.

"Them God-damned Brantleys!" he growled. "Be a good thing if this town was to get shut of 'em once and for all."

Fancy didn't answer him. She was too busy staring at the Brantleys.

The bridegroom was a tall, thin man, who, despite the fact that he was still young—thirtyish, Fancy guessed—was almost as bald as old man Wilkins. And the bride, half hidden in clouds of white veiling, was a girl not much older than Fancy. She looked like an angel, all pink and white like Dresden china, with masses of hair like pure sunlight peeping out from under her veil. But, somehow, Fancy had the feeling that she didn't look happy—not the way a bride ought to.

Then, a moment later, she saw the reason. Behind the newly-weds walked a young man—much younger than the groom, with a face so sad that just looking at it made Fancy want to burst out crying. For the life of her, Fancy couldn't tear her gaze away from that face. It resembled the groom's face so strongly that Fancy had no trouble in deciding that they were brothers. And it wasn't a particularly handsome face, either—the cheekbones were too prominent, and the mouth too wide, and tight-lipped, and droopy at the corners. It was a rawboned kind of a face, sort of like the pictures of Abraham Lincoln, except that the coloring was different—fair, instead of dark, with light, chestnut-colored hair and blue eyes. But it was the sadness in it that caught Fancy.

Bet my bottom dollar, she thought, that he's in love with her too!

"So Ty got her!" Duke chuckled suddenly. "Damned if I ain't glad. Ty ain't a bad sort. But that there Court . . ."

"Court's the light-haired one, with the sad face?" Fancy asked.

"Yep. And he's all Brantley—a no-good son of a biscuit eater if there ever was one. That old man's their paw—Jeff Brantley, and them two sad-looking female critters is the Brantley gals, Agnes and Saphira, what no man around here would have on a bet. That good-looking blond boy in the back is Philemon, and that human iceberg walking 'longside of him is his wife, Martha."

"Who's the bride?" Fancy asked.

"Oh, that's Fern—Fern Vance. Used to spark her myself, once in a while. Poor thing, she had a hard row to hoe, being Matt Vance's daughter—and then getting herself hitched to a Brantley . . ."

"You don't think much of the Brantleys, do you?" Fancy said.

"Don't nobody hereabouts think much of 'em. One of the oldest families in the State—and used to be one of the richest. Only they're poor as Job's turkey hen now—which still don't stop 'em from trying to lord it over everybody else. Court and Ty've been feuding over Fern for years—Court was ahead, I think, till he got highfalutin notions and went away to Harvard College. Ty made good use of his time. . . ."

"You seem like you like Ty," Fancy observed.

"I do. Only Brantley worth his salt. Holds his cards close to his nose and his liquor like a gentleman. But that little snot-nose, Court —hell's bells, baby, I used to lick the pants off of him twice a week when we was kids, him and that Tommy Wilson, whose paw was pastor of that church. Him and Court was great pals—always mooning around reading poetry and stuff. Only Woodrow—that's his real name—not Tommy—has run off to Atlanta to be a lawyer. Heard tell he's gone into politics—"

"Why don't you like the Brantleys?" Fancy said. "They look like real nice folks."

"Well they ain't. There's a saying hereabouts: 'The Brantley women die by drowning, the men by bullets, fire and the sword; but no good ever come out of the breed—not yet nor ever will.'"

"Who said that?" Fancy demanded.

"Old Jeff, himself. Said it so often that everybody in town's got it down word for word just like I told you. And it's true, too. The Brantley women always do drown themselves. . . ."

"Why?" Fancy said.

"On account of their men. Them Brantleys sure got roving eyes and taking ways. You take Phil, for instance. He's got himself a highbrown down in shadetown and three off-color yard children. Only that Martha won't drown herself—she ain't got blood enough in her veins to care."

"I still don't see what you got against Court."

"Always held himself up as being so fine. Every time me or my brothers, Buck and Tom, would pass by Hiberion, he'd start his niggers to singing the 'druther song.'"

"The 'druther song'?" Fancy echoed blankly.

"'Druther be a nigger, and work like heck,'" Duke quoted bitterly, "'than a poor Georgia cracker with a long red neck.' So naturally, I had to lick him. Now I'm top dog around here, and them Brantleys is plumb played out, only they don't seem to realize it. Still hold themselves up mighty fine!"

"Sure that Vance girl ain't the reason why you hate 'em so?" Fancy teased.

"Heck no! Pretty as Fern is, she couldn't of married anybody else —not being Matt's daughter. Matt was one of the biggest carpetbaggers in the State, and him and that nigger-loving Rufus Bullock— our reconstruction governor, was thick as thieves at a lawyer's funeral. . . ."

This, Fancy decided, was getting kind of mixed up, so she didn't ask Duke any more questions. Instead, she sat very quietly in the buggy and watched the houses drop away behind her until they were passing by the Negro shanties on the lower end of Gwinnett Street. Then, as the street ran through a vacant field, Fancy saw the flare of torches on the back of a wagon, and the short, powerful figure of a man haranguing the Negroes from it.

"A medicine show!" she cried. "Oh, Duke, let's stop and watch!"

"Some other time, baby," Duke said; "we got things to do."

Fancy looked back over her shoulder at the man on the medicine wagon.

"What a funny little old man," she said.

"Heck, Wyche ain't old," Duke said. "He's thirty—the same age as me. He just looks that way. Funny thing about him—his folks are just about the richest people in Carolina—but Wyche ain't got a dime. His paw disowned him over some scrape he got into with a

mill gal. Old man Weathers owns just about half of them Spartanburg mills. . . ."

"You know everybody, don't you?" Fancy said admiringly.

"Just about. Only there's just one person I'm interested in getting
to know real good. And that party, little Fancygal—is you."

"Oh," Fancy said.

They drove up Walton Way past the miles of crepe myrtle that
would bloom later in the summer, hiding the greens in the center
of the street with their small, cerise blossoms, past the newer and
more imposing houses built by the merchants and businessmen who
had supplanted the old planter aristocracy, each with its white or
pink dogwood blossoming in the front yard, and the rows of yellow
jasmine, and flowering quince. As they approached the Sandhill
section, with its distinctive cottages, all the earth flamed with color:
giant magnolias towered heavenward, their branches bent under the
weight of blossoms the size of small cabbages, creamy-white and
heavy scented; spreading mimosa blew down the wind, with its
fragrant powderpuff blooms and fern-like foliage; here were the
smaller Japanese magnolias now, and weeping dwarf cherries, and
redbud trees that were like deep pink flame. Along walls and fences
the Cherokee roses twined, and golden masses of daffodil, crocus,
forsythia, and marigold threw back the light.

"Lord," Fancy said, "what a pretty place!"

"There ain't nowhere like Georgia in the spring, babydoll," Duke
said smugly. He sounded exactly as if he owned it all.

As one end of Lake Olmstead came in sight, Duke turned the
buggy into a side road that wound out of sight into a pine wood. It
was very cool under the trees, and the wind blew through them picking up the rich pine scent and the smell of honeysuckle. Fancy felt
a little dizzy, and it came to her then that she hadn't eaten anything
except that charcolate soda all day long. Duke had said something
about taking her to dinner, but he must have forgotten it.

The sun had begun to set as they climbed up the crescent-shaped
Sandhill, and now it was dark. There was the twitter of night birds
among the trees, and far off and faint a whippoorwill cried out just
once; then a mockingbird answered him, imitating the sound, a little
sour and flat and not exactly on key.

Fancy felt cold, suddenly, and a little afraid. She turned and

21

looked at Duke's face, illuminated briefly as he drew in on his cigar. She thought it had changed somehow. Duke was just as handsome as ever, but his face looked harder somehow, and his lower lip curled about the end of the cigar in a way that Fancy found vaguely disturbing.

Bet he can be mean as old Nick, she thought suddenly.

"How come you got two houses?" she asked.

"That one on Campbell Street belongs to all of us," Duke said, "though by rights it's mine—since I paid for it. But the one up here is where I hang out. I can put up with just so much of the folks then I get a bellyful. Look—you can see the house now. . . ."

By squinting a little, Fancy could make out the outlines of a Sand-hill cottage, a type developed from a typical farmhouse but having lines so distinctively its own that it had earned its right to a name.

"We call this here village Summerville," Duke explained. "Reckon that was because folks used to live up here in the summer mostly to get away from the heat. Now lots of folks live up here all year round. Come on, lil' Fancygal, let's go inside."

He helped her down from the buggy, and she stood there waiting while he took her bundle out of the back. Then she walked a little ahead of him until she came to the porch and waited there while he unlocked the door. Inside, he scratched a match on the sole of his shoe, and lit one of the lamps. Then he lit several others and turned to Fancy with a broad grin.

"Well," he said, "what do you think of it?"

"Oh, Duke," Fancy breathed, "it's just too fine for words!"

The cottage actually was hideous; but Fancy had no way of knowing that. The heavy, ornate furniture, decorated with bows about the legs, and the painted fire screen and the tremendous gilt picture frames, and the wilderness of potted plants were all a legacy from her predecessor—one Myrtie Torrence, the last of Duke's many all too fleeting lights of love. Of course, Duke had bought the furniture, but Myrtie had selected it, so that the heavy hand of her ferociously bad taste lay over the decor like a blight. But Fancy had slept on corn shucks and sat on cracker boxes all her life. To her, they were beautiful.

Duke looked at her suddenly, keenly.

"Damned if you don't look right peaked," he growled.

"You didn't take me to dinner like you promised," Fancy said; "I'm right smart hungry, Duke."

"Oh damn!" Duke said. "I'm downright sorry, Fan. Maybe we can rustle up some grub out of the icebox."

Fancy followed him out into the kitchen and stood staring in awed admiration at the tremendous icebox, built to hold a hundred pounds of ice at one time. Up on the farm they had a spring house that really didn't keep things very cold so that food was always spoiling. But in this marvel of modern science, Duke had food enough to feed an army.

"Make a fire in the stove, honey," Fancy said. "I'll cook."

"Now ain't you a smart one," Duke beamed. "Just give me a minute."

Hungry as she was, Fancy didn't rush things. She wanted to show him what she could do. She fried the chicken in an egg batter, turning it a rich golden brown. She made hot biscuits, and steaming coffee, and green beans swimming in fat.

Duke tasted everything, then stared at her.

"Babydoll," he said, "you'n'me are going to get along."

"I hope so," Fancy said.

After supper, she washed the dishes, while Duke sat in his big easy chair and pulled at a bottle of bourbon. She took a long time about it, polishing each dish lovingly. When she came back into the parlor, Duke poured three fingers of bourbon into a glass, topped it with ice and water, and handed it to her.

"Here, baby," he grinned; "have a little pickup. You're going to need it."

"I—I don't drink," Fancy whispered.

"Time you was learning how," Duke said. "Go on, take it."

Timidly Fancy took the glass and tasted the drink. It burned like fire, going down. All the stories Maw had told her came back with a rush—of girls who took just one tiny, little one and then. . . . She looked at Duke and her blue eyes widened with real fear.

S'pose he didn't mean to marry her after all? S'pose he meant to get her drunk and—she groped for Maw's euphemistic phrase for that mysterious happening that caused girls to drop out of sight, ashamed to be seen again—and 'took advantage of her.' For a moment a lively curiosity over what were the precise details of being

23

taken advantage of, almost drowned her fear. It must be plumb interesting, she decided, since it happened to so many girls.

But she didn't like the look on Duke's face. She had the funny idea that her clothes were not there any more. The way he looked at her made her feel naked. She didn't like the feeling.

"Sure is a pretty place you got here," she said breathlessly, and started walking around the room, still holding the drink in her hand. The minute Duke turned his head away from her just a little, she dumped the contents of her glass into one of the potted plants.

"Yessir," she said; "it sure Lord is . . ."

"Come here, lil' Fancygal," Duke said thickly.

Fancy noticed that his eyes were getting bloodshot. She shot a quick glance at the bottle. To her dismay, it was already three-quarters empty.

Duke got to his feet, swaying a little.

"I ain't drunk," he grinned; "I can down three of them and never feel it. Now, babydoll, how about a lil' kiss?"

Better humor him, Fancy thought fearfully. I'll let him kiss me just once and then I'll start talking about something real fast, and— but Duke put out his powerful arms and crushed her to him in a grip so hard that she was sure every bone in her body was broken.

She struggled with him soundlessly, but he caught her face between his fingers and forced her head back. Then he kissed her, hurting her mouth, tightening his grip about her waist until she could feel the breath leaving her body. Her head was enveloped in a fog of whiskey scent and her lips felt bruised. She was getting a little dizzy and she knew that she had to do something right away or—

Then, very quickly, she lifted both her feet off the floor. Duke had bent her so far over backwards, that even her slight weight was enough to make him lose his balance. He felt himself falling, and turned her loose, so that she had the chance for a half heartbeat to throw herself out to one side and away from him, before he crashed to the floor like a felled oak. He lay there for a moment, dazed, then he pushed up on his hands and knees, and rested there, hanging his big head and shaking it from side to side.

Fancy put out her hand and picked up the heavy brass poker that stood in the rack before the fireplace.

24

"Duke, honey," she whispered, "I'm awful sorry to have to do this; but I can't fight you no more—I can't. . . ."

Then she lifted the poker and brought it down across his head with all her strength.

There was a little blood, but not much; and he lay there breathing noisily out of his open mouth. Fancy bent over him, and her breath was a hot tangle at the base of her throat and her eyes were scalded. Then she turned and ran out of the door and down the winding road under the pines.

She fell more than once in the darkness, so that the new dress was ruined; but she kept going until she came out on the main road, and continued on down that, breath-gone and sobbing.

What am I? she thought miserably. What kind of a creature when my own folks put me for sale for a few dirty dollars, and the first man I meet thinks I'm only worth the price of some ruffled dresses? I'm me—a person, can't they understand that—not nobody's shoddy goods. I ain't to be pawed over and hurt and shamed—I ain't! I ain't! Oh God, oh Jesus, I'd druther be dead than held cheap. . . .

She had no idea how far she had gone when she saw the lights coming toward her. Then the terror was back again, and she turned to leap from the road, when her foot caught in a projecting root, and she sprawled on the ground, with a pain in her left ankle that was like fire.

The big grays that drew the wagon must have sensed her presence because they whinnied shrilly, and the driver pulled on the reins and got down. He came over to where she lay and stood there looking at her and she tried frantically to crawl into the brush, and screamed up at him:

"Don't you touch me! Don't you dare!"

"What's the matter, little girl?" the man said gently. His voice was as deep as Duke's, but ever so much more musical. Just listening to the sound of it made Fancy feel better.

"I hurt my ankle," she wailed; "and I'm plumb scairt and . . ."

"Here," the man said, "let me see."

He knelt down and his fingers caressed the injured ankle gently.

"Hmmn," he said; "bad sprain all right. Reckon I'll have to pick you up and put you in the wagon."

"No!" Fancy gasped.

"Don't be silly, child. I got mixed up with a young gal once and it cost me my birthright. Right now when I see a good-looking woman —I run."

Fancy felt the fear ebbing out of her.

"You must be Mister Weathers," she said.

He stared at her curiously.

"How'd you know?"

"Duke—" Fancy began and stopped in great confusion.

"So," Wyche Weathers said, "that's what you were running from in such an all-fired hurry. That overgrown polecat ought to be shot with slops and arrested for stinking."

He bent down and picked her up. Fancy was conscious of thinking, My God, he's strong! just before he laid her gently down in the wagon.

He stood beside it, looking at her, and the flickering lanterns showed on his face.

Such a strong face, Fancy thought, and a good one too. Bet he wouldn't mash a crippled fly—but he'd kill a man quick as wink what got in his way. . . .

She studied him, seeing the enormously broad shoulders and the great arms thicker and bigger than Duke's, looking out of place on Wyche Weathers because he was scarcely a head taller than she was. She could see the white hair at his temples, and the small, neatly trimmed black mustache that outlined a mouth that was firm, but kind.

Wyche looked at her torn dress and all the kindness went out of his face, leaving it hard as granite.

"Did Duke Ellis—molest you?" he growled.

Fancy realized suddenly that she held a man's life in the hollow of her hand. It gave her a heady sense of power. But which man? Duke was so big and strong, and this short man, strong as he was, might not be able to—

"No," she said quickly; "I just got scairt and ran."

Wyche looked at her doubtfully.

"Your dress?" he said.

"I tore it coming through the brush," Fancy said.

"All right," Wyche Weathers said. "Come, let me help you up beside me and I'll take you back to your folks. . . ."

"I—I ain't got no folks," Fancy lied.

Wyche stopped still, staring at her.

"What on earth am I going to do with you?" he muttered.

"Take me away," Fancy begged. "Just take me a long way from here where he can't find me!"

Wyche Weathers studied that one for a long moment, then he sighed.

"All right, little girl," he said and taking her arm, half lifted her into the high seat beside him.

2

FANCY stood in the little tent about ten yards back of the wagon, and took off her clothes. Then she slipped on the tight-fitting little red pants, and over them the baggy oriental trousers that were made of some stuff like mosquito netting so anybody could see right through them. She took up the blouse, which, though thin, was not transparent, and drew it over her head. It was so short that it left her middle bare.

She worked furiously, putting on the ropes of bright glass beads, and the earrings that dangled more than six inches below each ear. After she had brushed her hair back out of the way, she put on her jeweled turban. These jewels were glass, too. Just before she adjusted the long, thick veil that hid all of her face but her eyes, she looked at herself in the mirror and blushed hotly. The only thing about her that was really covered up was her face. She didn't like the way the men looked at her. Something got into their eyes when they saw her rigged up like this—something hot and ugly. Looking at them, Fancy could see all the goodness in them drowning right behind their eyes, and the badness leaping up like fire. It was as if

28

they stopped being men, and became animals; as if everything that had been done in the world to tame the ugliness down hadn't been much good after all.

And it was more than the way they looked at her. After each show, Wyche had to use his big fist on some one or two of them, liquored up and determined. She put out her hand and took up the little tin box. Then she drew the little key which hung around her neck on a chain out of her blouse and unlocked the box. Sitting there before the mirror, she counted the money. It came to more than five hundred dollars, and she had earned every penny of it herself.

That was the only thing that made it bearable. Never having had any money, Fancy had a good, sound appreciation for it. And except for letting her share a few of the expenses, Wyche wouldn't touch a penny of it.

"You made it yourself, baby," he said; "it's yours to keep. . . ."

Wyche was such a funny kind of a man. The way he treated her now—as if she was a queen or something. Of course, there might be something in his idea that it was she who drew the crowds; but he didn't have to be so gentle with her; that made her feel a little ashamed.

What made her more ashamed was the tight, grim-faced way the women looked at her. She could see their mouths moving, shaping the word, "Hussy!" every time she went into her dance. "Traveling round like that with two men," she heard one of them say once, "and one of 'em a nigger!"

Fat lot of good it would do her to explain that for the first two months they had been together, Wyche had slept on the ground next to Mose, leaving her the whole wagon to herself. It was only after she had bought herself this little tent with its folding cot, that he had had a comfortable place to sleep. After four months, the only time yet that Wyche touched her hand was to help her up and down from the wagon.

Fancy didn't want it any different from that; but she wanted folks to know what a real gentleman Wyche Weathers was. Being honest, she more than half realized that if Wyche had tried to change things, she would have agreed—out of gratitude; because never before in her life had anybody been so good to her. But Wyche didn't try to change things; he seemed to like them well enough just the way they were now. Fancy might have felt a little pique at his indifference, only Wyche wasn't indifferent. The look in his eyes had a glow to it whenever he gazed at her; half the time he seemed to be on the point of saying something—of asking her—but then his strong jaw shut tight like a trap.

Outside on the wagon now, old Mose was striking up a chord on his banjo. Fancy shivered a little. She was quivering on the inside like a marsh reed in a high wind, and she knew why. It was because they were back in Augusta again after four months of wandering. Augusta meant just one thing to Fancy—Duke Ellis. And she was mortally afraid of seeing his face in that crowd out there. Of course, with this veil over her face he might not recognize her, but then again, he might. There was no telling.

Quickly she put the money back in the box and locked it with the little key. All that money, and all because years ago old Liz Elberton had taught her to tell fortunes with a pack of cards. Fancy didn't hold with such foolishness herself, but a mighty heap of other folks seemed to. She had told Wyche's fortune about three months ago, and that had given him the idea for this outlandish getup.

"Heck, baby," he said, "you're a natural! With that hair and those eyes, you'll knock 'em dead! Make yourself a fortune, and help me make one too!"

In the end, Fancy had consented, reluctantly, more because she wanted to do something to earn her keep than for any other reason. She hated it with all her heart. In a few minutes now, Wyche would call out from behind the flickering lamps, made of wicks stuck in old bottles, "And now friends, I present to you Madame Scheherazade —mysterious daughter of the East! Knows all! Tells all! Past, present and future!"

That would be her cue to step out on the wagon and go into her dance, which wasn't anything but a sinuous wiggle in slow time to Mose's flute. Fancy was a good dancer, but this wasn't dancing. This was something else, aimed at getting that ugly look into men's eyes, and common sense out of their heads. It lasted, only a couple of minutes; then the rush would begin as men came forward and plunked down their dollars to have Fancy read their future in the cards. Few of them left without making the suggestion that their future would be considerably brighter if she would consider taking a prominent if brief part in it; but Wyche had coached her well:

"I am dedicated to the gods," she would whisper, using the words that Wyche had made her memorize; "I am wedded to the mysteries. There must be no living man in my life."

Peeping through the curtain, Fancy could see Wyche arranging the jars filled with the ugly ribbons of tapeworms, pickled in alcohol. Where he had gotten them, Fancy did not know; but to the crowds he grandly proclaimed himself an expert who could cure them of such things. Next to them, he hung up the grisly human skeleton which had been worth its weight in gold to Wyche when he had specialized in rooking the Negroes; but since Fancy had joined his troupe, he played chiefly to white crowds. A Southerner born and bred, it would have been unthinkable to Wyche to have Fancy exhibit herself before the blacks.

But now Fancy had displaced the skeleton as his chief attraction; and Wyche made more money than ever. She saw his eyes narrow as he arranged the exhibit, and that look of cold contempt for everybody who drew breath came into them. It was the only thing about Wyche Weathers that Fancy didn't like. She suspected that it was put on, that down deep Wyche sort of felt the need of getting even with a world that had treated him so badly. At bottom, he was a good sort; she knew that well.

"Take 'em, honey," he used to say, "or they'll take you. Never give 'em an even break. . . ."

"I don't believe that," Fancy said. "Folks is mostly good when you get right down to it."

"Humph!" Wyche snorted. "Like Duke Ellis, maybe? Or like your paw who was going to sell you like a horse to a man old enough to be your grandfather?"

Fancy had to admit he was right about that. She was sorry she had finally broken down and told him the truth about running away from home.

"People aren't mostly good," Wyche said gruffly, "nor even mostly bad. Trouble is they're a weak bunch of polecats who don't like their own scent. And the crazy thing about it, baby, is that they think nobody can smell it but them. So they got to hide things—got to play-act, puff themselves up big in the sight of their brothers. Folks don't hunger and thirst after righteousness, honey—they pant after applause, they thirst after self-importance. They'll lie, steal, cheat, sell themselves for vanity's sake. Ever notice how they tie themselves in knots reaching after a dollar? Preachers are always condemning the love of money, but money isn't important, not in itself; it's what it will buy that counts. . . ."

"Money won't buy everything," Fancy said.

"Damned little it won't. It'll buy what most folks want—it'll buy their brother's envy, and a sickening kind of fawning servility that most folks twist into respect. Hide your money in the ground, and nobody respects you for it; but buy yourself two dozen ruffled shirts, and a coach and four, purchase yourself the prettiest gal in town for your missus, and one a little prettier'n that for your light o' love, and they'll kill themselves in the rush to embrace your backside. Hell, baby, the more I see of folks the better I like old Mose and my mules."

"And me?" Fancy whispered.

"And you, baby. You, thank God, are different. . . ."

But I'm not, Fancy thought bitterly as she peered through the flap in the tent, or else I wouldn't get up there half naked on that there platform and let 'em look at me like I was a prize filly and they was snorting stallions. . . .

"Friends!" Wyche was beginning now, in his deep, rich voice, "I don't need to tell you what tapeworm can do to the human body! You have seen it with your own eyes—people wasted away to pitiful scarecrows, thin almost as Mister Bones here—" He tapped the skeleton playfully with his cane, and the spectators' eyes bugged out.

Fancy searched that sea of faces, but Duke was not among them; nowhere was there a mustache like that, or eyes with that hard, confident look. She sighed deeply from pure relief, and waited.

"But now, at last, I have made an end to these hellish tortures which for so long have devastated the human race. After years spent in the Far East, I have finally found a sovereign remedy! It was given to me by an old seer, a prophet of the occult whose life I once saved from the wild tribesmen of the desert! He lived scarcely a month after the rescue—just long enough to divulge to me his priceless secret, and to leave in my care, his beautiful daughter, Madame Scheherazade, whose knowledge of the occult equals if not exceeds that of her late, lamented father. . . . You will make her acquaintance in a moment; but first, let us look upon the lighter side of life. Music, Mose!"

The old black stood up, strumming his banjo; then with an agility astonishing in one of his years, he began a buck and wing that soon had the crowd calling for more.

"Mose is a wise man, too, in his quaint unlettered way," Wyche said genially. "For instance, Mose, why do old maids go to church so early on Sunday?"

"I reckon, boss, sah," Mose grinned, " 'cause they want to be there when the hymns is given out!"

"And why do old maids wear silk gloves?"

"That's easy, boss. It's 'cause they don't like kids!"

Many a time Fancy had heard Wyche groaning in real anguish as he copied his fearfully unfunny jokes from Thomas W. Jackson's *On a Slow Train Through Arkansas*. But the crowd loved them. It seemed to Fancy that it was the way that Wyche sprang them that made them go over so big. Now they were roaring with laughter.

"And now, friends, I give you that mysterious daughter of the East; that high priestess of the mysteries, to whom the future is an open book—Madame Scheherazade!"

Trembling all over, Fancy ran the few short steps to the wagon, and Wyche reached down and helped her up the ladder. Mose picked up his flute and began a wild wailing. Fancy closed her eyes and allowed her supple young body to quiver like an aspen in a high wind, and again the crowd roared. But it was a different sound now, a hoarse, ugly, beast bellow. Fancy could feel the men's eyes, hot upon her; but she didn't look at them—she didn't dare. .

When at last Mose stopped playing, and Wyche started his chanted description of her powers, Fancy opened her eyes. She let her gaze pass over the faces in that crowd; then she stopped suddenly, held by one face, as though the pale blue eyes had turned her to stone.

It was a young face, haunted and thin, with big cheekbones, and hollowed cheeks, and a wide, tormented mouth. Under the tall hat, Fancy could see the chestnut hair, and the quick jerking of the knot muscle over the jaw, clear in the torchlight. It was a face she couldn't forget, a face she had seen before somewhere, had seen and marked, and that had troubled her in many a senseless dream.

33

And now, gazing into it, Fancy remembered just where she had seen that face. Even after all these months, that mouth hadn't lost the terrible sadness that she remembered. She had seen this man coming out of a church, at a wedding, watching his brother bear away the girl he himself loved. She searched for the name. Bran—Brantwell—Brantley! That was it—Courtland Brantley, whom Duke had hated so.

But how could anyone hate a man with a face like this—so pitiful, and so tender? It was the sort of face that made her fingertips itch to reach up and stroke his cheeks, that made her voice drop deep in her throat murmuring ancient, wordless, wonderful things. Looking at him now, Fancy found herself hoping that he would come to her little tent to have his fortune read. I could comfort him! she thought, I could drive out the misery. . . .

But she had almost given up when he finally did come. She had gone through her patter effortlessly, telling them all the things they wanted to hear: "You will obtain riches. Yes, yes, your sweetheart will come back to you. You will make a fortunate marriage—I see a tall, dark man in your life. . . ."

Lies, and rot and foolishness and she was sick of it! But when the last of them had gone, and he had not come, Fancy bent her head down upon the little folding table, and gave way to tears. She did not know how long she cried, but a hand rested gently upon her bare shoulder, and her head jerked upright, and joy leaped into her eyes and blazed.

"Why were you crying?" Court Brantley said.

"Because I'm plumb—" Fancy began and caught herself. She had started to say. "Because I'm plumb, downright lonesome," but people from the mysterious East didn't talk like that. "Because I'm lonely," she said in a husky whisper. "No one understands me. I—I need a friend. . . ."

A crooked grin twisted the wide mouth, suddenly.

"That shouldn't be hard, Scheherazade," he said. "Any man in his right mind would settle for even one of those thousand and one nights. . . ."

"You wish your fortune read?" Fancy said quickly.

"Not particularly," Court said; "actually I wanted a closer look at you."

"And now that you have seen me?" Fancy whispered.

"The catch is, I haven't. If only you'd take off that damned veil!"

"It is forbidden," Fancy said quietly, and began to spread the cards. Court watched her, his pale eyes never leaving her face.

"There has been much trouble in your life," Fancy murmured. "You have returned recently from a journey . . ."

"Bosh!" Court laughed drily; "who hasn't?"

"From a far-off place—a place of snows. I see buildings, many buildings, a great city, and a—a school. Tell me, Mister Brantley, have you not returned from the University?"

Court's eyes widened.

"Well I'll be damned," he said; "how'd you know that?"

"But you have come home to sadness. I see a—a girl. She is fair, with hair like sunlight, and she is dressed all in white. A bride, Mister Brantley? But not your bride. The bride of another—one who looks much like you—who bears the same blood in his veins . . . A cousin? No, closer than that—a brother!"

"Good God!" Court breathed. "I've never believed this stuff, still . . ."

"The voices speak to me, the cards do not lie. You love her, this fair girl whose name is that of a flower—Rose? Lily? No, no—not of a flower, but of a green plant that does not flower. . . ."

"Fern," Court groaned; "Fern Vance."

"So what is it," Fancy whispered, "that you wish to know?"

Court looked at her bleakly.

"How I can stop loving her," he said. "Whether there's any hope for me—No! Not that—she's my brother's wife, and I've got to stop thinking about her like that. But I can't. She's inside me, like fire—like poison, and I'm dying of wanting her so. Don't know when I've slept a night all the way through. I can't eat. I've got no mind for anything but her. That's it, Madame. Reckon I sound like a mighty big fool to you. . . ."

"No," Fancy said carefully, "only like a man in love. I will consult the cards. . . ."

She dared not talk too much. After three months of nightly coaching by Wyche, her command of 'proper talk' was still too unsure to risk it. But as she spread out the cards before her, her mind was racing.

35

It's her who's the big fool, not you, she thought. Any woman who could have married you and then let you go is a fool! If I'd been in her shoes, I'd have grabbed you so quick that . . .

"What do they say?" Court Brantley asked.

Fancy looked down at the cards, her young face frowning and troubled. They had a pattern. Usually the cards hadn't any pattern and she made up wild, improbable stories to tell her clients. But the cards that lay before her frightened her. It's all plumb downright foolishness, she thought. King of Hearts—that's Court. Jack of Clubs, that's his brother, followed by the Ace of Spades. Death. Then the Queen of Diamonds—that's her, damn her to hell, and back again. And the King of Hearts again followed by the Queen of Spades. Queen of Spades—a dark lady. Now who the devil—

Me? It could be. I'm dark—leaseways my hair is. Now she turns up again! Then Court, then—me, then her! Then her, and Court. Not me any more. And not the Jack of Clubs, his brother—not any more, not never any more because the Ace of Spades came and—Jesus God! Her'n' Court, and the Ace of Spades. Here it is again, her'n' Court and the Ace of Spades—and here I am again, but I'm all alone. . . .

She kept shuffling the cards, but the pattern held. Court, then Tyler—followed by death. Then Court followed by Fern Vance, followed by Fancy herself. Court and Fancy linked, paired. Then Fern Vance getting into the linkage, splitting it apart; then Court and Fern, and Fern and Court—then death, always death and Fancy left alone crying. . . .

"Well?" Court said evenly.

"I—I cannot read your fortune," Fancy whispered; "the cards are —mixed up, sort of. . . . Here, take your money back. Some other time, maybe."

Court stood up and pocketed the dollar.

"You," he said, "are a faker. But a damned clever faker. Good night, Scheherazade."

After him there were only a few more, and Fancy was able to go back to her tent and shut her ears to Wyche's lecture on the virtues of Doctor Weathers' Eastern Snake Oil. Before Wyche finished roping in the suckers, she had dressed in her own clothes again, and walked away from the noise and the shouting. She wanted time to think. There was something between her and Court Brantley. Something mightily powerful that got into the cards and made them fall like that. But cards were a joke, a trick, and had nothing to do with people's lives. Then why was she trembling so? If that were the pattern of the future, she could break it. All she had to do was to take one card, the Queen of Spades, herself, out of the combination and it was broken.

But she couldn't. There was that linkage between her and Court. Even if it didn't last long, it was there. And if that happened, it was the rest of the pattern she'd have to change—that Queen of Diamonds business, because that wasn't any good nohow, not with the Ace of Spades always there. Why this Fern Vance was a danger to Court! She could bring him death. Him and herself. But Fancy reckoned that wouldn't matter much to her, because she wouldn't believe it was really going to work out like that.

Her poor head ached so with all the thinking. She walked very fast away from the wagon until she came under the trees, and it was there that she saw him.

"Why, Mister Brantley!" she said.

"I was waiting for you," he said gravely. "Figured you'd have to come out of that stifling hole after a while. Come walk with me, won't you?"

"All right," Fancy said.

Court didn't say anything. He walked alongside her, towering up tall against the night, until they came out from under the trees into the fields, and the moon came up, too, red-yellow and huge, bigger than a pumpkin.

Court turned toward her, studying her face.

"I thought so," he said. "You're lovely. And young. That voice was a fake—it made you sound old. Who are you?"

"I'm Fancy Williamson," Fancy said. Then it all came out in a rush: "I'm from Ca'lina, and I can't really tell folks' fortunes. I knew about you before. . . ."

"I see," Court said, his face still and unsmiling. "But you wouldn't cheat me—why?"

"It—it wouldn't have been cheating," Fancy whispered; "I could have told yours. I don't know how come, but I could have. And I didn't want to."

37

"Why not?"

"Because—because I kept seeing myself in your fortune, and it didn't seem right proper to tell you that."

"You're telling me now."

"Now's different," Fancy said.

"You're Wyche Weathers' wife?" Court said.

"Oh, no!"

Court looked at her and his face was grim.

"You travel all over the state with Wyche and you're not married to him?" he asked sternly.

"What's wrong with that?" Fancy said.

"Plenty. You're young, but not that young. You must know what folks will think. . . ."

"I do know, and it riles me plenty. Not on my account, but on Wyche's. A truer gentleman never drew breath. Wyche ain't never so much as kissed me—I have that little tent all to myself, and he's never even seen the inside of it. 'Pears to me, Mister Court Brantley, that some folks got awful dirty minds!"

"People," Court said tiredly, "have realistic minds, mostly. All right it hasn't happened yet, but it will."

"It will not!"

"All right, all right—it's none of my business anyhow."

Fancy looked at him.

"What is your business, Court Brantley?" she asked. "What do you do, I mean?"

"I haven't any—really. I was planning to build a textile mill down here; but since Fern ran off with that precious scoundrel of a brother of mine, I've neither the heart nor the inclination. . . ."

Fancy caught his arm suddenly and clung to it.

"Then you got to get the heart!" she said almost fiercely. "You can't waste your life mooning over a girl you're better off without. You've got things to do, Tallman, and I aim to see that you do 'em!"

"Tallman? Why'd you call me that?"

"That's my special name for you. First time I saw you, I kept thinking, Gosh, how tall he is!"

"I see," Court said. "I'm flattered." But his voice sounded cold. "Come on," he said, "let's walk."

They crossed the field, and went through a grove of pines. When they came out of the woods this time the river was before them. The moon lay just beyond it, caught in the ragged pines of the Carolina hills. It left a yellow-silver track in the muddy water, and in the other places where the light didn't touch, the river was burnt copper, blue-shadowed by the low-hanging trees.

"Gosh!" Fancy sighed. "Ain't it pretty, Court? It's so—so romantic-like. . . ."

One corner of Court's big mouth twisted upward in a smile. Fancy didn't like that smile. It was hurt-ugly, pain-twisted.

"Reckon it is," he said.

The silence stretched out between them. Fancy felt like screaming. If only something would make a noise! In the stillness she could hear the rustle of her own breathing. It seemed to be coming disgracefully quick. And the muffled beating of her heart, racing like something half wild—could he hear that too?

"That's our house up there," Court said quietly.

Fancy looked up and saw the weathered old house sitting on a little hill about five hundred yards from the river. She saw that it had been beautiful once, and also that in a curious way it was still beautiful. It had a spirit of its own, like a grand old lady who had fallen on evil days. Its paint wasn't white any longer, but a soft, bluish-gray—and even from where she stood Fancy could see that the paint was chipped and cracked, and the house itself far gone in pitiful decay. She stood quite still and watched the rising moon-light crawling toward it. Then the light touched the house, and it blazed white once more, and the blossoms of the magnolias standing around it picked up the light, too, and threw it back in a glow like that of sea foam, pearls, snow. . . .

"Oh, Court," Fancy whispered, "it's lovely! What do you call it?"

"Hiberion," Court murmured, and his voice caressed the word, like a lover breathing the name of his beloved. "Reckon this is the end of it," he said sadly, "nobody's got the money to fix it up any more. It isn't even safe to live in now, but—"

"Then that's another reason you got to fight!" Fancy said. "What are you anyhow—a man or a mule? You got brains—use 'em! Go out and get the money. Start your mill, then fix up your house. Forget that girl—there'll be plenty more who'd be mighty proud to be your wife. . . ."

"They," Court said grimly, "would be mighty big fools, considering my chances."

"Oh, you!" Fancy said in exasperation. "Come on, let's be getting back now."

"No," Court said, "let's sit down by the water, and look at the moon."

"All right," Fancy said.

They sat on the root of an oak and gazed out over the water. Fancy could see the grief coming back into Court's face, there in the moonlight. She put out her hand and laid it gently upon his arm.

"Tell me about her," she said.

"There's not much to tell—not that a man can put into words, anyhow. Why do you want to know?"

"So—I can find out," Fancy murmured, "what it is about her that can 'most kill a man down inside his heart. Reckon if I knew that I could bring him back alive again. 'Tain't much fun keeping company with a ghost."

"You want to bring me back?" Court said. "Why, little Fancy?"

"Can't answer that—not right off the reel. Don't rightly know myself. Reckon it's 'cause I got a mighty heap of pity for suffering. Suffered a right pert myself. . . ."

"Well," Court said, "she's a little bit of a thing—no bigger than you are, all white and pink and golden. . . ."

The sound of his voice made Fancy shiver. Oh God, oh Jesus, she thought, if I could only make him sound like that when he's talking 'bout me!

"She never had much of a chance—not with being the daughter of the rottenest carpetbagger that ever abused the sovereign state of Georgia. Folks don't forget those days easily. I know—I grew up during them. Maybe that's why she was content with becoming the wife of a Brantley. . . ."

"And take her chance ending up in the river?" Fancy said.

Court stared at her.

"So," he said, "you know that too!"

"Reckon there ain't much about you I don't know."

"Why, Fancy?"

"Right now, I'm listening—you're talking."

"All right. Fern grew up to daily slights and insults. She was left

40

out of everything—she never had any friends, except Ty and me. It made her a little queer—too silent, and a mite too intense. It was settled all along that she and I were to get married. Then I went away to Harvard, and something I said in a letter gave Ty the idea that I was getting hitched to a Yankee heiress. That did it. He told Fern. I think she married him out of pique. . . ."

"And were you?"

"Was I what?"

"Getting hitched to a damyankee?"

"Blazes no! I used to see Hester, my employer's daughter, once in a while; but there was never anything much between us."

"I doubt that," Fancy said drily.

"Why?"

"Because 'twixt you and most any girl there'll always be something much going on."

Court looked at her.

"Including you, Fan?"

"That's plumb, downright unfair! All right Mister Tallman Court Brantley, since you've got to be so blamed nosy—including me. Now take me back to the tent; I don't like being made 'shamed of myself."

"No," Court laughed; "I think I'll shame you a little more. It might be—fun."

Then, very quickly, he took her in his arms and kissed her.

Fancy wrenched herself backward and away from him. The next instant colored lights exploded inside his head, as her small, hard right fist landed high upon his jaw. Court put his hand against the place where she had hit him, seeing her standing there both fists doubled and ready, and lightning in her blue eyes.

"Well, I'll be damned!" he whispered helplessly.

"You," Fancy said flatly, "shouldn't ought to have done that."

"Why not?" Court said.

Fancy looked at him.

"There's a lot of bad things in this world," she said; "but I don't reckon there's anything worse than being kissed because a man thinks you want him to—except one thing, Court. . . ."

"And what's that?"

"Being kissed by a man what closes his eyes and thinks about somebody else whilst he's kissing you! I'm me, Tallman! I ain't Fern

41

Vance. I got more blood and breath and blazes in me right now than she'll ever have if she lives to be a hundred! Now take me back, Court—and I hope I never see hair nor hide of you again!"

"All right," Court said quietly.

It wasn't until they were in sight of the medicine wagon that he spoke again.

"Did you mean that?" he said.

"Did I mean what?" Fancy asked.

"About never wanting to see me again?"

Fancy looked at him and the dark red corners of her mouth trembled a little.

"No," she said, "reckon I was trying to fool myself. Never was much good at it. But I don't want to see you right soon. I want to see you when you're over her—when you're capable of loving again —not before. . . ."

"And then?" Court whispered.

"Reckon I'll learn you what a kiss ought to be like. What it feels like when a body means it."

Court grinned at her then, a crooked, engaging kind of a grin.

"Couldn't you," he said, "give me a small sample—right now?"

"No!" Fancy began; then a little flame showed in her blue eyes. "Why not?" she said, and putting up her arms, she drew his face down to hers. When she turned him loose finally, letting his lean face slip gently upward between the palms and fingers of her two hands, he leaned back against a tree and stared at her.

"My God!" he whispered.

"Told you, Court," she said. "More breath and blood and blazes than anybody in this whole blamed world!" Then she turned and ran away from him through the ghost-shadowed trees.

When she came out into the clearing Wyche was waiting for her. At the sight of her the sick worry in his eyes vanished and thunder and lightning took its place.

"Where the devil have you been!" he roared.

"Out walking," Fancy said tartly. "'Pears to me you're spreading yourself mighty wide, Wyche. Ain't nobody appointed you my keeper."

"Sorry," Wyche said shortly. "I've just been worried sick, that's all. Thought maybe you'd run into Duke and—"

42

"Duke!" Fancy said. "Why Wyche, honey, I'd forgotten all about him. Jehosiphat! I could of bumped into him at that. I'm mighty sorry, Wyche—didn't mean to give you a turn. . . ."

"It's all right," Wyche said. "Your supper's ready, baby. Sit down and eat. Afterwards I want to talk to you."

"All right, Wyche," Fancy said.

All the time while she was eating, she could see him watching her. There was a funny look on his face—half fearful, half tender. She finished her supper, and sat there, waiting.

"All right, Wyche," she said.

Wyche leaned across the table and took her hand.

"Fan, baby, I've been a fool," he said. "Thought I could go on living in the same world with you, seeing you every day and not have it get me. Reckon I've been in love with you for a long time. . . ."

Fancy's blue eyes widened, and her breath caught somewhere deep in her throat.

"Knew I'd have to tell you some time," he went on; "but I figured I didn't have the right. I'm too old for you—that's one thing. And being dragged all over the face of this filthy earth, living from hand to mouth, without even a pillow to put your pretty head on, or a roof to keep out the rain—that's a mite too much, to my way of thinking. . . ."

Fancy looked at him, but she didn't say anything. She didn't know what to say.

"When you walked off like that tonight, it came to me how it would be without you. The whole damned world went hollow, Fan. There wasn't any light anywhere—just emptiness, and that darkness that Moses talks about in the Bible—the kind you can feel. So—right then I knew you had to be mine if anything was to make sense any more. I know you don't love me, but I'm hoping maybe you can learn to—not the man I am right now, not old Doctor Snake Oil Weathers; but the man I was—the man I'm going to be again. . . ."

"You couldn't be any finer," Fancy said, "than you are right now. To me you're just about the best man in the world—and one of the nicest. . . ."

"No," Wyche said somberly; "I've been a hypocrite and a coward

43

too long, baby. Thought I could run away from myself, but I couldn't. I was always there, pointing the finger of shame at myself. Nobody ever made himself bigger than the next man by cheating him; a framework of lies is a mighty flimsy foundation to build a life on. Reckon I always knew that—but I didn't care. Now I do care, and that's your fault, baby. . . ."

"What do you aim to do?" Fancy asked him.

"Go back to Spartanburg. Go to my father, ask him for a job. Hell, I'll doff bobbins to get started. I'll win him over again. Heck, it won't be hard—I happen to know he wants me back again, now that Sue has run off with that drummer. . . ."

"Sue was the girl who . . . ?"

"Yep. Paw's a right smart businessman, but he doesn't know a thing about women. . . ."

Fancy looked at him.

"Why wouldn't you marry her, Wyche?" she said.

"Sue was right smart free with her favors. I doubt seriously that I was actually the guilty party; but I was rich, and old Ted Weathers' son—which made me the most likely prospect. . . ."

"You mean to take me with you?"

"No. Paw wouldn't cotton to the idea. I've got seven hundred dollars saved—first money I've kept since I've been on the road. That was your doing, too. When I saw how you hung onto a dollar, it shamed me into doing the same thing. Now here's my idea: there's a woman in Atlanta named Tess Fullbright. She's a good, motherly soul who runs a respectable boarding house. I want you to take this money and stay there until I come for you. It won't be long, baby—I promise you."

"Couldn't I," Fancy whispered, "stay here? I like Augusta."

"And run the risk of having Duke Ellis get his filthy hands on you? Fat chance, Fan—it's got to be Atlanta."

"All right, Wyche," Fan said; "but I won't take your money."

"Why not, baby?"

"Like you said, I don't love you. I might learn to; but then I might not. I don't want to be held to a promise. If I'm still there when you come, you'll know I'm yours—all yours, fair'n' square. If I've gone don't look for me, Wyche—it wouldn't do no good. . . ."

Wyche's face was terrible suddenly.

"There's somebody else?" he said. "Another man?"

"Yes. And it ain't Duke Ellis, which is what you're thinking. I don't want to call no names, Wyche, 'cause I ain't sure. I know I love him; but I don't know if he loves me. I got to find that out. If he don't, I've got to learn him to—or try to, anyhow. Maybe it won't work out. Maybe I'll change my mind. If I do, I'll be waiting. . . ."

Wyche's eyes were bleak with misery.

"That all the hope you can give me, baby?" he said sadly.

"Remember what you said about being a hypocrite? Can't lie to you, Wyche—I think too much of you for that. I'm just trying to be honest. I'm plumb, downright sorry, but that's the way it is. . . ."

Wyche got up slowly.

"I see," he said. "But just one more thing, Fan, baby. Don't settle for nothing less than the real thing. Whoever this man is, make him put a ring on your finger, and stand up before the preacher. Promise me that—the real thing or nothing. It just isn't smart otherwise. And tell him one thing for me—if he tries to play fast and loose with you, I'll find him. I'll find him if he tries to hide in hell itself. . . ."

"And when you find him?" Fan whispered.

"I'll kill him," Wyche said. "'Night, Fan."

"'Night, Wyche," Fancy answered; but her voice was so low he didn't hear her.

3

When Fancy got up the next morning, she saw that Wyche hadn't done anything about getting ready to leave Augusta. She looked around for him, and saw him sitting under a tree, peacefully smoking a cigar.

"'Morning, baby," he said as she came up to him, and started to rise.

"Don't get up," Fancy said. "Wyche—"

"Yes, Fan?"

"How come you ain't getting ready to pull out?"

"We're not leaving—not until tomorrow, anyhow. And—"

"But, Wyche," Fancy wailed, "you said you was sick of cheating people! You said it last night. And I'm sick of it, too. Sicker'n you, maybe. You don't have to get up and wiggle around before a passel of menfolks with almost nothing on. . . ."

Wyche studied her, his brown eyes tender and grave.

"You hate that, don't you?" he said.

"Yes. Most anybody would."

"That's another thing I like about you," Wyche said. "You're

46

modest—really modest. It isn't anything you've been taught. It's just in you, that's all. You're a funny kid, Fan. You aren't dry behind the ears; yet in some ways you're as old as the hills. You always try to do what you think is right, don't you?"

"Yes. But, Wyche, about tonight . . ."

"We're giving our farewell performance, baby—free. I'm going to give the suckers all that fine, bottled branch water for nothing. I'm donating Mister Bones to the Medical College here. I'm selling the mules, and taking Mose with me for my personal valet. Then you and I, Fan, are going to get aboard a train."

"Do I," Fancy said in a low voice, "have to dance?"

"Yep. Put your heart into it tonight, baby. You'll be doing them a favor. Give 'em something to remember. Most of those poor, lecherous devils are starved for beauty—fresh young beauty like yours. Up there, behind those lanterns, you're every man's dream girl. You're beauty, and passion—tenderness and flame. That's what they want, but they don't know how to say it. They don't even realize what being tied to their timid, duty-bound wives has done to 'em. If any one of 'em ever in his whole life got a caress he didn't have to buy, he'd die happy. . . ."

"To buy?" Fancy said. "But you said—"

"That some of 'em's married? Right. Only there're various kinds of coin that a man has to pay his way with, Fan. For most of 'em the coins are patience and resignation—to the woebegone, sullen, dutiful, holier-than-thou expressions on their spouses' faces when they slip into their arms. They've got an inkling that love oughtn't to be like that—that it should be joy given and taken—shared. So all their lives they feel cheated by the counterfeits they have to accept—at some dim-lighted brothel off a side street, or their little sacrificial lambs' frozen faces as they prepare to do their repugnant duty. . . ."

"You're a funny man, Wyche," Fan said.

"Am I? Funny—amusing; or funny—odd?"

"Both. And funny wise, too. Wyche—"

"Yes, baby?"

"You said I always tried to do right. But what is right, Wyche? I used to think I knew; but now I ain't sure. . . ."

Wyche stared at her, his strong, square face working.

47

"You *are* in love with this man, aren't you?" he said gruffly.

"Yes, Wyche," Fancy whispered.

Wyche looked away from her toward where the sun was coming up over the pines.

"Being in love makes you unsure," he said quietly. "He stretches out his arms and you want to jump right into 'em. That's perfectly natural, Fan, baby; but society is agin it; and this time, society's right."

"Why, Wyche?"

"Several good reasons, too long to go into, and which wouldn't interest you. I'll tell you the one that I think will: when a man's in love, he wants to keep the one he loves—and cherish her. He wants to build a picket fence 'twixt them and the world. He doesn't want it temporary, secret, hidden. He wants the world to know. The one he loves is somebody to him, not a thing to be taken, used and tossed aside. Hell, I'm not saying he shouldn't be interested in your pretty ankles and what a nice sway your bustle's got. That's part of it, too; but only a part. The rest of it is the long years ahead, the laughing together, and the crying, bringing up your kids, nodding together under the lamplight when your heads have turned white, and finally lying together forever in the long dark. . . ."

"But Wyche," Fancy said, "s'pose I can't have those things? S'pose all I could look forward to is a little while with him? Shouldn't I take a little happiness in place of none at all? Is that wrong, Wyche? What is wrong and right, that's what I want to know?"

"The question of Pilate," Wyche groaned. "Only he wanted to know what truth was, which is only another way of saying the same thing, I reckon. Fan, I can't answer that. You have to answer it for yourself. All I can give you is a rough rule of thumb to go by. The whole history of man, baby, has been made up of his efforts to raise himself up from the ape he was into something approaching the angels. Somewhere along the line he acquired himself a brain that could think. Of all the animals he was the only one who knew he had to die, and he hated it. He's built the world we know by refusing to accept the blind accidentality of fate; by never admitting that he was a pallid worm crawling over the surface of a half burned out cinder in space. He couldn't be little, couldn't sink into dust. Some-

48

thing in that awful, blind cosmos had to care about him, so he invented God. Maybe there is a God—I don't know; but the very conception is noble. Man stopped gibbering around in trees, he came down to earth and mastered it; he stopped crawling on all fours, he stood up and looked at the stars. . . .

"The point is baby, the ugly, clownish ape-thing we were had a hunger after dignity. He'd licked the saber-tooth tiger and the woolly mammoth with nothing but his brain against their awful strength. He had a right to his pride. And every time he's let go of that pride, every time he's lost that dignity, the world has sunk in blood and chaos, the light has gone out, and men have groped in darkness for hundreds of years. . . ."

He looked at her tenderly, keenly.

"So here's my rule of thumb, baby: anything that exalts that dignity of yours, be it chants and ceremonies, a ring on your finger, the white of a veil, is good: anything that debases it—is bad. And you have tremendous dignity, Fan, baby; I've never seen anything like it in anybody so young. . . ."

"Thanks, Wyche," Fancy said gratefully; but her voice was sad.

"I know I haven't made you happy," Wyche said; "I only hope I've made you strong."

Fancy put out her hand and let it rest on his arm.

"I reckon maybe you have," she said. "You've given me something to hang onto, Wyche. Now, whatever happens, I'll be thinking: I can't shame Wyche, I can't!"

"You can't shame yourself, baby," Wyche growled; "it ain't in you to. Come on, now—let's go get something to eat."

They had supper at the Globe. Fancy was dressed well enough for that now, and her manners were at least as good as those of the wives of many back-county planters. They didn't talk much. In fact they were sitting there over their coffee, when Fancy looked up and saw that man coming toward them. That man. It was a funny thing that those were the exact words that her mind formed in connection with him, for she couldn't remember ever having seen him before in her life. Yet she had the feeling that she would have known that freckled face anywhere, it and the eyes that smiled even when the rest of that thin, exceedingly handsome face was still, and the carrot-colored, thick-curling hair.

49

"Howdy, Wyche," the man said. His voice was like the rest of him, high-colored, warm, with a half suppressed chuckle in it.

"You buzzard," Wyche said.

"Now, Wyche," the tall man said, "you ain't got no call to low-rate me like that—'specially in front of a lady. Haven't taken notice of you letting any suckers off scot-free yourself. . . ." He looked at Fancy, and that infectious grin that demanded an answer was there on his face.

"Howdy, Ma'am," he said, "I'm Jed Hawkins. Hope you'll forgive my introducing myself this way, but since Wyche here clearly has no intention of doing it for me, I reckoned I'd better."

"I'm Fancy Williamson," Fancy said, and put out her hand. "Pleased to meet you, Mister Hawkins."

Jed Hawkins took her hand and held it a long time.

Wyche groaned.

"Now I've got to ask you to sit down," he said. "Reckon that's the only way short of mayhem I can get you to turn Fan loose."

"Mayhem," Jed grinned, "wouldn't do. It would have to be murder."

"Don't tempt me," Wyche said.

Jed drew a chair from one of the nearby tables, and sat down. He didn't say anything. He just sat there, looking at Fancy.

"I—I've seen you somewhere," Fancy said. "Leaseways, I kind of think I have. . . ."

"Right," Jed said. "Savannah, Macon, Waycross, Columbus. I'm a traveling politician, Miss Fancy. And every time I heard your show was going to be some place, I kind of made it my business to be there, too. . . ."

"That's downright flattering," Fancy said. "Wish I could believe you was telling the truth. . . ."

"The truth and Jed Hawkins," Wyche said, "ain't even on speaking terms."

"What was that saying about 'honor among thieves'?" Jed groaned. "Wyche, as one crook to another, you ought to treat me a little whiter'n that."

"And have you make off with my girl? Not on your life, Jed. I'm having enough trouble in that direction right now. . . ."

"Do tell!" Jed grinned. "Handsome young feller like you?"

"Wouldn't be so bad," Wyche said soberly, "if men like you meant her any good. But Fan's no more'n a kid, Jed—and real inexperienced. But there's one thing I want to get straight right now. I know you don't know a lady when you see one; but Fan's a lady. A true-born, honest to God, lady. So I don't want any free and easy tomcats like you hanging around. Understand me, Jed?"

Jed stared at him.

"All right, Wyche," he said quietly. "You've had your say. So now I reckon I'll have mine. You're dead, damned wrong on several counts. Number one, because I ain't had any particular hankering to chase after any real ladies before, don't amount to a hill of beans in this case. Knew the first time I laid eyes on her that this little girl was a lady. Heck, man, anybody who's got one good eye can see that; and ain't a blamed thing wrong with my sight. Number two, I don't mean Miss Fancy a bit o' harm. Fact is, I mean her all the good in the world. . . ."

Fancy looked at him. It wasn't, she realized, a hard thing to do. Jed Hawkins was one handsome man. A mighty heap handsomer, for instance, than Court Brantley. Not that it made any difference. Nothing made any difference as far as that was concerned.

"I think," she said, "you'd better explain yourself, Mister Hawkins."

"I aim to. Straight. Wyche, you know that being single doesn't help my political chances. I ain't very old, and folks have the curious idea that a young bachelor is a mite too unsteady for public office. . . ."

"I get your drift," Wyche said grimly. "Go on."

"On the other hand, a highfalutin aristocrat wouldn't do me any good with the folks who're my chief support. So I've kind of been on the lookout for a—a bride. I won't lie to you, Ma'am. First time I saw you, I looked you over with the cold eye of calculation. Can't say I fell for you at first sight. I didn't. But it took just one of them cute little dances of yours to warm that cold and calculating eye up a mighty heap—yessir, a mighty heap. . . ."

"So?" Wyche said brusquely.

"I just moseyed over here, and butted in to ask the little lady one thing: whether I couldn't see her once in a while. Whether we couldn't get better acquainted. After that, who knows? She might not like my looks or my style. . . ."

"And you," Fancy smiled, "might not like mine, knowing me better. . . ."

"Fat chance of that," Jed Hawkins said. "Now you tell me, Miss Fancy—what kind of a chance have I got?"

Fancy looked at him with grave eyes.

"None," she said.

Jed stood up slowly.

"Congrats, Wyche," he said.

"Not me," Wyche groaned, "some other polecat."

"In that case," Jed grinned, "I'm going to keep on hoping. Wyche, here, is a mighty good man, for all that he's a mite unfriendly. If it was him, I'd give up. Somebody else—no. I can give somebody else a run for his money."

"Not this—somebody else," Fancy said. "You coming to the show tonight?"

"No'm. I'm due back in Savannah tonight. That's my home town. Next time you're down that way, I'd sure admire to squire you around. . . ."

"There won't be any next time," Fancy said.

"I'll keep hoping," Jed said. "My luck's always been good. . . ."

"Don't depend on it," Fancy said.

"I got to," Jed murmured. "I'm sunk now. Seeing you this close, talking to you—I'm sunk. Scheming's all gone now, Miss Fancy. It's just you. 'Bye, now—both of you. You'll be seeing me. . . ."

As Fancy watched him walk out of the dining room, her face was puzzled.

"Does he," she said, "always go around proposing to girls he just met?"

"No," Wyche said. "Jed's got a reputation of being cagey—hard to get. Many a little filly's set her cap for him before now. Only he wasn't having any. Damned if I don't believe he means it!"

"He's nice," Fancy said. "Most any girl would take a shine to him. So good-looking and all. Still . . ."

"Still there's this other bounder," Wyche said. "That's it, isn't it, Fan?"

"Yes, Wyche," Fancy said, "that's it."

Wyche looked at her a long time and very intently. But he didn't say anything. He stood up at last and took her hand. They went out of the Globe together and started walking back toward the place they'd left the wagon.

On the way, they passed Court Brantley. He stopped still and looked at Fancy, seeing her in daylight for the first time, her clear young beauty unmottled by the flambeaus. And he frowned, thinking:

If she's no good, it sure hasn't marked her. That's a child's face— a sweet child at that. God, but she's pretty! Blue eyes with black hair is unusual—sets her off. And her skin's like a blonde's. White as—as—and it came unbidden to his mind—as Fern's. But he didn't want to make that comparison. It was, to him, a kind of blasphemy to compare any mortal woman with Fern.

As for Fan, one sight of him and there was a sunburst in her cheeks. She looked away from him quickly, hoping that Wyche wouldn't see.

Wyche didn't. He was too troubled in mind to notice the people they passed.

Peering through the flap of the tent that night, Fancy was frightened by the size of the crowd. It looked like everybody in the world was there. Even from where she stood, shivering behind the tent flap, she could see Court Brantley, and after that she didn't look for anyone else. She could hear Wyche making his farewell speech. It was, she realized, a curiously honest speech, for Wyche hinted that most of the benefits to be gotten from any medicine lay in the minds of those taking it. "Have faith," he said, "and it will help you the exact extent of the amount of faith you have." He made none of his usual extravagant claims for the medicine. The crowd sensed his mood and was restless.

He didn't even call upon Mose to dance or to crack any of their miserable jokes. At the end he said very simply: "And now, the young lady known as Madame Scheherazade will entertain you with her dance of the mysterious East. She will not tell fortunes, tonight —nor any other night in the future. For this, my friends, is her last appearance before you—and mine, as well."

53

Fan could hear the disgruntled mutter rumble through the crowd. She could feel her heart beating like a wild thing, and despite the heat there were beads of icy perspiration on her forehead.

Mose picked up the flute and began, and Fancy raced over to the wagon and Wyche helped her up. This time she didn't close her eyes: she looked straight at Court Brantley. She couldn't make out his face, because he stood too far away from the lanterns, but she had the feeling he was frowning. Then, very slowly, she began to dance to the music of Mose's flute.

Tonight, for the first time, she actually listened to it, and her dance was beautiful. She had no idea what she looked like, but Wyche did. He thought she looked like a bride in some strange, primitive rite, entertaining her future lord. He tried to follow her gaze to see whom she was doing it for; but it was too dark, and the faces of all but the men in the first two or three rows were hidden. Wyche found the dance strangely touching. Even Fancy's young, inexperienced awkwardness was moving. It was like an oriental child bride trying to please, but betraying her innocence of the sensuality she had been trained to imitate with every gesture.

Then he heard a high, nasal tenor voice saying: "That her, Duke?" And looking out he saw the three men pushing their way through the crowd. Duke was the only one of the Ellises that he knew; but he guessed at once that the other two men must be his brothers, Tom and Buck.

He loosened the buttons of his frock coat, getting ready to take it off. Then Duke Ellis elbowed his way into the front row and stood there looking at Fancy.

"Hell, yes! It's her all right," Duke bellowed. "Now where'n hell-fire is that polecat, Weathers!"

Wyche stepped forward easily from the shadows alongside the wagon.

"Right here, Duke," he said quietly, "though how you can smell another polecat through your own scent is more than I can see."

"Well, well," Duke grinned; "if it ain't the little Doc, himself! Nervy little fellow ain't you, stealing my gal!"

On the platform, Fancy stood still, too frightened to move. The men in the front row broke away from Duke and Wyche like a wave. Only Court Brantley stood where he was; then after a second, he started forward.

"Hiyah, Fan," Duke laughed. "Time you came on back home, babydoll. Been looking all over for you ever since you run away from our cosy little cottage."

Court had moved up now so close that the light of the lanterns showed on his face. Fancy saw him stiffen when he heard what Duke said, and something inside her died, terribly.

Oh, no, Court! No! she cried inside her heart. He's lying, it wasn't like that at all—it wasn't!

"Appears to me," Wyche said, "that Miss Fancy's got a perfect right to say what she wants to do."

"Nobody asked you, little Doc," Duke said evenly. "Now move out of my way. I don't aim to hurt anybody so small."

"You mean you don't aim to get hurt, don't you, Duke?" Wyche said almost gently.

Duke stopped short and glared at him. If he had ever before bothered to notice Wyche, he would have seen that the short man was as big around the chest as he was, and was better muscled, with even bigger arms. Fancy had thought to herself more than once that the top of Wyche Weathers looked like it had gotten joined to the wrong bottom, for only Wyche's legs were short. And they were thickset and powerful.

"You're asking for it, Doc," he said. "Well, I'll make this short. Got better things to do. . . ."

Then he swung his big right fist like a sledge-hammer, all of his weight behind it. But Wyche wasn't there any more. He weaved downward to the left, letting Duke's blow whistle over his shoulder, and came up almost from the ground with his left so that it buried itself in Duke's middle. Duke doubled, and Wyche crossed with his right, the sound of the blow carrying clearly. Duke's big head turned halfway round on his neck, and he went down like a pole-axed bull.

The men crowded back, staring. Not Duke Ellis! Not the man who had spread terror from Pinch Gut to the Sandhill. Not the man who had wrecked half the taverns on Carmichael's Range single-handed. But a second later, a look of pleasure came into their eyes. More than one man there remembered how Duke's big fist

55

felt. And to see him sprawled out in the dirt was a real pleasure.

Duke sat up shaking his head. He stared at Wyche with astonished eyes. He had never been hit so hard in all his life.

"You want some more?" Wyche said.

"Why you stinking, ornery, woman-stealing little polecat!" Duke roared and came up off the ground in a rush. But a heartbeat later he was back on it again, for Wyche waited until he was close enough, and jabbed through Duke's clumsy defenses, with maddening ease, flattening Duke's nose against his face; then hooking a right to his jaw turning it sideways just far enough so that the left hook could turn it back again, then right, and again the left, smoothworking, swinging, Wyche's fists, the size of small hams, landing right, left, right again so fast that it was for all the world as though he were punching a bag in a gymnasium. Duke Ellis didn't land a blow. He hung there, his eyes glazing over, taking it; until Wyche stepped back and dropped his hands to his sides, watching with cool amusement while the big man bent forward slowly, as though bowing to Fancy, and continued on down, gathering speed as he went, until he toppled to the ground.

"Reckon that settles that," Wyche said, "unless you other two polecats want a taste of the same."

Tom and Buck didn't answer.

Wyche turned toward the wagon, and put one foot on the lowest step, before Fancy screamed:

"Look out, Wyche!"

He half turned, but he was too late. Buck Ellis lunged forward, the blade of the spring-operated pocket knife, clicking open as he touched the catch on the handle. Wyche's big fist grazed his jaw; but the blade, all eight inches of it, disappeared into Wyche's flesh, low on the left side.

Wyche backed away from Buck, holding his side, and Court Brantley came up from behind and slashed the knife out of Buck's hand with one blow of the short gutta percha cane he carried. Tom Ellis started for him. Then he stopped short, and Fancy saw the reason: Court was holding a short, ugly little pistol with four barrels mounted in two pairs one above the other pointed straight at his chest.

"Don't come any closer, Tom," he half whispered. "Shooting an

Ellis would give me a hell of a lot of pleasure." He looked toward where Wyche leaned up against the wagon, the color draining out of his tanned face.

"'Tend to him, Fan," he said; "he's hurt bad."

Fancy leaped down from the wagon, and clawed at Wyche's clothes with frantic fingers. They were wet, sickeningly wet.

"Got to sit down, baby," Wyche whispered; "can't stand any more."

He slumped down to the ground, and Fan tore off her veil, holding it against the wound.

"Reckon I'm done," Wyche muttered. "Fan, baby—" Then he went down.

Court stood there listening to Fancy's helpless crying.

"Oh Wyche, honey, don't die—not over me don't die! I ain't worth it—I ain't! Oh God, oh Jesus, Wyche!"

Court turned away from her.

"Some of you men go get Sheriff Bowen," he said. "And one of you get Doc Blumfeldt."

By the time the sheriff and the doctor got there, Duke was up again. Court held all three Ellises before him at pistol-point while the sheriff clicked the handcuffs about their wrists.

"You Ellises have gone a mite too far this time," the sheriff said; "if Weathers dies, by God, I'll see that you swing for it!"

"He won't die," Harry Blumfeldt said; "he can thank his wonderful constitution for that. All right you men, help me load him on the wagon. One of you drive to the hospital. I have to stay back with him."

"All right, you three," Sheriff Bowen growled; "get moving. Thanks, Court—you acted like a public-spirited citizen."

"Just a minute, Sheriff," Duke said. "Let me tend to one little personal matter, before you drag me off. The little lady's a friend of mine. Surely a Southern gentleman like you won't stand by and see her left without a cent and nowhere to stay. . . ."

"All right," Bowen said; "but make it fast."

"Be a good scout, Sheriff, and take my wallet out of my breast pocket. That's it. Now my keys, out of the side. Give 'em to her. Fan, honey, these are to the cottage. You stay there till I get out . . ."

Mutely Fancy took the wallet and the keys, and went back to

wiping Wyche's face with his own handkerchief. Then she saw Court staring at her, and realized at last what she held in her hand.

"No, Duke, no!" she cried; but Court turned away from her, his thin face filled with disgust. In the driver's seat, the man who had taken the reins flapped them over the backs of the mules. The wagon moved off through the dark, with old Mose trotting behind it.

Fancy wanted to jump out of it and run to Court, but she couldn't leave Wyche. There goes my future, she thought, and turned back to the unconscious man. But from time to time she turned her head toward where Court Brantley's tall figure stood in the darkness, now that the lanterns were gone. She kept watching him until she couldn't see him any more. And it came to her then that the place where he stood was awfully dark—the darkest place, maybe, in the whole wide world.

Then the wagon went around a bend in the road, and she couldn't even see the place where he stood.

4

"I⊤ was mighty white of you to write me about my boy's misfortune, Mister Brantley," Ted Weathers said to Court. "Yes, sir—mighty white!"

Court looked across the aisle of the train at the pullman berth in which Wyche lay. Wyche had his eyes closed, and his massive frame seemed drained of strength.

"Isn't it a little dangerous," Court said, "to move him so soon?"

"Well, the docs did want me to wait; but I've got to get him home where he can be properly attended to. Besides, I've wanted him back for years. 'Pears to me I treated him mighty harshly. I mean to make it up to him now—if it's the last thing I do."

"Is he conscious?" Court asked.

"Not fully. The doc gave him a little something so that he wouldn't feel the jolting of the train. He'll be back in Spartanburg before he comes to himself. Anyhow, I'm mighty glad to have him— it's been five years, Mister Brantley. . . ."

"I know," Court said gravely. "There's one thing I think you'd like to know, Mister Weathers: Wyche was planning to come home

59

of his own accord. The night he was attacked—he'd already announced he was giving up the medicine show."

"Was he now?" Ted Weathers' powerful old face brightened; then a worried look came back into his eyes. "But this—this girl," he muttered; "heard tell the fight was over some girl."

"In a way it was," Court said smoothly. "It seemed that—this girl had previously formed a connection with a local man. They quarreled, and she ran away from him. Then she joined Wyche's troupe—in a purely professional capacity. She was much younger than Wyche, and he seems to have treated her in a fatherly sort of way. That's what she says—and I believe her. In fact," and Court forced a convincing chuckle, "she seemed a mite disappointed."

He could see the old man's face clearing with relief. Strange how the desire to believe a thing increased a man's credulity. . . .

Outside the window, the conductor bellowed: " 'Board!" and Court stood up.

"It's been nice meeting you, Mister Weathers," he said; "and give Wyche my kindest regards when he comes around."

"Thank you, my boy," Ted Weathers said. "If there's anything I can ever do for you—if you should ever need a job or anything . . ."

"Thank you," Court murmured. "Take good care of Wyche. He was a friend of mine."

When the train had gone snorting and puffing out of the station, Court Brantley stood there a long moment looking after it.

"So long, Wyche," he murmured. "You're out of this now—back in the lap of luxury. While I—oh hell, thinking about it does no good. . . ."

He started walking slowly through the town, back toward Hiberion. What went on inside of his mind was a kind of ugliness, but he couldn't stop it. They're all alike, he thought, women are all alike. Fern lying with the sanction of church and state in my brother's lecherous arms, and Fan up there in that little cottage of Duke's on the Sandhill—waiting. Why am I concerned about that? Fern now, was something to me; but this little fluff of hill trash was nothing and less than nothing. Yet it hurts, damn it! I was beginning to believe her—she swore there was nothing between her and Wyche. Maybe there wasn't. Wyche was a strange man. But she didn't swear anything about Duke Ellis and she took that money and those keys without a murmur. . . . Watch it, Court, boy. When are you going to grow up? You should know by now that virtue's always a lack of opportunity, or the product of fear—never a real inclination. . . .

But Fern. My little Fern—with that blonde hair like new moonlight, and skin like snow with a dawn flush on it. How could she? How in the name of all that's decent and holy could she turn to Ty? She knew Ty—she wasn't fooled. She knew that he was all Brantley —blood and bone of this centaur breed of ours. But am I any different? I've tried to be. Hell of a heritage to live down, though—seven generations of men who died in those atavistic, ceremonial brawls we call duels, and always because of their poaching upon the preserves of men who were their neighbors and friends. Not counting the ones who broke their necks leaping from second-story bedroom windows, or were shot in the back while running away from their discovered dishonor. . . .

Some family, we Brantleys. The men a breed of satyrs, and the women haunted by a suicidal mania. The Brantley women die by drowning, Father says. And by poison, leaping from high places and any other method that's convenient. He laughed aloud. Fine lot I've got to offer any woman—and I've been eating my heart out because two of 'em beat me at my own treacherous game. . . .

He came to the gate of the house, and stood there looking at it. He had the feeling that he was seeing it, really seeing it, for the first time since he had come back from Boston. That was crazy. He'd been back better than six months now; but it came to him that he had never really looked at Hiberion in all that time—never seen it with eyes stripped of illusion, divested of emotion.

Well, he was seeing it now, and the sight made him sick. Hiberion had been a name that had meant something in Georgia once. Had been. But not now. The slim Doric columns that had soared up for two stories to hold up the roof above two lovely porches were chipped and cracked, and there was green mold in the cracks. The white paint was a dirty gray now, peeling in tattered flakes, and the upper porch hung down at a crazy angle, all that was left of it, that is. Its floor had rotted through, and somebody—the Negroes, or perhaps even the family itself—had been using the timbers for firewood. The delicate filigree tracery of the ironwork balustrade that had surrounded it was still intact, but it was red with rust.

There was Spanish moss dripping from the eaves, and through the roof of the porches, Court could see the sky. The bronze knocker was gone from the front door, and the holes from the bolts that had held it had been greatly enlarged by rot.

The grass on the lawn stood up waist-high, and the bird bath was choked with weeds. None of the riot of flowers that had surrounded the porch showed, gone, too, a prey to neglect and despair. Around the house, he remembered, the fields had stretched out time out of mind down to the banks of the Savannah. But the fields were gone now, filled up with ugly little breezeway and dogtrot houses, with shotgun cabins, even; and instead of the scent of jasmine, the rank stench of collard greens cooking assailed his nostrils.

He was aware of a movement in the tall grass and weeds that choked what had been the finest yard and driveway in the state of Georgia, and a sow marched triumphantly before him, her litter grunting and snorting behind him. Pigs, by God! In Hiberion's front yard. "'If ye have tears,'" Court quoted, suddenly, bitterly, "'prepare to shed them now!'"

It had been bad enough when he left, eight years ago. But he had been so little prepared for this that in all the months he had been home he had shut his mind to it, had refused to see it as it was.

He started walking once more toward the porch and stood looking up at the giant magnolia tree that stood beside it. The tree was as beautiful as ever with its glossy oval leaves, and its huge, heavy blossoms whose petals were like woman's flesh, creamy-white and soft; and the scent that came down from them was a thing that overpowered the reason.

He went up the steps, feeling them giving under his weight, their strength and solidity gone. When he reached the lower porch, he realized that it too, had rotted through, and that all the Brantleys had been able to do about it was to bridge the gap with rough-hewn planks. He pushed the door and it opened with a creak that was an agony to hear; then Court stood once more inside the foyer of the house in which he had been born.

He kept quite still, holding hard against the pain and sickness inside his chest, seeing the great patches of plaster that had fallen from the walls and the ceilings. The fine old wallpaper, brought from England at great expense, hung down in tattered ribbons; the wide, curving staircase, that soared unsupported in sweeping spirals to the upper floors, had a ten-foot section of its balustrade missing. That staircase had been the glory of the house, like the magnificent chandelier of cut Belgian glass that now was a tattered ruin, with numerous strings of crystal missing.

Court went very quietly up the stairs toward his father's room, but before he had reached it, he heard the old man weeping.

"How are the mighty fallen!" Jeff Brantley cried. "I should have been killed at Atlanta! I should have died in my blood on a muddy field with a Yankee bayonet through my guts! That it should come to this! Oh the shame of it all!"

Court stepped into the room. It was a little better than the rest of the house, but even so it was sad to see. Saddest of all, perhaps, was the face of his father, lined and sunken, a ruin, too, like Hiberion, a breed that had died at Appomattox Court House, that lived on only in this quaking ghost. Court glanced at the thin, shapeless figures of his sisters, at their pale faces, which even to call plain was a kindness.

It was Saphira who saw him at last.

"So you're home at last," she said tiredly. "Father, here's Court."

"Court?" the old man quavered, and Court knew that this time again his father wasn't going to remember him. He had been through it all before, but it wasn't pleasant.

"Court?" Jeff Brantley mused. "Oh yes, Court—another of my sons. The one that ran away to Boston. The one that had to become a Yankee and go to Harvard College. . . . Oh, how sharper than a serpent's tooth is an ungrateful . . ."

"Hush, Father," Agnes said.

"I will not hush! Let me howl like old King Lear. Let me bare my shame to all the world. Come here, Court. Let me look at you. Let me see what they've done to you, up there in that heathen land."

Court started toward the trembling old wreck who had been a Brantley, who had sat on his horse with the best of that centaur breed, who had been proud, and brave and fiery and handsomer far than any of his sons. Halfway across the room, he could smell the liquor fumes. Jefferson Brantley was drunk.

"Yes, Court," he whispered, turning his watery blue eyes upon the tall figure of his son. "You came back. That's good—that's better than the others did. Tyler running off to Martin in Savannah, and Philemon—Philemon—"

"Father!" Agnes and Saphira chorused.

"I'll not be silenced! Philemon wallowing with his nigger wench and begetting children with her! There are black Brantleys now—you know that, Court? The finest blood in Georgia is flowing now in nigger veins!"

Of course Court had known about it. He had been told the whole story with delicate malice by Fern the very day he got home. But it wasn't a thing that talking about helped. Nothing helped things like that really.

"Father—" he began.

"Tyler now," Jeff Brantley said, "I'd have expected this of him. He's a raffish nighthawk like all the Brantleys . . . but not Phil. Phil was always good. Should have known better, though—it's in the blood. The Brantley women die by drowning; the men by fire, bullets, or the sword—those that escape hanging, that is. But no good ever come out of the breed, not yet, nor ever will. . . ."

Agnes came up to Court quickly and whispered in his ear:

"We've been keeping it from him for years. But Mary Jane, our washerwoman, told him about it this morning. Oh, Court, why do niggers love so to be the bearers of evil tidings?"

"Revenge, perhaps," Court said, "for the way we treat them. Who knows?" Then to his father, he said: "Now, Father—it's not as bad as all that—"

"Not bad? Do you mate a thoroughbred with a jenny? Or the sons of men with female apes? Not bad, Court? I should have strangled in my mother's womb before I lived to see this day!"

"Well," Court said, "it's done now, and sitting here crying over it won't do any good. There's a lot more to be done around here than moaning over Phil's misdeeds—"

"You should talk!" Jeff Brantley roared. "You were the first of my sons to run away and leave us in poverty and despair."

Court could not repress a smile despite his misery. His father still talked, as always, like a back county orator.

64

"And the first to come back, Father," he said gently.

"That's true, that's true," the old man sighed. "Only what are you going to do, Court? What can anyone do now?"

"Well," Court said, "for one thing, I'm going to try to raise some money to build a mill—"

"A mill!" Jeff exploded. "Oh no—not another one! Not another of my sons stooping to engage in trade!"

"Engaging in trade," Saphira put in drily, "Father's quaint way of describing that store Phil was smart enough to set up. Have you been up there yet, Court?"

"Once or twice," Court said. "I didn't linger. Stores depress me—especially Phil's kind of a store."

"You're as bad as Father. Phil's done right well, Court. It's his money that has kept us eating and put clothes on our backs. In fact Father couldn't afford the disgusting state he's in right now if it weren't for Phil."

"I gather," Court said, "that you don't entirely disapprove of Phil, Saph."

"No, I don't. Any man who married Martha Tilton would have done the same thing. Of course, it's unfortunate that Phil had to turn to this colored girl. But he's been married to Martha six years, and still not a child in sight. Besides his mulatto yard children are quite pretty; I've seen them."

"Saphira!" Agnes said.

"Why not?" Saphira said. "Why shouldn't I see them, Agnes? After all, they are our own flesh and blood."

"I think," Agnes wept, "that you're being perfectly horrid."

"All right, I'll be horrid then. We've lived in illusion too long, my dear sister. Notice the crowd of men outside beating a path to our door? We're too good, we Brantleys. Good for what? You know why we're still here in this drafty, hideous old house, listening to the wails of this drunken old weakling who sired us? Because nobody would have us, my darlin' sister. Sneer at Phil's high brown wench if you want to; but she's better than us. She could at least get a man. Can you? Can I?"

"That, Saph," Court said quietly, "is quite enough."

"It is enough, isn't it, Court? It's a heap too much to my way of thinking. I'm through with this life. I'm going out and get myself a man—any way I can get him. In wedlock or out of it. And I won't be choicy. Any man I can get will do—even an Ellis. . . ."

"How are the mighty fallen," Jeff Brantley moaned.

I could have stayed in Boston, Court thought. With a little encouragement my friendship with Hester Snow could have ripened into something. I could be sitting down right now to a good dinner looking at her across a Hepplewhite table under candlelight. But I had to come back to a girl who wouldn't wait for me, to this plantation overgrown with weeds and white trash, to this lovely old house through which the wind blows without hindrance. I had to come back to this sodden old wreck of a father, to these two disappointed harpies I call sisters, to those tart-tumbling gallants, Tyler and Phil. It's something to be proud of, this family; there's nothing finer than this Brantley breed. . . .

"Please," he said tiredly, "we've quarreled enough, don't you think? I'm very tired. . . ."

"I'm sorry, Court," Saphira said at once. "That was rotten of me. You must be hungry, too. Anything to eat in the house, Ag?"

"Well," Agnes said, "there's some greens and sidemeat and corn pone. I'll make Court some coffee . . ."

"Nigger food!" Jeff Brantley snorted.

"No thank you, girls," Court said politely. "I'm not hungry now. I'm a little too tired to eat anyhow. I think I'll go out and wander around a bit."

"But Court," Agnes protested, "you just said you were tired."

"I am, but it's not the kind of tiredness you can lie down on. I'm all kinked up. I need to move about."

"Go see Phil," Jeff Brantley said suddenly. "Talk to him, Court. You always had great influence over him. Maybe you can get him to give up his wench. Maybe you can get him to see the light of reason."

"I'll try," Court said; "I'll stop by Ty's, too; I want to talk to him about the business I'm planning."

"Didn't you hear Father say he's down at Melody, Uncle Martin's place?" Saphira said. "Uncle Martin's sick, and our precious brother is trying to persuade him to leave Melody to him—instead of to all of us."

"I don't believe that," Court said. "With all Ty's faults, he wouldn't. Fern go with him?"

"Aha!" Saphira laughed. "So the wind blows still to that quarter! No, Court, darlin', she didn't. She's at home now, all by her pretty little self. Now you can establish a new record even for the Brantleys. Your brother's wife—that would be interesting, wouldn't it?"

"Saph, you're a devil," Court said; "I have no intention—"

"Haven't you, my saintly brother? Then you're the first Brantley in history who hasn't. Besides, I don't believe you. Considering the fact that you so nobly came to the defense of Wyche Weathers' fancy woman last week—or was she Wyche's? I heard she was originally Duke Ellis'. Anyhow, she's most likely yours by now—since Wyche is in the hospital, and Duke's in jail. What about it, Court?"

Court's face reddened; then, suddenly, he smiled.

"You won't believe me, Saph," he said, "but she isn't. Anyhow, thanks for the suggestion. Come to think of it, it's a mighty good idea."

"Court," Agnes wailed, "don't you go and get yourself in trouble! Somebody in this family has to stay out of trouble."

"Why?" Saphira said. "Appears to me it's a heap more fun to get into it—deep. Come on, Court, I'll walk you to the door."

They came out on the porch, and Court looked at Saphira, thinking: you've got grit in your craw; no wonder you're my favorite relative. But Saphira's hand was gripping his arm, hard.

"Court!" she whispered; "is that her?"

Court looked up, and saw Fancy standing at the gate looking at the house.

"Yes," he said brusquely, "that's her all right."

"My, she's pretty!" Saphira said. "Go ask her in, Court. I'd like to meet her."

"No!" Court said. "You don't want to meet that kind of a woman, Saph. Leave it to me—I'll attend to her."

"She doesn't look bad," Saphira said. "She looks like a child—sort of scared. Why, Court, she has a sweet face! I don't believe the things people are saying about her—I really don't!"

"Now, Saph—" Court began; but Saphira wasn't there any more. She was running down the path toward the gate.

Court started out behind her, then he slowed to a walk. He'd be damned before he made a scene. Let Saph meet Fancy if she wanted to. Not much harm could come of it.

"Hello," Saphira said breathlessly, "I'm Court's sister, Saphira. You're Fancy, aren't you?"

"Yes'm," Fancy murmured. "Mighty proud to make your acquaintance, Miss Saphira. . . ." Then, very shyly she put out her hand.

Saphira took it in a grip that caused Fancy to wince.

"How pretty you are!" she said. "Black hair and blue eyes—that's an odd combination, but it's lovely. I wish I were pretty. Oh well, there's nothing can be done about that. I do hope we're going to be friends."

"Me too," Fancy said.

That's Saph, Court thought. A tongue like a fiend out of hell, and the best, kindest heart in the world when you get right down to it. I'm glad she's being sweet to Fan. The poor kid needs it.

"I wish I could ask you in," Saphira rushed on, heedlessly, "but—"

"I know," Fancy said. "Court won't let you. He—he thinks I'm—bad."

"Well, aren't you?" Saphira demanded. "I should think it would be very interesting to be bad. I've often thought I'd like to be—very much."

Fancy stared at her, then at Court.

"Does she mean that, Court?" she asked.

"Reckon she does," Court grinned.

Fancy put out her hand and let it rest on Saphira's arm.

"Can you tell when a body's lying, Miss Saphira?" she asked seriously.

"Of course I can. I'm a woman, aren't I?"

"Then listen to me: I have never let a man so much as touch me in all my life. . . ."

"Ha!" Court snorted.

Fancy whirled and faced him.

"Listen to me, Tallman!" she said. "You're the first man I ever even kissed! Course Duke Ellis kissed me once, but that was 'cause he was twisting my arm fit to break it; and afterwards I hit him on the head with a poker to stop him from doing anything more! I let

68

you kiss me, and that was the first time! And I kissed you, and that was the first time for that, too!"

"You expect me to believe that?" Court said.

Fancy looked at him, and her mouth tightened.

"No, I don't," she said flatly. "That would be too much to expect, 'specially from a high and mighty Brantley. Reckon I'm a mighty big fool to care. But then I am a big fool as far as you're concerned, Court—so right now, I know exactly how Lem Waters felt. . . ."

"Lem Waters?" Saphira said.

"Yep—neighbor of ours in Ca'lina. They found him a-lying 'longside of Hannah Murray, and her dead—shot to death. Lem was drunk, and there was one bullet gone from his gun. Well—they hung him. Come protracted meeting time, Hannah's husband, Tim, got religion, and confessed that he'd shot Hannah, seeing her walking with Tim in the moonlight. That bullet Lem shot lit in a tree. But right now, I know how he felt sitting there in his cell a-waiting. You see, Court, nobody believed him either."

"Court," Saphira said, "she's not lying! Can't you see that, you big dumb ox? She's not!"

Court looked at Fancy, but he didn't say anything. He just stood there looking at her, and after a while he spoke to her very gently, but all he said was:

"All right, Fan, I'll take you home now."

They started off together walking slowly, and Saphira hung over the gate watching them. I believe her, she thought; don't know why I should, but I do.

Court didn't look at Fancy, or even speak to her; but from time to time he glanced at her out of the corner of his eye. His face was puzzled. Looking at her made it a hard job to do any kind of thinking at all. He kept seeing that her skin was just as white as was Fern's, except that the coloring of the cheeks and the mouth was warmer and richer, and that her hair was so black it looked blue. Every time he glanced at her he had the funny feeling that her eyes didn't belong to her; they were startling behind her sooty lashes, being the exact color of an October sky when she looked at him, and like flashes of light when she moved them.

Her mouth's too big, he thought, and sort of sullen. I've never seen that exact shade of red before. But that wasn't what he wanted to think of—he had to decide really whether or not she was telling the truth. She couldn't be. No man on earth would travel around for months with a girl like this one and not—Then, too, hadn't Duke given her his wallet and his keys and hadn't she taken them?

There was beyond this something else, something frightening to think about. Suppose she was telling the truth? What then? He thought about his choices in the matter if she were. They were very simple, and both of them very unpleasant: He could be all Brantley and heap upon her the misery that came to every woman who loved a Brantley without thought of herself, or he could play the fool and marry her and be forever the laughingstock of the whole town.

"Oh damn!" he groaned, and seeing her looking at him, he realized he had spoken aloud.

"Court," she said very simply, "why won't you believe me?"

"You took his wallet," he said, "and his keys."

"I know. I was beside myself what with poor Wyche hurt so. There was two hundred and fifty dollars in that wallet, Court. Here it is—count 'em and you'll see I haven't touched a red cent of that money."

As he took the wallet, it came to Court that he had absolutely no way of knowing how much money had really been in that wallet. But looking at Fancy, he knew suddenly she was telling the truth. About this, at least, she was telling the truth.

He handed the wallet back to her without even opening it.

"Why?" he said.

"I don't want to be beholden to Duke," she said simply. "Took this money back to him three times at the jail, but he won't take it."

"But you stay at his house," Court said.

"Yes. Tried to pay him rent, but he laughed at me. One sure thing, Court, I'm going to be gone from there long before he gets out of jail."

"Why do you stay there now?" Court said morosely.

"Where else could I stay? Can't come stay with you, Tallman. Can't stay in the streets. Leaseways, up there, I'm safe. Folks hereabouts so scairt of Duke, that they leave me be. That's the only good thing," she added bitterly, "I ever got out of knowing him . . ."

Court looked at her. He was frightened. He couldn't exactly put into words what he was afraid of, but he knew that if he started believing Fancy he was going to be in trouble—bad trouble.

"Why'd he say you were his girl?" he demanded.

"Reckon I was, kind of. I thought old Duke was just about the finest gentleman I'd ever seen. Way he talked, I thought he aimed to marry me. Then he got me up to that little old cottage of hisn, and tried to make me drunk and grabbed me. I hit him with the poker and ran. That's how I met Wyche."

"And he, of course, was not your beau either?"

"Wyche wants to marry me, Court," Fancy said gravely; "and he's willing to wait. He ain't one for putting in a crop before he's built a fence—not that I'd let him if he was. . . ."

Court stared at her, and nodded slowly.

"You know, Fan," he whispered, "I believe you. Damn my hide for a stupid fool, but I do!"

"Oh, Court, honey, I'm so glad!" Fan said; "I'm so blamed glad I'm scairt I'm going to cry. Heck, I am going to cry, darn it!"

They were passing the railroad station, and the train from Atlanta was in. But Court didn't pay any attention to any of the dozens of people he knew who were getting off of it. He stepped up close to her and took her in his arms. When they came apart finally, he heard the sharp intake of breath behind him and a woman's voice gasped:

"Why, Court! Court Brantley!"

Court turned his head slowly and looked over his shoulder. Fern stood there, her small, slippered foot beating a tattoo on the cobblestones. Behind Fern were still others, the women's faces twisted with rage, the men trying to keep the look of envy out of their eyes. Court turned then and made Fern a deep bow.

"I suppose," Fern said, "that you make a habit of kissing women in public places!"

"No," Court said; "no, my dear sister-in-law—not all women. Just the pretty ones who don't belong to me. The ones who do, I kiss in private. Of course, I'll admit the classification can be stretched a mite."

Fern took a backward step.

"Oh!" she said. "Her! That woman! Why, Courtland Brantley!" Court grinned at her wickedly.

"Now look, Mrs. Brantley," he said, "Mrs. Tyler Brantley—

you've no call to take on about Fan like that. Appears to me you've thrown away your right to be concerned about anything I do. And Fan's all right. At least she's honest, in her curious way."

"Honest!" Fern said. "Her!"

"Yes, her. It was because she'd just convinced me of that that I kissed her. I know the truth when I hear it, having had some recent experience with liars."

"I suppose," Fern said, "that you'll end up married to this—this circus snake dancer!"

Court looked at her.

"I could have done worse," he said quietly. "Reckon the way little Fancy made her living is kind of irrelevant. The point is, Fern, honey, I kind of think that she tells the truth—that she'd keep a bargain. I know some people who can't keep bargains, who forget important promises, whose sacred word doesn't mean anything. Maybe I'm no judge of such things, but I don't think Fan comes off so badly by comparison."

He turned to the others, smiling peacefully.

"And now that you've all had your fun," he said; "don't you think youall had better run along home? Night air's bad for the health, I'm told."

The crowd began to move off slowly. Ceremoniously Court turned to Fancy and offered her his arm.

"Oh, Court!" she said. "The way you took up for me—it was just grand!"

Court looked back over his shoulder and saw that Fern was still standing there. As he looked at her, the last ray of sunlight came through the open ends of the depot and lighted her face. She was crying.

Seeing her cry made Court feel good all over. It was, he knew, a bad, ugly sort of feeling—a cheap kind of triumph. But he couldn't help it. After what he had come home to, it felt good to make Fern cry.

A little while later, walking through the gathering darkness with Fancy, after they had got down from the horse car that had taken them up the Sandhill, Court didn't feel so good about it any more. You're a bad loser, Court Brantley, he told himself, and that was a mighty ugly thing. What good is it now to hurt Fern? What good is anything now, anything in this whole damned dreary world, now that she's gone?

Fancy tightened her grip upon his arm, and rubbed her soft black hair against his shoulder. He was so tall, this Court Brantley. Tall and brave and gay—a real gentleman. The Brantleys were the finest people in the state. Real quality, no mistake about that. But that girl—that Fern Vance who'd married his brother Tyler. She was so pretty. A body hadn't ought to be that pretty—it wasn't right. It wasn't fair to the rest of the women in the world—it wasn't fair to Fancy to have that white and golden beauty 'twixt her and the man she loved. . . .

Court had spoken to her right short like, though. But why? He had sounded a mighty heap like a hurt and disappointed man. I'll fix that! Fancy decided; I'll make him forget her if it's the last thing I do. . . .

But when they had come to Duke's cottage, the moon was already up and she could see his face. It frightened her. Fancy hadn't known any Brantleys before or else she would have recognized that look. Fern could have told her about it—Fern, and any of a legion of other women, living and dead, who'd seen that look on a Brantley's face. The Brantleys weren't the smartest folk in the world or the bravest or the best, as Fancy believed; what they were actually, was unbeatable—they were just a little too much for most other people; without knowing or caring how and why, they made better men than they, back water—give ground.

Fancy fumbled in her little handbag until she had found her keys. She unlocked the door and turned back to Court.

" 'Night, Court," she said quietly.

" 'Night?" Court laughed. "Heck, Fan—the night's not even a baby, yet. But you and I, honey, are going to age it—fast."

Then he stepped up to her and took her in his arms.

Fancy didn't fight him. She didn't because she didn't want to. And, after a minute or two she knew that what he wanted was what she wanted too, as much as he did, maybe, or even more. But Wyche Weathers had given her something; he had strengthened something that she herself had. And what he had given her was a very good thing, for even in the midst of this—this new thing that spun the night about her head, that made her want the dying, the melting, the awaited hurt, it came to her and cried out fiercely: no, not like this! In a veil, in the church—for always, not a playtoy, not your easy woman, Court Brantley, no more than Duke's—your woman, yes, because I love you; but only when you love me back, when you're willing to build that fence and stand up 'longside of me proud for the world to see. . . .

She tore free of him and stood there shivering and crying a little until her breath came back and then she said:

"No, Court—not like that. Not even you—like that." Then she turned and went through the door and slammed it shut and locked it behind her.

She stood just inside the door and listened to his breathing. It was an ugly sound. He didn't move or say a word. She stopped her own breath, holding it hard in her throat until she hurt from holding it so. There was a hot tingling feeling crawling over her flesh, and at the same time it was cold, too, so that she felt like she was scalding and freezing; but outside the door Court Brantley didn't move. Then, very quietly, she heard him turn, and his footsteps went slowly, lumpily across the porch and down the steps. She heard the gravel on the walk crunch once or twice, and the harsh, rusty squeak of the gate hinges. Then it was still.

She let her breath out, little by little. There was no sound in the room, no sound at all except the noise she made breathing, and the hammering underneath her ribs. She took a step toward the door, then another, and her fingers closed over the knob. Then, quite suddenly, her knees gave way, and she went down in a little heap before the door, one hand still stretched out and up, holding the doorknob, the knuckles of the other rammed into her mouth, trying to keep from crying aloud; but it was no good.

She let it out then, ugly and choked and noisy like a whipped child.

"Court!" she cried. "Oh, Court, Court, Court. . . ."

Then she lurched to her feet and went to the side window where she could see the road, curving down and away from the cottage in the moonlight. Court was walking down it, his head bent, shuffling his feet in the dust like an old man, and everything Wyche had told her, everything that she herself believed was nothing and less than

74

nothing, and she hurled herself against the door, twisting the key with stiffened fingers, and ran out of the house.

But, when she got to the gate, she saw it. A smart little road wagon came up the road toward Court. It was drawn by two dappled grays, and as it stopped, the moonlight came down between two of the pines, and fell upon the head of the girl who drove it. Where the light touched her hair, it looked like silver. Fancy stood there, watching her talking to Court. Then Court climbed up into the seat beside her, and she pulled the horses around in a wide circle, heading back down the road.

The moon still shone on the road after they had gone. But somehow a grayness had got into the light, dimming it. Fancy couldn't understand that. All she knew, as she turned away from the gate and started back toward the cottage was that the edges of everything were unclear, that there was no purity to the moonlight, or even to the light of the stars. . . .

5

FANCY looked at Court, seeing him sitting there upon the big Morgan that was the last of the fine horses for which the Brantleys had been famous. His face was frowning and sad. How long had it been? Six weeks now—maybe a little more. Lately he seemed to have given up trying—he just sat on the porch and talked to her, telling her his dreams. He's got big dreams, too—mighty big ones. A great cotton spinning mill to give jobs to the poor folks hereabouts— course it would make him rich, too; but he really didn't seem to care so much about that.

He's good, Fancy thought, down deep he's good. Here lately he's been treating me so sweet like. If only I didn't know about him going to her house, too—and her married to his brother! But he wouldn't—Court wouldn't, not my Court, not the one I know— better than he knows himself. Holding him off was the right way to handle him, only it was so blamed hard. How do you hold off a man you love? How do you make him keep his distance when what you wanted was him up close, so close, holding him hard and never letting go?

Only that would be the surest way of spoiling it. What she had right now wasn't much, but it was something. It was a chance, and it was getting better all the time. He's beginning to believe in me, now, she mused; he's kind of thinking that even if I ain't his kind I could learn to be. I could get to be a lady, too. I read all those books he brings me, and I try so hard to speak fair. He'll see some day that I wouldn't shame him—that I could move among all his fine friends and be at ease, that nobody'll ever know that I was just a hill girl from Ca'lina, and they'll think I'm a lady born. . . .

"This the place, Court?" she asked.

"Yes. This is Dry Gully. Notice how it runs, Fan—clear up to the river almost. If it weren't for that little hill there, the river would run down into it. That's what makes it perfect."

"How come, Court? I don't rightly understand."

"Textile mills," Court explained patiently, "are run by water-power. That canal down in Augusta was dug more than forty years ago for the same reason. It furnishes six hundred horsepower; but just look at the way this gully falls down and away from the river. Why it would be a millrace, Fan. It cost them a fortune to dig that nine-mile channel down in the city, and this one, short as it is would furnish more power—much more. A thousand horses at the least, or I miss my guess. I could build a series of dams, and spill the water over the wheels, and . . ."

"But there's no water in it," Fancy said.

"I know that. Look at the bluff, Fan. A few hundred sticks of dynamite and the whole thing would go up in the air, and let the river through. Don't you see?"

"I see all right," Fancy laughed. "I see you're one smart man, Court. Tell me one thing, though—who owns this land?"

"I do. I bought it as soon as I got back—took a lot too much of the money I'd saved. That's why I've got to borrow more."

"I've got four hundred dollars," Fancy said seriously. "Would that do?"

"Bless your sweet little heart," Court laughed. "No, Fan, it wouldn't—to build the kind of textile plant I have in mind would cost in the neighborhood of one hundred thousand. Fat chance I've got of getting that much."

"Why not, Court? The mill would pay it back in no time at all."

"Right. But you think the bankers believe that? I've maps to show this gully. I've led them over the whole thing point by point: see here, this natural canal doesn't even have to be dug—it's there waiting. One hour's blasting and you have more water power than all of Augusta—enough to power all the openers, breakers, finishers, cards, drawers, rovers, spindles, looms that a first-class mill requires with that. . . . Heck, Fan, do you know what I'm talking about?"

"No," Fancy said seriously, "I don't, Court."

"Neither did they. I'd start to describe all that beautiful machinery to them—tell them exactly what each one does, and they brushed me aside with, 'So sorry, but we can't see our way clear at this time' —or: 'Sorry, Mister Brantley, but since you don't have any security. . . .'"

He turned to her, his face flushed and angry.

"'Security.' What the hell do they want—a pound of flesh? What's a man's knowledge and integrity if not security? But they can't see that. What they want is mortgages and Hiberion is already mortgaged to the hilt. I've got nothing left to pledge. That fine family of mine has already mortgaged away my life and my future. almost before I was born. They sold me and my future down the river to pay gambling debts, to buy off outraged but surprisingly reasonable husbands, to try to hold onto a kind of life that was dead and rotten fifty years ago. . . ."

He pulled out his handkerchief and mopped the beads of sweat from his brow.

He's so wonderful when he's mad, Fancy thought. If there was only some way I could help him; but a hundred thousand dollars! Heck, there ain't that much money in the whole wide world. . . .

She rode the little mare she had rented from the livery stable up close to him and put one gloved hand on his arm.

"Don't give up, Court," she said. "You can do it. I know you can. If anybody in the whole state of Georgia can do it, you're the one. Wish I could be some help to you, instead of just getting in your way—don't look like I'm much good to you in no way atall."

Court looked at her.

"You're the only person in this whole filthy world who is any good to me, Fan," he said quietly. "You believe in me—and I need that, 'cause I don't really believe in myself. You stick by me although I've tormented you enough to make you hate me a thousand times over. I actually think you're really fond of me, though for the life of me, I can't see why."

"No, Court," Fancy said, "I ain't fond of you. Not just fond of you. I love you. There's a mighty big difference 'twixt the two words to my way of thinking."

Court grinned at her, mockingly.

"You sure don't act like it, sometimes," he said.

"That's where you're wrong," Fancy said. "Love is for keeps, Court. This—this other thing isn't love. It can be mixed up with love, and it ought to be. Between people who love each other, reckon it can be downright beautiful. But people what love each other ought to be proud of that love—proud enough to make it a going concern, not something cheap. The way I feel about you, Court, is a mighty handsome thing; the way you feel about me—ain't. . . ."

Court stared at her.

"You know, Fan," he said, "sometimes I think you're a thousand years old."

"I'm nineteen—and that's old enough. The way I love you, Court, honey, ain't simple. I want too many things. I want a house and kids and you walking 'longside of me to church, feeling proud that I'm yourn. . . ."

"Yours," Court corrected her.

"All right, yours. Like I said, the way I feel about you is beautiful, and I don't want it dirtied. Only you make it so hard for me. . . ."

"How, Fan?"

"In a way that shames me to think about, let alone say. Folks have been saying for years that men and women are different. Course they are, but not as much different as folks like to think. Men are supposed to be wild, and spirited and a little bad—but not women. Only that ain't—isn't—so. I know that now. You taught me. I've got a mighty heap of wildness in me, Court, and a lot more badness than I'd like to have to answer for. You kind of reach that, Court. From all I hear tell about youall, it's you Brantleys' greatest talent. Youall can make any woman feel like a hussy and be glad of it. . . ."

"Fan," Court said, "Fan, honey . . ."

79

"Wait, Court. I haven't finished having my say, yet. The times I've kept you outside that little cottage haven't been 'cause I didn't want to let you in. It would be a relief to let you in and get it over with—it would be nice not to have to feel so choked up and miserable all the time. But it ain't that simple. I don't want you like that. I don't like the idea of slipping around and being scared, and hoping that I don't have a shamed yard child, that you don't think enough of to own. . . ."

Court looked at her, but he didn't say anything.

"And I don't like playing second fiddle. I hate knowing that the only reason you come around at all is that the girl you love is married to your brother. I know you go to see her. I don't think nothing much happens betwixt you. Leaseways I hope not. I'm just living in hope, Court, that all that can be changed. . . ."

"You're a funny kid," Court said; "but damned if you aren't kind of fine at that."

"Yep, I'm funny. Likewise I'm a fool. I keep on hoping with everything against me. I didn't come from nowhere. My folks are hill trash. I don't have book learning. I can't even talk fair. The main reason why you never even thought serious like about taking me home with you is 'cause you think I'd shame you in front of your fine friends. . . ."

"You are nobody's fool," Court said grimly.

"Ever thought about one thing, Court? I learned myself to read and write without ever being inside a school. Just listening to you, I'm getting so I talk better. Don't you see I'd have sense enough to keep my mouth shut until I learned the ways of your kind of folks? It ain't where a person comes from, but where she's going that counts—and dangblast it all, I'm going up! With you, I hope; without you, if I have to. Come on now, let's go back—I've dangled my heart on my sleeve enough for one day."

Court rode along beside her silently, his forehead creased with thinking.

"You know, Fan," he said, "there's a lot in what you said. Where a person ends up is the important thing after all. Folks around here would die in their tracks before they'd admit it; but three-quarters of the aristocracy of Georgia were jailbirds and debtors who were shipped over here from England because they didn't have what it took to get along over there. I've heard my mother say when she was good and riled that the first Brantley was a common cutpurse, let out of Newgate Prison on his promise to leave England—and the girl he married was a slattern whose morals weren't anything to shout about. I kind of believe her. The Brantleys got to be rich and powerful, but lesser folk would have been hanged out of hand for half the things they did. . . . Yep, we're haunted by our origins, our souls are twisted because a tavern wench got tired of being paid for casual loves; there's a devil in us because a London cutpurse went unhung. . . ."

The way that they rode looped down Walton Way into Gwinnett Street, and cut through the edge of the Terry. Fancy looked at the Negroes curiously. Then, suddenly, she drew the rented mare up, and laid a hand on Court's arm.

"Those kids," she whispered. "My, but they're pretty!"

Court looked at the two little mulatto girls playing in a hard-packed dirt yard.

"They ought to be," he said bitterly; "they're Brantleys, too."

Fancy turned and stared at him.

"My brother Phil's yard children," Court said. "We're a tribe all right."

Before he could say anything or put out his hand to stop her, Fancy was down from the mare and running hard toward the wooden gate. A moment later she was kneeling in the dirt beside the two little girls, holding them both in her arms. They stared at her, their eyes round with wonder. Then one of them smiled.

"Lady," she said, "pretty lady . . ."

Court got down from the Morgan and strode over to where Fancy knelt. He stood there frowning at her; but when she looked up he saw her eyes were bright with sudden tears.

"Oh, Court," she whispered, "they're beautiful! They're just too beautiful for words!"

Court looked at the children. It was the first time he had seen them up close. They were the color of dark honey with the sun shining through it, and their hair was only a shade darker than that. He put his hands on their heads, feeling that hair as fine and soft as cornsilk, without even a trace of a kink to it, and it came to him that Fancy was right. The children were beautiful. And all they could look forward to, he realized bitterly, was to fall into the lecherous hands of some diseased black or twanging poor white and bring forth more victims to the eternal degradation to which we've consigned them. . . .

"I wish they were mine!" Fancy said fiercely. "Niggers or not, I wish they were mine!"

"Thank you, Ma'am," a soft voice said behind her. "You sound like you mean it. And that's a powerful nice thing for a white lady to say."

Fancy turned her head and stared at the young mulatto woman who had spoken. She had a baby in her arms, a child fairer than the others, with bright blue eyes, contrasting strongly with his pale coppery skin. Fancy got up at once.

"Let me take him!" she breathed. "Oh please let me hold him, won't you?"

Silently the young woman passed the infant over, and Fancy hugged him hard, crooning to him softly.

"Howdy, Mas' Court," the woman said. "This lady your Missus?"

"No, Belle," Court said gravely.

"Sure Lord ought to be," Belle sighed. "The way she do love chillun! I do declare, it's the beatingest thing I ever did see."

"What do you call them?" Fancy said. "They're such darlings!"

"I called the boy Dred, Ma'am. But I got real fancy with the girls. I call 'em Angel and Delight."

"Such pretty names," Fancy sighed, "and downright fitting, too."

Belle laughed pleasantly, completely at ease now.

"They sure Lord have taken to you, Ma'am," she said. Then peering more closely at Fancy's pale face: "You hongry, Ma'am? You looks right peakish to me."

"I'm starved!" Fancy said.

"Then you come right on in. I got dinner pretty nigh ready. You, too, Mas' Court . . . that is, if'n you don't mind."

Court frowned. He had doubtless eaten food prepared by Belle's hands many times when she had been a servant at Hiberion. What real difference did it make to eat it in her house? Southern custom was against it, but Southern custom had been against his going away to Harvard; it was against his going into the textile industry, and any of a thousand things he wanted to do. He smiled a little sheepishly.

"I don't mind, Belle," he said gently. "But don't go to any trouble."

"No trouble a-tall, Mas' Court. Youall just sit right there and play with them kids. I'll whip you up something nice in two shakes of a jackrabbit's tail."

She was as good as her word. Minutes later she laid the food before them—a half spring chicken apiece, golden-brown, rolls so light that they seemed weightless as they lifted them to put the butter in, and so hot that they reddened the tips of Fancy's fingers. There were peach preserves beside the plates and string beans with a piece of salt pork in them and coffee that was black and scalding and perfect.

"Belle, honey," Fancy sighed, "it's 'most too pretty to eat!"

"Tastes better'n it looks, Ma'am," Belle laughed. "You dig right in."

Afterwards, Fancy had a hard time getting up out of her chair.

"I'm fair about to bust!" she said; but a minute later she was romping with the girls over the well-scrubbed floor.

"We'd better be going now, Fan," Court said. "Thanks for the dinner, Belle—it was mighty good."

"You're welcome, sir," Belle said. " 'Bye Ma'am."

"Can I come and see them sometimes?" Fancy asked breathlessly. "They're so sweet, and I do love them so!"

"Yes'm," Belle whispered, blinking back the tears. "God bless you, Ma'am! God bless your good, kind heart. . . ."

"I don't understand it," Court said as they rode away. "Belle's not pretty. I've seen any number of high brown wenches who are prettier'n her. What the devil possessed Phil to . . ."

"She's kind of restful like," Fancy said. "Didn't you notice that, Court? And from what you've told me about Phil's wife, she's awful hightoned and fidgety. Maybe your brother needed somebody restful around him."

Court looked at her.

"You," he said with mock severity, "you are exactly one thousand years old!"

"Court," Fancy said.

"Yes, Fan?"

"What are you going to do about those kids? If you stand back and

83

let folks kick 'em around the way they do most niggers you ain't the man I thought you were!"

"I mean to do something for them," Court said, "or see that Phil does. Send them to a good colored school, Hampton or Tuskegee, maybe. I've been planning to ride up to that store of his for some time. Want to come along?"

"Yes," Fancy said. "Where is it?"

"In Pinch Gut," Court said.

"Pinch Gut?" Fancy said, "what a funny name!"

"It is, isn't it? It seems that during one of our eternal floods, a Jew named Asher loaded all the foodstuffs his boat could hold and went from house to house giving it to the starving people. Gave away his entire stock of merchandise. They say he kept saying: 'Oi, oi! the poor pinched guts!' That's how the section got its name."

"Poor folks live there, don't they?" Fancy said.

"Yes," Court said; "but most of Phil's clients are farmers—croppers and small acreage men. They come in on Saturday and let him cheat them—and he's got them so buffaloed that they think he's doing them a favor."

"You don't think much of your brother, do you?" Fancy said.

"Nor of myself. The world would be better off if somebody blew the whole shooting match of us plumb to hell."

"I think you're wrong about that," Fancy said, "and I aim to prove it."

When they came to Phil's store, Fancy was disappointed. Instead of the fine establishment she had expected, it was a ramshackle building filled to bursting with all sorts of goods. Here were plowshares and harnesses and hoes. Under glass, put there, Fancy guessed, to keep the flies out, which it didn't, were loaves of bread, and hogsheads of flour and sugar and tubs of lard stood opened in the aisles. There were smoked hams and sides of bacon hanging from the ceiling, most of them green with mold, and bolts of cloth filled the shelves. But above all the many smells, one stench rose up overpoweringly so that all the air was thick with it.

Fancy saw Philemon Brantley standing behind the counter. He was as tall as Court, and far handsomer. He was lean and broad shouldered, and his rich blond ringlets crowned a face that Fancy decided was a sight too good-looking for a man.

84

"Howdy, Court," he said. "Time you were paying me a visit. Jehosiphat! Who is this? No, don't tell me—it must be that girl everybody's connecting you with . . ."

"Miss Williamson," Court said stiffly, "my brother, Philemon. Phil, meet Fancy."

Phil put out a powerful hand and gripped hers hard.

"Howdy, Miss Fancy," he grinned. "Sure Lord wish I'd seen you first! You're about the prettiest little thing these old eyes have feasted upon in many a year!"

"Well you didn't see her first," Court said. "Besides you're tied up enough. Saw those yard children of yours on the way up here, Phil."

"Did you now?" Philemon said. "Cute little beggars, aren't they? More'n half the time I forget they're niggers."

There was, Fancy was sure, not even the tiniest bit of shame in his voice.

"What's Martha got to say about them?" Court asked.

"Nothing. What could she say? But it appears to me this ain't the kind of thing we ought to discuss before Miss Fancy, here."

"She was with me," Court said; "she saw them first. . . ."

"They're too sweet," Fancy said. "I just love them!"

"Me too," Phil said. "I feel kind of sorry for those kids, though. Hell of a thing to be born black."

"They're not black!" Fancy said.

"I know, I know. It's just a way of speaking. Much good it'll do them that they aren't."

"Phil," Court said slowly, "you have got to do something for those kids."

"Sure, sure, but what?"

"Give them an education. At least do that."

"All right, but where? You know of any school for niggers hereabouts? Besides, I'm not sure it would be good for them anyhow. Put ideas in their heads—make them uppity. And the South's a mighty bad place for uppity niggers to have to live."

"They don't have to live in the South, Phil."

"Jehosiphat! You're mighty concerned about those kids, aren't you?"

"I am. And I'm going to see that they get a chance, even if you won't, Phil. Race is one thing; but blood's thicker than water, boy."

85

"All right," Phil said cheerfully; "you do it, then. I don't mind."

Fancy wrinkled up her nose.

"What's that smell?" she asked.

"Guano," Phil explained. "Nowadays it's well nigh impossible to get a decent crop without it. The soil's bled white. Stinks like blazes, doesn't it?"

"Sure does!" Court said. "Let's get out of here!"

But before they could get away from the stench of the fertilizer, a man came into the store—a poor white that reminded Fancy so much of her Pap that her heart ached at the sight of him. The man was tall, but so bent over from his labors that his actual height seemed shortened by half a foot. His neck was red and seamed by wind and sun, and his adam's apple jerked fearfully as he came toward them. He held a hat in his hand, and he kept twisting it.

"Mister Phil," he began.

"I know, I know!" Phil snapped. "You want an extension. Why, damn it to hell, Adams, what do you think I am—a charitable institution?"

"No—sir," Adams said doubtfully. "But I got to have another loan, Mister Phil. Crops didn't do so well last year, and if I don't git some guano down, the seeds I put in ain't going to grow. You can't let me down now, sir. How you ever expect me to pay you off if I don't raise a crop?"

"I've been carrying you on the books for four seasons, now, Adams. If you'd attend to your farming instead of hossin' around with the old woman and raising a passel of bare-assed younguns you can't feed, you'd do better."

"I reckon I can't help that," Adams said tiredly. "Them there's the ways of nature. Mister Phil for God's sake . . ."

"All right, all right! Good thing for you I got a kind heart. I hold mortgages on your last three crops. Reckon you'll have to give me a note on your land and your mules. Don't reckon I'll take one on your old woman, seeing how you've plumb wore her out with younguns."

Adams smiled feebly at this last joke.

"Sure," Phil said affably, "take all you need. I'll have Lawyer Cummings draw up the papers. You come in here tomorrow and sign them."

"All right, Mister Phil. Thank you, sir—thank you kindly. What your time prices going to be this time?"

"Forty percent, you lucky devil. Most of the merchants are charging fifty-three; but as I said, I've got a kind heart. How's Sal and the younguns?"

"Right pert, thank you. One of the gals ain't so good though. She's got a misery in the chest—yesterday she was a-spittin' blood. . . ."

"You send her right down to Doc Blumfeldt," Phil snapped. "Damn it, man, why didn't you tell me about this before? Tell Doc to send me the bill. I'll take the money out of your worthless hide, later."

Adams' thin face broke into a wide, grateful smile. For a moment Fancy was sure she saw tears in his eyes.

"Can't thank you enough, Mister Phil," he husked. "Mighty white of you, sir—yessir, mighty white!"

"Forget it," Phil said grandly. "You seen anything of that good-for-nothing Tom Watts?"

Adams hesitated.

"Yessir," he said, "sure have. He's kind of hiding out from you, sir—seeing as how he can't pay. He's afeared he'll lose his land."

"Damned right he'll lose it," Phil said. "But what can I do? I can't carry him any longer. Tell him to come on in—I already talked to Burke Cameron, and he's got an empty shareholding out on his east section. Nice house on it, too; heap better than the one Tom's living in now. Hell, 'cropping ain't so bad. Tom will be better off as a tenant for Mister Cameron than he ever was on his own. . . ."

"I'll tell him," Adams said. "You sure are good to us folks, Mister Phil."

He left the store then to get one of his grown sons to help him carry out the hundred-pound sacks of guano. Court looked at his brother, his whole face pale with rage and shame.

"Forty percent!" he said. "And a mortgage on his land for a few bags of that filth. God in glory, Phil—what's come over you?"

"Got to live," Phil said complacently. "And I'm good to those ragged-assed crackers. They're the worst people in the world to collect from—worse than the niggers, even. What in hellfire's wrong with you now?"

"Sick," Court said. "I'm puking sick. Our folks have had their faults, but mostly they were the kind of faults a man could understand—like getting mean drunk and wrecking a saloon, and chasing after anything in skirts. But they were brave men in their way. They might kill a man over his wife and take his last cent in a game of cards. But they never figured they had to live at the cost of blood spitting from a young girl's lungs, or children getting soft bones and potbellies from eating swill. Not even the Brantleys were that rotten low!"

Phil's face reddened.

"You're a fine one to talk, Court," he said. "However I do it, I'm the only one who's been keeping the family alive, while all you do is to chase from vinegar bend to bitter creek after this little bit of hill trash, here!"

Fancy saw Court's mouth tightening, and his hands doubling into fists, so she stepped in quickly and caught his arm.

"No, Court," she said quietly. "Don't fight him—not over me. If that's what he thinks, let him. Come on now—let's get out of here."

But it wasn't until Fancy stumbled as they stepped out on the sidewalk that he saw her eyes were tear-blinded. He turned to go back into the store, but Fancy looped both her hands through the crook of his arm and swung down hard.

"No, Court!" she said. "I told you—no!"

"Damn him to hell and back again!" Court roared. "What right had he . . ."

"All the right in the world, I reckon," Fancy said wearily. "We were poking our noses into his business—so we kind of had it coming. Anyhow, Court—I had to find out some time. It's better that I found out now. . . ."

"That you found out what?" Court demanded.

"How your family feels about me. Take me home, Court—I got packing to do."

"What the devil do you mean, Fan?"

"I'm getting out—Court. Out of your life. All I could ever do for you would be to spoil your chances and make you 'shamed. I—I love you too much for that. . . ."

"God damn it, no! I'll show them. We'll go down right now and

88

find Reverend Mister Barrish. They'll have to accept you, Fan; damn them all to hell, I'll make them!"

Fancy looked at him wonderingly, and her blue eyes were very wide. Then, slowly, she shook her head.

"No, Court," she said.

"I thought you said you loved me?"

"I do. More'n anything in this whole blamed world. More than life itself. Too much to cheat you. Too much to let you marry me because you're mean-mad and hurt. If the day ever comes when you want to marry me—for good reasons, like loving me, and thinking that nothing's any good without me, I'll marry you. But until then, no, Court."

Court studied her small face.

"You're something kind of special, aren't you?" he said gravely. "Promise me one thing, Fan. . . ."

"What's that, Court?"

"That you won't run out on me. Give me time to fix things up—straighten out my crazy, snake-bit hound dog's mind . . ."

Fancy waited a long time before she answered him.

"All right, Court," she breathed. "I won't run out on you 'cause I can't. I'm your prisoner, just like you had me locked up in jail. Got to be near you, got to see you, got to touch your hand—I can do without food and water better'n that. I think sometimes if I had to go 'way where I couldn't see you no more, I'd plumb curl up and die. . . . Now take me home. I got to be by myself for a while."

On the porch of the little cottage, Court kissed her solemnly, and turned to go.

"What you going to do now, Court?" she asked fearfully.

"I'm not going to whip Philemon, if that's what you're thinking. I mean to have a talk with my brother Tyler. He came back to town yesterday. If we can get this business about my Uncle Martin's place straightened out, maybe I'll have enough security to make a start. Anyhow, it's worth a try."

Seeing him riding away down the road, Fancy thought suddenly, wildly, I'm a fool! A mighty big damned fool! I could have had him —he'd have learned to love me afterwards. . . . Oh God, oh Jesus, why didn't I?

Court didn't have to go to his brother's house to see Tyler. He met him walking down Broad Street, a valise in his hand.

"Don't tell me you're going back already, Ty?" he said.

"Yep," Tyler grinned, pushing his hat back on his bald head. "Uncle Martin's a mighty sick man. Might kick off any minute. I got to be there to show him how us Brantleys love him!"

"You bastard," Court said. "How you love Melody, you mean."

"Now don't be so finicky, Court," Tyler laughed. "You wouldn't want to see him leave that lovely plantation to an orphan home, would you?"

"No, I wouldn't," Court said honestly, "still . . ."

"I'm being plumb, downright practical. And I am good for the old man. You'd think I was his maw, the way I gentle him. Come on boy, let's go into Riley's and have a snort of bourbon and branch water."

"Won't you miss your train?"

"Hell, no—I got an hour yet. Come up here to try to get Fern to go with me, but she won't budge. Thought for a while you had something to do with that—unprincipled scoundrel and lady-killer that you be; but Saph told me about your little bit of fluff from the Ca'lina hills. Black hair and blue eyes—boy! When do I get to meet her?"

"Never, if I can help it. How long you plan to be away this time?"

"Long as necessary. Can't tell, boy—the old man's weakening fast. Still, he might last another month or so. . . ."

"I see," Court said drily. But inside his heart he was crying: don't go, Ty! Don't leave Fern here alone any more. She's been dangled in front of my eyes too much now. You're my brother. Of course you're a polecat and worse, but what Brantley isn't? It won't be good for you to go away again. You're my brother. We're the same flesh and blood. But I'm a Brantley, too, remember. How in hellfire do I know I can keep my hands off her even if I want to? And I do want to. She loves me—me, not you, you bald buzzard! She's admitted it to me, hanging in my arms a-crying! But she's good and sweet and loyal, and she'll hate me. I don't want that. Don't want any bad blood between us. Because what will happen will be killing business, and our whole history's muddy with ill-spilt blood. . . .

"Come on," Tyler said. "A little bourbon will cheer you up."

90

"All right," Court said. "But this time, I'm buying."

They walked up Broad Street toward Campbell, and turned down it once they had reached the saloon. Then they went in the swinging doors, and stood together at the bar, resting a foot upon the brass rail.

But the liquor did Court no good. All his Brantley blood rose up in him hot and angry. He looked at his lean, pale face in the mirror that hung behind the bar. His wide mouth was twisted in a scowl, and his brows crowded his eyes.

Still he lifted his glass with a steady hand and proposed a toast. "To you and Fern," he said.

"And Melody," Tyler answered. "Unc hasn't said so outright, but he's hinted that he's leaving the place to you'n'me, Court. We're going to be rich, boy."

"Fat lot of good that'll do me," Court said.

"Why not? Then you'll be able to build your mill."

Court looked at him, hard.

"So you know about that?" he said.

"Yep, Phil told me. Appears to be a right smart idea. Do us Brantleys a mighty heap of good and no mistake. You can count on my help, Court."

"Thanks," Court said ironically, lifting the clear amber liquor to his mouth. He gulped it down, feeling it choking off his breath like fingers of fire; then that passed, and it lay in his belly like lava, from which fumes rose black and evil into his head.

I can count on your help. Your help. Know how you can help me, Ty? Give me my Fern back. Give her back, damn you! My mill. My big, sprawling mill with the machines clattering and the white fluff growing smaller and smaller until it's no more than a single thread winding itself onto the bobbins. Like life, Ty—you card it free of illusions, you comb it clean of dreams, you twist it tight, rove it down, spin it down until it's narrow and fine and has direction, then you warp it with the threads of other people's lives, pulling them down off the creel, winding them on the beam, then you weave them into the pattern of your destiny, all the bright and dark threads and when you're through, you've got something fine. . . . Hell yes, I'm drunk. Going to get drunker yet. Only in this case, you ugly, bald-headed buzzard of a brother of mine, the only thread I need is missing; you, Ty, have stolen the golden skein.

There's a code, I know; I'm supposed to be gallant and wish you luck, and keep my chin up and breathe the air. Only I'm a Brantley, too, and we Brantleys talk about gallantry, never act it and I don't wish you luck a damned bit and what the hell good is the mill anyhow without Fern for whom I was going to build it? The mill was going to give me back Hiberion, white under the trees, with the music and lights and dancing in the big hall. But I don't care about Hiberion, Ty—it's dead; it's lost its soul. I'll get it back, I reckon. I'll build that mill. But every time I look up, I'll be listening for Fern's footstep on the stair. I'll be watching for her to come and sit down across the table from me so I can see that hair soft golden under the candlelight, and hear that lovely voice of hers saying what she says to you, now, my brother—or at least what she's supposed to. . . .

"I reckon," Tyler drawled, "you've had enough."

Court threw back his head and laughed aloud.

"More than enough, Ty," he said. "Of the bourbon, of the Brantleys, of all the things that have happened to me."

"Go home, Court, boy," Tyler said. "Don't slip your block. Go home and stick your head under the pump. Drink yourself a quart of scalding black coffee. You'll feel better in the morning."

Or worse, Court thought. But aloud he said mildly, "Reckon you're right, Ty. Now you go catch your train."

Court rode very quietly under the pines, with the river rolling on toward the sea on his right hand. It was rising now, but this year it wouldn't be very bad; the signs were against it. Still it boomed bass-voiced and angry, and the drifting logs ground their ends ragged against the Sand Bar Ferry landing. There was a mule, dead and floating, being borne southward on the flood, and behind it a coop of chickens came, the rooster standing on the wire top and crowing lustily.

Like me, Court thought, crow while you're drowning, boy! Crow your lungs out and who'll hear you? Not the river, not the pine trees, maybe not even God. . . .

But where the road wound downward from Augusta, it was quieter under the trees. The scent of honeysuckle drifted sweet, and yellow jack in the pulpits brightened the swampy places, and along the roadside were wild verbena, red clover and reddish grass. Court felt himself growing quieter, too, there in the cool shade, where the winds came down brimming with pine scent and all the air was clean and good.

When he came up the drive to Hiberion, he suddenly touched his crop to the Morgan's flank, and came thundering up to the gate in a cloud of dust. When he was close enough, he hauled back on the reins and the great stallion lifted, flying over the broken gate, thudding to earth beyond it, and pounding around the house to the stable. Court sawed at the bit cruelly, and the horse reared, pawing the air and neighing shrilly.

That was a mighty fool thing, he thought; but I had to let it out somehow. . . . He fought the horse down, and dismounting, led him into the stable. Then he took the saddle off, threw a frayed blanket over the Morgan's steaming sides and walked up to the back porch.

Inside the kitchen, Saphira saw him coming.

"You're late," she snapped. "Here I've been slaving over this range like a nigger, and nobody shows up to eat. Father, dear Father —is not hungry. He prefers a liquid diet. And our sweet, delicate Agnes has a headache. Wonderful things, headaches. They allow you to lie on your back and pity yourself, and at the same time avoid doing any hard work. You hungry, Court?"

Court glanced at the greasy, lumpy corn pone growing cold on the stove, the turnip greens with the white fat congealing on the top, and the thick piece of sidemeat, white and salt and disgusting. Nigger food, his father had said; but even Negroes ate better than this.

"No," he said quietly, "I'm not."

To his chagrin, Saphira started to cry.

"I'm no cook," she wailed. "I'm the only decent white woman in this town who has to do her own cooking. We can't afford a colored woman. We can't even afford our laundress, except that Phil pays her. I can't even go to church any more, because I've made over those rags of mine so many times that even the children snicker when they see them. I'd like to get married, Court; but who'd marry a woman with hands like these? And nobody wants a woman my age, especially when she's so broken down with scrubbing floors and making beds and cooking and nursing a drunken old imbecile that . . ."

"Saph, please," Court said.

"It's the truth," Saphira said. "Now where are you going?"

"Up to see Father," Court said wearily.

"He's in no fit condition to see anybody. He's quiet now, but this morning there were lizards in his room. Lizards! Now, Court, I ask you. . . ."

Court didn't answer her. He was already halfway down the hall toward the stairs. As he passed Agnes' room, he could hear her crying. It went on and on, never rising, never falling, in a dull, endless monotone. He stopped quite still and listened to his sister's weeping; then he shook his head and went on up the stairs. No wonder Father's drunk, he thought, and pushed open the door.

Jefferson Brantley sat in the big chair with his head sunk forward on his chest. He was asleep and as he slept, he snored. His mouth hung open, toothless and weak, and a thin line of saliva crawled down the corners of his mouth into the dirty whiteness of his beard.

Court stood there looking at his father, his chest tightening so it was hard for him to breathe. He took a step forward, two. The old man did not even stir. Then Court put out his hand and took the second bottle from the table, the one that had scarcely been touched; and, putting it in his pocket, went back down the stairs.

He started walking then, toward the center of town, stopping every few feet to take a long pull at the bottle. Drink it down, Court, boy, he railed at himself, get yourself some Brantley bravery. Drown your mind in this gut-corroding poison—it stops thinking, boy, it stops it dead in its tracks, and after a while, you're free. After a while you forget about Fern lying soft and acquiescent in your brother's hairy arms. After a while Hiberion's beautiful again as it was when you were a child, and being a Brantley means something. . . . So drink deep, Court Brantley, and when you're drunk enough go find yourself a girl on the town. That to a Brantley fixes everything. That always was our sure cure for hunger and hopelessness, lost love, and present despair. . . .

But he wouldn't. He knew that. It wasn't as easy as all that with him. He was a Brantley, all Brantley, but he was something else too. Something different. Reckon I've got a weak stomach, he thought;

but it wasn't that, either. What it was wasn't simple. It was complicated in the same way that he himself was complicated. Inside his head was a brain that worked like no other Brantley brain had worked before it. Inside his body were nerves stretched tighter than nerves ought to be stretched and still hold together. Depending on how things (and people) struck them, they twanged like music, or jangled in discord. And not just anybody could strike that note. No hot tangle of alien woman's flesh, rented for an hour. Not for him. The woman had to mean something, be somebody. And it came to him that had Fern been as ugly as homemade sin, he would have loved her still.

Ty was gone. Back to Savannah. Back to keep his ghoulish watch beside his uncle's bed. Fern was alone in a house on Telfair Street, and he, Court Brantley, was drunk—mean drunk and full of hell. This, Saphira had said, would mark a new low, even for the Brantleys. It wasn't a thing to be thought about; he must push it out of his mind—go back to Riley's, blind himself into speechlessness and stupor. But his footsteps traveled, steady and slow, down McIntosh Street, past Broad, past Greene, until he stood on the corner of Telfair looking at the light that shadowed in her window. . . .

Being alone was one of the bad things. Fancy knew that. It wasn't late yet—only a little after nine o'clock. Maybe he would come back again. It would be a good thing to sit on the porch and hold his hand and not even talk. Just knowing he was there was a kind of a comfort. Where was he now? With her? Oh God, oh Jesus, Fancy prayed, please don't let him be—anywhere but with her. It wouldn't be a good thing, on a night like this most anything could happen and afterwards there would be killing.

For a half-second the image of Court Brantley lying dead in his blood rose up in her mind so clearly that she was sick. She got up from her chair and went to the edge of the porch and clung to one of the pillars until the dizziness went away. And, as she straightened up, she heard the sound of the horses.

She went down the porch steps so fast that she almost fell; but she caught her balance and reached the gate running and threw it open. Then she stopped. Horses. Two of them from the sound. The irregular clip-clop of a team, and the sound of wheels whispering through the sand. But Court always came horseback, riding his big Morgan like a prince. She didn't know anybody who drove a team, and this was the last house on the road, so—whoever it was had to be coming here. Fancy stood very still waiting until the little road wagon came round the bend and she could see the woman who sat in the driver's seat. And even through all the questions that rose in her mind, one thing sang aloud: he's not with her! He's not, 'cause she's here!

Fern drew the wagon up before the gate.

"I hardly expected," she drawled, "to be greeted with so much enthusiasm. However . . ."

"You're here, and it can't be helped," Fancy said. "Come in, won't you? Or would you rather sit up there on that wagon and feel high and mighty?"

"You have spirit, haven't you?" Fern laughed. "As a matter of fact, I will come in. I have a certain amount of curiosity—and it isn't often that one gets the opportunity to see the inside of a—love nest."

"Then come and take a good look," Fancy said. "Reckon you'll find it kind of dull though—can't be much of a love nest where a woman lives alone, can it?"

"That," Fern said coolly, "depends."

Fancy put up a hand and helped her down.

"Started to let that one pass, but I reckon I won't. Just what does it depend upon, Mrs. Brantley?"

"Why upon her visitors, of course—and on just how long they stay."

Fancy looked at her. This one, she decided, has a tongue like a snake. For all her looking like an angel out of Glory, she's bad— she's mean bad, and capable of wrecking most anything to get what she wants.

"But I don't have visitors," she said simply. "Just one visitor. He's all I'm interested in. Reckon you're interested in him, too—for all that you've got no right to be. So let's bring it right out in the open, Mrs. Brantley—let's talk about your brother-in-law. That's what you came way up here to do, ain—isn't it?"

"You are quite right," Fern said.

Fancy pulled up one of the big rockers on the porch.

"Sit down," she said.

Fern slipped gracefully into the big chair.

"I," she said, "don't know quite how to begin. . . ."

"Then I'll do it for you. You came up here to get me to give Court up. You were going to tell me that since I'm not quality, and because Augusta people with tongues joined in the middle and loose on both ends have done a mighty heap of mean talking about me, I might kind of hurt his reputation, and keep him from doing what he aims to. . . ."

"You are a mind reader!" Fern breathed.

"Your kind of mind. Small, greedy, and kind of dirty. The main trouble with all of those things is that none of 'em is so. Want me to tell you what is so?"

"Why yes, I think it would be very interesting."

"You're in love with Court yourself. You married Ty because you was mean-mad and hurt, thinking Court had ditched you. Now you're sorry. You want Court back, and you aim to get him. Your husband ain't no hindrance. To your kind of woman a husband never is. Too easy to fool. You're the kind what passes along every twisted lying thing what folks say about a girl like me—a girl what has no man to shoot or horsewhip folks who use her name in public; and goes right home to wait for your lover to slip into your house the minute your husband is out of it. . . ."

"Go on," Fern said.

"All right, Court comes to see me. But he sits right there in that chair you're sitting in, and never sets foot on the inside of the house. Maybe he kisses me good night—which ain't wrong, seeing that I'm a single girl with a right to a gentleman friend. What riles me up plenty is that when he leaves here, where he can't come inside, 'cause I don't aim to make of myself nobody's easy woman in spite of all the talk—he goes right smack dab down to your house where he can come in, and does! So now, Mrs. Brantley, while we're on the subject of giving Court up, why don't you give him up? Appears to me that I have more right to him than you. Tell me, why don't you?"

Fern looked her straight in the face, and her eyes were utterly naked.

"Because I can't," she whispered.

97

"I see," Fancy said. "So it's like that, eh?"

"It's like that. I was going to say all the things that you mentioned. And, in all fairness, most of them are true—you wouldn't be good for him and you know it. You're not his kind. But you're not stupid. What's the good of lying to you. I do love Court. I always have. I expect to go on loving him till the day I die. If it's any comfort to you—there's nothing actually between Court and myself—which is why I believe your fantastic story of his never entering your house. I know from experience that he's an honorable man. But tell me one thing, Miss Williamson—do you mean to marry Court?"

"Yes," Fancy said, "if he'll have me—yes."

Fern stood up. There was something curiously unreal in the grace of the motion. She lifted one hand and patted a stray lock of her silvery blonde hair back into place.

"I don't think you will," she said quietly. "I don't even think that there's much danger of it. But if the danger ever arises, I'll prevent it. You see, Miss Williamson, Court loves me, too. That there's been nothing between us is my doing—not his. So if I ever think that he's getting too lonely, too desperate—I'll—remedy the situation. Good night, Miss Williamson. You've been very kind."

"There ought to be a name," Fancy said bitterly, "for women like you—but offhand I can't think of it."

"So little imagination," Fern Brantley said. "What a pity!"

I feel sick, Fancy thought, death-sick. How can you fight a woman like this one? Used to dream about people like these—so fine and sweet 'cause they didn't have to root hog or die like us. But where we get mean-mad and liquored up and raise holy ned, the meanness inside of people like her stays there and kind of festers so that everything they touch or even breathe on—dies. . . .

"I'm glad we understand each other," Fern said. "In your quaint, unlettered way, you're not unintelligent. I think you know now that you can't win. So, good night again, Miss Williamson—and I hope that you won't think too badly of me. . . ."

Fancy watched her climb into the smart little wagon.

"I don't think about you," she said, "in any way a-tall. Maybe, like you said, I won't win; but it won't be because I stopped trying."

She turned then and walked back into the house, hearing the sound of the wagon turning on the road behind her. By the time she reached the porch, the sound of it had dimmed, so she turned once more, thinking:

There's no way to get down there now. The horsecars aren't running. And me like a big fool, turned that horse back to the livery stable. If I went what could I do, anyhow?

But all the same she knew she was going. There was no question about that. She went into the house and changed her shoes, selecting a pair that were low and comfortable, suitable for walking. Then she tied her big hat under her chin and started out. The walking itself was a good thing; it required enough attention to keep her from thinking too much. But she knew somehow, in a way that left absolutely no room for doubt that something was going to happen that night—she could feel it in the very marrow of her bones.

It had been a long time now since she had done so much walking. By the time she came down into Augusta, it was very late and she was tired. She leaned against the foot of the fire alarm tower, called Big Steve by everybody in Augusta.

Then it came to her that standing on this brightly lighted corner of Greene and Jackson Streets wasn't the smartest thing in the world for her to do—so she moved on slowly, wearily in the direction of Hiberion.

When she got there, it was dark. She stood at the gate a long time, looking at the house, thinking: I've been a fool. You can't just go to a man's house in the middle of the night and ask for him. His folks'll think you're crazy or worse. And Court would get mighty mad. . . .

Nothing for me to do but turn around and go back, she mused. But that was all of seven miles, and she was so tired. . . . She started walking, just the same, away from the house back toward the river, but she hadn't gone fifty yards, before she heard the rich, dark voice chuckling:

"Looking for Mister Court, lil' Miss Fancygal?"

Fancy whirled and stared into the face of the old Negro woman. She knew this old scarecrow, old as the hills, and black as original sin. Everybody in Augusta knew old Maud. They all said that the old woman was crazy; but Wyche who was very friendly with old Maud laughed at the idea.

99

"Crazy like a fox," he said. "Maud just won't take low for nobody —and since she's near eighty, and a woman, nobody's got the heart to put her in her place. So to hide the fact that they don't know how to handle one old colored woman who thinks that whitefolks are both fools and hypocrites and says so, they take refuge in pretending she's insane."

"No," Fancy snapped at her. "Anyhow, what's it to you, old niggerwoman?"

"Ain't a thing, honeychile. I just happens to be on your side. And I hate to see you a-worrying thataway when you ain't got a thing to worry about—not a thing."

"What you mean I ain't got nothing to worry about?" Fancy demanded. "'Pears to me I got plenty!"

"Just 'pears that way—that's all. Lil' gal, you got everything. You got a face like an angel out of Glory, and a figger what would make the 'piscopal minister lay his Bible down. You got a way o' walking what would make a young man itch all over and plumb nigh drive an old man wild. So how come you worrying?"

For the life of her, Fancy couldn't keep from smiling.

"Can't help it, old woman," she said. "I kind of think I'm going to lose my best gentleman friend."

"And I kind of think you's crazy, 'specially if you's talking about Mister Courtland Brantley."

Fancy looked at her.

"How'd you know it was him?" she said.

"Got ways of knowing. Listen to me, chile. Done knowed them there Brantleys since 'fore they knowed themselves. Ain't never been one of them, from their great grandpappy right on down, what a pretty woman couldn't wind round her little finger. You listening, honey?"

"Yes'm," Fancy whispered, "I'm listening."

"Good thing you is. 'Cause I'm agonna set you straight. Ain't never been no woman what had any luck with a Brantley—you know why?"

"No," Fancy said. "Why?"

"'Cause the wrong kind of gals married 'em—poor lil' critters what couldn't manage 'em nohows! Listen to me. Just like old Mas'

Jeff says, the first one of 'em mated with the devil's daughter and the strain is in the blood. But I kind of think you's a match for Mister Court. First place, he ain't as wild as the rest; secon', you got spirit. Wild devil horse need a wilder mare. Be good for Mister Court if you was to git him hooked—heap better than gitting shot over his brother's wife. . . . But listen to me, chile—don't let him get too close beforehand—not even 'cause you loves him, and he wants to—or maybe 'cause you wants to, which though folks won't admit it, sometimes crosses a woman's mind. Marry him, lil' Miss Fancygal! Make him stand up in front of the preacher man. Git him hooked legal—then give him hell!"

"How can I?" Fancy said. "He don't love me none. . . ."

"Then he's a mighty big fool—'cause he sure Lord ought to. You's a mighty sweet lil' old gal. But just the same it's your bounden duty to hook him—'cause he needs you, Miss Fancy—you be good for him. That lil' yaller-haired gal his brother married is going to ruin him sure. She ought to know that one Brantley is more'n any woman can handle, let alone two!"

"Is he," Fancy breathed, "with her—now?"

"Don't know. Saw him a-heading in that direction, 'bout an hour ago—maybe two. If'n he is—you go right in that house and pull him out—yank out some of that yaller hair whilest you's at it. Snatch her bald-headed—teach her some respect—go on, lil' Miss Fancygal, go fight for your man!"

Fancy stood there a long moment after Maud had gone, disappearing quickly into the night. Then she, too, turned, and started walking toward Telfair Street. But this time she went very fast.

The minute she got to the house, she saw him. He came through the gate so fast that he was almost running, and something caught hold of Fancy's heart and tore until she could feel the sinews giving and the inside of her lungs filled up with brine and fire and there was a taste in her mouth like blood.

The cards were wrong, she thought. They said afterwards. Only there wouldn't be any afterwards. There won't be anything else after tonight, not even me. . . .

Then she turned up McIntosh Street toward Broad and Reynolds. She went down Reynolds past East Boundary into the countryside where Hiberion was, and on past it until she came to the place where the willows were and the Savannah flowed quietly, blue-golden in the night.

Court slowed his pace after a time. Above his head the great stars hung low and close, so close that he could almost touch them with his outstretched hand. The earth rolled away under his feet, and the sky swung about his head in ponderous rhythms. But it was no good, none of it was any good, or even real. Nothing was real except the sickness down inside of him.

That was a near thing, he thought bitterly. Another minute and it would have happened and damn my stupid hide I don't know whether I'm more ashamed of the fact that I nearly pulled another rotten Brantley trick, or of getting cold feet and running out of there like a man pursued. She was willing—great God—she was willing! And now I'll die remembering her mouth like that, and the way her eyes looked melting under her lashes. . . . I should go back. Who'd know? Ty would never find out and . . .

Ty, my brother. There are many kinds of dishonor, but this one, I reckon, beats them all. . . . I've got to get out of town, leave Augusta—go back to Boston . . . marry some Yankee girl, bank the fires that consume me with her; but Fern—yes, Fern—oh God, oh Jesus, I—

"Looking for your lil' Miss Fancygal?" old Maud drawled.

Court looked at her.

"Yes," he said tiredly. "Where is she? You've seen her?"

"Yep, sure Lord has. She gone to the river—like all the Brantley wimmen. Look for her there, Mister Court Brantley—look for her there!"

Court caught hold of the old woman's arm, holding it hard.

"Where?" he roared; "where'd you see her?"

"Turn me loose, Mister Court," Maud said drily. "You's hurting my arm. Then I'll tell you, but not until then."

Court turned her loose.

"Down in back of your house," old Maud said. "I seed her standing out in front looking at it a few minutes ago. Then she started running—straight for the river. I 'spects you better be getting down there, Mister Court."

Court didn't answer her. Already he was off, running down the road in the direction of Hiberion. He passed it and went on down the gentle slope until he came to the clump of willows.

Almost at once he saw Fancy. She was sitting under a tree, her back resting against the trunk, staring out over the water. Court stopped short. Then he started walking toward her.

Fancy heard him and looked up, her face white and still, the corners of her mouth down-drooping, her lips trembling.

Court knelt down beside her and caught her shoulders hard with his hands. But she turned her face away from him.

"No," she said.

Court sat down beside her.

"What's got into you, Fan?" he said gruffly. "What made you run off like this?"

"None of your business," Fancy said.

"Well, I'll be damned," Court said. Then he put out his arms to seize her, but her hands came up, raking at his eyes.

Court stared at her.

"You *are* riled up!" he said.

She turned toward him, her young face bleak and fierce.

"No," she said, "just hurt, that's all. Still don't know me, do you? Still think you can come to me with her kisses all sticky on your mouth!"

"So that's it," Court said.

"That's it, all right. I ain't going to preach at you. You know what you're doing, I reckon. Just going to tell you a few things—like how it feels to love a man what doesn't love you back. It's no fun, Court. I found myself walking by your house at night—just to look at it. It's a mighty nice old house. And I kind of started to wish that I lived there—with you. That I was really yours—that's not it exactly. I reckon what I really mean is that I wish you were mine, like I'm yours. I belong to you, Court; but you don't belong to me. You don't belong to nobody, I reckon, excepting maybe—her."

"No," Court said, "not even to her."

Fancy leaned forward suddenly, and pillowed her dark head on his knees. She hid her face and whispered: "Found myself a-wondering the other night how it would be to have your baby. I'd like that, Court; I'd like it very much. . . ."

"Good God!" Court said.

"I know, I know," she went on. "You think I ain't fitten. But I'm more fitten than her—than a woman what marries one brother and plays fast and loose with the other!"

"That isn't so, Fan."

"Think I'm a fool? Saw you coming out of her house two o'clock this morning. But no matter. What you do isn't my concern any longer."

"Why not, Fan?"

"It's her you love, not me. Not this damnfool hill gal mooning around dreaming how it'd be to hold your son in my lap—and him so little and sweet with light-brown hair like yours and a mouth like yours and eyes. . . ."

"Fan, for the love of God!"

"I'm sorry, Court, if I shocked you. Shocked myself, too, when I thought of it. But that's how I feel—all gentle like and tender, a-looking at you. All wanting you and not wanting you at the same time. Know what? It's even nice just like this—a-sitting here looking at you. You don't have to say anything, do anything—to make me happy. All you have to do is to be here, alive and breathing the same air I breathe. . . ."

Court didn't say anything. He looked at the delicate white oval of her face, framed in her black hair.

Fancy took his big hands and turned them over, palms upward. Then she ran a soft finger over them.

"Rough," she said. "You worked hard once, Court. These ain't gentleman's hands. Yet you are a gentleman—a real gentleman through and through. Even I can tell that. Sometimes I want to cry, looking at you. You look so sad and mad with yourself for getting mixed up with poor white trash like me. And I look at you and think, how beautiful he is! Like an angel sent down out of Glory. Only your eyes got a little bit of devil in 'em, Court. And your mouth —why it's the wildest, cruelest, sweetest, wickedest mouth in the whole wide world!"

She bent down suddenly and kissed his upturned palms. Court felt something stirring in him—something like pain. He put his hands under her armpits and stood up, raising her with him until she was facing him. He stood very still, looking down at her. Fancy did not move or speak, but lay back against the circle of his grasp, and the big tears hung in her black curling lashes, and made streaks down her face.

"Now what the devil are you crying for?" Court blustered.

"Because I love you so much," she wept. "I love you so hard I want to die!"

Court kissed her.

"No," she whispered, "not any more. Don't kiss me again, Court. It hurts too bad. Thought I could give you up—thought I could let her have you and stand by and see Tyler kill you and laugh. But I can't. I got to stop that two-timing hussy. I got to keep you safe. All right you don't love me, but I'll learn you to—you've got to see the light of reason, Court. There's only one way to fix things so she can't get her thieving hands on you—so that you won't even want her no more. . . ."

"And what's that?" Court asked mockingly.

"You can marry me," Fancy said.

Court turned away from her very slowly, and his face was terrible.

"Court," Fancy said. "Don't look at me like that. I'm shamed to my soul, that I had to say it, but it's true. I'd make you the best and sweetest and most faithful wife in the world. We're alike, you and me—we suit each other. . . ."

Court started to move off then, under the dark trees, where the first morning light was beginning to show.

"Court!" Fancy said. "Court—where're you going?"

"Home," Court growled. "After this, I'm going to get drunk."

Fancy stood up, facing him. She had a little lace handkerchief in her hand. Her fingers moved, tearing it to shreds. When she spoke finally, her voice was little more than a whisper.

"Good-bye, Court," she said.

"You'll be seeing me," Court mocked her.

"No, I won't," Fancy said. "Know why, Court? 'Cause deep down inside, I'm yours. That makes me one of the Brantley women, doesn't it? And you know what happens to them!"

She whirled then, almost before the words were out of her mouth, and hurled herself down the steep slope, running very fast, stumbling over roots and stones until she came to the river and went into it still running, splashing it up about her in great silver sheets, until it was above her knees, her waist, her shoulders.

Court came after her. As he splashed through the muddy water, he could see her small head, black against the water, her long hair floating out behind her in a cloud, then she threw herself forward and the yellow water rose up like wings, and came down closing, and the eddies moved out in circles, spreading, spreading, out to the shores of forever.

Court went in then in a clean dive, and swam powerfully under water, his fingers groping, groping until he could stand it no longer and had to come up for air. As he gulped his lungs full, he saw Fancy break water, yards downstream, her white arms thrashing helplessly about. He started after her, eating up the distance with mighty strokes, and caught her just as she went under again, fastening his fingers cruelly in her hair. Then he started for shore, dragging her behind him. He got her out at last, and struggled up the slope. Then he lay her face downward across a log and pumped at her back until she turned her head on the side and vomited black water and started to cry.

He picked her up, and marched up to the house with her. Saphira heard him kick the door open and started down the stairs.

She saw Fancy lying drenched in his arms, and stopped still.

"Oh, no, Court!" she whispered. "Not another one!"

"She's all right," Court said. "Take care of her, won't you, Saph?"

"Why certainly. The poor little thing! What made her do it, Court? Tell me, what?"

"That," Court said, "is none of your damned business, Saph." Then he put Fancy down upon his sister's bed.

She lay there upon the bed shivering, her lips blue with cold, until he covered her with a blanket, and went out of the room and came back with some whiskey.

"Here," he said, "drink this."

Fancy drank the whiskey, never taking her gaze from his face. Her blue eyes were very big behind her sooty lashes, and the look in them was a thing that Court wasn't going to want to remember.

"Don't try that again," he said. "Promise me, Fan—don't try that again!"

"You love me, Court?" she said. "Say you love me—even if you lie!"

"I love you," Court said. It was almost the truth. He bent down then and kissed her lightly. Then he started for the door.

"Where are you going?" Saphira said.

"To get some dry clothes," Court said. "Then—out."

"You coming back?" Fancy asked faintly.

"No," Court said.

Fancy raised herself up on her elbows.

"Come here, Court," she said.

Court walked back.

"Now kiss me," Fancy said.

Court bent down and kissed her lips. He straightened up, staring at her. He hadn't known there was that much tenderness anywhere in the world.

"That's how I love you, deep down inside," Fancy whispered. "All softlike and sweet. Oh, Court, if you only love me, too . . ."

"If he doesn't," Saphira said angrily, "he's a fool!"

"I do," Court said; then very quietly, wonderingly, half to himself: "God help me, I really do!"

He got up then and walked out of the room. Saphira sat on the bed and put her arms around Fancy. And Fancy rocked back and forth on the bed, hugging her knees with joy.

He didn't come home all that day. When it was night, Fancy went out to find him. She had gone to her cottage first, and changed her clothes, putting on a dress of scarlet lace that did wonders for her complexion. Her hair was smoothly knotted in a little bun on the base of her neck. Then she climbed upon the nag she had rented and rode back down the hill toward Augusta.

She found Court where she expected to find him, standing in front of the bar in Riley's Saloon on Campbell Street. Riley looked up in astonishment as she entered, holding the rag he was wiping glasses with in mid-air.

"Now what th' divil is all this?" he roared. "No females is allowed inside me bar!"

"I—I want to talk to him," Fancy said, pointing.

"You talks to nobody in me place," Riley said. "Now git out of here before I summons the law, and have you pulled in as a common—"

"Softly, Riley," Court said. "You're talking to the girl I'm going to marry."

"Th' divil you say!" Riley bellowed. "You're in no fitten condition to know what you be a-doing! And be damned and be jasus if I'll be a party to . . ."

Court grinned, swaying a little as he spoke, "You aren't a party to anything, Riley."

"You mean to stand there and tell me that you're going to git yourself hitched up to that—"

"Now, now, Riley," Court said, "no hard names. Appears to me that Fan's a heap better than the fine ladies of this town who think that a nicely printed piece of paper gives them the privilege to sneer at her. A piece of paper whose provisions they abuse constantly in their husband's absence. Well, little Fan's going to have her little piece of paper. And I don't think she'll abuse it—being a curiously honest girl. Will you, Fan?"

"Never," Fancy breathed. "Oh, darling, I'll never leave your side. . . ."

"Come on, Riley," Court said, "shut up your grog shop for the evening. You're going to be best man—and a witness. No argument, now."

Riley didn't argue. In fact, he was moved to do what he hadn't done in twenty years. That is, he took a drink of his own poison. Then he shut up shop and followed Court and Fancy to Hiberion.

Court tiptoed up the stairs, taking care to wake neither his father nor Agnes, and came down with Saphira. She came running into the kitchen and threw her arms about Fancy.

"I'm mighty glad!" she said. "You're going to be good for Court— I just know you will!"

"Just a minute, everybody," Fancy said quietly. "Saph, honey, is a fire laid in that stove?"

Saph looked at her wonderingly.

"Yes," she said, "why, Fancy?"

"Light it," Fancy said. "Where's your coffee pot?"

"Over there," Saphira said. "But, Fan, I don't understand . . ."

"Appears to me that Mister Riley here said the only thing that made sense all evening. He said Court's in no fitten condition to marry anybody. I don't want him to wake up tomorrow and be sorry.

108

So I'm going to make him some coffee—strong as the dickens and black as old Maud. After I get him sober, if he still wants to marry me—all right. If not, I won't be around to bother none of you. Mister Riley, I'm sorry to keep you waiting; but I kind of think you agree with me—don't you?"

"I do, Ma'am," Riley said, "and I want to say I'm sorry, Ma'am —I kind of had you wrong."

"I'm used to that," Fancy told him.

Half an hour later, Court Brantley gulped the last of four cups of steaming black coffee, and sat there shaking his head.

"Court," Fancy said tremulously, "do you remember what you said—in Riley's?"

"Heck, yes," Court grinned; "I was drunk and I wanted to marry you. I always get my best ideas when I'm drunk. Come on—let's go. . . ."

"Where?" Fancy said.

"To Judge Harris, of course. He's the nearest Justice of Peace, isn't he?"

"You mean that, Court?" Fancy said.

"If I don't, I'm crazy—and I don't think I'm crazy. Come here, Fan."

Several minutes later, he looked down into her eyes, that were hazed over with tears.

"Do I mean it?" he looked at her tenderly.

"Yes," Fancy said. "Yes, oh yes!"

When Riley left the parlor of Judge Harris, he ran all the way home. Mrs. Riley listened for a breathless five minutes. She didn't even wait until morning. Neither the whispering wires of the telegraph nor the even newer telephone that Augustians were only beginning to get used to after four years of watching a few advanced citizens grind a crank and shout into a long-necked mouthpiece, could have spread the news faster. By mid-afternoon of the next day, the only people in Augusta who did not know it were the dead in the local cemetery.

It had, of course, certain consequences. Among other things, Fern Vance Brantley took to her bed and stayed for three days. And for all of that time, not for a minute did she stop crying. . . .

6

So i was drunk, Court thought bitterly, but I wasn't that drunk. Can't even tell myself I didn't know what I was doing. I knew all right—Fan saw to that. Mighty decent of her—or mighty smart— which? Now I can't say she tricked me, 'cause she didn't. Outsmarted myself, I reckon. Any way I play it, it comes out wrong. If she's honest, she's still a millstone around my neck, because she's going to keep me from reaching the very people I need to go to for help. If she isn't, I've been the world's biggest fool. . . .

Wonder what in hellfire got into me? Reckon I was lonely and there was that business about Fern, but even so was that reason enough for this? I'm a failure, but the Brantleys have mostly always been failures when it came to anything practical. Yet not one of them, not a single one that I ever heard tell of ever made this kind of a mistake. The Brantley women have always been something—something very real and sweet and fine, and our mistake has always been on the side of not treating them as well as they deserved, of making the lives of good women into pure hell while we followed our natural bent on the side. We're a proud, wild, wrong-headed breed all right; but none of us has ever been this stupid before—not a single one. . . .

He looked at Fancy as she bent over the blackiron range. Her face was flushed from the heat, and her black hair hung down stringily into her eyes as she worked. Court noted with acute distaste that there were yellow sweat rings at the armpits of her dress. She looked, he thought, like what she was—white trash.

But, he had to admit, it was not her fault. That stove was enough to drive a mule mad. It was very old and it never drew properly, and either burned or undercooked the food. Fancy could cook, he knew that. And she had thrown herself wholeheartedly into the role of wife and homemaker. Truthfully Court had no complaints. That made it worse. If Fancy had turned out badly as he had confidently expected her to in her new position as his wife, he would have felt better about the whole thing. But she had tried so hard to live up to what was expected of her, and on the whole her failures had been few.

Court suspected that the dismal little shotgun house he had rented on the edge of town gave her as much of the horrors as it gave him; but so far she had not complained. Duke's cottage had been so much more comfortable. That was another thing that bothered Court. Did she ever in her mind make comparisons?

"Oh, Court, honey," Fancy wailed suddenly, "I can't do a thing with this stove!"

Court got up and worked gingerly with the damper. Finally the fire caught up and blazed.

"There," Court said, "nothing to it, Fan."

"I'm so dumb!" Fancy quavered. "I try so hard to do everything right—for you, Court—and it looks like everything I try turns out a mess. Reckon you're plumb, downright sorry you married me. I make you such an awful wife. . . ."

"No," Court lied, "far from it, Fan. You're just tired, that's all. Besides it won't be like this all the time. One of these days real soon you're going to have a colored woman to cook for you, and a decent house to live in, and a maidservant to clean. . . ."

"Oh, darlin', will I?" Fancy breathed. "That would be just too wonderful. You're smart. Soon as you find somebody who's got sense enough to back you with that mill, we'll be just about the richest folks in town. I'll have the finest, nicest clothes—all silks and satins, and all the best people in town will come to call. . . ."

That, Court thought grimly, will never happen—no matter how rich we get. Didn't know you had ideas like that, Fan. Guess all women are alike in some ways. They never learn anything in this town, but they never forget anything either. When I do make my pile, we'll have to go away, little Fan—far away where people never saw you dancing half naked on the back of that wagon. . . .

He stood up and reached for his hat.

"I'm going out for a while," he said. "Couple of things I've got to attend to. . . . See you later, hon. . . ."

"Court," Fancy whispered, "know what? This is the second time this week you've started out of the house without even offering to kiss me good-bye."

Oh, damn, Court thought; but aloud he said mildly: "Sorry, hon —got a lot on my mind, I reckon. Come here and kiss me then, because I have things to do."

Fancy slipped into his arms, and her mouth clung to his with easy, accustomed passion. That way she never fails me, Court thought wryly; God, no—not that way. . . .

"See you later, Fan," he said, and went out the door.

Court had nothing to attend to and nowhere to go. He had to get out of the house, that was all. Away from the smells of cooking and poor ventilation. Away from Fancy's woebegone little face, trying so hard to be cheerful. Away from anything that reminded him of his folly.

He started walking through the shaded streets of the town, feeling the thick heat of the Georgia summer beating down upon his head. He had the curious sensation that the streets through which he passed emptied themselves as he entered them; and a little while later he saw that he was right. He turned quickly into the upper end of Broad Street. The scattered crowd of passers-by suddenly and with a single mind discovered they had business elsewhere. Court found himself striding through a street emptied of all but the aged and the infirm. And they had all become concerned with the ancient, fly-specked signs in the show windows. . . .

Rage mounted up out of his collar and beat about his ears. So they'll snub me, he thought bitterly. Who do they think they are?

I had more than half decided to leave this town, but I'll be damned if I will now. Going to build that mill if I have to steal the money to do it. I'm going to get this damned place so sewed up that they'll have to come a-running when I crook my little finger. I'll fix it so that these pious old she-dogs will have to dance attendance upon Fan—damn their hypocritical souls. . . .

But a little while later the rage drained out of him, and he was oppressed with an awful sense of loneliness. Here, a few blocks away on Greene and Telfair Streets were the houses of his friends —men and women whom he had played with in childhood, school-mates, good people all of them, and he realized suddenly that there was no longer any house in Augusta with the possible exception of Hiberion itself that he could enter and be welcomed. And for this, he had only himself to blame. Of all the Brantleys, only he had crowded the town too far. Of course the sins of the family had been many and black, but they had stayed within the larger, looser bound-aries of convention; theirs had been the sins expected of a vigorous headstrong breed. But this was too much; Augustians might whisper behind their gloves and fans about his openly consorting with a woman like Fancy; but asking them to accept that woman upon their own level was something else again. . . .

He got tired of his aimless wandering finally, and started back to the little house where his wife waited. He looked at his watch and swore bitterly under his breath. He had been gone far longer than he intended. Fancy must have had his supper ready for him hours ago, and to Fancy the little suppers she fixed for him were very important. They were an expression of her love for him; burnt of-ferings, he thought wryly, upon the altar of domesticity.

When he came into the house, he found her crying.

"It's all cold," she wept; "and I tried so hard to keep it warm. The one time it turned out well, too. Oh, Court, why couldn't you come back on time?"

"I got all tied up," Court said. "It's all right, hon—I'll eat it cold."

"No, you won't!" Fancy said. "My husband is not a-going to eat cold food!"

I could have done worse, Court thought, as she busied herself, thrusting the pots and pans into the oven, and poking up the dying fire. Oh yes, I could have done much worse. . . .

Later, Fancy sat across the table from him and watched him with her great blue eyes as he ate. She ate very little, but it pleased her greatly when Court had, or feigned, a good appetite. Tonight, Court forced himself to eat two helpings of everything, though he really did not feel like eating at all.

When he had finished and sat down in the big rocker, she brought him his cigar case and stood behind him with her arms around his shoulders.

"Court," she said plaintively.

"Yes, hon?" Court said.

"Myrtie Torrence was by here today and she said . . ."

"The devil you say!" Court roared. "How many times do I have to tell you I don't want you associating with Myrtie Torrence?"

"But Court," Fancy said, "I really don't have any girl friends, and I couldn't rightly put Myrtie out. It would of been a mighty mean thing. She ain't really bad, and—"

"All right, all right," Court said. "What did she say?"

"A lot of things. But only one of 'em made any sense to me. Court, why don't we live up at the big house? It is part yours, ain't it?"

"Myrtie put that bee in your bonnet?"

"Yes. Why can't we, Court?"

"For one thing, my father lives there. For another—so does my sister Agnes. Saph, of course, is all right—she liked you. But you don't know Agnes or my father."

"But it's such a big house. It's got lots and lots of rooms."

"Damn it all, Fan, you're no fool! You know what would happen if I brought you there?"

"What, Court?"

"My father would have heart failure. And Agnes would walk out into the street. You're a good kid, Fan; but people are the way they are. They don't forget things easily."

"I see," Fancy said sadly. "Court, ain't there no way we can win them over?"

"None," Court said grimly.

"Not even if you was to get rich and . . ."

"I said none," Court growled.

Fancy didn't say anything more.

Looking at her, Court had the thought that even when it was still her face was lovely. Given a little better chance in life, given the good fortune to have been born into a different estate, Fancy might have queened it over Georgia society.

"You're going up there tomorrow?" she asked.

"Yes," Court said. "It's about time I paid the folks a call."

"Oh," Fancy said. "You won't be long, will you? I do get so lonesome, Court."

"No, Fan," Court said gently, "I won't be long."

"Want to hear me read now, Court? I've been studying real hard."

"Yes," Court said. "You can read to me, Fan."

Fan went and got the book and sat down on his lap. That was one of the first things that Court had done, once he'd gotten used to the idea of being married to her. If he were going anywhere, his wife couldn't shame him. So he had begun teaching Fancy. He was surprised at how much she knew already and how quickly she learned. Listening to her now as she raced over the page, making only a very few mistakes in pronunciation, Court nodded his head in slow approval.

She'll make it, he decided. Oh, yes—Fan'll make it all right. . . .

That night it took him a long time to go to sleep. And when he did sleep he dreamed. He wasn't afraid of his family, but this first visit to Hiberion after his marriage was something to think about. He had no guarantee that his father or Agnes wouldn't show him the door. Yet he had to go. Common courtesy demanded that much.

He dressed very carefully in the morning. Fancy sat upon a low footstool and watched him. He kissed her lightly and went out walking under the great oak trees whose leaves hung down listlessly from the heat. Not a breath of air was stirring, only the zigzag lines of heat rising from the cobblestones as he crossed the street, only the sun beating down mercilessly where there were no trees, and he remembered wryly his father's story that in the beginning the devil had been given both Georgia and Hell, and after spending one summer in Georgia he had promptly rented it out and lived in Hell. At the moment, Court didn't doubt it.

He took a longer time to reach Hiberion than he could remember ever before having taken. Even then he stood in front of the gate a long time before he pushed it open.

Hell, he thought, it's done now. And nothing they can say or do can make any difference. So thinking, he mounted the steps to the front porch and opened the door.

Agnes and Saphira were both sitting in the high-ceilinged living room, crocheting. Agnes saw him first and stood up, letting her work fall to the floor.

"Court!" she exclaimed. Then: "Oh, Court—how could you!" Then she turned and ran up the stairs. Saphira got to her feet more slowly, and came toward him with a slow smile that was half tenderness—and half spite.

"The prodigal returns," she said. "Well, Court—welcome home. Sit and chat with me a spell. . . . You must have *so* much to tell me!"

"I don't have a blamed thing to tell you, Saph," Court said. "How's Father?"

"Prostrated. How'd you expect? He declares that his sons will put him in his grave yet. I think he slightly underestimates his daughters —or at least one of his daughters. How was she, Court—fun? Now you can tell me the things I ought to have learned from my husband. Only I don't have a husband. So you tell me."

"You are mad."

"Then I'll ask Fancy. She'll tell me. I'll get her to teach me the secret of her black arts."

"You don't need any teaching. All it takes is the temperament and the inclination, and you, Saph, darling, have both. Father's upstairs?"

"I told you he was prostrated. But don't go yet, Court. Seriously, I'm curious. You're happy?"

"Very," Court said. "Fan's really been wonderful. Don't think I could have found myself a better wife if I had searched the pages of the Almanac de Gotha."

"Trying to convince yourself, Courtie-pie? You don't sound that happy. Fan's a sweet child—but she's a child. And I'll bet you're too strait-laced to teach her all the tricks you've learned from your lights o' love. Well, you've succeeded in out-Brantleying the Brantleys, with, of course, my hearty approval. That's quite an accomplishment."

"I am going up to see Father now," Court said, "with your kind permission, Saph. . . ."

"Or without it, brother dear. I shall be waiting for you when you come down."

Jefferson Brantley, Court observed the moment he entered the room, was neither more nor less prostrated than he had ever been. And what was wrong with him was the pint and a half of bourbon he had consumed as usual, rather than any sorrow.

"Court," he said. "Glad to see you, boy. Heard you'd gotten yourself married and to a rather disreputable woman at that. Well, I'm not going to quarrel with your choice. A good man can do wonders for a woman who loves him—set her feet on the right path, raise her up again to respectability. Shows you're honest at least—that you don't regard your fellow human creatures as mere playtoys for your pleasure. That's good. Have a drink, son—have a drink!"

Court picked up the bottle of bourbon and poured himself a stiff one. He hadn't expected this. Not this.

"Perhaps this will change the Brantleys' fortunes," Jeff Brantley went on. "We've been rather cruel in our dealings with women, Court, boy—yessir, rather cruel. Our wives have suffered—and the lesser women who have given way to our impetuosity have suffered even more. Yessir, son, the Brantley women die by drowning—we drive them to the river, or to the madhouse. We're a satanic breed; we've got centaur blood in our veins. Well, here's to you, Court, boy—to you and your new bride!"

Court lifted his glass to his lips. But he didn't drink. He heard the noise start below.

"Don't you go up there!" he could hear Agnes' voice shrieking, "don't you dare!"

"Now, Ag," Saphira laughed; "she's a perfect right to—"

"Now what in the name of the lustful daughter of Satan who gave birth to the first Brantley is that?" Jeff Brantley roared.

Court took a stride toward the door, but he was too late. Fancy stood in the doorway, clad in an enormous black hat with quite outrageous yard-long ostrich plumes, and holding a feathered muff of the same black plumes in her hands. Her dress was of black silk, plentifully garnished with even blacker sequins, and it was cut in extreme décolletage, being intended for dancing instead of street wear. Court knew that dress and that hat. Fancy had bought them out of her own savings, and he hadn't had the heart to tell her how bad they were. To her simple country heart, they were elegance itself. She probably saw Myrtie Torrence in that professional tart's costume, Court groaned, and thought it looked so fine. . . .

He started toward her grimly, but his father's anguished quaver stopped him dead in his tracks.

"This the girl you married?" the old man whispered. Then, suddenly, astonishingly recovering the full power of his lungs, he roared: "You're welcome to visit me any time you like, Court boy, but get that—that—creature out of here!"

Court could see Fancy quite visibly crumpling under the impact of the old man's savage scorn, so he came up to her and took her gently by the arm. She did not say a word as he led her down the stairs and out into the street, but came along quietly in all her bedraggled finery, her tears streaking her pale face.

When they reached the little house, Court looked at her.

"Go wash your face," he said coldly. "And take off those rags and burn them."

"But Court . . ."

"Do as I say! They make you look like—like the kind of woman Myrtie Torrence is."

"Oh, Court—no!" Fancy said. Then she ran into the bedroom and shut the door. He could hear the water splashing in the basin on the washstand. He sat down miserably in the big rocker and thought about the expressions on the faces of all the people they had passed in the street. He knew then that he was doomed in Augusta. If he ever wanted to get his mill started, if he ever were to rise in life, he'd have to go somewhere else. He knew that now.

Fancy came out of the bedroom then, wrapped in a soft, pink robe. She looked absurdly young and penitent and fearful all at the same time.

"Court," she said timidly, "I'm so sorry. . . ."

"It's all right," Court said gruffly. "You had to find out some day."

"But I shamed you, Court. I shamed you in your own house in front of your father. I reckon I got too lonely—and started thinking about what Myrtie said and . . ."

"And you came to my father's house," Court finished for her.

"He and my sister behaved precisely the way I told you they would. You got your feelings hurt, damned badly, which was what I was trying to avoid. Oh well, it's done now. Let's forget it, shall we. . . ."

"I can't forget it!" Fancy cried. "I'm so shamed I could curl up and die and . . ."

Court stood up then, and took her in his arms.

"Forget it, Fan," he said.

But the next day, he noticed the change in her. She was silent. Moodily and sullenly silent. The breakfast she gave him was awful. Court thought she hadn't tried to make it any better. He stood her pouting until mid-afternoon, then he spoke to her sharply.

"What the devil's the matter with you, Fan?"

"A whole lot of things," Fancy said tartly. "Been thinking what a fool I am. What call had your pap to speak to me like that? After all him and all the Brantleys except your brother Phil is poor'n Job's turkey hen. How come they hold themselves so fine?"

"Look, Fan," Court began patiently.

"You, too!" Fancy raged at him. "You stood there and let him call me bad names and never said a word—nary a living word! I reckon you're shamed of me, Court Brantley. Reckon the best thing for me is to get myself out of this house right now!"

"Fan, for God's sake!"

"Thought I was doing myself proud when I married you! Well, I didn't. You ain't got a ghost of a chance of doing anything big in this here town. You know why, Court Brantley? In the first place, you ain't got it in you, and in the second, nobody's going to give you a helping hand—because of me."

"There are," Court said, "other places. . . ."

"You've been to 'em, and what good did it do? I don't aim to be poor all my life—and that's all I'll ever be with you. I'll be slaving over that miserable, rotten little stove till the day I die. And you ain't even got the gumption to get out and get yourself a job of work. What we going to do when your savings are gone, Court? Tell me, what?"

She is more than a little right, Court thought bitterly, on all counts. So, now the honeymoon is over.

"You can leave," he said coldly, "any time you want to, Fan."

The rage went out of her at once, like air from a pricked balloon.

119

She started to cry, terribly. Court went over and took her in his arms.

"I'm mean," she wept. "I'm meaner'n a sidewinder! And you, Court, honey, are just about the sweetest and the nicest and the best . . ."

"No, Fan," Court said gently. "Reckon most of what you said was just about right. But I haven't given up trying. And you mustn't give up either. If we can't make it here in Augusta, we'll go to Macon or Savannah or some other place far enough away so that nobody ever heard of us. We can start clean, that way. Make a new life for ourselves. Come on, now—dry your eyes."

Fancy obeyed. But that night, for the first time since they had been married, she pushed away his encircling arms.

"Just don't feel like it, Court," she whispered. "I'm plumb wore out, and I don't feel so good. . . ."

Yes, Court decided, the honeymoon was definitely over.

He couldn't sleep. He kept thinking about what Fancy had said. He thought about it a long time and very carefully. And the next morning he got up and caught a train for Atlanta.

But a week later, sitting in his room on the sixth floor of the Kimball House, Court was ready to give it up. He had his shoes and socks off and was bathing his swollen feet in a basin. He had no idea how many miles he had walked, or how many men of wealth and prominence he had talked to. Now, from the railroad depot diagonally across Pryor Street, he could hear the whistle of the trains.

Go back North, Court Brantley, he told himself angrily. Go back where you've got a chance!

It didn't help to be a Brantley. Not here in Atlanta. They had the fever here already. There were all kinds of factories and plants in and around the city. And that prophet of Southern industrial progress, Henry W. Grady, had bought a one-fourth interest in the *Constitution*. From the editorial chair, he was shouting industrialization to the rooftops. Court, earlier in the week, had visited the offices of that newspaper, and Grady, himself, had offered support.

But even that hadn't helped because of two things: the capitalists of Atlanta were quite willing to back another mill—in Atlanta. They had no intention of seeing the profits and wages going to benefit another section of the state. That was the first thing. The second was that too many of them knew the Brantleys of old.

"Court Brantley—Brantley did you say? Not old Jeff Brantley's boy? I knew your father well, son. Finest horseman and best shot in the state. And women—Lord! So you want to go into business— W-e-l-l, now—that's right strange. First Brantley I ever heard tell of that had any interest in making money—mighty good hands at spending it, though. . . . Now, son, don't take on. I've got nothing against your family. I'm sorry, son, but since you put it that way, I'll have to admit that I would rather invest money with people who have a better reputation for steadiness. Fine people, the Brantleys; but you got to admit that all of 'em I ever heard of was a mite wild."

The dead hands of the past, strangling the future. The sins of the fathers. . . . Oh, hell, Court thought, I'm going home.

It was hard, telling Fancy of his failure. What made matters even worse was the fact that that very next morning, Tyler came back from Savannah. He stood on Court's front porch at half past eight in the morning, tall, lean, hook-nosed and laughing, the sunlight gleaming on his bald head. Seeing him there, like that, Court groaned. In all of Tyler's thirty-seven years of life, nobody had ever been able to pull him out of bed before noon.

"This the lil' gal you married?" he grinned. "Mighty nice. Yes-sirreebob-tail, mighty nice! Sweetest lil' bit o' fluff I ever did see. But tell me, boy, all things being considered, did you have to make it legal?"

Thereupon, Court hit him.

Tyler wiped the blood that was streaming from his nose, and the wide grin never left his face.

"Why you snotty little pup," he laughed, "I used to tan your hide come weekdays or Sundays, and I can do it again."

"Think so?" Court said, and started out of the house.

But Fancy caught hold of his arms.

"No," she said. "You ought to be used to what folks think about me by now, Court. Don't take on about it. Shouldn't rile you up none, nohow—'cause you more'n halfway believe the same thing yourself. . . ."

"Fan, please," Court said.

"It's all right, Court," Fan said quietly. "One of these days you're going to find out that I didn't lie to you—that I'm not and never was the kind of woman you think, then you're going to be mightily ashamed of yourself." She stopped talking and put out her hand.

"Howdy, Mister Tyler," she said. "Mighty proud to make your acquaintance."

"Likewise," Tyler grinned. "Sorry I opened my yap like that, Ma'am; but bedeviling Court is one of life's dearest pleasures."

"How's Fern?" Court asked.

"Just fine. In fact, she's sitting out there under the oak waiting on me."

"I'll go invite her in," Court said. "Excuse me a minute, hon."

He started down the walk toward the gate, and Tyler came with him. Fancy watched them go, her face troubled. Didn't ask me to come along, she thought. Thought marrying him would be enough; but it isn't. Got to work at it yet—got to get her out of his mind. . . .

"Look, Court," Tyler said as they came up to the buggy, "I got news for you, boy—big news!"

Court ignored him.

" 'Lo, Fern," he said.

"Court—" Fern whispered.

Tyler looked from one of them to the other, and he didn't like what he saw.

"I said I had news for you, Court," he said drily. "Would you like to hear it? Or would you rather just stand there and make sheep's eyes at my wife?"

"Mighty pleasant occupation," Court said. "All right, Ty—what's your news?"

Tyler grinned shamelessly.

"Uncle Mart," he said, "kicked off a week ago and left Melody to the two of us."

"Why, Tyler!" Fern said sharply, "is that any way to talk about your uncle's passing?"

"Reckon it isn't honeychild," Tyler said; "but the old man wasn't doing any good here below. He'd been sick a long time, and I reckon going was a relief to him. Sure was to me," he added looking at Fern. "If I had had to stay down there one minute longer without seeing your pretty face, I'd just about busted a seam."

"Tyler Brantley!" Fern said.

"Come into the house and have a seat," Court said. "It doesn't seem right somehow to stand up out here talking about Uncle Martin like this. You, too, Fern; you'd be mighty welcome."

Fern shook her head.

"No, thank you, Court," she said stiffly; "I'll wait right here. You boys run along and have your talk."

Court looked at her.

"Why won't you come in, Fern?" he said. "Because of—Fan?"

"Because of Fan," Fern said flatly. "Marrying her was your business, Court. But associating with her—would be mine. Go ahead, youall. I'll wait."

Court stood there a long moment, then he turned back toward the house. Tyler looked back at his wife and whistled softly.

"Boy," he said to Court, "you sure got yourself in a spot. Reckon you better take lil' Fan to some other place where she ain't so well known."

Court's face was bleak and fierce.

"Be damned if I will," he said. "Money talks, Ty. And before I'm through I'm going to own this town—lock, stock and barrel. Then watch them. They'll put up with Fan all right; they'll come a-crawling on their bellies to kiss her fingertips."

Tyler shrugged.

"Can't blame you for being pig-headed," he drawled. "I'm right pert stubborn myself. Runs in the family. But it 'pears to me that you're barking up the wrong tree this time, Court, boy. This here is bigger than you. There are rules, you know—main one is not to get caught. But you got yourself caught, and that's bad. On top of that, you forget one thing: never has been a man born what needed a home or a family. Most men get them accidentally, because some smart little filly holds out long enough and teases bad enough to convince him that her particular equipment must be a heap better'n any other gal's—which it ain't, as he soon finds out. Marriage, Court, is woman's vested interest. She's the only one what gains a damned thing by it. And she gains a hell of a lot—security—financial that is—and freedom to give way to her natural impulses, 'cause she's got a man to hang the results of her sins on, even if no two of 'em remotely resembles the other. What I'm driving at, boy, is that nothing on earth is meaner and fights dirtier than a good woman—

123

and little woods fillies like Fan are her natural enemies. She can smell 'em five miles to the windward. They're always there, a-threatening to break up her closed corporation, and she doesn't like it one damned bit. The men, now, that's different—they'll cotton up to a cute little bit of fluff like Fan in a minute, but if you think any woman in this town is going to accept Fan, even if you roll her in diamond dust and gild the seat of her pants, you're crazy!"

There was, Court realized grimly, a lot of truth in this.

"Come on up to the house," he said. "Fan'll be wondering what we're standing her jawing about."

"With pleasure," Tyler said. "I'm right smart partial to your little Fancy myself."

"Come in, Mister Ty," Fancy said shyly. "I'm mighty glad you're here. We ain't had no visitors in the longest time."

"I aim to," Tyler grinned. " 'Sides I'm hungrier than a hound dog on a nigger 'cropper's section, and believe me, that's some hungry!"

Fancy's face brightened at once.

"I'd be mighty proud to fix some breakfast for you, Ty," she said. "Your brother don't rightly 'preciate my cooking."

She went into the house, and Court and Tyler sat down on the steps.

"Reckon Melody is saddled with mortgages, too," Court said, "like all the big plantations nowadays. . . ."

"Not so many as you'd think," Tyler said. "I got some ideas about that, boy. Given my head, I'll clear them off in less than a year."

"Tell me about Melody," Court said.

"Tell him about Melody!" Tyler echoed, rolling his eyes skyward. "Ask me to tell you about heaven—that's easier. Court, boy, that there Melody is just about the prettiest spread of land these famished old eyes ever feasted on—lying there in the Savannah river bottom, a-stretching itself out in the sun from vinegar bend to bitter creek, plumb from hell to breakfast! Black bottom land, Court; hell, you can smell the good stuff in it. Every inch of topsoil what's washed from these starved-out holdings up here around Augusta is piled up down there eighteen inches deep—cotton grows so damned fast that you throw in the seed and jump back to keep the stalks from cracking you on the jaw."

"Yet," Court drawled, "there are debts. . . ."

"Your Uncle Martin," Tyler said, "knew about as much about planting as the left side of my hindquarters. His methods—" Tyler stopped, groping for the words—"Heck, the only way I can describe them is to say that they existed in a state of urinal poverty. Doggone! That's what I call turning a phrase. I sure put that plumb politely!"

"But you could do better?" Court said.

"Court, boy, if I don't clear that place of debt in one growing season—hell's bells, if I don't show us a good-sized profit, I'll lay my worthless carcass down in a coffin and let you nail the lid shut."

"You've got your chance," Court said. "I'm no planter, God knows. But Ty, if you can't straighten that place up, I'll have to sell my half to raise the money for the mill."

Tyler stared at him in genuine alarm.

"Don't do that!" he said. "Don't you even think that way! Why, Court, boy, that there plantation is a-going to make us so damned rich. . . ."

"All right, all right," Court said tiredly. "Take the damned place. Run it for a year and show me the profits. You've got the land in your blood, Ty—like all Southerners. I'm sick of the old life. While I was up North, I saw a few things, including why they were able to whip the pants off of us. We've got to have more industries down here—we've got to give these rednecks half a chance at a decent job and wages in their pockets. The South's got to have enough to eat in its belly for once in its history—all the South, Ty, not just a few fortunate aristocrats."

"Damned if they didn't make a Yankee out of you, up there," Tyler grinned. "You sound like one of those abolitionists."

"I am," Court said, "but it's human misery I'm trying to abolish, Ty—the misery of white humans, just like you and me. Maybe I'll even get around to the blacks, before I'm done."

"Do tell!" Tyler chuckled. "I'll be right there when you do—to wave you good-bye as you start off on your journey—a-riding on the topside of a fence rail, all dressed up in that suit of tar, and all them pretty feathers!"

"That won't happen," Court said. "Ty, how'd you happen to marry Fern?"

"How'd I happen to beat your time, you mean? You helped—writing home about your pretty Yankee heiress."

"That was a lie!" Court growled.

"Well, maybe I did exaggerate a mite—but all's fair in love and war, boy. Appears to me you ain't got no right to complain."

"I'm not complaining. I'm just remembering what you said. Stuff like marriage being a woman's vested interest."

"Don't miss a thing, do you? It's the truth, boy. But the point is, what in hellfire makes you think any Brantley's got a mite of sense in his head as far as women are concerned—even me?"

"You were talking mighty wise a minute ago," Court said. "Thought you were above such things."

"Well, I ain't. That little yaller-haired filly gave me the itch so damned bad I nearly went plumb out of my mind. I was plumb burning to find out if her hidden talents were as delectable as they looked from the outside. Course I hinted more than once that between such high-minded, modern enlightened people as her and me, the book and the preacher weren't really necessary; but Fern wasn't having any—not that girl!"

"So, like the rest of us damned fools, you had to build your fence around her to find out that her talents were just as mediocre as any other woman's?" Court mocked him.

"Partly," Tyler drawled; "but only partly. As a matter of fact, Fern ain't mediocre. But there's more to it than that. I just like to have that little gal around anyhow. She's stimulating. She'll help me git up and git somewheres. Besides, boy—ever thought about the fact that after us there ain't no more Brantleys? Phil and that girl he stole plumb out of the chilling room of the Augusta ice plant ain't got a chit or a child—and you and Fancy ain't likely to do no better. Seems like it's up to me to keep the breed going."

"Phil," Court said, "has done that already."

"You mean his nigger yard children? Hell, boy, they don't count. What this town needs is a passel of true-born Brantleys to turn it up on its ear. So it's up to me—if you'll give me half a chance."

"Me?" Court said brusquely; "what the devil do I have to do with it?"

"You know damned well what you have to do with it," Tyler said calmly. "Fern ain't over you, yet. And there ain't a doggoned thing you can do about it." Tyler grinned half teasingly, half fondly at his younger brother. "I'm getting old—and you always was a heap prettier'n me. So lay off, won't you? Give me a chance to set Fern right."

Fancy put her head out of the door.

"Your breakfast is ready, Ty," she said. "Come on in, won't you?"

"Sure Lord will," Tyler groaned. "My belly was just asking my backbone whether my throat was cut."

Court stood up along with him.

"That—business we were talking about," he said; "don't worry about that, Ty—I have no intentions at all in that direction."

"Good!" Tyler said, and they went into the house.

Half an hour later, he sat back, the last hole in his belt completely by-passed.

"Honeychild," he said, "sure you don't want to leave this nit-wit and run off with me? Girl what can cook like that—whew!"

"Ty, you're the beatingest old thing!" Fancy giggled. "It's sure nice to cook for a man what enjoys it."

"I always enjoy your cooking," Court pointed out.

"You!" Fancy snorted. "You eat like a bird, Court."

"I will try to do better in the future," Court said.

Tyler pushed back his chair and got up. Court walked through the hall with him, and a moment later Fancy came, too, putting the dishes she had started to gather up, back on the table.

On the porch, Tyler stood a moment, looking at the two of them.

"You swing a wicked fist, boy," he said, feeling his swollen nose gingerly. "Good-bye now." He crossed the porch, and started down the steps, but on the second one he turned.

"Oh, by the way," he said, "heard they turned Duke Ellis loose this morning. Didn't have a thing to hold him for—'cepting disturbing the peace. He was unconscious when Wyche got knifed, so they couldn't hold him for that. Good-bye, Honeychild—you, too, Court —be seeing y'all."

Then he turned very quietly and went down the path out of the yard.

7

THERE WAS no wind. The flame in the kerosene lamp stood straight up. Above it, Court Brantley's face glistened with sweat. He sat across the table from Fancy and in his hands he held a revolver. He worked over it carefully, oiling it, then slipping the cartridges one by one into the chambers, and giving the magazine a slow, deliberate whirl with his thumb. He picked up an oily cloth and began polishing it, although it already glinted bluely in the light of the lamp.

"Court—" Fancy got out, "oh, Court . . ."

"Yes, Fan?" Court said somberly.

"Maybe he won't come . . ."

Court stood up slowly and walked to the windows. There was no moon and the chinaberry tree hooped its umbrella shape, black and tremendous across half the sky. Under it the shadows were inky, sooty, crawling with secret, unheard sounds. A man creeping up through that blackness with a gun in his hand would have all the advantage, Court knew. Even if I blew the lamp out now, he'd still be able to see better. Wearily he turned back to Fancy.

"He'll come all right," he said.

"Maybe he won't," Fan moaned.

But he would. Court knew that. Duke Ellis was no coward. Buck and Tom, yes. Without Duke they were nothing, and less than nothing. But not Duke. Duke was something—absolutely something. Looking out of his window into the crawling dark, Court Brantley thought that the something Duke Ellis was, was a thing the human race should have gotten rid of twenty-five centuries ago. Well, it hadn't; and what lay between him and Duke now was killing business.

He, Court, had married Fancy. But he knew exactly how much difference that would make to Duke. Tonight, within hours, minutes, maybe—one of them was going to die. Tonight, in this year of Our Lord, 1880, in modern times, in a civilized country, he and Duke were going to pump bullets into each other's guts until one of them went down and stayed.

And to the victor would belong the spoils.

Looking at Fan, seeing her face white in the lamplight, her black hair running off unedged into the blackness behind it, her full, sullen mouth trembling in little uncontrolled jerks at the corners, Court wondered. If Duke gets me, he thought, will she step across me and fly into his arms? Will she? Why not? He was something to her once, how much I don't know, will never know, don't even want to know. I'm a Brantley and any pretty woman can lie to us and make us believe it. It's bad enough to die any time in any way even when you're dying for something, but I never thought I'd die like all the rest of the Brantleys in dubious battle over second-hand goods . . .

He looked at her.

I shall save one shot, little Fan, he thought. And if I live long enough, I'm going to pump it right between those lovely breasts of yours. You'll lie beside me, Fan, in the long dark, and I'll share those lips of yours, but only with the worms, the dampness, and the crumbling mold . . .

Fancy backed away from him.

"Court," she whispered, "don't look at me like that! Oh, Court, honey, you make me plumb scairt!"

"Don't be frightened, Fan," Court said gently. "There's nothing to be afraid of. Not now, not any more."

"But I am scairt!" Fancy wailed. "Right then, I thought you was going to kill me."

Court shook his head.

"No, Fan," he said. "Not now. Not until you deserve it."

Fancy stood there looking at him, her fine nostrils flaring with her breathing. Then she came up to him, her face very white, her blue eyes behind their sooty lashes, enormous in her small face. She was so close to him that he could feel her breath rustling against his throat.

"Duke can't win," she said quietly. "Maybe we'll all lose, but he can' win. I'm not a thing, Court. Not nothing a man can have for fighting over—like two dogs a-snarling after the same bone. I'm me, darling—and maybe I ain't much, but I'm all yours."

"Suppose," Court said cruelly, "he kills me?"

"Then he'll have to kill me, too. Kill me—or watch me night and day. 'Cause I'm a Brantley now, Court, love—and the Brantley women always know just what to do."

"You'd die because of me?" Court demanded.

"That's one way of putting it. I don't think about it like that. What I think is I couldn't live without you. Not one minute, Court."

Court looked at her. Then he put down the gun.

"Come here, Fan," he said.

She came away from his kiss, crying. He held her by the shoulders, hard.

"Go to bed, Fan," he said. "It's going to be all right—believe me."

"All right, Court," she whispered. But she didn't believe him. She didn't believe him at all. . . .

Court sat in the big chair, waiting. His eyelids stung. They felt as if they had sand under them. His head nodded once or twice. He stiffened his neck until his head jerked against the taut-held muscles. Then, ridiculously, it was morning, graying in through the windows, and the gun lay on the floor under his loosened fingers, cold and unfired, and Duke Ellis had not come.

But he did come in the afternoon, in full sunlight, as Court, who knew the man, should have known he'd come. He came up the path, slowly, dressed in a suit of the finest white linen, a cigar stuck between his teeth at an angle, having somehow an air as jaunty as a plume.

He stopped on the porch long enough to fan himself with his soft, rich Panama hat, then he lifted his big hand to knock on the door. But he never brought it down, for Court stepped out on the porch and faced him.

Duke looked him up and down slowly.

"Where's Fan?" he drawled.

"That," Court said, "is none of your damned business, Duke."

"Now do tell!" Duke said. "That's a mighty poor way of greeting an old friend. What I want to know is how come it ain't, Court?"

"Fancy happens to be my wife," Court said. "I don't think I'd have to tell anybody else this, Duke; but I know you. I don't want you hanging around my place. I don't want you trying to see Fan. If you do . . ."

"What?" Duke drawled. "Tell me what, Court, boy? Sounds right pert interesting."

"I'll kill you," Court said. "I'd do it now and save myself future trouble, but I see you don't have a gun."

"A gun?" Duke chuckled. "Since when did I need a gun for one puking puppy of a Brantley? You Brantleys are played out. Not that you ever was much, Court. Anyhow, so's you'll know, I'm taking Fancy back, any time I get the notion to."

"Why don't you get that notion now?" Court said quietly.

"Some other time," Duke said. "Ain't had my vittles yet. Course I could break your stiff Brantley neck on an empty stomach, but it'll be more pleasurable after I've et."

Court looked at him.

"I am not that particular," he said. "I'll send you and any other Ellis whatsoever to hell any time at all. Before breakfast or after it. I'm warning you, Duke."

"Well, I'll vow," Duke said happily, "that you do talk big for such a little fellow. All right, boy, I'm warned. I'll tend to you later. You —and Fan." Then very calmly he turned and walked down the steps and out of the yard.

Court watched him go, his own fingers tightening on the trigger of the pistol he had in his pocket. Couldn't miss him from here.

He's half as big as a barn anyhow and I could drop him now so easy that . . .

Only I can't. All the men that we Brantleys have killed—not one of them ever died with a bullet in his back. Or unarmed. No—we've always faced them down on the Sand Bar Ferry and took their shot first and then shot back, sometimes even with a bullet already in our guts. The Brantleys don't run to cowardice or murder. Which is the reason, maybe, that so many of us have died violently in very bad ways.

He turned then and went back into the house.

There began then what Court always thought of afterwards as the bad time. For Duke Ellis stayed in town and did nothing—absolutely nothing at all.

The heat lay along the land like a blanket, and the chinaberry tree in the yard sent down its thick, sickening scent. The river grew shallow and stank and there were mud flats in the middle of it. And the rains did not come. Night after night the moon came up big and yellow, dimming the stars. The songs that the Negroes sang down in the Terry seemed to get sadder each time Court heard them. And Court Brantley sat by his window each night, holding the gun in fingers that dripped with sweat, but Duke did not come.

Every day, all day long in the thick heat he did not leave the house. Outside the sun flamed down, smashing the red Georgia earth with hammer blows. Nothing moved. Even the crows were still in this heat-killed, sun-stricken land. Court ate nothing, wasting away into gauntness, and Fancy's sullen mouth drew down more and more at the corners. And always they quarreled. One minute they were still, and the next the air was alive with sharp and bitter words that ended with Fancy sulking in a corner or dissolved in acid tears that settled nothing and left her eyes reddened and ugly.

But at night they did not quarrel. No, never in the night.

The days crawled into weeks until it was fall, but the heat did not lessen. When the rains finally came, they came in great thunderstorms like those of midsummer that turned Fancy's face ghostwhite with fear. Having to stay there like that in that ugly little house was a bad thing. Court hated the sight of her, now. He wondered if he couldn't go to Savannah, Macon, Charleston—any place where there might be men with money who would listen to him.

He came into the house one day with the rain dripping off his broad-brimmed hat, and looked at the dinner that she had fixed for him. He didn't even sit down.

"Fan," he said, "I'm going down to Savannah. There's a man down there—a friend of Tyler's . . ."

"Oh, Court," she whispered, "no!"

"I've got to go some time," Court said. "Looks like old Duke has just about given up. You stay in the house, and you'll be safe."

"Please, Court," Fancy said, "please, darlin'—don't go! I'm scairt! He might come. . . ."

"He won't come," Court said, and went into the bedroom to pack his bag.

When he came out, Fancy was curled up in the big chair. Her mouth was sullen.

"Go on," she said, "leave me. But I want to tell you one thing, Court Brantley. Won't be my fault what happens."

"I know," Court said; "nothing ever is from a woman's point of view. I'll be back in two or three days. You stay in the house, Fan."

"I won't promise you," Fan said tartly.

In Savannah, it was the same thing again—failure. Court rode out toward Melody, telling himself that he wanted to talk to Tyler; but it was Fern he wanted to see.

Melody was a beautiful plantation. Riding through the mile-long drive bordered with water oaks that led up to the house, Court had the feeling that it was even more beautiful than it had been before. The oaks dripped gray moss that shredded the morning sunlight, and on both sides of the road, the fields stretched away out of sight, with the cotton plants, bursting with bolls, standing in the cleanest rows he'd ever seen, and the earth between was blacker than the heart of darkness. It was good land, rich bottom land, river silt piled up with the compost of all the earth that the Savannah drained. The yield, he could see, would be great.

But there was something else about Melody—the miles of fences freshly whitewashed, the clipped, pruned, orderly look about it—all the thousand small evidences that here was the hand of a master planter. In his uncle's time, it hadn't been so.

133

Ty's good, Court admitted. Now if he can only give me a lead on something . . .

But there was something missing. For the life of him Court couldn't tell what it was. Then the house came in sight as he turned a bend in the road and he knew quite suddenly what it was.

Nobody sang. You expected singing on the land. The field hands timed their work to the rhythms of the lead hand's song. Negroes sang all the time: when they were happy, when they were sad; when they were sick, or drunk, or dying. Something had to be mighty amiss for a black man not to sing. But he didn't see anything wrong—not at first, not until he was only fifty yards from the house.

A line of Negroes crossed the road with hoes in their hands, and picking sacks slung from their shoulders. They looked up at him, sitting on his rented horse, and Court saw that their eyes were dead. The brownish whites of their eyes were red-streaked and dull, their gaze listless. There was not a fat man among them. Some Negroes ran to fat. One of Martin's best workers had been a black who weighed three hundred pounds. But these hands weren't fat. They were black skeletons walking. They were a line of unkempt scarecrows. They were filthy. His uncle's hands had been decently dressed in blue jeans or overalls, but these had rags and gunny sacks for clothes. Looking at them Court felt sick.

Then the last of them crossed over into the field and a white man came behind them. He was tall and dressed in faded khaki, and a double-barreled shotgun lay in the crook of his arm. He had a muleskinner's whip about fifteen feet long coiled about his shoulder. And he had three dogs with him: two bloodhounds and a bull mastiff.

Court looked at the dogs and the sickness left him. What took its place was a different thing. Like murder.

Bloodhounds were bad enough. Court knew that bloodhounds wouldn't attack a man. They'd only track him to hell and begone, corner him, and wait for the man and the mastiff to come up. The mastiff. Big as a yearling calf. Ugly. Able to pull a full-grown man down and worry him to death.

His feelings must have showed in his face, for the man stopped and looked at him.

"Now who in hellfire," he drawled, "might you be?"

Court looked him up and down, slowly.

"That," he said very quietly, "is none of your God-damned business."

He could see the overseer's hand tightening on the triggers of the shotgun. And he didn't have a pistol. He had left it behind with Fan.

"Reckon I'll have to make it my business, Mister," the overseer said. " 'Pears to me you're trespassing."

"And it appears to me that you're exceeding your authority. Whoever told you to stop and question people on the drive?"

"The owner," the overseer said. "Mister Brantley."

"The half owner," Court corrected him. "You're looking at the other half right now. And if you aren't off this place by sundown, I'll take the greatest pleasure in throwing you off, personally."

"I reckon Mister Ty'll have something to say about that," the overseer said.

"Reckon he will," Court said. "But if he doesn't sing a tune I like, I'll throw him off along with you. Now get out of my way; you're blocking the road."

The overseer fingered the gun. Court touched his heel to the nag's flanks and bore down upon him. Then the man stepped aside. Court rode on toward the house thinking what a wonderful target his back made at that distance. But he didn't turn his head. The man stood there looking at him; then, swearing softly, he plunged on into the field after the blacks.

The house had been painted. It had the same trim, well-kept look as the rest of the plantation. Court got down from the horse and climbed the porch steps. He pushed open the screened door and went in.

Tyler was sitting before the dining room table, his food untouched before him, staring off into space.

"You bastard," Court said.

Tyler grinned at him, wearily.

"Funny thing," he drawled; "I've just been calling you that same thing. But now I'm willing to apologize—'cause I see I had you wrong. Sit down, boy. I'll have Matilda rustle up some vittles."

"No," Court said. "We've got a crow to pick, Ty."

"Thought so; but what I want to know is—is it the same crow?"

"Those Negroes," Court growled; "convict labor, aren't they? Farmed out to you?"

"Yep," Tyler said. "Different crow . . ."

"All right, what's yours?"

"Fern."

"Fern?"

"Yep, Court. She left me. Got the Pinkertons out a-looking for her. They trailed her far as Boston, then they lost her. Boston—that's what made me think it was you."

"Well, I'll be damned," Court said.

"Don't reckon you were planning to join her later, were you?"

"First I heard of it," Court said.

Tyler looked at him.

"You're telling the truth," he said at last. "That makes it worse. Don't reckon I'll ever find her now. Though it's kind of nice not to have to shoot you, boy. Blood is thicker than water, ain't it?"

"Sorry, Ty," Court said quietly. "I'm mighty, damned sorry."

"You are, like hell. Oh, skip it. Now, what about the niggers?"

"Get rid of them. Get rid of that redneck. He was itching to take a shot at me."

Tyler put out his hand and took a cigar out of the box on the table. He stuck it into the side of his mouth and passed the box over to Court.

"Sit down," he said. "Have a smoke. No need your being so riled up over something you don't know about, and damned sure don't understand."

Court sat down. He took a cigar. Tyler bent forward and lit it.

"Well?" Court said.

Tyler took his wallet out of his breastpocket and counted out ten new one-hundred-dollar bills.

"Here," he said, "that should run you for a while."

Court looked at the money, then pushed it back toward his brother.

"Don't change the subject, Ty," he said.

"Hell, it's yours. Part of an advance the Savannah factors offered me against the crop. Go on, take it—I know you need money."

"I do," Court said, "but not this kind."

"What other kind is there? It's all dirty. Look, boy, to make a profit after paying off our debts, I had to cut expenses to the bone. That's how come I got those convict niggers. All right, it ain't right.

136

I feel sorry for those poor devils, too. But you're young, Court. You got a mighty heap to learn. Show me anything on this God-damned earth what ain't got a little evil mixed in it. The line between what's good, and what ain't is mighty unclear. Look, right now—by November, in our first growing season, I'm going to pay off all the debts and show a profit, too. Next year, maybe, we'll clear enough to start your mill. Is that good or ain't it?"

"It's good, Ty—but not like this."

"I'll send those jailbirds back to the pen right after next harvest, Court. I don't want 'em around. By then, we can afford to hire hands—pay 'em good, too. I want you to build your mill. Even if the money did start off wrong, what difference does it make when it ends up right? Them nigger jailbirds catch hell—all right. But you think my getting rid of 'em is going to do 'em any good? They'll catch it somewhere else—more hell than here, because I keep a kind of tight rein on that redneck. Besides, here, they're making it possible for somebody to have a chance. . . ."

"How?"

"By getting us started to build that mill of yours. That mill will do the whole town a mighty heap of good like you've been preaching for years. What's more it'll keep on doing those starved-out crackers good; be the first time in history they ever got enough to eat. And the money they spend will do the merchants good, and through them, the whole town. Like I said, I won't renew my contract with the State after next harvest time—a year from now."

"And that overseer?"

"State man. He goes with the niggers. You'll buy that?"

Court looked at him. No unmixed blessings. In a few years, with luck, he could start to build his mill. He could remain in the land he loved. His sons would grow up Southern men. The Brantleys would again be a power in the State. And Hiberion would again be what it had been. No more pine-barren children, spitting death from their lungs. No more supply store with his brother living by choking the life out of the starving. It was good. From this there would come good. This blood money, earned in the hot sun under the chaingang guard's lash. This filthy pile of paper that had cost the blood beaten out of black men's backs—and inside them no more singing.

But Tyler had said there would be no more of that. No more after a year.

Slowly Court put out his hand and picked up the money.

"I'll buy it," he said. "Hope you find Fern."

"Me too," Tyler said.

THAT WAS a mighty foolish thing, Fancy thought. How come I had to go and say that? Telling Court what happened wouldn't be my fault. . . . Now s'posing something was to happen? S'posing Duke was to come and—oh Lord, oh God, oh Jesus, no!

Court would think I planned it. No matter what, he'd always believe that I cottoned up to Duke—that I opened up the door and let him in. Only it ain't a-going to be like that. Duke come here while Court's gone, I'll kill him. Can't do that—I'll kill me. Better be dead than shame Court. Be no good nohow a-sitting here seeing him looking at me—thinking. . . .

She got up and walked to the window, holding Court's revolver in her hand. It was too big. She could scarcely lift it. Going to get myself a gun of my own, she thought. Little lady's pistol what I can handle.

She turned back and looked in the bureau drawer under the pile of socks until she found the money. Then she went out of the house and started walking toward the upper end of Broad Street where the pawnshops were. They had pistols there, she knew that.

The shopkeeper looked at her through his thick spectacles.

"What can I do for you, Ma'am?" he said.

"I want a gun," Fancy blurted. "A little old gun—what I can handle."

The storekeeper stared at her. She saw him looking at her hand where the ring was.

"Planning to shoot somebody?" he said.

"No," Fancy said. "My husband travels—and I'm just plumb scairt in that house all alone. Feel better if I had a gun."

"That's right," the storekeeper agreed. "Mighty heap of prowlers and vagrants about these days. I can see your point, pretty little girl like you. . . . All right—which one?"

"That one," Fancy said and pointed.

The storekeeper got the small revolver with the ornamented stock, and the trigger that folded forward without any guard.

"Bullets?" the storekeeper said.

"Yessir."

He got down a box of the tiny cartridges, and laid them beside the gun.

"You know how to load it?"

"No," Fancy said, "show me, please."

He did, and Fancy went out of the store with the little pistol in her handbag.

She didn't want to go back home. Not now. It was mid-afternoon, and she didn't believe that Duke would come in the daytime. Besides, she didn't like to stay in the house alone.

Now where could she go? She couldn't visit Myrtie Torrence, because Court wouldn't like that. Myrtie was bad, just like Court had said. Fancy shook her head thinking of it. Howcome a girl like Myrtie could do such a thing? Myrtie was pretty and soft-spoken, and always acted nice around Fancy. It was a hard thing to understand. What love was, what a body was made for, couldn't be bought and sold. It was a good thing, kind of holy, even, 'cause that was how life started—a new life, part of Court, and part of me, and the rest of it God and the angels. Anybody who'd ever seen a child, sleeping in his mother's arms could understand that. How could people put a price on such a thing?

But thinking about children gave her an idea. She hadn't seen

Belle and those kids of hers in the longest time. Well, she'd go see them right now. She'd hold little Dred in her arms and rock him to sleep. And anybody what didn't like it because those kids had a drop or two of the wrong kind of blood could go hang!

She loved them. More than that, they meant something to her. What they meant was a thing she couldn't exactly put down in words, because she didn't even know the words for it. But what it was, was a simple thing. They stilled her hunger for children of her own.

Today, as Belle's little house came in sight, she realized that for the first time. Oh, Lord, she prayed silently, why can't we have one? A little boy what'll look just like Court. So little and sweet. One I can hold and sing to, and love. . . . He'd need me. Court doesn't need me or even really want me, I reckon. But a baby'd change all that. Man can't hate the mother of his son. . . .

"Howdy, Miz Fancy," Belle said. "Thought you'd plumb forgot all about us."

"That's something you don't need to worry about," Fancy said. "Can't forget those kids. Can't get 'em out of my mind. How are they?"

"The girls are fine; but Dred's been a mite poorly lately."

"Sick?" Fancy said. "Oh, Belle, why didn't you come to me before now?"

"Don't take on so, Miz Fancy. Reckon it's 'cause he's teething. Though he do feel awful hot. . . ."

Fancy went into the house at once without saying anything else. She bent over the crib and picked up the child. He was burning with fever, his tiny face flushed.

"Belle!" Fancy said, "this child's sick—death-sick! You run right out of here and get the doctor!"

"Miz Fancy," Belle said sadly, "I ain't got no money for no doctor. . . ."

Fancy stared at her.

"You mean to tell me that Phil . . ."

"Mister Phil would give me some all right. He's good that way. But he ain't been around here lately—and I can't go up to his house and ask for him."

"I've got some," Fancy said. "Now run!"

"Doctor ain't a-going to come in no hurry for colored folks," Belle said. "Do my best, though."

"Tell him," Fancy said, "that Mrs. Courtland Brantley wants to see him—right away. Tell him it's a—a emergency."

Belle went out of the house at once. Fancy turned back to the child thinking, that was a real proper word. Court would be proud of me, if he'd heard me say it. Then she began to strip the clothes off the feverish little body.

Twenty minutes later, Belle was back with Doctor Benton. Fancy could hear his voice, gruff and angry, saying:

"You told me Mrs. Brantley, gal. Who're you trying to fool? Mrs. Brantley doesn't live in a shotgun cabin in the nigger section!"

"She's in there, all right," Belle said. "You go see, Doctor."

Fancy got up and walked to the door.

The doctor took off his big hat.

"Howdy, Ma'am," he said. "What's the matter? You get sick all of a sudden while you were passing through?"

"I'm not sick," Fancy said. "It's a child—her child."

"Well, I'll be damned!" the Doctor exploded. "You don't mean to tell me you made me drop everything to come attend to a picka-ninny!"

Fancy stared at him.

"I sent for you to come attend a baby," she said. "A helpless baby who's death-sick. But right now I don't think you could do any good. Man with that kind of a heart couldn't do nobody any good. You can go. I'll get somebody else."

Doctor Benton studied her. Then he said:

"Where's the child?"

"In here," Fancy said and led him to where little Dred twisted on his crib.

"Light skin," Doctor Benton muttered, "blue eyes. Another Brantley yard child, by God!"

"Another baby, what's sick," Fancy told him. "Now you get busy, damn you!"

Doctor Benton examined the baby. Then he opened his bag and took out a bottle of pills.

"Give him this," he said. "Cut the pills in four pieces. Crush one

142

of the pieces. Give it to him in water. *Boiled* water, dammit! Every half-hour till the fever breaks. Bathe him with cool water and alcohol. That'll help. You got sense enough to remember all that, gal?"

"She's got sense enough, all right," Fancy told him. "But *I'm* going to do it. Now how much do I owe you, Doctor?"

Doctor Benton got up and snapped his bag shut.

"Not a red cent," he growled. "Charge it up to my bad heart." Then he marched out of the house.

Fancy turned back to the baby.

"Get a pot of water on the stove," she snapped. "Quick, Belle! You got any rubbing alcohol?"

"No'm," Belle whispered.

"Then take this and get some. Go down to Oertel's Drugstore. But put the water on first."

"Yes'm," Belle said.

It was after midnight when little Dred began to sweat, and a half-hour later, he was sleeping peacefully, cool and quiet.

Fancy was tired—dog-tired; but she knew she had to get home. Even then she didn't think about Duke Ellis. She was thinking about Doctor Benton, wondering what made a man get like that. But he ain't all bad, she thought; he's got shame left. I reached that. Good thing—else that poor little fellow would be dead by now. . . .

She walked on. Wonder when Court's coming back? Lord, I do miss him so. Wonder what he's doing right now? If he even thinks about me?

Court was thinking about her all right. He had gotten back to Augusta a little after ten that night. Coming into the house and finding Fancy gone hadn't been a good thing. The waiting had been worse. He left the house at midnight and went down to Hiberion. But Fancy hadn't been there. Then, gripping the gun in his pocket, he went to the Ellises'. Duke wasn't at home, either. And there was the thing that Fancy had said: "Whatever happens, won't be my fault, Court."

Walking the dark streets of Augusta, Court Brantley was just a little crazy. All the things he'd thought, all the times he'd cursed himself for a fool for marrying Fan, were gone now. He was sick

143

inside. He was filled up with death and bitter hell. And only one thing would do the way he felt any good.

Killing.

But he couldn't find Fan or Duke. Not anywhere at all.

Fancy trudged along, so lost in her own thoughts that she didn't hear the buggy until it drew up alongside her.

"Howdy, Fan," Duke said.

Fancy looked at him and kept on walking.

Duke flapped the reins over the horse's back, lightly. The buggy moved off slowly, keeping pace with her.

"Riding's better than walking," Duke said.

Fan didn't answer him.

"Don't you trust me?" Duke said. "I wouldn't do you no harm."

"No," Fancy said.

"I'll take you home," Duke said earnestly. "I swear by my mother I'll take you home."

Fancy looked at him. Then she remembered the little pistol in her bag. And it was a long way home.

"All right," she said tiredly. "But don't try nothing, Duke. You do, and you'll be sorry."

"I won't try nothing," Duke said.

Fancy climbed into the buggy.

Five minutes later, they passed Court Brantley, standing in the shadow of an unlighted street.

He came after them, running.

But Duke was driving fast.

At the house, Duke got down and helped Fancy from the buggy.

"Good night, Duke," she said. "And thanks. I'm surprised. Didn't know you could be decent."

Duke looked at her and laughed.

"Said I'd take you home, didn't I? But I didn't promise nothing after that. Nary a damned thing."

Then he stretched out his big arms and picked her up, as lightly as a leaf.

"Duke!" Fancy said. "Please, Duke!"

"Please what?" Duke rumbled. "Don't tell me to let you go, 'cause

I ain't a-going to. Thought you could run out on me, eh? Got yourself married to a real aristocrat! Mighty fine, ain't you? Only, baby, you're my kind. Soft little boy like Court Brantley don't know how to treat you. Big damn fool even to try. . . ."

"Duke," Fancy wept, "oh, Duke, please!"

"Which way is the bedroom, hon?" Duke chuckled. "Kind of ironical, ain't it? Thought he could balk Duke Ellis, huh? Well I laid off a long while, but it's time I learned him! Which way, Fan?"

Fancy's blue eyes narrowed. They looked shrewd, but Duke didn't notice that.

"In there," she said.

Duke marched into the bedroom.

"Now," Fancy whispered, "put me down, Duke. I ain't a-going to fight you. Know it ain't no use."

"Now you're talking sense," Duke said, and put her down.

Fancy's hand went into the bag and came out with the little gun.

"You get out of here, Duke," she said. "Get out or I'll kill you. I ain't fooling. Get out."

"Well, well, well," Duke grinned. "Good thing that the light is on, or I wouldn't even be able to see that little toy. Don't reckon it can shoot nohow."

"It can shoot all right," Fancy said. "Be mighty sorry to kill you, Duke. But I will. Believe me, I will."

"That lil' toy couldn't even dent my hide," Duke said, and started toward her.

Fancy backed away from him.

"Don't come no closer," she said.

Duke took another step, and stopped, his eyes widening.

"Now," he growled, "what the devil is that?"

Fancy half turned to see what he was staring at, and he was upon her, his big hands twisting her wrist until the little gun clattered to the floor.

"Now, babydoll," he said, "you're going to pay for that—with interest!"

"Turn her loose, Duke," Court Brantley said.

Fancy's lips moved, shaping his name.

"Court," she whimpered. "Oh, Court . . ."

145

"True to form, eh, Fan?" Court said. "The minute my back was turned . . ."

"No, Court!" Fancy said. "Oh, no, darlin', no!"

Duke looked at the gun in Court's hand. It was very steady, pointing at his heart. Beads of sweat broke out on his forehead.

"Reckon you got me dead to rights, Court," he said. "Only there's two things I'd like to ask you."

Court nodded.

"Let Fan out of here," Duke said. "Don't reckon even one of you Brantleys is up to shooting a woman. . . ."

"And the second?" Court clipped the words.

"Give me a chance at my gun. More sporting that way, it 'pears to me."

Court looked at Fancy, seeing her lips blue, her whole body shaking.

"Get out of here, Fan," he said.

Duke pulled his own big Colt from the pocket of his pants. He looked at Fancy and grinned.

"Blow the lamp, honey," he said; "then git!"

Fancy looked at Court. Her eyes were imploring.

"Blow it out, Fan," he said.

Fancy bent over the lamp, but she couldn't blow it. She didn't have the breath.

"Blow it!" Court said.

All the breath came out of her at once. The flame bent back against the wick, scattered. And the darkness came down.

She ran out of the bedroom, through the other room, and out on the porch. She leaned against the pillar trying to get her breath back. From where she stood she could see the chinaberry tree humping its umbrella shape, black and tremendous across half the sky.

She didn't think about anything at all. She didn't feel. She just hung onto the pillar so hard that her nails broke against the wood.

It was quiet. From the hills above the town she could hear the whippoorwill crying. Then a mockingbird answered, closer at hand, imitating the sound. He didn't get it quite right. He was a half note off, and a little flat.

A dog howled.

Death, Fancy thought, that's the sign of death. Oh God, I—

146

Then there were the shots.

Fancy clung to the pillar, hearing them, feeling them. Her body jerked each time they came.

Then—silence.

But she couldn't move. She had to move, but she couldn't.

Then she tore herself away from the pillar and ran back into the house. Into the bedroom. She put her hand out and groped across the table until she found the box of matches. Her hand shook so that she dropped them, spilling them all over the floor. She bent down and found a couple. The first one broke. The second one flared briefly, while she lifted the shade and ran it along the wick. The wick spluttered. Caught. Fancy turned the knob. The glow spread through the room.

They lay on the floor—both of them. Fancy didn't move. Then Court Brantley put one hand down and pushed himself up half-way. She ran to him and put her arms around under his chest and pulled.

"Get your hands off of me," he said.

Fancy stepped back. Her hand felt funny. When she looked at it, she saw it was wet. Wet and sticky and red. She looked over at Duke Ellis. He lay in the other corner with a grin on his face and four little blue-rimmed holes in his chest. He was dead.

Court got up stiffly and went out of the room. But when he got to the porch, he had to sit down. Fancy followed him.

"Court," she whispered, "Court . . ."

Court looked at her.

"You little tart," he said.

"No, Court," she said. "It isn't like that. You're wrong, Court. There wasn't nothing. . . ."

"I saw you in his buggy," Court said.

Fancy sat down beside him, and pillowed her head on her knees. The way she cried now was a bad thing. Court couldn't bear listening to it.

"Wait here," he said. "I'll be back with the sheriff."

Then he lurched down the steps. The pain in his shoulder had been very bad to begin with and now it was worse so that he had to lock his teeth together to keep from groaning. Every time he took a step, he jarred the wound so that he could feel the smashed splinters of the bone digging in. The blood pumped out faster. He could feel the sickness starting down in the pit of his stomach. There was a gone, hollow feeling spreading out in both directions from his middle so that when he moved his legs he didn't feel them. But the black shapes of the trees jerked toward him and passed and fell away behind him and the road curved out before him.

She looked so small, sitting there. So small and childlike. Crying. Innocent-looking. Sweet. What made her do it? God in Glory, what?

How far is it? Got to rest—got to. Don't sit down, boy. Never get up if you do. Lean back against this tree—that's it. Steady now. Can't be much further. Christ! Didn't know a man had so much blood. . . .

The inside of his sleeve was sticking to him along all its length, but he had a feeling now the flow was slowing. He moved off again, almost running, his head low, snatching the air into his lungs in great gulps while the far stars and the black-shadowed trees and the shapes of the houses did a slow and stately dance before his eyes, and the road curved out white before him and curved again and there was the sheriff's house.

He walked up on the porch. Hammered at the door.

The sheriff came down in his nightshirt with his thin, hairy legs sticking out from under it, and stood there yawning at him with a lamp in his hand.

"Who is it?" Sheriff Bowen said. "Court! Court Brantley—what's the trouble, son?"

"I killed a man," Court said. "Duke Ellis."

"You don't say! Well, I reckon I ain't surprised. Somebody was a-going to do it sooner or later. But how come it was you, son?"

"Good and sufficient reasons," Court said. "He's up at my house. You coming?"

"Just a minute till I get dressed. Come on inside, boy."

"I'll wait here, thank you."

"You ain't a-going to run away?" Sheriff Bowen said.

Court laughed bitterly.

"The time to run was before now," he said. "Why in hellfire would I come to tell you if I meant to bolt?"

"That's right. Set down there in the rocker. You look plumb tuckered out. I'll only be a minute."

Court sat down. He felt sick at his stomach. The bleeding had stopped, but the shoulder was bad, very bad. He heard the little whimpering sound start and after a moment it came to him that he was doing it. He set his teeth hard and straightened up in the chair, staring out into the night.

Sheriff Bowen came down, hitching a last gallus over his shoulder.

"Where's your gun, boy?" he said.

"Right here," Court said, and passed it over.

"Well, I reckon we'd best be getting down there. Son, I'm plumb sorry it's you what done this. Your paw and me was boys together; don't reckon I know a finer man."

"Thanks," Court said drily. He got up stiffly and came down the steps with the sheriff, but in the street, in spite of all his efforts, he swayed a little.

The sheriff looked at him.

"You drunk, son?" he said.

"No," Court said, "not drunk."

When they got to the house, Court dropped down on the steps.

"I don't want to go in," he said. "I don't want to see it—again."

Sheriff Bowen looked at him, then shrugged. Court heard his footsteps receding as he went through the front room. Three minutes later, he was back.

"Where's your wife?" he drawled.

"Gone, I reckon," Court said tiredly.

"This on account of her?"

"Yes. Duke was—molesting her."

"With, or without her consent?" Bowen snapped.

"Without, of course," Court said. "He thought I was out of town and kind of broke in. . . ."

"I see." Then he passed Court back his gun.

"Better load it, son," he said. "Tom Ellis is out of jail now—and old Rad ain't no slouch with a gun. Other than them, you ain't got a thing to worry about. Ain't a jury in the whole South what wouldn't bring in a verdict of justifiable homicide in a case like this." He lowered his lantern suddenly and stared at Court's left hand.

"And self-defense," he added. "You come along with me to Doc Brewster and git that fixed. Wasn't going to take you into custody, but I reckon I better. Keep you up at my house. You ain't in no

149

fitten condition to defend yourself. I'll send a wagon up for Duke in the morning." He looked at Court. "And when it's over—go easy on that little gal, won't you?"

Court stared at him. He thinks I'm lying, Court thought. He thinks I caught them together. That's what they'll all think. Everybody—the whole town.

"Don't worry," he said, "I will."

9

"I CAME as soon as I read it in the papers," Wyche Weathers said. "Always thought Court Brantley was a good sort. But then I read the other part—about Mrs. Courtland Brantley—née Fancy Williamson. . . . So I caught a train."

"I'm glad," Fancy whispered. "Oh Wyche, I'm so glad."

Wyche looked at her. Then he put his hand in his pocket and came out with a packet of letters, tied with a string.

"Wrote you to that boarding house in Atlanta. They came back. So I wrote you here—General Delivery. Figured you'd ask at the Post Office. I figured wrong. Picked these up myself this morning. Don't know why the devil they didn't return them. . . ."

"Give them to me," Fancy said. "I want to read them."

"No," Wyche said. "Water under the bridge, Fan."

"I'm sorry, Wyche."

"Don't be. You told me the score before I left. And you did it right, married him. These go in the grate. Now, tell me about it. Knowing you, I know you weren't playing around with Duke Ellis. I'd bet my life and my hope of heaven on that."

"Thanks, Wyche," Fancy said.

"What's the trouble, baby?"

"Court doesn't believe me. He won't even see me when I go to see him."

"Then he's a fool. Why won't he?"

"He—he saw me in a buggy with Duke Ellis—that night."

"Damn!" Wyche said. "What the devil were you doing there?"

"I'd been down to that colored girl, Belle's house. Her baby was sick. I got a doctor for her. On the way back, Duke offered me a ride. Swore he'd be good."

"And you believed him?"

"I had a little gun in my handbag, Wyche. Figured I could take care of myself."

"I see. Can you prove that you were at Belle's house?"

"Yes. Belle will tell them . . ."

"No good. A colored woman's word ain't worth a dime in court."

"The doctor," Fan said. "Doctor Benton."

"Good! Come on."

"Where're we going?"

"Down to Bob McCullen's office. He's Court's attorney. I want him to know this."

"Why?"

"Got a hunch that District Attorney Carter's going to say some mighty mean things about you."

"Oh, Wyche, no! Why should he?"

"To pin a murder charge on Court instead of justifiable homicide. Next year's election time, Fan. He can see himself in the governor's chair. And this case is big. If he can make the jury believe that your marriage wasn't exactly—legal, the whole thing becomes a scrap between two men over a woman—of, I'm sorry, Fan—of doubtful virtue. You see?"

"I see," Fancy said. "But my marriage to Court was honest and I can prove that, too."

"How? They're saying about town that Court was drunk."

"Riley stood up with us. He saw me pour a whole pot of coffee into Court first to get him sobered up. I made Court ask me again, Wyche, after he was sober. Judge Harris can testify whether or not Court was drunk. And Saph."

"Saphira? Hell, baby, that's best of all. His sister. Good! Right now I feel damned good. Carter hasn't got a chance."

"Wyche, won't they say that—that you'n'me were . . ."

"You bet your boots they will. But I'm going to demand to be called. Another reason I want to see Bob."

Fancy looked at him. He was dressed up. Fine—real fine. The nicest clothes she reckoned she'd ever seen on a man.

"You look mighty nice," she said. "Heap of difference from the way you used to look."

"Thanks," Wyche said. "Things have changed, Fan. I run the Weathers Mills, now."

"You run them? But I thought . . ."

"That my old man was mad at me? Heck, he was. But he got over it when he found out the truth about Sue Wells. Then he saw the handwriting on the wall, baby. Six months before I got hurt, he suffered a light stroke. While I was laid up, he had another one. Nothing much, left him with a twitch in the right corner of his mouth, and the shakes in his hands. . . ."

"Wyche, he ain't a-going to die?"

"No. The doctors say he can live to be ninety, if he's careful. But being careful includes giving up running the mills. So soon as I got up, I took over. The old man's as pleased as punch at the way I handled things. So he signed over the mills to me. I'm his only child anyhow, and he was going to leave them to me when he died. Mills are making more profits now than any time in their history. The old man brags about me all over town. About once a month he comes down and interferes with what I've changed. We argue like hell, then he grins and admits that I'm right and goes out and brags some more about how smart his boy is."

"That's wonderful, Wyche. Sure wish that Court . . ."

"That Court what, Fan?"

"Could get started with his mill. He owns a piece of land up in Dry Gully that would make a perfect mill site. Only nobody'll back him. The Brantleys have got too bad a reputation."

Wyche looked at her.

"Want to show me this place, baby?" he said.

"But, Wyche—what about Lawyer McCullen?"

153

"Heck, Bob'll be in his office all day—we got time. I want to see this place."

"Why?"

"Because it'll tell me a few things about Mister Courtland Brantley. Things I need to know."

"What kind of things, Wyche?"

"How much he knows about textile mills. A good site means a whole lot. You can locate a mill most anywhere, Fan—but a man who knows the business will put his plant close to a source of cheap power. Come on, I got this buggy for the length of my stay."

"All right, Wyche," Fancy said.

Looking at him, as they drove northward out of town toward Dry Gully, Fancy was thinking: I was a fool. Knew what kind of man Wyche was. Knew he'd get there. But love and horse sense's got mighty little to do with each other. Man like Wyche—good, kindhearted, sure. Got grit in his craw. Got get up and get in his makeup. Smart—steady. But I'm in love with a man that's crazy wild like all his family, and who'll never get anywhere, and who's 'shamed of me. Only he can look at me and I melt all over. What can you do against a thing like that? . . .

"This the place?" Wyche said.

"Yes—little further up. We'll have to leave the buggy though."

"All right," Wyche said, "come on."

A few minutes later, they stood above Dry Gully, looking down into the steep, twisting ravine, Wyche didn't say anything.

"Court says that water used to run through here once," Fancy said. "Water from the river. Then something—an earthquake maybe, raised up that bluff, and cut it off. Says that a few sticks of dynamite could blast through that bluff and the water would race through down here—real fast. Fast enough to turn the mill wheels and run all the machinery for a mill."

"He's right," Wyche said quietly. "Seen a lot of mill sites in my day, but I've never seen a better one than this. He'd have more power than he could possibly use. Heck, baby, this gully would run three full-sized mills, let alone one."

"That's what Court said."

"How much does he need?" Wyche said.

"A hundred thousand dollars," Fancy said sadly.

Wyche grunted.

"He's got it," he said.

"Oh, Wyche!" Fancy said. "Wyche, honey—you don't mean . . . ?"

"That I'll back him? Heck, no, baby. Far as I'm concerned, Court Brantley is an unknown quantity, beyond the fact that he evidently knows the textile business. What I'm backing, is you, Fan. Want to see your future assured. It'll be a straight business deal—Court'll have to pay me back say—seventy-five thousand, and keep me in on this as minority stockholder. But I want the thing set up so that no matter what happens to him, you'll be protected. And if he has an ounce of sense in his head, he'll see it my way."

"Wyche," Fancy said, "I don't know what to say."

"Don't say anything—especially not to Court. Let me talk to him. You put it to him, and he'll get his back up, sure. Come on, now. We got to see that lawyer."

Bob McCullen looked up as they entered. Fancy thought he looked worried.

"Howdy, Mrs. Brantley," he said. "And Mr. Weathers. Glad to see you both. Yessir, mighty glad. Hope you can help me out. The case comes up tomorrow, and I haven't a thing to go on—not a thing."

"Why not?" Wyche said.

"Court clams up every time I ask him questions. He's not doing a blessed thing to make it any easier. Ordinarily it would be an open and shut case. Unwritten law, you know. But Carter's got something up his sleeve beside his arm. He's going around grinning like a crazy bobcat."

"What could he have up his sleeve, Mister McCullen?" Fancy asked.

Bob McCullen looked at her and flushed.

"Ma'am," he began, "I don't exactly know how to put this. . . ."

"Speak your piece, man," Wyche growled.

"The fact is, Ma'am, that you're the big question mark in this case. Nobody in Augusta knows anything much about you, and what they think they know sure Lord doesn't help. . . ."

"I see," Fancy said. "I used to dance on the back of Wyche's Medicine Wagon—and tell fortunes. That makes me—bad. A man's got a right to protect his wife, if she's a good woman—if she's really his wife. But if a man in high society marries a nobody, that's different. If the whole town believes he only married her because he was drunk and crazy, that's different. And when the man who got killed was supposed to have been more'n a mite friendly with her before she got married, kind of throws your unwritten law out of kilter, doesn't it?"

"You have stated District Attorney Carter's case—beautifully," McCullen groaned.

"All right," Fancy said. "Only the trouble with all that is that none of it is so. I never had anything to do with Duke Ellis—never in my life. Not him nor any other man. When I met Wyche, here, I was running away from Duke after I had hit him on the head with a poker to keep him from—I don't have to say what, Mister McCullen. . . ."

"Which only brings up another point, Mrs. Brantley—the question of your relations with Mister Weathers here."

"Let her tell you the whole thing, Bob," Wyche said. "The whole dad-blamed story. It's kind of sad—how a whole town can go out of its way to persecute an innocent kid on nothing more than hearsay. How her marriage has been hurt by gossip, completely unfounded gossip. Don't interrupt her; just listen. Then call me to the stand. Let me have my say. Call Judge Harris who married 'em, and Riley the saloonkeeper, and Saphira Brantley, then see if that polecat Carter can make of this marriage a drunken farce. Call Doc Benton to prove where Fan was on that night, and the colored woman Belle —Doc's word will make hers stick. Then call Fan to the stand, and see if even those stupid oafs they'll make a jury of won't be able to see she's telling the truth."

"I could use more light," Bob McCullen said, "and less heat, Wyche."

"Tell him, Fan," Wyche said.

When she had finished, Bob McCullen leaned back, grinning. Then he got up and went to the telephone. He turned the crank and barked into the mouthpiece:

"Operator, get me Burt Benton's office. Number? Hell, honey, I

156

can't be bothered looking up numbers. You get it—there ain't that many telephones in town."

That next morning was bright. The courtroom was packed. Sitting beside Wyche, Fancy could see people who looked important; people dressed in their finest clothes. The case was big. She remembered what McCullen had said to Wyche as they left the office:

"Heck, Wyche, put your money up. For a case like this, I ought to pay you. If I'm not sitting in the governor's chair next term or the one after directly as a result of this case, I'll resign from the bar."

Fancy looked at all those people. Some of them she recognized. Philemon and Martha. Jed Hawkins. It gave her a queer feeling seeing him here. Agnes and Saphira. Tyler. Old Jeff wasn't there. Home, drunk, Fancy guessed. Across the aisle on the front row sat Rad and Sary Ellis. Fancy couldn't keep from looking at them. She thought she'd never seen a man look madder than Rad Ellis in her life; but Sary Ellis' face was sad—terribly sad. Fancy couldn't look at her. With all his faults, Duke had still been her son. Tom, Duke's brother, sat beside them; but Buck was still in jail. It would be years before they let him out, Fancy reckoned. . . .

But some of these folks were mighty fine. She looked at them keenly, studying their clothes.

"The Brewsters," Wyche whispered; "the Wagoners, the Waltons, the Phinizys, the Cummings—the flower of Georgia, Fan. This case is really something. Saw folks outside from Macon, Waynesboro, and Brunswick—got here too late to get in. Why right now you can name your price for a seat in any of the windows. . . ."

Bob McCullen paused by their seats and whispered to Wyche. "Notice the crowd?" he said. "And you asked me about my fee!"

"Couldn't we," Wyche asked wearily, "kind of keep Fan out of this as much as possible?"

"Are you crazy, Wyche?" Bob said. "That's going to be our main defense. The unwritten law. Leave it to me, Wyche. I'll do it right. Play for sympathy for her. The poor, downtrodden lower-class girl who never had a chance. Build Court up big, too—his decency, his nobility in marrying her, the respect he showed for her simple, innate goodness by making her his wife instead of just sneaking around like so many of our so-called respected citizens. Boy, I won't leave a dry eye in this courtroom!"

"Don't doubt it," Wyche said grimly. "Notice that Tom Ellis is leaving the courtroom?"

"Damn!" Bob McCullen said. "Not even waiting for the trial, is he?"

"Do you think what I think?" Wyche growled.

"Yes. Probably gone to round up some of his boys. Mob violence. Well those Ellises aren't popular—don't reckon they'll get very far."

"I have a mighty shiny piece of persuasion in my pocket," Wyche said. "You have the police ready, Bob."

"Right," McCullen said.

Judge Richardson was entering the court now, and all the people stood up until he was seated. Then the bailiff began his cry:

"Hear ye! Hear ye! The case of the People of the State of Georgia versus Courtland Brantley, charged with the murder of Duke Hently Ellis, on the night of September 7th, this year of Our Lord, 1880! The Court is now in session!"

Fancy put out her hand and gripped Wyche's wrist, squeezing it hard.

At once Granville Carter, the prosecutor, was on his feet.

He turned to the Court and looked each juror in the face, slowly. Then he began.

There were, he told the jury, and the spectators, in the city of Augusta, two well-known families. The members of one of them had been citizens since the founding of the city; the others, late-comers, had had the sagacity to found the great turpentine industry upon which so many of the good people of Augusta depended for livelihood. One of these families, being aristocrats, had been venerated, though throughout their history, they had lived the lives of drunkards, profligates, and lechers. . . .

Fancy stared at him.

"The Ellises," Carter went on, "though vigorous, high-spirited men, given to the playful excesses of youth, have aided in keeping Augusta economically upon her feet, despite their humble birth. They are the type of men who have made our democracy great, while the Brantleys have produced nothing, and destroyed much! Who is it, I ask you, that have driven their wives to suicide or the madhouse? Which of these two clans has figured in scandals without number, in endless duels, in drunken orgies? Which, I ask you?"

Bob McCullen got slowly to his feet. He looks lazy, Fancy thought. But that other lawyer's awful. They listen to him and Court ain't got a chance. . . .

"Your Honor," McCullen said quietly, "I object. It seems to me that the learned counselor is laboring under a wee mite of a misapprehension. Didn't the bailiff read a charge against Court Brantley? Or was it against his ancestors? Maybe we ought to recess while my eloquent opponent goes down to Magnolia cemetery and digs 'em up so that they can be properly charged. . . ."

"Objection sustained," Judge Richardson said. The whole courtroom rocked with laughter.

McCullen made the prosecutor a sweeping bow and sat down. Granville Carter's face was beet-red.

"I see," he grated, "that we have to deal here with the tactics of a mountebank!"

Judge Richardson leaned forward.

"Mister Carter," he said, "you will please withdraw that remark, or I shall be forced to hold you in contempt of court."

"Very well, then," Carter snapped; "I do withdraw it. Is my worthy opponent satisfied?"

"Quite," McCullen said.

"My opening statements," Carter went on, "were intended merely as introductions to more pertinent matters. From past experience, I know exactly what to expect in this case. Counselor McCullen intends to sway you with his matchless eloquence; he intends to portray the defendant in the role of the poor, deluded husband, defending the sanctity of his home; he intends to work upon your sympathies for his distinguished lineage, his good looks—to present Court Brantley, in fact, as a man of probity and honor!

"It must be, therefore, regrettably, my task to prove to you that such was not the case! I am going to prove to you that the poor, unfortunate young man who was brutally bereft of his life in the full bloom of his youth was merely trying to repossess what was rightly his! I tell you, Gentlemen of the Jury, that it is known by nearly everybody present here that a common-law relationship existed between the deceased and the woman called Fancy. I tell you further, that the defendant, Courtland Brantley, took advantage of Duke Ellis' absence to alienate the notoriously fickle affections of the woman, Fancy. . . ."

"Your Honor," Bob McCullen said, "I reckon I'd better object again. Mrs. Brantley ain't on trial here. Her husband is. Besides which, Prosecutor Carter's remarks are downright ungentlemanly—even if they were true, which they aren't. Furthermore, they have very slight bearing on the case, if any."

"Will the prosecutor," Judge Richardson said, "please explain the pertinency of his procedure to the Court?"

"It's very pertinent, Your Honor!" Carter said. "I intend to prove that far from being a case of an outraged husband rightfully defending his home, that Court Brantley actually engaged in a marriage of doubtful legality for the purpose of safeguarding his hold upon his paramour, and that upon learning from the deceased that he intended to have back the woman on whom he had much more valid claims, Courtland Brantley did wilfully murder Duke Ellis! Yes, I said murder! And I intend to win from this court the highest penalty —that Courtland Brantley be hanged by his neck until he is dead!"

"Objection overruled," Judge Richardson said.

Carter turned, smiling.

"Call Courtland Brantley to the stand!" he said.

"Courtland Brantley to the stand!" the bailiff echoed.

Court got up and walked to the chair. The bailiff lifted the Bible and said: "Do you solemnly swear to tell the truth, the whole truth, and nothing but the truth, so help you God?"

"I do," Court said.

"Mister Brantley!" Granville Carter began, "I want you to answer me carefully! Isn't it a fact that you met the woman, Fancy, during the absence of Duke Ellis? Answer me, isn't it?"

"No," Court said, "it isn't. Duke was right here in town when I met—my wife. He didn't leave until later. Reckon I had a hand in his leaving though. That was when he and his brothers got high-spirited—I believe that's what you call it, sir—and tried to murder Wyche Weathers. I sort of helped send them to jail."

"You answer my questions!" Carter roared. "The information I want, I'll ask for!"

"And what you don't want, you'll conceal," Court said drily.

"Mister Brantley," Judge Richardson said, "please confine your remarks to answering Attorney Carter's questions."

"Yes, Your Honor," Court said.

"Courtland Brantley," Carter began again; "did you not pursue this woman," and Carter pointed at Fancy, "until you succeeded in your sole aim—which, due to the fact that there are ladies present, I can only hint at—not state?"

Court turned to the Judge.

"Do I have to answer that one, Your Honor?" he asked.

Judge Richardson nodded.

"Well, Attorney Carter, I'd better warn you that I can't answer that with a yes or no. It's a little more complicated than that."

"Answer my question!" Carter roared.

"All right. I did pursue Miss Williamson night and day. And my motives don't do me any credit. I'll admit that. But that I succeeded in my aims—no, sir. Miss Williamson shamed me out of 'em. She pointed out to me that I had unmarried sisters; that I sure Lord wouldn't like it if any man tried with them, what I was trying. She reminded me that she was all alone in the world—and that people had been using her name mighty unkindly already. . . ."

"Ha!" Granville Carter snapped, "you expect these gentlemen to believe that?"

"Why not?" Court drawled, "since it's the truth?"

"Will you tell the Court, please, just where you were on that evening that this so-called marriage took place?"

"No," Court said grimly.

"Then I will!" Carter shrieked. "You were in Riley's saloon. Furthermore, Gentlemen of the Jury, the aristocratic Mister Courtland Brantley was so drunk at the time he could scarcely stand—thus conclusively proving that he had no intentions of marrying this woman in the first place. Isn't that the truth, Court Brantley!"

"No!" Court roared.

"This marriage which the defendant did murder to defend, or so we're asked to believe—started in Riley's saloon. The woman, Fancy, dragged him from that saloon, and married him before he could recover his senses. You can readily see, gentlemen, how a handsome young aristocrat must have seemed quite a prize to her. Furthermore, Riley himself, our good barkeep, upon whom, God knows, I wish to cast no aspersions stood as witness to this touching and sacred ceremony! Gentlemen, I ask you! Your witness, Counselor!"

Bob McCullen got up.

"I notice," he began, "that Attorney Carter has carefully refrained from determining exactly what happened the night of September 7th, which after all, is what concerns us here. But I'm going to follow the line of questioning he has indicated. I'm going to for two reasons: Attorney Carter has persistently and with malice aforethought, tried to blacken the name of a sweet, innocent girl whose only crime was that she was poor and from a humble background. And my second reason is that Counselor Carter's procedure is made to order for determining my client's innocence . . ."

McCullen was good, Fancy could see that. But he had gone through a long list of questions before she realized how good he was. He asked Court questions about his marriage. Then he dismissed him from the stand, and called Riley, Saphira and Judge Harris to back up what Court had said.

"That takes care of the drunken marriage," he said. "But I've got to take care of something else. Attorney Carter said first that Mister Brantley was safeguarding his hold on his paramour—and then contradicted himself by saying that the defendant married Miss Williamson because he was drunk. I'm going to finish the job, with the Court's permission—even if this line of questioning doesn't seem exactly germane. We believe in the sanctity of womanhood down here, Your Honor—and I mean to see that no slur is cast upon this woman whose only mistake has been to underestimate our feeble understanding—and who has committed no sins!" Then he turned to the bailiff. "Call Mrs. Courtland Brantley to the stand," he said.

Fancy got up. She could feel the trembling down inside her. The way the people looked at her! Like—like their eyes were hot. She understood why Bob McCullen had gone so far as to pick out her dress. It was black and plain and simple. He'd even made her brush her hair down tight, too, so that her face looked like a child's.

"Mrs. Brantley," McCullen said, "what exactly was the relationship between you and Duke Ellis?"

"There wasn't any," Fancy said. "I met him when I first came to town. He made a big fuss over me—bought me things, made out like he aimed to marry me. Then he tried to get me to drink liquor, and grabbed me—I—I—got away from him and ran. That was how I met Mister Weathers."

"I see," Bob McCullen said. "Why did you come to Augusta, Mrs. Brantley?"

Fancy told him, trying hard to use proper speech. She could see after a while that folks were believing her. Some of the women were crying, as she told how she ran away from a loveless marriage, only to land in even worse trouble.

"Reckon I was foolish," she said; "but I'm a hill girl, with no booklearning, and I thought folks mostly meant what they said. I trusted Duke Ellis, and I was wrong. Then I trusted Mister Weathers, but that time I was right."

She told them about her travels with Wyche. How he'd respected her, given her her own private quarters, protected her from bad men. He'd asked to marry her, but by that time she'd met Court Brantley. She told them how she hated to do that dance, but she didn't know any other way of making money—and there were worse ways.

"What I didn't figure," she said in a barely audible voice, "was because I did something that looked wicked, folks would think I had to be bad. . . ."

She straightened up and looked at the hushed spectators.

"There's one thing I'd like to say," she said quietly; "I hope Your Honor'll forgive me if it ain't in order. I'd like to ask you folks, all of you, to give me a chance. You've got fathers and brothers and husbands to take care of anybody who uses your name in public. I—I haven't anybody. The things I've done came of not knowing— not out of badness. Didn't know what they'd lead to—didn't realize that my husband's life could be put in danger because he tried to protect me; that a whole case could turn on whether or not I was worth protecting. That wasn't a fight 'twixt two men over a—a street woman. That was a man trying to defend his home."

She had them now, and Carter saw it. He was on his feet crying, "Object, object!" before she could finish her words.

"Overruled," Judge Richardson said.

"Mrs. Brantley," Bob McCullen said, "was the night of your marriage the first time Court Brantley had asked you to marry him?"

"No sir. It was the second."

"What happened the first time?"

"I—I turned him down. Not because I didn't love him. I did—I do —so much! But because he asked me for the wrong reasons. Had an argument about something with his brother Phil, and Phil made a remark about me. Court was set to show him—to show the whole town. But I couldn't marry him because he wanted to show people. It had to be because he loved me—no other reason."

"I see—but you were convinced he did love you, after you and his sister had sobered him up that night with black coffee, and he asked you again?"

"Yes. I tried to let him alone before. But every time I saw him, I loved him more and more. And then I saw some other girls paying attention to him, even some who had no business to, 'cause they were already married, and I got so jealous I thought I'd die. So I got real riled up and had some hard words with him, but he only laughed at me for being so foolish. But, Your Honor, I was so sad and mixed up 'cause I thought I'd lost him, that I told him I was going to be like the rest of the Brantley women, and I ran and jumped in the river. Court saved my life then. . . ."

"Your Honor," McCullen put in smoothly, "we are prepared to introduce two dozen corroborating witnesses, who saw the defendant walking through the streets dripping wet with Miss Williamson in his arms."

"That won't be necessary," Judge Richardson declared. "Proceed," he added.

"That was when he decided to marry me. Reckon that kind of forced him into it—'cause I really ain't his kind, and Court could have most any girl he wanted. But afterwards, he was so good to me! He knew I didn't know anything, so every night he would sit down and bring out the McGuffey Reader and teach me to read and spell and even to figger a little. . . ."

"And this, Your Honor," McCullen said, "was the marriage that my distinguished opponent would have you believe was no marriage at all! This tender, heart-warming romance, in which a man of honor tried to lift up a simple, lovely woman to his own high estate in life! This is what Prosecutor Carter tries to reduce to mere bestial lust! Your witness, Counselor! I'll get back to the night of September 7th, after a while."

164

Granville Carter stood up. Fancy thought his face looked ugly.

"Mrs. Brantley," he said, "I'm not going to take you back over the points that my opponent has introduced so skilfully—though I doubt most of them. I'm going to take up the night of September 7th, 1880—a few hours before the murder. Isn't it a fact," he thundered, "that you spent those hours away from home—in the company of the murdered man? Answer me, isn't it? And isn't it also a fact that your husband, along with half a dozen other citizens, whom I have here in this Court, and whom I will call upon to testify, saw you riding through the streets at a most unseemly hour in the buggy with Duke Hently Ellis? Did he not then follow you home from your rendezvous with the man who, despite all testimony to the contrary, had once been very dear to you? And did not the fatal shooting take place," Carter paused, spacing his words with terrible clarity, "in the bedroom of your home?"

Fancy looked at Bob McCullen. He was grinning. Carter had slipped his head into a noose of his own making.

She looked the prosecutor straight in the face.

"I was in Duke's buggy that night, late. That's true. And he was killed in my bedroom. That's true, too. But none of the rest of the things you've said. Not one of 'em is true. . . ."

"Ha!" Carter exploded; "you expect anyone to believe that?"

"Yessir," Fancy said evenly, "I do. I'm not quality. Never learned how to lie and cheat like quality folks do. Folks who know me, know that."

"Then maybe," Granville Carter sneered, "you'd better tell us exactly where you were."

"I was at the house of a colored woman named Belle Fisher. Her baby was sick. I got Doctor Benton to come and 'tend to it. Then I 'tended to it myself until after midnight. . . ."

"You can prove this, Mrs. Brantley?" Judge Richardson asked.

"Yes, Your Honor."

Bob McCullen stood up.

"If Your Honor will allow the irregularity, I'd like to make a motion that Belle Fisher and Doctor Benton be called to the stand."

"Permission granted," Judge Richardson said.

Fancy kept watching Court's face during their testimonies. It was stony, unchanging. He doesn't believe them, she cried inside her heart, he thinks they're put up to say that!

But Carter was not satisfied. He called Fancy back to the stand.

"I think," he said, "that the Court would still like to know what you were doing in Duke Ellis' buggy."

"I was walking home from Belle's. It was late, and I was tired. Duke came by and offered me a ride home. Spoke real nice, but I didn't trust him, not at first. Then he swore by his mother that he'd be good and take me home. After we got there, he told me that he hadn't sworn anything about after that. Then he picked me up and walked into the house with me. That was when Court came home. . . ."

Carter dismissed her. Then Bob McCullen called Court once more to the stand.

"I found my wife," Court said, "struggling in Duke Ellis' arms. I started to kill him then. But Duke asked for a chance. . . ." Then he told the story of the duel in the dark. He didn't say anything much about his wound; but McCullen dragged that in, too. The lawyer called Doctor Brewster to the stand.

"An inch lower, and it would have been fatal," the old doctor said. "As it was, Court had damned near bled to death when he got to me. Pretty brave boy, I'd say—walked all the way up to Sheriff Bowen's and back to the house with the sheriff without saying a word about a wound of a type that three times in my experience I've seen put men in their graves. Obviously Ellis fired first, because Court's bullets killed him instantly—he couldn't have fired that shot after he'd been hit."

Sheriff Bowen was next. He testified that Court had made no effort to run away, that he had reported the killing to him, and had given up his gun without protest. He described the scene at the house, and stuck to every detail under Carter's furious cross questioning.

Carter was beaten and he knew it. But he tried hard. He called back every witness. He tried to find holes in the testimony. He kept it up so long that Bob McCullen was moved to drop a bombshell. He asked the Court's permission to call Sary Ellis, Duke's mother, to the stand.

As the tiny, frail old woman took her seat, there was not a sound in the courtroom. Looking at her, Fancy thought, Oh no, this is mean, this is too mean, not that poor old lady, grieving for her boy. . . .

"Mrs. Ellis," McCullen said, "I'm sorry to have to call on you. I sympathize, and I'm sure everyone here sympathizes with your grief. You're a good woman, and a fine mother. I called on you because I know you're not vengeful—that you don't want to see a man punished unjustly, not even over your son.

"But the prosecution has tried to color the whole case with the idea that your boy was only trying to take back a woman who'd been his common-law wife. Mrs. Ellis, this is painful, I know; but you and your son were unusually close. How much did you know of Duke's private life?"

"Everything," Sary Ellis said tiredly; "Duke warn't close-mouthed."

"You knew about Myrtie Torrence?"

"Yessir. Him and me had words over that. Tried to get him to straighten up and do right."

"Then you—didn't agree with your son's behavior?"

"No, sir. Duke was mighty wild. Knew he'd get hisself kilt if he kept it up. Cried over that boy many a night—over all my boys. . . ."

"Your Honor!" Carter spluttered, "I—"

"Sit down, Attorney," Judge Richardson snapped. "The testimony is germane. You introduced this line of questioning yourself."

McCullen smiled.

"Mrs. Ellis, did your son at any time say anything that led you to believe that a—relationship existed between him and Miss Williamson?"

"No, sir. He was all steamed up over that. Said she'd balked him. Said she was the sweetest, best lil' gal he ever did know, and that he'd even get hitched with her before he'd let anybody else have her. 'Maw,' he used to say, 'you ought to meet her. She's driving me wild. . . . Done looked all over the State for her, and ever' time, I just misses her. But she's a-coming here,' he said—'then I'm going to get her. Going to bring her here for you to see. She ain't like my other gals,' he said. 'Maw, you'll just love her.'"

The old woman turned and looked at Fancy, seeing her sitting there, crying from joy. "I kind of reckon he was right," she said sadly. "That little girl would of been the making of him. . . ."

The jury was out less than five minutes.

They filed back in, and Fancy strained forward, a tiny white line around the corners of her mouth.

"We find the defendant," the foreman said, "not guilty!"

Fancy collapsed against Wyche's shoulder, shaking all over. Then all the people started shouting and laughing and crying at the same time, and men fought their way forward to shake Court Brantley's hand.

Court shook hands with them, thinking: you polecats. You'd have watched me hang with just as much glee. It was a good show, wasn't it? Either way it came out it was a good show, and none of you, not a clinking one gives two hoots up a hollow stump that it was my life that was in balance here. . . .

When he left the courtroom, a free man, he saw Wyche Weathers waiting for him with Fancy. Tyler and Philemon were there, and several other men—friends and schoolmates of his.

"Heard tell," Wyche said, after he'd almost broken Court's hand in his grip, "that Tom and Rad Ellis and a bunch of their cronies is out to get you. Me 'n' the boys decided to walk you and Fan home, and stay there with you tonight, seeing that you're in no fit condition to defend yourself."

Court looked at Fancy and frowned.

"Thanks, Wyche," he said. "That's mighty decent of youall."

"I'd like to be excused, if you don't mind, Court," Tyler said. "Got a little crow to pick with that there shyster, Carter."

"No you don't!" Court said. "There's been killing enough, Ty. You come along with the rest. It's been a long time since I had a chance to talk to you fellows, anyhow. . . ."

"'Pears to me," Nick Cohen drawled, "that we might not have to sit up tonight after all. Them Ellises ain't waiting for night. Here they come now."

Fancy saw them, then, heading toward the place where she stood with Court and the others. Tom Ellis was leading them, and behind him came old Rad.

The crowd that still packed the courthouse square fell apart.

Fancy saw men pushing their womenfolks into buggies, and fat, rich-looking men running off like clumsy bulls.

Tom came on, drawing ahead of his followers.

"We want Court Brantley," he said. "And we aim to get him. You fellows give him up peaceable like, and won't nobody git hurt."

Wyche stepped out of the group.

"Now do tell!" he drawled. "Reckon I'd better tell you a thing or two, Tom. Court was tried fair and square for killing that hound dog of a brother of yours, and acquitted by due process of law. That's enough for me and every other law-abiding citizen in this here town. We ain't giving him up, Tom. And you and them rednecks you got with you better turn right around and git out of town while you can. . . ."

"Take care how you talk, Wyche," Tom said. "They's more of us—and we're armed."

Wyche loosened his frock coat so that the butt of his big revolver showed plainly in its holster under his armpit.

"Reckon you think we ain't?" he said quietly. "Another thing, Tom. You'n' your brothers have made this town a mighty unpleasant place for decent folks ever since you come out of them backwoods where you belong. We'd be mighty happy to be rid of you Ellises once and for all. There's more'n twenty-five men here, and I'm going to tell 'em right now that if you start anything half of 'em is to aim for you, and the other half for old Rad. And out of all these fellows, somebody ain't a-going to miss. Reckon I've said my say. You want Court, here—come and get him!"

Fancy moved over to where Court stood and put her arm through his. He didn't move. Then he put his hand up and pushed her hand down and away from his side.

Tom stood there, staring at Wyche.

They're nothing, Fancy thought. Like Court said, without Duke, they're nothing.

"You win—this time," Tom said. "But you ain't heard the last of this, Court Brantley—you neither, Wyche!"

"I'll wait," Wyche said.

"I feel like a fool," Court said, "standing here letting you stick up for me like that, Wyche. Don't reckon you fellows will have to stand guard over me tonight. Those yellow polecats won't come back."

"Don't think they will," Wyche agreed; "but Ty and Phil and me'll walk you home just the same. And we'll kind of set on the porch. The rest of y'all hear any shooting tonight, come a-running— all right?"

"All right," the others said. "So long, Court. So long, Ma'am— good luck."

Luck, Fancy thought bitterly; I'll need luck. He ain't right yet. Wouldn't let me take his arm—even after what Maw Ellis said. . . .

"Don't mean to horn in on your talk with Fan, Court," Wyche said; "but I got to get back home. I got some business to talk over with you. Fan showed me that Dry Gully of yours, while you were in jail. That's the best damned mill site I ever did see. How much will you take for it?"

"It's not for sale, Wyche," Court said.

"Didn't think you would sell it, and I don't blame you. All right then, boy—here's another proposition. How about letting me advance you the money for that mill? I don't even want it all back. I aim to keep a minority share in the concern—that's how good I think the chances are."

"No, thank you, Wyche," Court said quietly, "I owe you enough already."

Wyche stared at him.

"You owe me?" he said. "For what?"

"Those witnesses you bought. Belle. Doc Benton. Maybe even old lady Ellis. They must have cost you plenty, Wyche. I'm grateful, of course. You did it for Fan—I know that. Even so it was mighty handsome of you; 'cause it was your chance to have me out of your way."

Wyche's big fist doubled. Then he loosened his fingers, slowly.

"You better thank God for that bad arm, boy," he said quietly. "I sure Lord was tempted to separate your fool head from your worthless shoulders."

He looked over at Fan, seeing her face white, the look in her eyes like that in a trapped animal's, dying in terrible pain.

"I withdraw my offer," he said. "But I'm going to make another one—for Fan's sake. Since you've shown me that you ain't got sense enough to appreciate what you've got, I'll put it this way: I'll advance to Mrs. Courtland Brantley, any time she wants it, the entire amount of money needed to build a textile plant in Dry Gully—that mill to remain in her possession, and in the hands of her heirs—forever. She can hire you as general manager, if she wants to. She can even sell or assign you a minority share. But it's got to be down in black and white that Fan keeps the controlling interest. Because I don't trust you, Court Brantley. I don't think you're wicked. You're something worse—you're a fool."

Court looked at Fancy, mockery in his eyes.

"Well, Fan," he said bitingly; "want to be a rich mill owner?"

Fancy didn't answer him. She was looking straight at Wyche.

"No, Wyche," she said; "not like that. It's got to be Court's."

"Pearls," Wyche said bitterly, "at the feet of swine." Then he turned and marched away from them.

"Ty," Fancy whispered, "Phil—I don't think they'll come back. I want to be alone with Court for a while. He's got a gun. If you hear shooting, you can come with the others. . . . All right?"

"All right," Tyler growled; "but I don't like it. I don't like it at all." He looked at his younger brother. "For the record, boy," he said, "Wyche is right. You're a fool."

Then he and Philemon turned and went away together.

Inside the house, Fancy came up to Court and stood there looking at him.

"Court—" she said.

Court didn't answer her.

"I'm glad you got off," Fancy said breathlessly. "I reckon I would of died if they had sent you to jail or—oh, Court . . ."

Court moved past her deliberately and sat down in his big chair. Fancy moved over and stood in front of him. Court didn't even look at her. He groped in his pocket with his one good hand and came out with a cigar. At once Fancy ran into the kitchen and came back with a match. She lit it, and held it out.

Court drew his head back and looked at the match in her hand until it burned down to her fingertips. She dropped it, shaking her hand, and blowing on her burned fingers. Then he put his hand in his pocket and came out with his own matches and lit his cigar. He shook the match out and threw it out into the yard. Fancy came up to him in a rush and put her arms about his neck.

"Court," she whispered; "I'm so glad you're safe. Oh, Court, honey, I'm so glad!"

Court put up his right hand, and locked the fingers around the flesh of her arm. Then very slowly he pulled her arm away from him.

Fancy stood there looking at him. Then, very quietly, she turned and walked into the bedroom, and closed the door behind her. She lay there all night, awake, listening every time he moved in the big chair in the next room. Then, just before morning, she got up again.

She came into the room, and walked over to the chair. He was awake, but he didn't move. Fancy bent down and took the dead stump of the cigar out of his mouth. Then she kissed him, achingly, longingly.

Court's mouth was as cold as death.

Fancy stood there looking at him, trying to keep from crying.

He got up out of the chair, easing his heavily bandaged left arm up with the aid of his right hand. For a moment, pain showed in his eyes. Then he straightened up and went on out the door.

It was quiet in the room after he had gone. Fancy stood in the middle of the room for a long time. Then she couldn't stand up any more so she went and sat down in his big chair. She sat very still, with her hands on the two arms of the chair and stared out into the empty yard.

And the sun came up over the chinaberry tree like a blast of trumpets.

10

It wasn't until she saw Jed Hawkins coming up the path toward the house that Fancy remembered that he had been at the trial. That wasn't strange, after all that had happened. She watched him coming toward the porch, and she didn't move. Her mind was too sunk in dull misery for that. Court was gone—God knew where—hating her, believing her guilty of all the ugly things that Lawyer Carter had said about her. All she could think of, seeing Jed now, was that he had acted mighty funny afterwards.

He hadn't come forward like Wyche and the other men to help Court out. She hadn't even seen him after the trial. He had simply slipped into the crowd and disappeared. Wouldn't have done Jed any good to try to help, Fancy thought. Court would have just spoke mean to him like he did to Wyche and made one more enemy. And Court had enemies enough already—all the Brantleys did. Still it was mighty ungentlemanly of Jed not to help. But then she stopped thinking about it altogether because Jed was standing there on the porch looking at her.

He wasn't smiling, and that made him almost a stranger. He had

173

the kind of a face that was meant to smile. When it was serious he looked different somehow. Older—harder, she couldn't decide. . . .

"Fan," he said.

"Yes, Jed?"

"Heard that husband of yours had left you. That so?"

"Yes, Jed."

"Good. Good riddance for bad rubbish. Listen, Fan. . . ."

"I'm listening," Fancy said.

"Damn! When you look at me like that you make it hard for me to talk. My tongue gets thick. And I'm supposed to be the original silver-tongued boy. . . ."

"Get to the point, Jed."

He leaned forward and took her hands.

"Come with me, Fan," he said tensely.

Fancy tried to pull her hands back, but she couldn't. He was holding them too tight.

"I'm a married woman, Jed," Fancy said. "You want to make of me all the things that mean old lawyer said?"

"Heaven forbid. Look, Fan, let's reason this thing out. You're married—legally, technically. Only you ain't—not by a long shot, when your husband gets in a huff and leaves you. I'm a lawyer, remember. Even under the law that changes things. I've got friends in high places. This here marriage of yours can be dissolved because of Court Brantley's action. I'm not asking you to do anything dishonorable. Appears to me all the dirty tricks have been done to you already."

Fancy didn't say anything. She just sat there looking at him.

"I don't want to make a mistress of you. If I wanted a mistress, you think I couldn't have half a dozen right now?"

"No," Fancy said, "I don't think that."

"All I want you to do is to come with me to Atlanta. I'll put you in a nice respectable boarding house with a bunch of other working girls. Woman there watches over them better'n their own mothers would. Then I'll petition the Supreme Court for an annulment or a divorce. And I'll get it for you, too. Then, after a decent interval, you'n'me can get hitched—legal and proper. And damn it, honey, we'll stay hitched until Gabriel blows that horn of his. . . . Come on, Fan—what do you say?"

"No, Jed."

Jed stared at her, wonderingly.

"Why not, Fan?"

"He—might come back," Fancy said.

"Good God!" Jed exploded. "Hell, Fan, where's your pride?"

"Haven't any. People in love never do."

"Oh, damn!" Jed Hawkins said. He straightened up, and watched her face. "All right," he said, "but I'm not giving up, Fan. I'll wait. You just might change your mind. . . . I don't believe you dislike me."

"No," Fancy said, "I like you very much."

"Thanks," Jed said drily. "That gives me a hell of a lot of hope. Anyhow, just in case you do change your mind, I'll give you my address in Savannah."

"I don't want it," Fancy said. "I'm not going to change my mind."

"Suppose he doesn't come back?"

"No, Jed."

"Fan, honey—isn't there any way on earth . . ."

"Yes, Jed. Just one. If you ever hear that I'm a widow—wait two, three years, then ask me again. I like you a lot—better'n anybody else next to Court, except maybe Wyche . . ."

"Third fiddle!" Jed groaned; "that's a fine thing."

"No—second maybe. I don't like Wyche that way. He's a fine man—a mite too fine for me, maybe. He's like a big brother—or a father. Don't think I could ever think of him any other way. . . ."

" 'For this relief, much thanks,' " Jed quoted bitterly. "So now I'm supposed to spend my life waiting around for somebody to shoot that Brantley polecat."

"You aren't supposed to spend your life doing anything as far as I'm concerned," Fancy said. "Your life's your own, Jed Hawkins. Smart thing for you to do is to forget all about me. Find yourself some nice, sweet little girl and . . ."

"You stop talking damned foolishness, Fan."

"What's foolish about that?"

"Everything. You've got me as mixed up as a snake-bit hound dog baying a summer moon. Got your face in my eyes like two silver pennies. I'm blind, honey. Every time I look at another woman, all I see is—you."

175

"I'm sorry, Jed."

"Don't be. Loving you is a kind of a glory. Living on like this, hoping against hope, is God-damned awful, but I wouldn't live any other way. Every morning is a new day, and the sun comes a-blazing with hope. I keep telling myself, today it'll happen—something will change, something will. . . ."

"But it won't, Jed," Fancy said; "you've got to see that."

"I'm blind, honey," Jed said. "I told you that before. 'Bye, now. I've bothered you enough for one day."

Fancy didn't think about him much after he had gone. All she could think was: Where is Court? Where is he now—right now, this minute? What's he doing, thinking, feeling . . . ?

Court Brantley at that moment stood in the cupola above the dome of the State House and looked out over Boston. He did this every time he came there. It was a kind of a ritual with him. He had been in the city three days now, but this was the first time he had gotten the chance to do it.

Maybe that's why I haven't had any luck, he thought. Hope this changes it. God knows it needs to change. . . .

He looked down on the Common, seeing most of the expanse of fifty acres that slopes down from the State House to Boylston and Tremont Streets. He could see the broad estuary of the Charles, with the Harvard crews rowing on it, and he had almost the feeling of being home.

He couldn't see Harvard from where he stood. It was too far away; but he had visited the campus already, walking the lanes alone, looking at the place where of all his life he had been happiest. Court loved Boston. It was the only city he could ever remember where he had been entirely at peace. There was something about the old city, with its rows of well-built brownstone and brick houses, each with its two squares of neatly trimmed grass between it and the street, and all the quiet, cultured people he had grown to like so well, once their almost impenetrable armor of reserve had been broken through. Life went smoothly here; he had been a fool ever to leave it. He could remember how the quiet and dignified servants had opened the doors for him in the homes of his friends; homes so solid and forbidding from the outside, yet radiating warmth and welcome on the inside. He remembered his friend, Stan Woodbury, standing under the plaster cast of the *Winged Victory* of Samothrace on the high, marble mantel, and lifting his glass of steaming punch to drink his health.

Those were good memories. Much better than his last ones. But he didn't like to think about that.

As he came down into the street, he had the feeling once more that he had behaved badly—that Wyche hadn't lied and Belle hadn't lied and Doc Benton hadn't lied and that nobody had paid them. Fan—least of all had she lied. He couldn't explain it even to himself: the wave of revulsion that had risen up in him afterwards, the natural, instinctive Brantley cruelty.

Well, it was done now. Fan was down in Augusta and he was in Boston—more than a thousand miles away. He'd come to get backers for his mill. Afterwards, I'll make it up to her, he thought. Poor kid, she's sure seen hell on account of me. . . .

He started walking rapidly toward State Street, where the business offices of Woodbury Textiles Incorporated, were. Stanton had slid easily into the position his father had reserved for him. And, Court had found out, he had done well. His fortune, now, was one of Boston's largest.

Court arrived with minutes to spare. But the bespectacled young man who served Stanton as clerk and receptionist did not keep him waiting. He had, he informed Court, orders to show Mister Brantley in at once.

Stanton Woodbury stood up the moment Court entered the oak-paneled office, his hand outthrust. He had put on flesh with the years, but his ruddy face was the picture of health.

"Court!" he said. "This is a pleasure!"

Court took the hand Stan put out to him and shook it hard.

"Sit down," Stanton said. "Have a cigar. They're good Havanas right off the very last boat."

Court took the cigar and sank down in one of the leather-covered chairs.

"It's good to see you, Stan," he said quietly.

"Same old Court," Stanton said cheerfully. "A little thinner, maybe. Big a devil as ever, I'll bet. They'll never forget you at Harvard, Courtland."

"I was kind of hoping they would," Court grinned.

"We'll have to get together and talk over the old days," Stanton said. "But Rileton, my clerk, says you wanted to see me on business. What's it all about?"

"I've been trying to raise the money to build a textile mill, near my home in Georgia. So far—no luck. I need a lot of money—nearly a hundred thousand. People don't listen to that big a proposition easily, Stanton. I've been trying for years. I've seen every man of wealth in the whole South. No luck. It's a perfectly safe deal, Stan. With cotton growing right in my back yard, the mill would show a fantastic profit. Labor's cheap down home, too; but you know all that. The point is, as I said before, it's a perfectly safe investment; but I've been turned down all over town, and I don't know why. So I thought of you. Would you consider it, Stan?"

The smile left Stanton's face, and he looked at Court, soberly, seriously.

"The answer, old boy," he said quietly, "is no. But I'm going to be a little different from the others. I'm going to tell you why. And after that, I'm going to make you a counter-proposition. All right?"

"Shoot," Court said.

"Since you Southerners got interested in textile manufacture, we've lost a fistful of money here in New England. The conditions down there all favor you: climate, cheap labor, and accessibility of raw materials. If we could compete with you on anything like an even basis, I'd let you have the money in a minute. But, Court, I think that when you consider the matter, you'll see that it just isn't sound business to finance something that's going to cut your own throat."

"So," Court said, "that's it!"

"That's it, all right. I'm sorry to have to tell you that you haven't a Chinaman's chance of raising that money in Boston. Give it up, Court—it's a bad deal."

"I reckon I'll have to," Court said sadly, "if that's the way it is."

"That's the way it is. But don't look so downcast, old boy. To me, you're a gift from the gods!"

"What do you mean, Stan?"

"My manager in chief of all my mills, has just retired. He was a crotchety old beggar anyhow; I'm glad to be rid of him. But I've been driving myself mad trying to find a man to replace him. Court, old boy, the job is yours if you want it. You know more about mills than I'll ever learn. I'll give you fifteen thousand dollars a year to start with. What do you say?"

Court frowned.

"Damned if I know what to say. I've been offered three jobs since I've been calling on folks trying to raise that money. I turned them all down because I thought that I would be able to raise it, finally. But now, I don't know. . . ."

"Believe me, Court, you won't be able to," Stanton said seriously. "It's a good position and I don't believe you can call the pay bad. Besides, it would be wonderful if we could make a proper Bostonian of you. This town needs a little of your spirit. What do you say?"

Court got up slowly.

"Give me a couple of days to think about it, won't you, Stan? If I take that job, it's going to change my whole life. A man oughtn't to do a thing like that too fast."

"Right you are, old boy," Stanton Woodbury said cheerfully. "You can drop in on me here when you've made up your mind. Or you can telephone me. The office has one of those infernal machines, now. Ah, progress! By the way, Court—where are you staying?"

"The Vendome," Court said. "See you, Stan."

He didn't go back to the hotel at once. Instead he went back to the Common and sat down on a bench. Near him a group of children were feeding the pigeons. It was a clear, autumn day, with just a hint of a bite to it. Court stared straight ahead of him without seeing anything at all. He sat there until he began to feel stiff, then he got up and started up Beacon Hill. That part of the Hill had already been overrun by the Irish. If the signs meant anything, the rest of it would go, too. No longer would it be the dwelling place of aristocrat, poet, philosopher, and sage. The old order changeth, he mused. But not to change was, in the long run, a kind of death. . . .

I've changed, he thought. I've gotten harder, and meaner'n Satan himself. . . .

But for the life of him, he couldn't come to any decision about the job. I could send for Fan, he thought; nobody knows her here, and it would be much better. . . . But he couldn't make up his mind. Maybe, he thought, because I don't really want to make it up. . . . So he turned and went back toward the Vendome.

As the hotel came in sight, a sudden oddity of memory struck him. Martha, his sister-in-law, had asked him where he would be staying in Boston. On the surface, there was nothing queer about that. Nothing—but the way she had asked it. A little too intensely. A mite too much interest. Then it was a little strange that she had asked him at all. Martha Brantley wasn't going to write him any letters. Phil, either. The Brantleys never wrote letters. Then why the dickens had she wanted to know?

He had asked her that same question, and her answer was queerer than her question: "I've got reasons," Martha had said.

He shook his head, thinking about it. Women loved to appear mysterious. Once inside the hotel, he dismissed the matter from his mind and went straight to his room. He pulled off his shoes, his coat, and his tie, and stretched out on the bed, staring at the ceiling.

It was a hard decision to make. He had dreamed about that mill so long. Even when he'd been an undergraduate at Harvard, he'd haunted textile mills, and learned all he could. Afterwards he'd worked for Jonathon Snow and really learned the business. Then there had been the trips to Atlanta, Savannah, Macon—even Charleston, all failures. He hadn't wanted to come North for capital. He had wanted to keep the Yankee mill owners out of it. But they were the only people he knew who might be interested. Or so he had thought.

Of course, he could get the money from Wyche Weathers. Or rather, Fan could. But he couldn't do that. It was unthinkable. You didn't take money from a man who is in love with your wife. Not even from a man like Wyche, who almost certainly would never try to do anything about the way he felt. And the terms Wyche had set were downright insulting. I insulted him first, Court thought bitterly, reckon he had a right to hit back at me. . . .

The half healed wound in his shoulder ached dully. His head ached, too. Groaning, he got up from the bed, and picked up a glass from the dresser. He opened his valise, and took out the bottle of bourbon. But he never got it open, partly because it was a hard thing to do with no strength in his left hand, and partly because a bellboy knocked on his door while he was still trying to get it open.

"Lady to see you, sir," the bellboy said. "Downstairs in the lobby."

Court groped in his pocket and tipped him. Then he put his shoes and his tie and his coat back on. It took him a long time because his left hand was awkward and weak. And all that time he was thinking, Now who the blazes? Can't be Hester, because I heard yesterday that she'd married Horace Clayton. All the rest of the girls I knew here didn't know me well enough to look me up at my hotel. Come to think of it, that's a funny thing for any Boston girl to do. . . .

But he was halfway down the stairs before it hit him. No Boston girl. No girl reared in the rock-ribbed conservatism for which Boston was famous would even think of such a thing. But a girl who'd lived all her life outside the pale of society because of the fact that her father had been a New Englander and a Carpetbagger, might think of anything. "They trailed her as far as Boston," Tyler had said. "Then they lost her. Boston. That's what made me think it was you."

She stood up as he came into the lobby, and extended one small, gloved hand.

" 'Lo, Court," she said.

Court didn't answer her. He just stood there looking at her. She was dressed all in brown and the color became her. It matched her eyes, for Fern was one of those rare blondes with brown eyes so dark they look almost black. Her brown velvet hat had red and yellow artificial flowers in it. The angle it was cocked at above her silvery blonde hair was damnable, Court thought. She had on a brown plush pelisse instead of a coat, with big sleeves that fitted the upper part of her arms, the rest of the sleeves forming the back and sides of the cape itself. It was trimmed with brown beaver fur. So was her skirt. Her collar was beaver, too. It fitted close around her neck. She'd tied it with a tie of light brown silk. As she came toward him, Court could hear the ruffles of her silk petticoat rustle as she walked.

"I said, hello, Court," she whispered.

"Come on," Court said, "let's get out of here."

He stepped to the edge of the sidewalk to call a cab, but she stopped him.

"I have a buggy," she said. "There it is—over there."

Court looked at it. It was a smart little rig—spanking new. The horse that drew it was something, too.

"I see," he said; "you're making your stay here—permanent."

"Yes, Court."

Court helped her up into the buggy, then he climbed up beside her.

"Suppose," he growled, "I were to write Ty. . . ."

Fern smiled at him.

"You won't do that," she said. Then she flapped the reins over the horse's back.

Court didn't say anything. He sat back watching her. It came to him that Fern knew Boston as well as he did. She paused at Old North Church, from whose tower Paul Revere's lanterns had been hung. Then she turned the horse slightly eastward to Old South Church and the State House from whose balcony the Declaration of Independence had been proclaimed. They stopped at the Granary Burial Ground, almost under the shadow of the tower of the Park Street Congregational Church that Sir Christopher Wren had designed.

"I want to stop here," Fern said.

Court stared at her. Then he got down and swung her down after him. She took his arm, keeping the other hand in the fur muff and they went through the graveyard together. Court looked at the headstones. They were weathered, chipped, brown. And on nearly every one in this section was the name, Vance. Most of the dates were from the time of the Revolution or even before. Three of the stones listed battles in which the men lying below had been killed.

"Funny," Court said, "I never realized. . . ."

"That Father was a Bostonian? It isn't strange. Nobody ever bothered to find out anything good about us. The Vances of Boston. Only I was born in Augusta, Georgia, of a Southern mother, who hated my father."

"My God," Court said. Then: "Are all your folks buried here?"

"No," Fern said. "Only the first ones—and not all of them. Some of them are over there. . . ."

She pointed to King's Chapel, not a stone's throw away. King's Chapel, Court knew, had been the church of the Tories.

"King's men, eh?" he said.

182

"Yes, Court. Your precious Civil War that you Southerners will never be done with fighting wasn't the only one in which brother took up arms against brother. Two of my great grand-uncles died in the same battle—on opposite sides. I only hope they didn't kill each other. Come on, let's go."

"You had a point," Court said, "in bringing me here."

"Yes. Boston is my home. It always has been, I reckon. Father used to bring me here often as a child. He left me a brownstone—on the Hill. And a trust fund that'll take care of me the rest of my life. Here, I have friends—like the Woodburys. I'm accepted. . . ."

Court stopped her.

"Did Stanton tell you that I—"

"No, Court. I had a wire before you even left Augusta."

Court stared at her.

"Martha!" he exclaimed.

"Yes, dear—Martha. She hates Ty almost as much as I do. She hates all the Brantleys, including that precious husband of hers—except you. She thinks that you and I were made for each other. I agree with her."

"But," Court said, "I have a wife. You have a husband."

"I know," Fern said. "Come on."

They rode toward the Charles. Neither of them said anything. Court put out his hand and laid it on Fern's arm.

"All right, Fern," he said. "Speak your piece."

"All right," Fern sighed. "You have a wife. I have a husband. Let's take them up in that order. Your wife. A nobody from the Carolina hills. A medicine-wagon mountebank who danced nude before hundreds of men."

"Not nude," Court said.

"Almost. Required precious little imagination on their part. Duke Ellis' mistress. Wyche Weathers' mistress. Your mistress. Your marrying her, Court, was one of the most fantastic businesses I ever heard of. . . ."

"Go on," Court said grimly.

"A woman who made you do murder. Who nearly got you killed. The list is endless, but that's enough. Too much, to my way of thinking."

"And Ty?" Court said.

183

"A drunkard. A balding satyr. An ugly egotist who imagines himself to be God's gift to women. . . ."

"You married him, remember."

"I know. On the rebound, Court. I was a fool."

"Go on."

"A man whose manners would disgrace a pig. Sloppy, unkempt. Loud, boorish, vain. A man," Fern paused, looked at him, "who isn't even a man any more. Not even half a man. . . ."

"What the devil do you mean, Fern?"

"You stopped in New York for a week, didn't you?"

"Yes, why? I was laid up—my arm went back on me. What's that got to do with it?"

"Tyler stayed in Augusta. He made all his trips between Riley's and Hiberion on that big Morgan of yours. Somebody—who didn't know you were out of town, took a shot at him. You do look alike, you know. And everybody knows that horse. In the dark it must have been easy for him to get confused."

"You're lying," Court got out. "Dammit, Fern, you're lying."

"No, Court. Martha wired me this morning. Told me to tell you. The man who shot at him didn't hit him. Only that Morgan of yours reared and threw him—not all the way. His foot got caught in the stirrups. The animal dragged him half a mile. His back is broken —he'll be paralyzed from the waist down—the rest of his life. . . ."

Court stared at her.

"And your reaction to the news," he said flatly, "is to desert him."

"I'd done that already. I see no reason to go back, now. Pity is a kind of sentimentality I can't afford, darling. The point, Court, which you've been so stubbornly evading, is that there's no reason for your going back. I had dinner with the Woodburys last night. I dropped a hint or two that you'd do admirably for that manager's job Stan is trying to fill. Stan was delighted. And what makes it perfect, Court, is the fact—" she stopped, looking at him.

"I'll bite, Fern. What makes it so perfect?"

"The fact that nobody in Boston, so far as I know, has the slightest idea that you're married. Do they, Court?"

"No," Court said. "Not a living soul in this whole blamed town." Then very quietly he got down from the buggy.

"There's a word," he said, "for what you're suggesting, Fern."

"There is? What is it, darling?"

"Bigamy," Court said.

"A word," Fern said tensely, "made up of sounds, letters, syllables. Meaning as little as any other word. Meaning nothing considered against the actuality of—us."

Court lifted his broad-brimmed hat.

"Good-bye, Fern," he said.

"Where are you going?" Fern said.

"Back to the hotel. Then home. I'm going to see what can be done for Ty. I'm going to ask my wife to forgive me." He smiled, suddenly. "She should be grateful to you. You've made me appreciate her."

Fern shrugged.

"A risk I had to take," she said calmly. "But don't say good-bye, Court. Good-bye is the wrong word."

"Why is it, Fern?"

"Because you'll come back." She pulled at the reins, turning the horse gently around in the direction from which they had come. When she had him all the way around, she pulled up, briefly.

"Oh yes, Court," she said; "you'll come back." Then she drove off in the direction of Beacon Hill.

"Fan," Tyler said, "I'm dry as a bone. Get me a drink, won't you?"

Fancy went back into the kitchen and came back with a glass of water. She put one hand under Tyler's head and raised him up so that he could drink.

"Damn!" Tyler swore. "Call this a drink, babydoll? Ain't Court got no bourbon in this shack?"

"Yes," Fancy said; "but you can't have it. Doc Benton says it's bad for you."

"To heck and tarnation with Doc and what he says! Fan, a spot of bourbon and branch water wouldn't harm a baby, let alone . . ."

"No, Ty."

Tyler watched her, moving about the room, and his eyes were dark with adoration.

"Anybody ever tell you," he whispered huskily, "that you're an angel?"

185

"Don't be silly, Ty," Fan said.

"My brother," Tyler said, "is a fool. A hairy-eared jackass. A mule. A stubborn, good-for-nothing, Brantley mule. Than which there ain't no worse breed. . . ."

"That's enough, Ty," Fancy said.

"He'll be back, though," Tyler said. "Not even a Brantley could be that stupid. Any day now the doorbell'll ring and . . ."

Fancy sat down on the edge of the bed and wiped his face with a damp cloth.

"You—you don't hurt none, do you Ty?" she said.

"No," Tyler said. "Wish to God I did, Fan."

"Why?"

"Pain would mean feeling. And there ain't any feeling. Did you see Doc Benton sticking pins in my feet and legs? Just like puncturing so much beef. Didn't feel a thing. Fan, remember what I asked you?"

"Yes. Only you don't have a gun any more, Ty. I took it last night and threw it in the river. Didn't see how you could get to it, but some fool might give it to you. Couldn't have that, Ty. You see, if you blew out your brains in my bedroom, I'd have to clean up the mess."

"I'll have to think of some other way," Tyler said cheerfully. "Can't mess this place up. Not after the way you've fixed it up."

Fancy looked around the room. It glowed with fresh paint. There were curtains, that she had made, on the windows, and hooked rugs on the floor. Belle had made the rugs. They were real pretty, Fancy thought. Outside in the yard, she had a flower garden. There weren't many flowers blooming in it, because late October was a little cool for them, even in Georgia; but next spring it was going to be something.

Next spring. If there ever were any spring again.

Looking at Tyler lying there, she felt like crying. But she couldn't. That would be bad for him, too. She'd brought him down from Hiberion when she saw how low his spirits were. Agnes' hysterics didn't help. Nor old Jeff's drunken wailing. Saph had been mighty fine, though. She still came in at night to sit with her brother. Other people came, too. Mister Wittly, the Episcopal Minister. And that, Fancy was beginning to see, was a good thing.

People were changing. Getting to be on her side. Old Mrs. Cummings had passed by last week and seen her up on that ladder, in overalls, whitewashing the house. She'd stopped and stared. Then she'd climbed out of her buggy and come into the yard.

"God bless you, child," she'd said; "you've got spunk."

Fan took her in to see Ty, and she'd prayed over him. Then afterwards, she'd gone out and told the members of the Ladies Auxiliary:

"We good Christian people of Augusta have done that girl wrong. Everybody has deserted poor Tyler but her. If you want to see goodness in action go up to Court Brantley's little house. Go there and be convinced, like I was, that she's innocent of the things we've said about her."

I've got friends now, Fancy thought. I've got a chance. I've got everything but what I need most, want most—everything, but—Court.

She saw that Tyler was sleeping at last, so she put her face down against the covers and cried very quietly. She didn't make any noise. Nobody could hear her. She was sure of that.

But she felt hard hands gripping both her arms, and she came up, winking her eyes, trying to get the tears out of them, trying to see. And when she did see, she started crying harder than ever.

"Court!" she sobbed. "Oh, Court, honey, sweetie, Court . . ."

Court held her against his chest, tight.

"Come on," he said, "let's get out of here. We don't want to wake him."

They went out on the porch, and Court held her and kissed her but she couldn't stop crying.

"You came back," she said. "Oh, honey, you came back!"

"Stop it!" Court said gruffly, "and listen to me! I've been a fool, Fan. Didn't know until the other day, just how big a fool. I'm going to ask you to forgive me. I want to make it up to you. 'Cause Wyche was wrong about one thing: I can recognize a pearl when I see one. Will you forgive me, Fan?"

"Forgive you?" Fancy whispered. "You're back and you talk about such foolishness? Oh, darling, there's nothing to forgive. . . ."

Inside the house, Tyler groaned.

"Fan!" he called. "Where are you, baby?"

"Coming, Ty!" Fancy said.

They went in together, and Court stood looking down at his brother.

"Is it bad, Ty?" he said.

"You bastard," Tyler said.

"Look, Ty," Court said, "it won't stay like this. I'm going to get the best damned doctors in the world, and . . ."

"With what?" Tyler said. "I made a crop before this happened. Paid off my debts. But no profit, Court. Not even money enough for seed for next spring. What are you going to pay 'em with, boy? Your looks?"

"No," Court said. "I'll get the money, Ty. Don't worry about that. It may take me two years, but I'll get it. I'll see you on your feet, walking, if it's the last thing I do."

"Big words, boy. How's Fern? You saw her in Boston, didn't you?"

"Yes," Court said, "I saw her. You want me to write her?"

"No," Tyler said. "I never want to see her again. Not as long as I live. Kind of expected that you'd stay up there, too. Would have been downright cozy for you two. Me crippled, and Fan tied down here taking care of me."

"I came as soon as she told me about you, Ty," Court said quietly. "It's better like this. Fern—in Boston—and us, here. Take it easy, boy. I've things to do."

Court and Fancy went back out on the porch, and stood there, looking at each other.

"Fan," Court said, "I've got to go away again. Right away—tonight."

"Where?" Fancy said.

"Spartanburg."

"No, Court! You're not going to Wyche and . . ."

"Yes, Fan. I'm going out and get you that mill. I'll manage it, if you'll hire me. Think I'll do, bosslady? I've had a lot of experience and . . ."

Fancy looked at him. Then she shook her head. Slowly.

"No, Court," she said.

Court didn't say anything for a long while. Then, he said, very quietly:

"Why not, Fan?"

"I know you. You're all Brantley—a mighty heap too much, sometimes. The mill's all right. It's a mighty fine idea—but not this way. Not with you eating your heart out over the way you had to get it. Learning to hate Wyche, who's always been your friend. Maybe even hating me because the mill would be mine and the only way you could get it would be through me. It just isn't worth what it would cost . . ."

"I see," Court said. "You prefer for Ty to stay crippled to save my feelings. You'd rather us stay poor than to make this little sacrifice."

"It's not little. And the trouble is you can't make it—not for keeps. Right now—sure. But later on, you'd get to thinking. Besides, Court, if you'd use whatever that is you've got betwixt your ears you'd realize that there's another way."

"Such as?" Court said.

"Melody. Ty can't farm it. You're going to let it go to seed? All right you don't have any money, but you could even sell part of it to get the stuff to plant the rest. And any banker would let you have a loan if you gave him a mortgage."

"That's true," Court said, "still . . ."

"Still nothing! Listen to me, Court Brantley. I lived on a farm all my life. I know as much about planting as you do—more maybe. Ty's got it out of debt. First growing season we could make us a handsome profit—four or five seasons we'll have enough money to start building the mill, and Melody as security to borrow more."

"What about Ty's share?"

"Make him part owner of the mill. Pay him—do anything; just you get going!"

Court looked at her a long time.

"All right," he said. "I'll do just that."

11

But it wasn't that easy. Nothing ever is. You make your plans, then all the things you hadn't figured on kick them into a cocked hat. Things like the boll weevil. Like the supply merchant whose interest rates, apparent and hidden, were never less than forty percent, sometimes as high as eighty. Like the sharecroppers, white and black, beaten down by the heat and the kinds of things that they ate until it took three of them to equal the work of one Yankee farm hand. Things like the other most important fact of all, that Courtland Brantley was a gentleman born and bred and cotton planting in the 1880's called for a taskmaster meaner than a sidewinder and tighter than the Georgia Railroad Bank.

So that first season they failed. Miserably. Completely.

Sitting in the house, just before that second planting season they talked it over. It was raining and that didn't help. It had been raining too long. By now even the sound of it got on their nerves.

"You can do it, Court," Fancy said; "I just know you can."

Court looked at her.

"Yes," he said, "I can do it. But do you know how, Fan? Do you know how Tyler made this place pay?"

"No," Fancy said, "how did he, Court?"

"He used convict labor farmed out to him by some of the crooked-est officials that ever disgraced the State of Georgia. Five out of six plantation owners hereabouts do that still. You pay those crooks a pittance, and they send you the dirty, starved-out niggers, complete with an overseer—with a whip."

"Oh, Court—no!"

"Damned right they do. Even your highfalutin friends, the Gil-mores, use convict labor. And do you know who has his crooked fin-gers deep into that stinking mess? That would-be lover of yours—Jed Hawkins."

"I'm glad you said would-be," Fancy said tartly. "Besides, I don't believe Jed would do a dirty trick like that. Why it's no better than slavery."

"Why pretty it up? It *is* slavery. Hell, it's worse. In slavery times a good Negro was a valuable possession. You fed and clothed and petted him like a good horse. But who gives a damn what happens to these chain-gang niggers? Kill 'em off, work 'em, starve 'em, beat 'em to death. There're always more. And don't take up for Jed Hawkins. If I see his red freckled face around here one more time, I'm going to remove his spots—with buckshot."

"Don't be a fool, Court," Fancy said. "Jed means nothing to me."

"Oh no? Seems to me you do a sight more cottoning up to him than is necessary or seemly. I tell you, Fan—"

"Don't tell me. I'm sick of your telling me. I married you, Court Brantley, because I loved you. I do still, which is downright foolish, maybe. But you haven't anything to fear from Jed Hawkins. I like Jed, but it doesn't go any further than that. But every time you sit here snarling at me over your own mistakes and failures, I like him a little better. It isn't Jed you ought to be afraid of, Mister High and Mighty. It's your own stupid, stubborn, stiff-necked self!"

Court looked at her. Then he grinned, wryly.

"You sure have got guts," he said.

"Thanks," Fan said. "Court—please don't let's fight any more. That's all we've done all winter. We got to make some plans. There ought to be some way we could make a go of Melody."

191

"There are several," Court said slowly, looking away from her, "but they all stick in my craw like bile. All right, we've got one advantage down here in these bottom lands—we don't have to buy guano—not yet. But we have to buy damn near everything else at rates that would make any Ohio farmer reach for his teamster's whip. So we have to reduce expenses—which means taking it out of the hides of our people. And they're good people, Fan, black and white, they're all good."

"I know," Fancy said sadly.

"Their living standards are the ones they got used to in slavery. The Negroes, anyhow. The whites didn't even have it that good. You'd think a body couldn't live any lower than that. But they can. Every planter who doesn't use convict labor has proved that. All right, corn pone, molasses, collard greens and fatback gives the grown-ups pellagra and the kids soft bones—even when they have enough of it to fill their bellies. But now, cut out the collards—you need even that little garden patch to plant more cotton. Don't ever give 'em enough of the other swill—hell, Fan, even the hogs refuse it. In the wintertime give even less. Don't listen to 'em whining from hunger—it might soften your heart. And planters with soft hearts don't make profits. . . .

"Cabins don't cost much to build, do they? Hell, even that little is too much, now. You've got to make a profit, remember. The supply merchant is breathing down the back of your neck, and the damyankees with their railroad freight differentials, and their factories that make the things he sells, and their high tariffs are breathing down his. So you don't build your 'croppers' cabins even as good as nigger slave cabins were built before the war. You build 'em like hillbilly cabins, stand green pine planks on end, running 'em vertically, and make 'em a one-room box that after one season of rain and sun has warped and shrunk so that the winter rain blows through it without hindrance and the wind plays tunes up and down their backbones. . . ."

"Court, it doesn't have to be like that. I tell you . . ."

"Doesn't it? Ever seen the Tilton hands? God damn it, Fan, even a nigger should have a suit of overalls once in a while. Not now, not down here. Put gunny sacking on him. Let him make his shirt from flour bags. Shoes? Hell, I bought the black bastard a pair three years ago. If he was big enough jackass to wear 'em every day, let him do without.

"Oh, yes, Fan. I keep the books. And my 'croppers, black and white, can't read or figure. I can do it all right. I can get the money to build my mill. Only every time I see my face in the mirror afterwards, I'm going to get sick—puking sick."

"There's some other way," Fancy said stubbornly. "Some other decent, honorable way."

"Is there? At best it's no good. I'm no damned planter. The old place was gone before I was born. I hate it. Getting out of bed before sun-up, pounding on the doors of the shanties, dragging old women and kids barely toddling out to the fields, standing over them all day cursing at them, driving them worse than animals. God damn it now, Will, get the lead out of your black ass! Get moving Ras, what the hell do you think this is—a square dance? And you, Tildy, you're missing a sight more weevils than you get. Look at that damned grass—which one of you burr-headed black bastards plowed this row? You think I like that, Fan? Hell, the mill's not worth that—not even that."

"Then what are you going to do?" Fancy said.

"I'm not going to plant this season. I'm going out and raise that money for the mill even if I have to put a gun in their faces! Stealing is better than this. There's a sight more risk to it, and a hell of a lot more honor."

"Then I'll plant," Fancy said. "I can do it. I was raised on a farm and I know how."

Court looked at her narrowly.

"Damned if I don't believe you could," he said. "But we'd have to go further into debt to get supplies, and we'd be the laughingstock of the county—a woman running a plantation."

"Who cares about that? I can do it—without abusing the hands, or starving them. And it would leave you free to try to raise some money elsewhere. Court, give me a chance. All along I've been nothing but a drag on you. I want to help you. It would make me mighty proud if I could . . ."

"I'd be away all summer," Court said. "And if I came back and found out that Jed Hawkins has been hanging around here, I'd have to shoot him."

"And you," Fancy said bitterly, "would have to go to Boston. So I reckon I'd have to shoot Fern. Only shooting's too good for her. Reckon I'd just notch her nose and her ears, cut her tongue out, scratch out her eyes and snatch her bald-headed."

Court looked at her. Then he started to laugh. He stretched out his arms and drew her to him. She could feel his body against hers, shaking with laughter.

"I don't have to go to Boston, hon," he said. "Fact is, to Bostonians, the Southern mills are a threat. I wouldn't have a Chinaman's chance there. New York—Philadelphia, Baltimore. God knows where else. But not Boston. That I promise you."

"And if Jed comes here while you're gone, I'll chase him off even if I have to put the hounds on him. I promise you that, darling. Is it a deal?"

"It's a deal," Court Brantley said.

Afterwards, after he had gone, Fancy was sorry. She knew farming all right, but not big farming. It was ten times harder and more complex. And doing it herself, she learned how right Court had been about the bitter needs that had all but destroyed all over the South the ancient sense of *noblesse oblige*. To keep alive now, with high tariffs, time charges, taxes, high freight rates, and the boll weevil destroying a quarter of the crop, it was dog eat dog down to the naked bone.

But Fancy was a woman, and that made a difference. There was a way—so simple that the men never thought of it. Fancy deliberately ignored cotton's endless demands for land and more land until nobody even had flowers around their doors any more, planting the white enslaver up to their porches. She returned a full twenty-five acres to the growing of foodstuffs. All kinds of foodstuffs. She diverted some of the money she borrowed into a small dairy herd. And chickens. She put the old men and women and the children into the garden acreage. And she fed her people, after the quick-growing truck vegetables were up, better than any hands had eaten in the South in fifty years.

Twenty-five acres hardly scratched Melody's boundless sweep. But it made the miracle she was praying for. It and Fancy and God.

It changed sullen, shuffling hands into workers who loved the ground she walked on. Who never had to be cursed or driven. Who worked from before dawn until after dark—singing.

Then there was nothing else to do, after the crop was in but wait for cotton weather. Fancy knew the signs, and waited. She wanted that long, hot dry weather. She prayed for it. While it's damp, early planting time, spring time, raining, the crop gets a good start. But so do the weevils and the weeds, and the grass. But when the dry weather sets in you work like a dog, like a Negro, like an ox. It's nip and tuck, between the cotton and the weevils and the weeds. You don't let up a minute all day every day. Fancy knew that, and she waited.

She rode out every day with the black hands, making them turn over a row or two, so that she could feel the earth, seeing when it was dry enough. Then one night, she got on her horse and rode around to all the cabins, telling the tenants to be ready. This was it.

She knew that absolutely, perfectly without even knowing how and why she knew. Something about the air—so hot and dry you had to sit on the back porch and gulp at it to get enough. Something about how the sun went down flaming orange down the sky. The lightning bugs bobbing over the Johnson grass. The frogs begging for rain, deep-voiced and moanful. The way the corn curled up from the heat.

She was up before the sun, out in the fields with the Negroes and the white 'croppers—the two races in different fields, of course. She knew better than to work them together. She watched them pushing the plows between the rows turning the grass back into the soil, and behind the big, earth-breaking plows the women and children came, digging out the ugly boll weevils. Fancy didn't say a word to them, she just sat there on the horse, watching them. But she had a hog already killed and roasting over the barbecue pit, and watermelons, and fish a-frying. They worked like dogs, like demons, singing all the time, grinning up at her. After a while, she got tired of sitting there. So she got down and bent through the rows with the black women, breaking every law of etiquette ever heard of in the South, every custom, and tore the ugly weevils loose until her fingers ached. And the hands kept working faster.

They piled the weevils up and burned them with coal oil. They smelled awful, burning. The water boys came and went, bringing the buckets. Some of the Negroes didn't drink. They just poured it over their heads and let it soak their shirts for coolness and kept on working.

They had lunch in the middle of the fields, and afterwards Fancy went over and worked with the white 'croppers. They hadn't been working so fast, but after she joined them they started to work as fast as the blacks or maybe even a little faster. And that night, they all sat down to the barbecue, the whites on one side, the blacks on the other. And they all told jokes and sang.

But Fancy couldn't sleep. She went out to the barns and watched old Josh rubbing down the mules so they wouldn't get too stiff. Then she went out into the fields and under the light of a moon you could read a newspaper by, she started picking more weevils. One of the house servants missed her and came looking for her. When she saw what her mistress was doing she went back and roused out the others, roaring at them, black arms akimbo on her massive hips:

"Lil' Missy ain't a-going to lose this heah plantation! Not with that kind of spirit! Git up, you lazy rascals and let's go help her!"

They did. By morning they'd almost cleared the south acreage of the pest.

And the next day, red-eyed, sleepless, Fancy started all over again.

So it was that when weeks later, Jed Hawkins rode out to Melody, he stared at Fancy with real concern. She was down to skin and bones. Her white skin that wouldn't tan, because she had a blonde's lack of pigment despite her black hair, had reddened and blistered and peeled, so that her blue eyes looked twice as bright.

"My God!" Jed whispered. "You—you look like a damned cracker!"

"Which is exactly what I am," Fancy said. "Didn't you know?"

"Yep. But you never looked like one before. All you need now is a corncob pipe between your teeth, or a wad of snuff under your lower lip. Fan, for the love of God, do you have to do this?"

"Yes."

Jed stared at her, his face working. He looked hurt and mad, and sick all at the same time.

"The woman I love," he said, "down on her hands and knees in the rows with the niggers—for that long-tall polecat. And him gallivanting around begging for money to start a mill, and letting his wife do his work. . . ."

"That's enough, Jed Hawkins!" Fancy said.

"It's a damned sight too much to my way of thinking. Fan, how long are you going on being such a fool?"

"As long as he's alive," Fancy said, "and wants me."

"Jesus!" Jed said.

"What would you suggest? That I leave him and run off with you, and live in luxury off the money you get out of farming out your convict niggers?"

"So," Jed muttered, "you know about that. . . ."

"I know about that and a lot more of the dirty, rotten things you've done, Jed. I'm sorry I found out. I like you a mighty heap. It shames you for me to work in the fields like the poor white trash I am; but it sure Lord shames me to have a friend of mine turn out to be a side-winder and a polecat and a dirty, rotten crook. Reckon that makes us even, doesn't it?"

"No," Jed said. "After today, I'm getting out of that shady deal. I'd rather be tarred and feathered and ridden out of town on a rail than have you hate me, Fan."

"I don't hate you," Fancy said; "I like you. I don't expect folks to be anything much. When they are, it always surprises me."

"Prepare to be surprised," Jed said. He came toward her, his eyes pleading. "Fan—Fan, honey," he said.

"No, Jed. There's just one thing you can do for me. Get off of Melody and don't come back until my husband's at home. I don't want talk. And I want to keep your friendship. Court's got a good gun eye and a mighty short temper. And there's been enough killing —over me."

"Right," Jed said sadly. "But one of these days . . ."

"Forget it, Jed," Fancy said, and put out her hand.

Jed took it, feeling it rough, toil-worn, calloused. He held it a long time, looking at her. Then he swung himself into the saddle and rode away without saying anything at all. Not even good-bye.

By the end of August, Fancy knew she had won. The crop, she could see, was going to be more than double the yield that Melody had ever produced before even from its entire acreage. And before it was all picked, Court came home.

She could see from his face he hadn't got the money. It was worn with bitterness. And when he looked over the fields, white with the bursting bolls, seeing the pickers working smoothly, rhythmically in time to the lead hand's song, he didn't congratulate Fancy or thank her or even say anything about the thing she had done.

That hurt. Fancy brooded over it while Court attended to the picking, baling and ginning, and rode with the long line of wagons into Savannah to the factors to sell it. When he came back Melody was out of debt. He had bought supplies for the next season, and paid off all the debts and they still had a small profit. But he didn't thank her. And then, finally, Fancy knew why.

He had failed. She had succeeded. He was a man, all man, and a Brantley—prouder even than other men, and it had taken his wife, this hill girl he had married to show him how to run a plantation. He was, deep down inside, grateful to her. But he would never forgive her. Never.

When he came back from the factors, his face was black with anger. He came up to Fancy and caught her by the wrist, hard.

"So," he said, "Hawkins was out here! First thing I heard in town was . . ."

"You are hurting my arm, Court. Turn me loose."

"He was out here, wasn't he?"

"Once. And I sent him packing. I'm sorry I did now. I was a fool." Court turned her loose and stared at her.

"You mean that?" he said.

"Yes, Court."

"Might I ask why?"

"Yes. You're an honorable man and a gentleman, but you're not nice. You're meaner than old hell. Jed is a crook and a scoundrel, but he's nice. Very nice. He thinks nothing on earth is too good for me. Came out here and saw me working in the fields with the hands, and he almost cried. You don't give a damn about that. You don't even care that I saved Melody for you—that I gave you the chance you needed. Jed thinks nothing's too good for me—you, I reckon you think everything's too good for this poor white trash you made the mistake of marrying."

Court stepped back and stood there, bleak misery in his face.

"You're right, Fan," he said. "I haven't even said thank you, have I?"

"No, Court—you haven't."

"Then—why didn't you run away with him when you had the chance?"

Fancy looked at him and her blue eyes were very clear.

"Because I love you, Court—not him," she said simply. "Funny I have to tell you that."

The next second she was in his arms, held so hard she couldn't breathe.

"You won't be sorry, Fan," he muttered hoarsely—"not ever!"

After that, it all went very smoothly and very well. Court learned what Fancy had to teach. He humbled himself even to asking her advice on the crops and the weather, and the next season the profit they made was better than fair, and the one after that it was so good that Court could buy guano to fertilize the already rich land so that at their fourth picking time the other planters came out to look at their fields with wondering eyes.

They didn't make enough money to start the mill. Not yet. But at the end of their fourth year at Melody they had an excellent chance of getting it. If in the fifth season they had any kind of luck at all, if the weather held, and they beat the weevils, and the high spring grass, if . . .

"Just one more year, Fan," Court said. "Just one—that's all."

Fancy didn't answer him. She came up to him and tied the white tie that he had been struggling with for nearly five minutes. Then she stepped back and looked at him.

"Now," she said, "now you really do look nice. You'll be the handsomest man at the Gilmores' tonight."

Court grinned at her.

"No I won't," he said. "Know who's going to be there? Your light o' love—Jed Hawkins. Sometimes I think I ought to shoot him off-hand and save myself the trouble of doing it later—when he's deserved it."

"That," Fancy said, "will be never. Besides, he can't deserve it without me being mixed up with him some way, and I don't aim to get mixed up with anybody. You're enough trouble, Mister Court-land Brantley." She stopped and stared at him. "You know," she said softly, "that's plumb, downright strange."

Court ran the comb through his hair.

"What's strange, Fan?"

"That we—haven't had any children," Fancy said. "It's been five years, Court."

"We're young yet," Court said; "I've known of cases where couples after fifteen years . . ."

"Court—"

"Yes, Fan?"

"You aren't sorry, are you?"

"Sorry about what?"

"That you married me. I'm just getting so that I can mingle with your kind of folks without making a fool of myself. And—you ought to have a son."

Court turned around and looked at her.

"It could be my fault, Fan," he said. "The Brantleys are an old, and worn-out line."

"You—worn-out?" Fancy said; "ha!"

Court picked up her evening wrap and held it out for her. Fancy slipped into it and sighed.

"Five years," she said.

"Five good years," Court said. "One more will make six. If I hadn't had to borrow to run that first year, we'd be away from here now."

"I'm glad we're not," Fancy said. "Didn't know I could love any place on earth like I love Melody."

"We'll keep it," Court said. "We can come down here in the summer, as soon as the mill gets to running smoothly enough."

"Court," Fancy said, "what do we need with a mill—now?"

That was the wrong thing to say. She saw that at once. Court had that mean Brantley look in his eyes, and that stubborn set to his jaw.

"We don't," he said flatly. "We're on the top of the heap right now. Melody is a success. I could get any price I named for it. But it isn't that simple. What does a man need with any particular woman as a wife? Or with any of his dreams?"

"I don't know, Court," Fancy said. "I'm sorry I asked you that."

"It's all right. And the answer to that question is that he really

200

doesn't need any of those things—except that something inside of him dies if he doesn't get them."

"You'll get your mill," Fancy said; "I just know it."

"Thanks," Court said. Then he looked at her with grave eyes.

Fancy was dressed all in white. The dress was made of white satin, cut just a little way off her shoulders, very tight in the waist, and decorated with lace that was just off white. The collar was of lace, and the short sleeves that came to a little below her shoulders were trimmed with it. Great masses of the same lace went around her hips and were tied in a bow at the back, and then trailed down alternating with the white satin to make her train. More of the lace was sewn in foot-wide ruffles all around the full skirt, and the hem of the ruffled satin skirt was edged with it. Fancy had a puff of ostrich feathers and aigrettes in her black hair. She looked, Court thought, damned lovely.

"Merry Christmas, darling," he said, and kissed her.

It was Christmas Eve of 1885, and they were going to the Gilmores' to a party. The Gilmores were a power in Savannah, but right from the start they had accepted her. That was one of the things Fancy liked about Savannah. Nobody down here knew her history. Except Jed. And he wouldn't tell it. None of them had ever seen her dressed in those baggy, transparent trousers, doing that awful dance on the back of Wyche Weathers' Medicine Wagon. She was Court Brantley's wife, and that was enough. All the women went out of their way to be nice to her, including the ones who were too nice because they were envious. They—the envious ones—were looking for an opening, a chance to get in their barbs; but Fancy never gave them any. She had learned the difficult trick of answering questions very politely without telling the person who had asked them what he wanted to know. So it was that all their efforts to find out who she was, what her family connections were, how she had met Court and any of the ten thousand other things they asked her that were none of their business, met with the same lack of success. They never gave it up, being Southern women and endlessly curious; but they never found out anything.

It was raining when they came out of the house, and the air had that bottom land chill to it. In other places the cold was dry and biting, but in that part of Georgia it crept in upon you through your very pores until after a while your bones ached with it. But Court had the closed carriage brought around and wrapped her in the buffalo skin robe; so it wasn't too bad.

She was nervous about going to the Gilmores'. They had the finest house and their plantation was the biggest of all and they were richer than anybody else. One of the Gilmore girls had been in love with Tyler and she never failed to ask after him with real sympathy. But all the while she was busily engaged, perhaps unconsciously, in transferring her affections to Court. Which, Fancy realized, wasn't at all hard to do, because Court was ever so much better looking than Tyler, and besides, he had all his hair.

Amos, the Gilmores' butler, announced them, and Fancy could see people all over the place turning to look at them. When they did, the same things always happened: the women's eyes narrowed a little, and their gaze traveled quickly up and down her, so that tomorrow her gown would be the subject of many a conversation. But the men's eyes widened, and when they looked at her, it wasn't the gown they saw. They were indulging themselves in the pleasant masculine speculation over how she must look out of this gown and indeed out of any gown whatsoever. When she had been younger, before she had married Court, Fancy had hated that look; but now she had gained a certain security of spirit, and knowing how men were, and how natural and right it was for them to be like that, even, in the case of this tall man she loved and had married, how exceedingly pleasant it was to be wanted until you began to want back, she gloried in it.

She was a grown woman now. She didn't place too much importance upon female envy or male desire, but she wouldn't have been a woman if she hadn't liked being the object of both attitudes. Then she saw Jed Hawkins looking at her, and a little spot of color came into her cheeks, and moved upward until it reached her eyes. She had, oddly, the feeling that it wasn't right for the young lawyer-politician to look at her like that. She didn't know why. The reason was very simple: Jed Hawkins existed for her as a person. The others didn't.

Jed disturbed her. He was tall—not so tall as Court, but still tall. And he was so good-looking that in spite of all the times she had seen him, his looks still surprised her. Looking at him now, she had again that feeling of annoyance that he always provoked in her. She had worked and fought and studied to gain her easy assurance, and Jed wrecked that in half a second. She couldn't understand it. She loved Court Brantley more than life itself, but every time she came into a gathering where Jed was, she found afterwards that she could remember precisely what he had worn, whom he had danced with, and every careless word he had said. Jed had red hair and freckles. Jed had a most engaging grin. He had two ways of talking. At the Gilmores', he talked like the cultured, educated man he was; but when he made a speech, he twanged like a backcountryman, became deliberately ungrammatical, and talked about his 'Pap,' who he swore had been a sharecropper, spat tobacco juice through his teeth, hitched up his galluses, and told them he had been twelve years old before he had ever worn anything but a gunny sack, and eighteen before he crowded his big feet into shoes.

All of which was a pure lie. But it got the votes.

He's nothing but a crook, Fancy thought hotly. But that grin of his is kind of cute, the other part of her mind said. She had those thoughts about him and they horrified her. They rocked her hard-won assurance to its foundations because it made her think that she was wicked. She didn't realize, being a woman of her generation, that no man born of woman has ever been able to rid himself of his natural inclination toward polygamy. The best most people are able to do is to refrain from acting upon it. She didn't even suspect that the same nature that had given her certain natural responses to being looked at certain ways, to being kissed, to being caressed, was entirely too efficient to place the key to those responses in the hands of any one man. A species was too damned difficult to evolve to have it perish from lack of propagation while its members spent lifetimes hunting around for their one and only true love. . . .

Decency was never lack of temptation, but Fancy didn't know that. I'm bad, she thought, I'm awful bad; but all the time, she was looking at Jed Hawkins out of the corner of her eye.

She danced the first waltz with Court. Then Court went away to dance with Laura Gilmore, and Fancy saw Jed coming toward her. She wanted to run, to hide. Then she realized that she was being a mighty big fool, and took the hand he held out to her, and swirled into the giddy strains of the waltz.

"You're beautiful," he said.

"Please," Fancy said, "don't make fun of me."

"I'm not. I mean it. Also, at the risk of having you think me a blackguard, I'm going to tell you I love you."

"Take me back," Fancy said.

"No," Jed grinned. "You know I'm a scoundrel now. So I'll make the best of it. If I could steal you from your husband, I'd do it. If I could find out what nights he's away from Melody . . ."

"Jed Hawkins!"

"Don't act so shocked," he said. "I'm only telling the truth. And the truth is always respectable."

"Nothing about you is respectable," Fancy said.

"You're mean," Jed teased; "now I'm going to get even!"

He whirled her through the door into the dining room. Then he kissed her, a long time, and very thoroughly. And when he turned her loose, she didn't slap him. Jed had already raised his hand to point at the mistletoe as a means of defense, but then he saw he didn't need to. So he took her arm, and drew her through the dining room and out on the big gallery that went all around the house. He started down the steps toward the garden.

"No!" Fancy whispered. "Oh, no, Jed!"

"Oh come on," he said. And Fancy went.

He kissed her again. She kissed him back very honestly. He tightened his arms about her waist, and kissed the hollow of her throat, her bare shoulder, the nape of her neck, and finally raised his head to find her mouth, but the moonlight was very clear and he saw that she was crying.

"Now what the devil . . ." he said, and turned her loose.

Fancy went on crying.

"I'm sorry," Jed said.

Fancy didn't answer him. She couldn't. She was crying too hard.

"I said I was sorry," Jed said, desperately. He was lost. This was out of his depth. A belle of Savannah might slap your face when you kissed her, but she wouldn't cry. Not like this.

And it came to him that he was in a bad spot. Because of this nothing—this thing that hadn't happened, he was now in danger of being shot or horsewhipped by a man who came from a family known for its murderous tempers.

"Please stop crying," he whispered. "Fancy, please!"

He took out his handkerchief, and dabbed clumsily at her cheeks. His freckled face was so filled with concern that he looked funny. Fancy suddenly found that she wasn't crying any more. She was afraid that now she was going to laugh. But then she remembered that she had allowed him to bring her out here without resistance, that she had kissed this man who was still a stranger, that she had liked kissing him very much, and after that she didn't feel like laughing.

"Take me back now," she said.

He took her arm and they went back into the dining room. "Let's not go in together," Jed said, and Fancy looked at him.

Why, she thought, he's afraid! He's scared stiff. . . . Then she stepped very quickly ahead of him and went back into the ballroom. Court was dancing with one of the McQuinizys. He seemed to be enjoying himself.

I'll go to him, Fancy said. I'll tell him I have a headache.

But she didn't have a headache. All she had was this sick feeling. This feeling of being dirtied in some peculiar, unseen way. By herself. By her own act. Jed had only been a man, playing a man's game. But what had she been—and what was the name of the game she had been playing?

I'll stick it out, she thought. I won't spoil Court's fun.

She danced with several of the guests. Jed didn't come near her for a long time. When he did, she started to refuse to dance with him, but it came to her that he might think she was afraid. So she got up and danced with him. He didn't talk at first. He seemed to be thinking, sketching out in his mind what he was going to say.

"I'm sorry," he said at last; "but only that I made you cry. I'm not sorry I kissed you. I'd do it again. I'm going to do it again the first chance I get. . . ."

"You won't get another chance," Fancy said.

"Why not? You didn't seem particularly offended—not at first."

"I wasn't," Fancy said. "That's why you won't get another chance."

"Want to bet on that?" Jed Hawkins said.

Going back home in the carriage, Fancy lay back against the cushions, listening to Court's cheerful whistling. He was a little drunk, and he looked very happy. Fancy pretended to be asleep, but she kept watching him.

"He's so fine," she thought. "He's got some funny ways, but he's all man, mine. He's worth ten of that damned little. . . . Oh God, oh Jesus, why did I have to think of that? All it proves I reckon is that from white trash, comes more trash. And me thinking I could be a lady. . . . Made Court kill Duke Ellis, but that wasn't my fault. I felt terrible over that, but what I felt was pity, not shame. But this— what in heaven's name got into me? Oh, Lord, please don't let me ever do anything like that again!"

Court opened the door for her, and they climbed the stairs together. Fancy took off her wrap and stood there watching Court while he yanked off his tie and his stiff-bosom shirt. Then he flopped down into the armchair and pulled off his shoes.

"Thank God," he said. "Now I can breathe!"

Fancy stood there looking at him a long time. Then she went over and sat on his lap. She put up both her hands and held his face between them. She came up very slowly from his lap, so slowly that Court didn't know the precise instant that her mouth closed over his. But afterwards he knew.

Afterwards, when the night was graying into morning. When he was very sweetly, softly, loosely, warmly, completely dead. When there wasn't a muscle left in his body. Or a nerve. Or a care.

"Court," Fancy whispered.

"Yes, Fan? Yes, darling, honey, sweetie . . ."

"Court, listen! Let's go back to Augusta. Right now—tomorrow. Let's start the mill. We've money enough—almost. And most anybody would lend you the rest now."

"I thought—" Court said.

"Don't think! Let's go!"

Court raised himself up on one elbow and looked at her. He could see her very clearly. There was light enough for that now.

"Thank God from Whom all blessings flow," he said fervently.

"Are you that glad I changed my mind?" Fancy said.

"I am glad. But that wasn't what I was thanking God for. . . ."

"What were you?" Fancy said.

"For giving me eyes," Court laughed and put out his arm to her. She came to him and lay with her head pillowed on his shoulder.

"Fan," Court said, "why do you want to go all of a sudden? Only last night you said . . ."

"I know. But now I want to. I can't stand this place any longer!"

Court raised himself up and stared at her, frowning.

He was no fool, and Fancy knew that. In about a minute he was going to start asking some very pointed and leading questions which it wouldn't be good or wise or safe for her to answer. She knew how to stop that. But it wasn't all calculation. With his face frowning and intent, Court Brantley to any woman—any real woman—was irresistible.

A minute later, he discovered he wasn't dead after all. Not completely.

12

FANCY sat in a big chair on the rise about one hundred yards above Dry Gully. She sat very still, with both her hands resting on the handles of Tyler's wheelchair. Everybody else was standing up.

Except us, she thought, except us two cripples. Then it came to her that that was a bad thing to think—that what was wrong with her was not like being crippled. It was, actually, a kind of glory.

But Fancy was young. On that July day of 1886, she was only a few months past her twenty-fifth birthday. And all her life she had been slim and good to look at. It was kind of hard to believe that very soon now, in a month or so, she'd be slim again. She'd be slim, and Court would have his son, and everything would be just about perfect.

She could see Court standing with Philemon and Martha and the Mayor and several other important people. Below them, in the valley, was the mill. It was the biggest building that Fancy had ever seen. The hills on both sides were covered with people—mostly the men and women and children that Court had already hired to work in Dry Gully Mill. For more than two weeks now, Court had been teaching them to use the machinery. Fancy had wanted to watch that, but he wouldn't let her. Of course, most of the machines couldn't be worked anyhow, because they didn't have the water-power yet; but Court had even got around that by having a little steam engine brought into the plant to turn them over enough for the people to learn to work them.

He'd used up a thousand dollars' worth of cotton that way; but those folks sure had learned fast—Fancy had to give them that. Many of the women in that crowd, Fancy knew, were wearing dresses from the cloth they had made while learning. It wasn't good cloth, but they were proud of it. They and their sons and their husbands had made it down to the last thread.

Tyler half turned in the wheelchair and looked at her.

"Feeling all right, babydoll?" he said.

"Just fine, Ty," Fancy said. But she wasn't. She felt terrible. Her legs hurt, and her feet and ankles were swollen. She had a misery in her back, and she was so heavy that it was uncomfortable to move. But she was very happy. On the inside she was melting with happiness. Every time the child stirred, she could imagine what it was going to look like. It would be a boy, and right from the first it was going to look just like Court. It was going to be so sweet to hold it in her arms and sing to it and feed it and watch it kick and laugh and gurgle. It wouldn't cry much—not Court's son. No, it would laugh all the time and be happy and she was going to love it so. . . .

She looked at the mill wheels waiting in the gully for the first rush of the water. The dams stood there, bone-dry and dusty. But in a little while they were going to blow that bluff sky-high and the water would come tumbling in and the mill wheels would turn over. A little further up on the ravines and hills, she could see the half finished houses that Court was having built for the mill workers. They weren't much, but Fancy knew they were a heap better than anything these folks had had before. In the middle of the hollow square that Dry Gully Village would form, two bigger buildings were going up—one a church, and the other a school. That was mighty nice, Fancy thought, Court sure was taking good care of his people. But she looked over at a still larger building that stood a little further off, and frowned. The General Store, Philemon Brantley, Manager. That was Phil's own idea, and Fancy didn't like it. He'd told Court it wasn't a good idea to make the mill people go all the way down to Augusta to buy their stuff. He'd even promised to run it fair and square, but Fancy didn't believe him. She didn't trust Philemon. He just didn't have an honest face. . . .

Agnes and Saphira were coming up the hill now. They had on new dresses, and there were two escorts with them.

"Look at 'em," Tyler snorted, "proud as punch of themselves. Got themselves a couple of beaux. Hell, baby, ain't they got sense enough to realize that them boys are just cutting themselves in on a good deal?"

"I think they have got sense enough," Fancy said quietly. "But I think now they don't care much. They're both over thirty, remember. Besides Saph's friend is right nice."

"Breath and britches," Tyler said, "that's all, Fan."

"What else is there to a man?" Fancy mocked him.

"Nothing, I reckon," Tyler said sadly. "And in this case the britches don't even work."

"Ty, please! Don't take on. You know Court's doing all he can."

"Yep. Damned fine of him. Sending me all the way to the University of Edinburgh in Scotland, because Doc Fleischer said that O'Donnell of the Scottish Medical College was the one man on earth who could operate on me and get away with it. Doing it on borrowed money—money he can't rightly afford to use—and the mill still in the gambling stage. . . ."

"No it isn't," Fancy said. "This morning Court showed me more than two hundred orders that had come in. Most of them from Atlanta and Birmingham, and other places where they make ready-made clothes—and linen. We've been getting orders right along. A few of them from as far away as New York and Chicago."

"Two hundred orders is chicken feed, Fan, baby. What about the rest of the year?"

"Court says it's simple arithmetic that we'll make a profit of fifteen percent clear the first year, and double it the next. Phil agrees with him, and Phil is one smart businessman."

"One smart crook," Tyler said; "but he knows how to milk the suckers."

Fancy put her hand on Tyler's arm and squeezed it hard.

"Oh, Ty!" she said, "here they come!"

The two men climbed the rise with the heavy black box between them. A plunger stuck up out of the top of it, and the men were unrolling the wires as they came up the hill, paying them out behind them.

They came up to Court, grinning.

Even from where she sat, Fancy could hear them.

"Here you are, sir!" they said. "It's all yours."

Court put his hand on the plunger. Then he straightened up and said something to the men. They grinned at him and picked up the box again. Fancy could see that they were coming straight toward her. Court came behind them a little more slowly.

When he was close, he smiled at her. Fancy didn't like that smile. It wasn't altogether a good one. She thought that his face looked hurt, smiling—and a little bitter, too.

"It's your baby, Fan," he said. "Blow it!"

"No, Court," Fancy said. "I couldn't. I just couldn't. It's yours—all yours. You've done so much and waited so long. . . ."

"Put your hand on the plunger, Fan," Court said.

Fancy stretched out her hand and let it rest on the wooden handle, but she couldn't push it in. For the life of her, she couldn't.

Court bent down and covered her hand with his own.

"Now, baby," he whispered. "Now!"

Then he pushed her hand down, hard.

Fancy saw the earth leap up in the narrow place that was all the diggers had left between Dry Gully and the river. It went up high in a black, solid cloud, and afterwards she heard the boom of the explosion. It felt like someone had cupped two big hands, and pounded against both her ears at the same time. It crowded down inside of her body so that the child stirred, and she hurt, suddenly.

"The water!" Tyler roared. "God, boy—the water!"

Fan saw it then, tumbling through the gap in a yellow torrent, pushing the red clods of earth ahead of it, spreading out between the broken earth rubble the dynamite had left. It ran very fast in the sunlight until it came to the first dam and stopped there. Then it began to rise in the channel. Fancy watched it creeping up the dry, dusty wall of the dam until it got to the top and ran across that, and fell down the other side with a roar that she couldn't hear very well because the explosion had deafened her.

Her fingers worked on Court's arm as the water hit the first of the mill wheels. Even from where she sat, Fan could hear it creak. Then the bucket-shaped upper blades filled up and the wheel began to move ever so slowly as the weight of the water tripped the buckets over, spilling the water down and out and the next bucket-blade filling up and spilling and the next, and the wheel turning now, faster, faster. . . .

Fancy looked at Court and saw that his lips were moving, shaping words. But they never came out. She could hear Philemon's husky:

"Good God, Court, look at it! There goes the second wheel!"

The second wheel's blades dipped into the whirling millrace, so that they were pushed around by the force of the current; but beyond that was another dam with even more of a drop. The water went over it and now the biggest of all the wheels began to turn, ponderously, and even further down the last wheel was beginning to stir. The people on the hills saw it turn too, and now they took off their hats and cheered.

Then all at once, without anybody saying anything to them at all, they came together in bunches and formed into lines, and the lines moved forward raggedly down the hill, and crowded together in front of the mill's gates.

Court looked at Fancy and saw that she was crying, and a little way off Phil was trying to dry Martha's eyes and Agnes and Saphira were bawling in each other's arms.

"Stop it, you all!" Court roared at them. "We've got enough water!"

"Can't help it!" Martha sobbed. "After all we've been through to see this started—to know we're going up again. Court, you'n' Phil will be the biggest men in the State!"

"Oh yes, you will!" Fancy breathed. "The biggest man in the whole South, Court—not just in Georgia."

Court stared at her.

"I don't know," he said. "I don't even think I care. See those folks down there going through the gates? Well some of those families, working together, are going to have more money at the end of this week than they've ever seen in any one year. I wonder what it'll do to them. . . ."

"I'll tell you," Tyler drawled. "The women are going to blossom out in shoes too tight for their feet, and fancy dresses and all kinds of gewgaws. The men'll be buying bowler hats and striped pants, and nickel cigars. There is going to be a mighty heap of drinking done, and somebody's going to use a knife on somebody else, and there'll be a shooting scrape or two, maybe, and Myrtie Torrence and gals like her are going to get rich. . . ."

"Who is Myrtie Torrence?" Martha asked.

"Our local daughter of joy," Saphira told her without batting an eye.

"Saph," Court said, "one of these days I'm going to take a buggy whip to you."

"Why?" Saphira said. "Appears to me there's a heap less harm in saying what she is than patronizing her the way you men do."

Court took half a step toward her, but Fancy caught his arm.

"Leave her alone, Court," she said. "This is such a wonderful day; don't let's spoil it."

Court smiled at her.

"You're right, Fan," he said. "Come on, all of you, and I'll show you Dry Gully Mill going full blast!"

"It's not dry any more," Martha said. "That's just about the wettest gully in the State of Georgia."

Fancy got up slowly, looking down at the earth. Even the special dresses didn't do any good, she knew. I'm just plumb, downright ugly, now.

Philemon got behind the wheelchair and pushed Tyler down the hill. Then they went into the mill, together with the mayor, and Mister Phinizy, the banker, and the pastor of the Episcopal Church, and all the people who were anybody in Augusta. They went past all the whirring, clattering machinery. Fancy looked at it in a way that made Court think she understood it. Then they stopped before the slashing bath, and Agnes asked:

"What on earth is that for?"

"They're starching the yarn to make it strong," Fancy said, and Court stared at her. Of course there was much more to it than that. The hot, bubbling bath that the yarn went through had other things in it besides starch. There were lubricants in it, and a preservative and—but Fancy was right in the main. Slashing yarn, when all was said and done, was starching it.

"How the devil did you know that?" Court said.

"My Aunt Tilly used to work in Horse Creek Valley Mill," Fancy said. "I used to go over there and take her stuff Maw had baked. I even doffed bobbins myself couple of times in rush seasons."

"I see," Court said.

Fancy thought he sounded mad.

They all stayed until one o'clock when the whistle blew for lunch. But when the workers poured out of the gates into the open air, they found that sawhorses had been set up, and long planks stretched across them, and a crew of Negroes in white aprons and caps were busy with the pigs spread out over the pits. They all started toward the pits, but long before she got near them, Fancy could smell them. They smelled wonderful. There was a black iron pot where the Negro cook had put in the heads and the livers of the hogs mixed up with beef and seasoned with a lot of different kinds of hot spices to make the hash. The pot was propped up on bricks over a low fire, but beyond that was a big fire of oak logs that the Negroes kept blazing by throwing in new logs as fast as it burned down even a little. They didn't cook anything over this fire. One of the cooks came and went, taking the clear, glowing embers from it with a shovel. He spread the embers out in the bottom of the pit. Over the pit the pigs turned on green hickory spits. That way the pork was cooked in clean, smokeless heat. Other Negroes stood by the pits and didn't do anything but turn the pigs over and over again. There was one man who stood next to the pit with a mop made of clean rags tied to a hickory stick. He kept dipping his mop into a pot filled up with vinegar, salt, pepper and spices, and smearing it all over the roasting pigs. The pigs were turning golden-brown and their skin puckered up in little blisters that would become very hard and dry and would crackle when you ate them, Fancy knew.

"You women will have to serve," Court said. "We've got to start these folks off feeling good."

"Oh, Court!" Agnes said, "not in my nice new dress!"

"Dress be damned," Court said. "These pine-barren crackers are a touchy lot. They're prouder'n all hell. You'll find the majority of the men who come up to get served will call me by my first name. In their way, they're the world's staunchest democrats, within certain limitations, of course."

"Limitations?" Fancy echoed.

214

"You've got to have the right color to your hide, and belong to the right church. Beyond that, a man can be poorer than the dickens, or richer than old Commodore Vanderbilt, and they'll treat him just about the same. Of course, they'll listen a little more carefully to the opinions of a man who's rich and powerful; but the next day, when they repeat those opinions, they'll give them as their own—and believe it. Here come the others, now."

Fancy looked and saw buggies and carriages and riders still coming into the mill grounds. All the people got out of their carriages or off their horses and came forward to shake Court's hand.

Court introduced her to Judge and Mrs. Richardson, though he didn't need to, because Judge Richardson remembered her from the trial. But he was too polite to say anything. She shook hands with Bob McCullen, Joe Cummings, all the Phinizys, the Waltons, and Tom O'Mallory. After that she lost track of the names. A big stage came up and an orchestra climbed out of it, and a brewery wagon brought keg after keg of beer.

Fancy was surprised to see how all the fine ladies in their new summer dresses joined in and heaped up the plates of the mill workers. Then the mayor got up and made a speech; he said that Court was a public benefactor. After a while, Fancy stopped listening, because the speech was dull.

Fancy saw Court standing up now, but when he started talking, it was to the mill workers, not the important people, that he spoke.

"I don't have to tell you," he said quietly, "what the price of guano is today—or what kind of a crop you can grow on these starved-out lands without it. I don't need to remind you what your chances were of keeping your lands another two years, or even another one when the supply storekeeper tallied up his accounts. You know these things as well as I do. You've seen the red earth bleed away along the gullies, and the crops come in smaller every year. You've seen the blights come, and the cotton fail. You've heard your children crying in the night from hunger, and put your hands over your ears because there was no food. Your old woman got a misery in the chest. Your oldest daughter died—spitting blood. . . .

"Then you lost the land and became a 'cropper on another man's place. That was bad even when he was a good man, because the mills up North set the prices on his bales. When he was a bad man, the exact difference between you and the niggers he used to drive before the war was the color of your skins, that was all. . . ."

Fancy could see them nodding, as Court touched their deepest fear.

"That's what this mill is for, folks. No more depending on the weather, praying there won't be a drought, that it won't rain too much, that the Savannah'll behave itself and not sweep you clean away. No more hoping that you'll make enough bales to pay off the debts and have a little something left over besides. Every week now, you're going to have cash money in your jeans—money to buy food, and clothes—to call the doctor if your folks get sick, money to lay aside for your old age. More money than any of you have ever seen.

"This mill doesn't belong to me. Not alone. It belongs to you—all of you. Now let's see what you'll make of it!"

He sat down then, and Fancy caught his hand and squeezed it hard, and all the mill workers stood up and cheered him so loud that Fancy couldn't even hear herself think.

All the barbecue was gone by now, and one of the storekeepers set up a row of caged turkeys, and Court pointed out a wagonload of borrowed guns. The mill workers, hill men all, could shoot. None of the turkeys got past three contestants though only the head was in sight.

Then the orchestra started up, playing the toe-tickling hill tunes. One of the oldest mill workers started calling the sets and Fancy was astonished to see that all the fine ladies danced with the sweaty, linty mill hands. She wished that she could dance because she did love dancing, but it was too late for that now. So she sat beside Tyler and watched Court dancing with the mill girls. She didn't like the way they looked at him—as if they could eat him with a silver spoon, but Court looked bored, so she felt better.

She heard Tyler swearing softly under his breath.

"And I used to be the best God-damned dancer in the State of Georgia," he said.

She laid a hand on his shoulder.

"You'll dance again, Ty," she whispered.

"No," Ty said. "No, babydoll—I'll never dance again. All I want to know is why in hellfire that Ellis bastard had to be such a rotten shot!"

"That's a wicked thing to say, Ty," she said gently. "Wicked and foolish. Dead you wouldn't have a chance. But now there's still that doctor in Scotland, and you've still got hope. . . ."

"No, Fan," Tyler said. "I haven't any hope—nary a drop. I'll be sitting here in this dangblasted wheelchair till they roll me through the pearly gates—or into bottom pits, which is a sight more likely. Don't reckon it'll be too long, neither. A man don't hang around when he ain't got nothing to cling to."

"Ty, please," Fancy began; but the whistle blew, and the music stopped. Court stood up and raised his hand.

"Go on playing!" he called. "We'll make cloth tomorrow!"

The dancing lasted until after dark. When it was over, Court got up and told his workers that they would be paid for the whole day, and they all clapped and cheered.

Even after that, when Fancy rode back with Court to Hiberion, the carriages of the important people followed them, and the party went on in the big hall until morning. The hall had been cleaned, and a few repairs had been started on it.

"It's beginning to look like its old self again," Thomas Cummings, Joe's father, said. "Tell you what, Court—suppose I send a crew of men down from my lumber yard tomorrow. Good carpenters, all of them. Fix the old place up . . ."

"I'd like to," Court said; "but every cent I have is tied up in the mill and—"

"Hell, boy," Tom Cummings boomed, "your credit's good. Pay me when you get it. Take two years—heck, take three. You're the biggest man in Augusta now; you can't go on living in this old barn."

"Thanks, Tom," Court said, "that's mighty kind of you."

Agnes and Saphira were surrounded. Agnes was flirting with all the young men, but Saph's gaze rested only on Peter Lewis' face. Fancy soon found out that neither the fact that she was Court's wife, nor her delicate condition stopped the young men from paying her compliments.

"Ma'am," young Joe Cummings was saying; "I'm plumb, downright sorry that Court saw you first. Now if it had been me . . ."

"You'd have tripped over your own big feet," Fred Walton chuckled. "One good thing, though—old Court's going to be mighty busy with that mill. So if you ever get lonesome, Mrs. Brantley, just let me know; I'd be mighty proud to squire you around town."

"You sure don't aim to live long, Fred," Nick Cohen said.

"Oh well, a short life, but a merry one, I always said," Fred laughed.

Life is going to be good now, Fancy thought. Oh yes, it's going to be good.

In the morning, she was sure of it. Because that next morning, the noise of hammering woke her up. When she looked for Court, she found that he was already gone. She put on her robe and went downstairs. The whole house was filled with carpenters. They had torn both of the rotten porches down, and were putting up new ones.

Inside the hall, other men were ripping down the last of the wallpaper, and knocking down the broken plaster. The furniture had been covered, but the floor was white with plaster dust. Two men excused themselves and went past her up the stairs and started squinting along the broken section of the balustrade, and one of them made marks upon a piece of paper.

Two others came in with a tall ladder, and began rigging a block and tackle over some scaffolding to let the damaged chandelier down to the floor. Another man was taking the broken windowpanes out one by one. It seemed to Fancy that they were tearing the house all the way down instead of building it up. But all the broken things had to be cleared away before they could start to fix things.

She went up to her room and got dressed. When she came down again Agnes was watching the work. Saphira wasn't there, because Saph didn't live at Hiberion any more. She lived with Tyler in the cottage where Court and Fancy had spent their honeymoon. She took good care of Tyler, Fancy had to give her that. A few minutes later, Jefferson Brantley came tottering down the stairs, leaning on a cane.

"Court's a good boy, Missy," he said. "What in tarnation did you say your name was?"

"Fancy," she told him.

"Fancy. Yes sir, Court's a good boy. Best of the Brantleys. Reckon he took after his maw. Never thought I'd live to see this day—never thought it. Now Hiberion's going to look like it did before the damyankees came down here and ruined everything."

"Father," Agnes said crossly, "you talk too much!"

"Why? She ain't a Yankee. She's as Southern as you are, Missy. Course she come from a poor family, but that doesn't matter." He turned to Fancy, smiling. "We'll make a Brantley out of you yet. We can do it, too. You've got the makings. Got the build and the carriage and the grace. Don't reckon Court went far wrong, marrying you. But then, us Brantleys always did pick out the best. Got a talent for horseflesh and women."

"Thank you, sir," Fancy said, laughing.

"Course I'm mighty sorry Court has to get his money by engaging in trade. No occupation for a gentleman. We Brantleys have been planters for well nigh onto two hundred years, most of it right here on this spot. Ty was the only one of my sons who was carrying on in the old tradition. Poor Ty—didn't seem to have no luck, nohow. But Court's a better man than Ty. Course he's made his mistakes. . . ."

"Father," Agnes snapped, "will you please hush!"

"Reckon I will," the old man said. "Didn't mean to hurt your feelings—Fancy. There! I got it!"

"You didn't hurt my feelings," Fancy said. Then seeing he was turning, trying to go back up the stairs, she took his arm.

"Here," she said, "let me help you."

"Thank you, daughter," the old man said, and his old eyes misted over, suddenly. "Nobody's tried to be nice to me in so long," he quavered. "Nosirreebobtail, Court didn't make no mistake in marrying you—no mistake at all. . . ." He leaned forward suddenly, until she could smell the whiskey on his breath.

"If it's a boy," he whispered loudly, "name him after me, won't you?"

"I will," Fancy promised. "And after Court, too. Courtland Jefferson Brantley—how's that?"

"Just fine," Jeff Brantley said. "Yessir—that's a mighty fine name."

For the rest of the week, when Court came home, late at night, he was too tired even to talk much. But from the few things he said, Fancy gathered that things weren't going as well as he had expected. Finally she got it out of him.

"It's the damned climate," he said. "I thought it would be an advantage, Fan; but it isn't. There's so blamed much static electricity in the air that the yarn breaks if you look at it hard. I'll have to go down and see old man Phinizy tomorrow."

"Why, Court?"

"We'll have to put in humidifiers to moisten the air. You'd think that in a river valley it would be wet enough, but it isn't. And that won't be good for the workers."

"You mean the dampness will make them sick?" Fancy said.

"Damned right it will; but what choice have I?"

"But Court—they're humans, just like us. Some of 'em are little children!"

"I know, I know! But Fan, they were starving before the mill came. It's a choice of evils. I'll have to hire a company doctor to take care of them. Not all of them will get sick, and even so, it's better than starving the way they used to."

"Reckon you're right," Fancy sighed; "but it's a pity—isn't it?"

"Yep. But the point that's worrying me right now is the fact that I'll have to borrow more money. That's why I'll have to see Mr. Phinizy."

"He'll lend it to you, won't he, Court?"

"Sure. There's no doubt of that. He's a mighty fine man. But what's worrying me is having to pay it back."

"You'll do it, Court," Fancy said; "I just know you will."

Court's lips brushed her cheek, and he was gone. Fancy stood there staring after him. He didn't used to kiss me like that, she thought.

She didn't go upstairs again, but stood in the hall looking at the repairs the workmen had already made. There was so much more to be done, but already she could see how it was going to be. It made her feel good all over just to look at it. She was going to live in a house now, the kind of a house that she had dreamed of.

She turned at last to go up the stairs, but before she reached them she heard the sound of high heels. So she came back toward the door, thinking that it was Saphira, and she was glad. She liked Saph. But in the doorway she stopped. It wasn't Saphira.

It was Fern.

"Mind if I come in?" Fern said. "No, don't answer that. You've an uncomfortable habit of telling the truth. And I shall come in for a moment. Is Court here?"

"No," Fancy said.

"Too bad. I did so want to see him. I hear he's done it—built his mill and all. I wanted to congratulate him."

"That wasn't all you wanted," Fancy said.

"How true," Fern sighed. "And I always do get what I want, did you know that? But don't worry, I'm very patient. I can wait—for years."

"You'll have a long wait," Fancy said. "Too long, to my way of thinking."

"Who cares about your way of thinking—Mrs. Brantley. I suppose I have to call you that. It has a singularly ill-fitting sound—applied to you."

"Don't you think you're wasting your time?" Fancy said quietly. "My mother always told me—see nothing, say nothing. And dirt is still dirt even when it's all dressed up and speaking proper. Appears to me you'd look a mighty heap better in folks' eyes if you'd go and take care of your own husband—who needs you."

"Thanks for the sermon," Fern said, and stepped past her into the hall. She looked around her, seeing the scaffolding, and the partially completed repairs. Her brown eyes lighted.

"Hiberion restored," she exclaimed. "You know, Fan, I've dreamed of this. Only it was I who lived here in those dreams, not you."

She turned and looked at Fancy, seeing her in the light of the gas-lights clearly for the first time.

"My God!" she whispered.

"Yes," Fancy said, "I'm going to have a child—his child. Now how long do you think you're going to have to wait, Fern Brantley?"

"Too long," Fern said. "I'm afraid you've won. The Brantleys have great pride of family. They might betray their wives with a casual light o' love—but not one of them has ever left the mother of his sons. I congratulate you. I didn't believe it was possible. Now if you'll be so good as to tell me where Ty is . . ."

"I'll do better than that," Fancy said; "I'll drive you over there."

"But you're in no condition to—"

"Don't worry about my condition, Fern. I'm white trash from the Carolina hills, remember. We have our babies and go on plowing. Come on."

"Even so," Fern said as they walked toward the stables, "I don't see why you're putting yourself out this way—for me."

"I'm not putting myself out. This is going to be plumb, downright interesting. Reckon I've got a hankering to hear what Ty says when he sees you."

"I can imagine," Fern laughed, "that he won't be overly polite. But why should that amuse you, when it isn't going to bother me in the least?"

"We'll see," Fancy said.

When they reached the cottage, Tyler was shaving. He looked at Fern and closed the razor, taking a long time about it. Then he laid it very carefully on the washstand, although one half of his face was still covered with lather. Saphira stood up and stared at them, but she didn't say anything either.

" 'Lo, Ty," Fern said.

"Get out of here," Tyler said. He didn't raise his voice.

"No, Ty," Fern said; "I've come—home."

"I said—get out."

"But, Ty," Fern said, "you need me now. You can't expect Saph to—"

"When I was a man," Tyler said, "I needed you. Now I don't. I don't need anybody but the sexton to toll the bell, and the Reverend Mister Wittly to say a prayer. I don't want you now. I hate the sight of you. Looking at you makes me sick—puking sick. Now will you go?"

"No," Fern said.

"I reckon you won't," Tyler said. "It gives you a delicious tingle way down in your little pink guts to see me here crippled—less than half a man, doesn't it? And you won't go back to Boston. That would take you too far away from my precious brother. You little witch. Don't you see you haven't a chance now? Court's a fool, all right. Before you might have been able to steal him away from the sweetest, best little gal who ever drew breath—the Brantleys have always been weak in that direction. But do you think you can steal him from his son? I ask you, Fern—do you think that?"

"No," Fern replied almost inaudibly. "No, Ty—I don't think that."

"Good. Stay in Augusta if you want to. But not here. Being hanged would be a blessing to me—a whole lot better than sitting here rotting. And if you stayed here, you couldn't sleep. You wouldn't—dare."

"All right, Ty," Fern said, "if that's the way you want it."

"That's the way I want it," Tyler said.

That month of August was one long nightmare to Court Brantley. Nothing seemed to go right. There was too much time and labor lost because the raw cotton did not flow smoothly enough from bale to finished cloth. There were still too many trucking operations, and the loss in unsalvageable lint was high. So Court shut down parts of the mill for a few days at a time, and changed things. He moved the openers, breakers, intermediate and finisher pickers into the carding room and connected them to the big carding machines by a shute; then he had a hole knocked in the wall between the carding machine and the drawing equipment, and fed the cleaned fiber slivers into the drawers mechanically; but the combs stopped him—as they were used only for the very finest fabrics. He worried over that problem for a week, but finally had to content himself with a v-shaped conveyor line into the roving, spinning, spooling, twisting, warping and slashing processes. He set up an endless smooth-flowing chain movement on the last three processes, warp drawing, mercerization and weaving, and last of all he reorganized the cloth room where the finished bolts were prepared for shipment.

By the time he was through, the whole month was spent; but the work served its purpose: the mill produced a quarter more fabric than it was designed for, and the supposedly undiminishable material losses were cut a full five percent. And Court had done another thing, too: he had kept himself from thinking throughout the more than twenty days that Fern, his brother's wife, waited for him every night outside the gate. Those hour-long rides with her were something he didn't like to think about. He was all Brantley, and Fern was lovely; but there was Fancy at home waiting to bear his son. That stopped him. Nothing else could have.

Still it wasn't a good thing to ride with her night after night down by the river where the willows were and the water went by murmuring. When the moon pulled itself loose from the river, and the silver spilled down, and the wind talked in dark voices, what could he say to her? What were the words?

I want you I need you I love you. But not spoken. I always have I always will and what has happened is an ugliness but it's a strong

223

thing and I cannot break it. It is flesh of me now blood of my blood bone of bone my big dreams and all the far, sweet hungers. It's a woman waiting. A good woman, true to me, in whom I can find no blame. A woman who loves me needs my love, who deserves a better man than I. The mother of my son to be, Fern, and that's a strong thing. A woman whom I ought to love but cannot (but only because of you because of you) and all the oft-mouthed words—honor, faith, decency—meaning nothing, Fern, meaning everything. I can't say them, don't know what they mean, they have departed from the house of my fathers and all that is left is I cannot because there will be a son of my loins and that is stronger than this—than even this. . . .

But all he said was, gruffly:

"Come on, we've been out long enough."

And all Fern said was:

"All right, darling—whatever you say."

Meekly.

He came home that night of August 31st and lay beside Fan in the dark a long time before he went to sleep. And even when he did sleep, hands caught hold of him and shook him. They were very big hands and they didn't have any arms or face or body. They held on to him very tight and shook him so that every bone in his body rattled. Then he heard Fancy scream.

"Court!" she cried. "Court! Wake up! Oh—Court—the house—the house!"

He sat up in bed and the hands let go of him.

"What's the matter with the house?" he said.

"I—I think—it—it's falling down!" Fancy said.

"You're dreaming," Court said; but there was the enormous shaking again and the pictures fell down from the walls and the bricks came down from the chimney and hit the roof and it was still again so that he could hear his own breathing, then one more brick fell.

"Come on," he said. "We'd better get out of here!"

They went down the stairs very fast but when they were halfway down it started again and the windows crashed in and there was the smashed tinkle of broken glass and the big door slammed open without anybody's touching it. Court pulled Fancy away from the house, seeing the shapes of the trees bending far over as though there were a hurricane but there wasn't any wind. Then one of the biggest broke in half and came down making a noise like thunder. Behind the house in the quarters, they could hear the Negroes screaming, then the horses started screaming too, and there is no sound anywhere worse than that. It stopped, then started again. Court pulled Fancy further away from the house but he had to stop because the ground at their feet opened up in a wide chasm, so deep it had no bottom; then it closed up again and they couldn't even see where it was.

"Court!" Fancy cried. "Your father!"

Court started running back toward the house, his dressing gown flapping about his long legs. Fancy stood there looking after him, hearing the Negroes screaming, and watching Hiberion sway from side to side and inside glass breaking and the booming noise from underneath the ground.

She was standing there like that when she felt the first pang. She sat down at once, waiting. She remembered that Maw had said that after the first one it took hours, sometimes all night, so she didn't worry about that part of it. She was too busy worrying about Court.

Then she saw him coming out of the house with Jeff Brantley in his arms, and when they were close she could hear the old man shouting:

"What's the matter with you, boy? Here I was sleeping the sleep of the just and you come a-busting in and snatch me out of my bed like a wild man! You drunk, Court? You must be! Look not upon the wine when it is red. . . ."

Then it stopped, and Fancy started to laugh. She didn't know why she laughed. She felt more like crying.

But she knew that Maw was wrong, because the pangs hadn't stopped, they were coming quicker now, and she tried to time them, and then she was scared. Because they weren't fifteen minutes apart like Maw had said, nor even ten, nor five. They were coming one after the other.

"Court," she said, "you better get Doc Brewster. I—I think it's coming."

Court stared at her.

"What's coming?" he said.

"The baby. Oh, Court, hurry! It's coming soon!"

Court started off, and the minute he left the house, the ground started to shake again. He ran through the streets toward the doctor's house, dodging the bricks from falling chimneys, and jumping over the rubble where whole walls had fallen down. When he got to Broad Street, he saw that people had left their houses and were putting up tents in the middle of the street. He heard voices:

"Worst quake in the history of the State!"

"The hospital's overflowing—don't know how many's dead. . . ."

"Tell me the colored folks have started a prayer meeting in the middle of the Terry. They aim to keep it up all night!"

"Damned if I blame 'em!"

"I'd say a prayer myself—if I knew a prayer. . . ."

Court Brantley was saying a prayer as he ran. He didn't need to know one. It just came.

But he couldn't find Doc Brewster. Doc was far too busy. He was treating the injured, riding through the broken streets, giving help where it was needed.

Just before morning, it started to rain. The sky opened up and the rain came down in sheets. Court trudged through the mud back to Hiberion, afraid to look, afraid even to ask; but when he got there, Fancy was lying under one of the trees with the child in her arms. She was wrapped in three blankets.

"Aunt Matilda helped me," she whispered. Then she started to cry.

"Oh, Court," she sobbed; "it—it's a—girl!"

Court bent down and pushed back the blanket and gazed at the tiny wrinkled ugly thing Fancy held. It had a button for a nose, and its eyes were shut tight so he couldn't see them. But its mouth was like a rosebud, and its head was covered all over with long, soft curling black hair. Like Fancy's. Even then he knew his daughter was going to be beautiful. He felt something come loose inside of him, and he was filled with something like singing. He leaned forward and kissed Fancy's mouth. She opened her blue eyes and stared at him.

"I'm glad," he said. "She's just like you. God, baby, I'm glad!"

Fancy stared at him unbelievingly. Then very slowly she smiled.

"The next one will be a boy, honey," she whispered; "I promise you."

"And the one after that?" Court teased.

"Whatever you want, darling," Fancy said.

13

It was a good thing, Fancy saw, that the men hadn't got any further with the repairs to Hiberion. Because now, they were going to have to do them all over again and more besides. She was lying on a couch in the hall, because Court didn't want her taken upstairs until he was sure that the house hadn't been weakened by the earthquake. The Negroes were cleaning up, and Lynne lay beside her, sleeping peacefully. Every minute or two Fancy would pull back the blankets and look at her.

So little and so sweet. There are a lot of ugly things in life, Fancy thought, but a lot of beautiful things too. This was one of the beautiful things. Of course Court teased about the baby's being red and wrinkled and ugly, but Fancy couldn't see that. She was sure that she had never seen anything quite so lovely.

She heard Court's booted feet on the half finished porch. He came through the door, his arms filled with flowers.

"How nice!" Fancy said, "are they for me?"

"Course not," Court laughed. "They're for my little sweetheart

there. You play second fiddle in this house from now on, Mrs. B."
Then he bent down and kissed her.

Aunt Matilda took the flowers and went to look for a vase. It took
her a long time to find one that wasn't broken. Court sat on a chair
beside the couch and poked at the baby's tiny hands with his finger,
trying to make her grab it, until Lynne woke up and howled.

"She's a Brantley all right," Court grinned. "Noisy little beggar,
isn't she?"

"Court," Fancy said, "what about the mill?"

"It was untouched," Court said. "Apparently the quake didn't
extend that far."

"Thank goodness," Fancy said.

Court sat there looking at the baby and grinning. Fancy thought
he looked right foolish, but she reckoned that all new fathers looked
that way.

Court stood up finally.

"I have to be getting back," he said. "The mill's going full blast,
Fan. We won't even miss a day's production."

He was bending down to kiss her good-bye when they heard the
sound of high-heeled slippers clattering up the porch steps and
Saphira came into the house.

"Thank God you're here!" she said. "Oh, Court—you've got to
come at once!"

"Where?" Court said. "What's this all about, Saph?"

"Ty," Saph whispered. "Half of the house fell in last night. He
wasn't hurt, but I couldn't move him. Everybody was so scared I
couldn't even get help. . . . And this morning early it rained
so. . . ."

"Is he sick?" Court said.

"Terribly. He's got to be moved up here. That house is dangerous
and he's burning up with fever and. . . ."

Court turned to one of the Negroes.

"Tell Ernest to hitch up the carriage," he said.

It wasn't until then that Saphira saw Fancy lying on the couch.
She came up to her at once, and when she was close, Fancy lifted the
baby up so that Saph could see her.

"Oh no, Fan!" Saphira said. "Don't tell me! When?"

"Last night," Court grinned. "Didn't you hear the celebration? We kind of shook up this town, I'm told."

"Oh let me take him! He's beautiful! Oh, Fan, you darling, I'm so happy I'm going to cry. . . ."

"It is not a him," Fan said sadly. "It's a girl, Saph. I called her Lynne."

Saphira stopped and stared at her, then she smiled broadly.

"Good!" she said. "There's been too blamed many Brantley males now. Come to Auntie, Lynne, and let's start showing the world what a female Brantley can do."

"Saph," Fancy whispered, "what about Ty?"

"He's very sick," Saphira said, "and the awful thing about it is—he—he's glad of it, Fan. . . ."

"Does she know?" Fancy said.

"No. He won't let me send for her. Fan, I'm scared. I don't like the way Ty looks. It's a dreadful thing to want to die."

"We'll snap him out of that," Court said. "Here's Ernest now. Come on, Saph, we'd better go get him now. We'll pick up Doc Brewster on the way."

Two hours later when they came back with Tyler, two of the Negroes had to carry him into the house and upstairs to bed. When they passed the couch where Fancy lay, she could see his face. Then she was sure.

"Why," she said aloud so that the sound of her own voice startled her a little, "he's going to die."

Hearing her say that, Court stared at her, and Fancy could see that he knew it too. There was no doubt of it; Tyler Brantley was dying.

Doc Brewster came down the stairs looking a little sick himself.

"Doc," Fancy whispered, "is there any hope?"

"None," Doc Brewster snapped. "Ty's a strong man, and even in his present condition he ought to make it. But he won't. He won't because he doesn't want to. I've seen cases like this before. And every time I meet up with a new one, I say the same thing. I swear I'm going to quit practicing medicine and take up planting!"

"But you never do," Fancy said.

"No," Doc Brewster said; "I never do. Now I reckon I'd better check up on you and the little lady."

There were times during the next five days when they began to

229

hope. But when Tyler started to go, he sank very quickly. Fancy saw Court tearing through the hall on his way to get the doctor. He didn't say anything to her, but she knew. So, although she wasn't supposed to, she got up and went up the stairs.

Tyler looked at her out of eyes that burned like lights in the sockets of his skull.

"Fan," he said, "babydoll."

Then he made a grimace that she knew was meant for a smile.

"Ty," Fancy said, "please try. We all love you so. For us, please try. If you don't, we'll never feel right again. . . ."

"Fern," Tyler said. "Get Fern."

"All right, Ty," Fancy said.

She sent one of the Negroes over to the boarding house where Fern was staying. Fern came at once. She got there only a little after the doctor, himself.

Doc Brewster took one look.

"Pneumonia," he said. "He hasn't got a chance."

In the doorway Agnes and Saphira started to cry, and Court's face was hurt ugly. But Fern Brantley didn't cry. She just stood there, looking at her husband.

My God, Fancy thought, how can she . . . ? But then she saw that Tyler was trying to force himself up on his elbows. Doc Brewster tried to push him back, but he couldn't. Even dying, Tyler was too strong.

"Fern," he said, "Fern."

"I'm here, Ty," Fern said.

"Loved you," Tyler said. "So much. You left me. All right. Just want to tell you one thing. . . ." His mouth opened, gulping at the air. It wasn't a pleasant thing to watch. Then his voice came back. When it did, it was clear and strong.

"You're going to see hell, Fern," he said.

Then he died. Like that. Like someone turning off a light. It was so quick that none of them knew it except Fancy. She was watching his eyes. She saw them stop burning, dim. She walked with quick, jerky steps over to the bed. Then she sank down and pillowed her face against the covers.

Behind her, Agnes started to scream, but the sound of it was cut off suddenly, as Saphira brought her hand hard across her sister's mouth. Fancy turned her face so that she could see Fern.

Fern hadn't moved. But all the color had gone out of her face. Even her lips were white. Then without saying anything at all, she turned and went out of the room. Fancy could hear her footsteps going down the stairs. The front door slammed, then there was the whirr of wheels on the drive.

Court knelt down beside Fancy and put an arm across her shoulders.

"Poor Ty," he whispered.

"He was a good man," Fancy said.

They buried Tyler Brantley among his ancestors in Magnolia Cemetery. All the Brantleys were there, and they wept for him. All the Brantleys except one—the one to whom he had given his name. For Fern had taken the train for Boston the same night that he died.

Going back from the cemetery to Hiberion, Court tried not to think of her. He tried very hard and very sincerely. But all the way back to Hiberion, one thing echoed through his mind like a refrain:

She's free now. Fern is free. . . .

14

The earthquake, actually, hadn't done too much damage. It was centered near Charleston and the shocks that had struck Augusta had been relatively weak. A few citizens had been hit by falling bricks, or cut by flying glass. Nobody had been killed. But many buildings had to be torn down as a result of it, and the topography of the whole region changed. The Sandhill rose many feet, and the downtown district of Augusta dropped, so that afterwards, buildings in the lower section of the city that had never been visible before could be seen from the hill. Of course, it did cause a few deaths, indirectly, Tyler Brantley's, for instance.

All that winter the work went on at Hiberion. By spring it was finished and the gardeners started landscaping. Fancy took an active interest in this, because she had her own ideas how she wanted the place to look.

Court was too busy at the mill to pay much attention to the house. All the advantages he had thought would come from having the mill located close to the cotton fields proved in practice to be no advantages at all. The differential in freight rates that Northern railroad owners saddled on the South, canceled out the advantage of being close to the cotton. The high static electricity in the air forced him to install expensive humidifiers, and the climate, which he had boasted of to Stan Woodbury, was so depressing to human spirits that his workers turned out to be less than half as productive as the Yankee mill workers he had known. Yet, he made a profit. The wages he paid his hands—wages no better and no worse than those paid by the rest of the Southern mill owners—made that certain. Court didn't feel bad about it. He was a man of his times. Grover Cleveland sat in the White House, ready to use the bayonet upon men who struck for better wages, and the people of Court's native Georgia were getting ready to elect John Gordon, of the famous triumvirate, to the governor's chair, knowing that he had gotten rich from his share of farming out convict labor. And bad as the wages were that Court paid his people, they were better than they had ever had before. No, Court didn't feel bad; he felt like a philanthropist.

It was April of 1887 when they finished the restoration of Hiberion. By early June, the gardens were done too. From her window, Fancy could see nearly all of it. She glanced quickly at Lynne, sleeping like a cherub in the wicker crib beside the big bed. Lynne was so beautiful. She had Fancy's black hair and blue eyes, but the expression in them reminded Fancy of Court. Looking at her, Fancy fairly ached to pick her up; but she did not. It was much better for the child to sleep.

She turned once more to the window, looking toward the river where the willows were. They reminded her of women washing their long hair in the water. Outside on the lawns the sunlight dappled with leaf shade lay along the moist green of the grass. Fancy let her gaze wander over the formal garden with its winding brick walks, broken into different levels, connected by low steps. There were fountains down there now, flashing in the sunlight. There was also a little garden house in the Japanese style, built of diagonal lattices with a pagoda roof. Fancy loved her garden house. It was very cool there, and she could sit and watch the little cherubs mounted on stone dolphins out of whose mouths the water arched into the gold-fish pool. There were water lilies and hyacinths in that pool and the fish were so tame that they came up and nibbled at her fingers when she trailed them in the water.

She got up from the window and started out of the room. She wanted to go out into the garden now, and stand again to look at Hiberion under the trees. Then she decided that she'd better take a parasol, because it was already hot. She turned and hurried to her closet without even pausing to look at the blue wallpaper with the silver fleurs-de-lis in it. All the furniture in her room was Louis Fourteenth—delicate and fine, brushed very thinly with white so that the gilt underneath showed through. There was a crystal chandelier in the ceiling, a copy of the one in the big hall, but much smaller of course, and the pictures on the wall and her mirror had massive frames of the same rococo white and gilt.

She had picked out the decorations herself, which had surprised everybody because she wasn't supposed to know about such things. She didn't know really, but since the mill had become a going concern, a great many doors had been opened to her, and she had copied everything that she liked best in the houses of the wealthy people.

Her blue and white and gold room became her, but Court was a little out of place in it. He didn't complain, because he had his own retreat in the library on the second floor. It was paneled in dark oak, and had a rack for Court's assortment of fine guns, and another rack for the pipes he had taken to smoking. Fancy hated those pipes. Not only were they smelly, but she had heard Fern say once during those terrible five days while they were trying to keep Tyler alive, "I love to see a man smoke a pipe—especially a tall man. They're so becoming. . . ." And a couple of months later, Court had taken up pipe smoking.

The library was crowded from floor to ceiling with books. Although Lynne kept her busy, Fancy had read many of them. Some of them she didn't understand, but she was beginning to. She had found Shakespeare hard going, but Court had read some of it aloud to her, and she had caught the lovely music of the poetry—deep-voiced and strong, like the sea, and after that, whenever she didn't quite understand a passage, she tried reading it aloud. It nearly always helped. The Bible and Shakespeare were her favorites. She was slowly working her way into other books as well, and without her even knowing it, the books were changing her. By great effort, she had mended her speech to the extent that it was now usually more precise than Court's, although she didn't have half his vocabulary.

She went down the stairs. As she came down the staircase that spiraled down into the big hall without anything holding it up that a person could see, she could see Court in the dining salon, having breakfast with Governor Gordon. The governor had come last night with several members of his staff. They were, Fancy knew, only a few of the hundreds of guests that would fill up the great hall tonight. There was going to be a reception in honor of Agnes and Saphira and their new husbands. The girls were getting married this morning—both of them.

The breakfast was being served, Fancy saw, not on the big banquet table, but on the smaller one that had a revolving circular leaf in the middle, so that if anybody wanted anything, all he had to do was to give the leaf a whirl and the dish he wanted would fly around in front of him. And there was plenty of food on it—too much to Fancy's way of thinking. There was oatmeal and bacon and eggs, or ham and eggs, if a guest would rather have that. At the moment, the governor was almost hidden behind a stack of buckwheat cakes soaking in butter and syrup, while a pile of biscuits stood smoking on a platter beside him. The servants ran back and forth between the dining hall and the kitchen, keeping the plates filled. But those senators and lawyers were emptying them almost as fast as they were being filled up.

Court wasn't eating much—as usual. He never ate much, Fancy knew that. He sat there talking to his guests, with a big cup of scalding coffee in his hand; but the slice of smoked ham and the one thin pancake on his plate went untouched.

He'll never get fat, Fancy thought. That's good; I hate fat men.

While she was standing there on the stairs, watching them, a servant came in with a stack of letters. Court put them aside, barely looking at them and went on talking. But he glanced at the top one and something about it made him frown. He picked it up, and looked at the writing. Then he said something to the others—an excuse, Fancy thought, and opened it. He read it quickly, and even from where she stood, Fancy could see his face change.

But only for a moment. It was so quick that she thought she was imagining things, and tiptoed on down the stair and out onto the veranda. It was cool and white and there was no way that anybody could tell that it hadn't been built along with the rest of the house.

235

Fancy stood there, looking up at the graceful Doric columns, then she went out into the front yard where the rose bushes were, and stood by the bird bath looking back at Hiberion.

It was something now. Really something. Just like it had been—only better. For the gardens were finer than the original ones. Court had hired an Italian landscape artist, whom Stanton Woodbury had recommended, to do them.

"Yep," old Jeff Brantley said; "Hiberion wasn't this pretty before. Court's outdone us. It's kind of different, but I like it."

As she walked toward the gardens, she could see that even the out-buildings were finer than many a house that the quality of Augusta lived in. Then she went down the first of the low steps and took her seat in the pagoda-roofed garden house and looked out across the pool on the side view of Hiberion.

She loved Hiberion now. It was the kind of house that she had dreamed of. Only it was more than she had dreamed of because she hadn't been able to imagine anything like this. She thought about the girls, and made a face. She didn't care much for the men they were marrying. Both Thomas Wilson, Agnes' fiance, and Joseph Plainfield, whom Saphira was marrying, seemed a little too sharp to her. They had both jumped at the high-paid jobs Court had offered them in the mill. Tom Wilson was the worse of the two. Joe wasn't so bad. Fancy thought that she might even learn to like him eventually.

She got up after a while and came back to Hiberion. There was so much to do. Most of it could be done without her help, but tonight had to be just perfect—for Court's sake. This reception for the girls was going to put him back where he belonged—right on top of the heap. Everybody was coming. They said that Court could deliver the vote of all of Richmond County through his mill workers. In a close election, that meant he could actually see to it that the man he wanted sat in the governor's chair. And Georgia elections were pretty nearly always close. People were saying that he was the richest man in the State, which wasn't so, because rebuilding Hiberion and improving the mill, and paying the interest and part of the principal on the debt had left them with precious little money. Enough to make the show that was expected of them—but not much more. Next year it would be better, and the year after that and all the coming years would be better and better until finally they would be as rich as people thought they were now. But Fancy knew it was a good thing for them to think so—Court could get the loans he needed, and the help of people who wouldn't lift a finger if they knew how things really were. . . .

Fancy made her way into the kitchen where the regular cook, Tildy Mae, and a crew of five more, hired especially for the occasion, were already hard at work. The baking was being done now, the pound and raisin cakes, as yellow as old gold with thick dark crusts were coming out of the oven. Tildy Mae was busily stirring the chocolate frosting for the chocolate layer cakes, and another girl was making a snowy covering of confectioner's sugar, egg whites and shredded coconut for others. Pies cooled on all the window sills and half grown black boys took turns at the cranks of the ice cream churns. Once the ice cream was hard, it would be packed in ice and rock salt and taken out to the spring house to stay frozen until tonight.

The other foods, the ones that had to be served hot, would have to wait until after the guests came, but the scalding, plucking, and cleaning of plump frying chickens filled the back porch with steamy, unpleasant odors. Boys ran back and forth to the smokehouse and came back laden with hams, many of which were rejected by Tildy Mae after one contemptuous glance. Potatoes were being peeled, and the yams were already being boiled into softness. Tonight they would be candied, and come out a golden-brown, silvered over with a rich crust of sugar, and dotted with spices. Bottles of wine were being brought up from the wine cellar and hurried down to the spring house to cool in the cold water. Later they would be thrust neck down into the buckets of ice that Jonas was busily cracking on the back porch, while the delivery wagon from the Augusta Ice Company unloaded still more cakes.

"Anything I can do?" she asked Tildy Mae, timidly.

Tildy Mae gave her a look that was only a little short of a glare. All black house servants were a little arrogant, and the cooks were the worst of the lot. And their snobbery was colossal and complete. Everybody else in Augusta might forget that Mrs. Courtland Brantley wasn't really 'quality'; but Tildy Mae wouldn't forget it. And she wouldn't let the rest of the Negroes forget it either. Only Matilda,

Lynne's nurse, was immune to her influence. As for the rest, Fancy had to call twice to get an answer; to be sternly demanding to get any kind of service at all. If it hadn't been for Matilda and Belle and her children, Fancy might have developed the same feelings about Negroes that everybody else had. But they, and her own good heart prevented that.

"No'm," Tildy Mae said sullenly. "Just get yourself all hot 'n' bothered in here, Ma'am. You go rest and 'tend to your dressing—I'll take care of things down here."

"All right, Tildy," Fancy said; "but see that it's done right."

As she left the kitchen, she pretended not to hear Tildy swearing under her breath.

She went back out into the garden and got Moses to cut the flowers for the tables and mantels. Then she went back upstairs and bathed, and started dressing. It was almost time for the wedding. When Court came into the bedroom, she was already dressed, and Candy, her maid, was putting the finishing touches to her hair. Candy had drawn it back from her ears and curled it into a bunch of soft, cascading curls down the back. These were held tightly close to their roots by a small, light blue ribbon, and Candy at the moment was fluffing the front of her hair into bangs, which lightly shadowed her forehead. She had a string of pearls around her neck, and two big pearls set in her earrings. Her dress was light-blue silk, cut low and square across the bodice, and edged there with shimmering white lace. The same kind of white lace was made into an outer skirt that covered but didn't hide the blue silk skirt beneath it and was tied in an enormous lace bow above the bustle. Her slippers were a darker blue, and her soft kid gloves that went up above her elbows a delicate off-white.

Court stood there, staring at her.

"You're lovely," he said. "Blue becomes you."

"Thanks, honey," Fancy said. Then to Candy: "You may go now."

Court sat down tiredly and felt the bristles of his beard.

"Damned lot of trouble," he said. "I'll have to shave again."

"We couldn't do any less for the girls," Fancy said. "Go on and shave and I'll help you get ready."

She went out to the upstairs hall closet and got his dress suit. When she came back, Court was burning something in the grate.

238

"What's that?" Fancy said.

"Nothing that concerns you," Court said flatly. "All this rigmarole because the gals are getting hitched. . . ."

While he was in the bathroom, Fancy laid out his dress suit. It was jet black with an even blacker silk braid running down the sides of his trousers. The trousers fitted very tightly, but thin though Court was, he had well-shaped legs. Fancy was glad of that. She didn't want him to make a poor appearance. The lapels of the jacket were of quilted black satin, and the stiff-bosom shirt was made of the finest kind of linen. Fancy laid the white piqué bow tie and the high, stiff winged collar and the stiffer cuffs on top of the shirt. Then she opened the little plush-lined box containing his diamond studs and cuff links.

He'll look so nice, she thought, as she put out his black silk socks and the patent-leather pumps with the black grosgrain bows on them.

"Oh, bother!" she said as she saw the jacket of his business suit lying in a heap where it had fallen from the back of the chair where Court had tossed it. She bent and picked it up and as she did so, her gaze fell on the grate. Whatever it was that Court had been burning had gone out, and it hadn't burned all the way up. She picked it up quickly and saw that it was part of an envelope. There was no letter in it. When she looked again, she saw that Court had burned the letter separately from the envelope, and that it was gone—only a heap of gray-white ash was left to tell where it had been.

She bent over the ash, seeing the words, "My own darling—" on the very top where the good rag paper had hung together in spite of the burning. Then she made the mistake of touching it, and it went to pieces so that she was left only with the piece of the envelope in her hand. The postmark hadn't burned. It said, "Boston, Massachusetts, June 10, 1887." And in the corner that was burned a part of a name was left: ". . . . tley," it said. She knew what it was then: Brantley. Fern Brantley.

She felt sick. So sick she had to sit down. Then she heard Court coming out of the bathroom, and got up quickly.

"What's the matter, Fan?" he said. "You look like something's bothering you."

"No," Fancy lied. "It's nothing, Court. I—I guess I'm just nervous, that's all. All these important people coming and . . ."

"Don't let it fret you, hon," Court said. "Come on, now—help me into my monkey suit."

A few minutes later, Fan gave a last pat to his bow tie and stepped back to look at him. He looks like a prince, she thought. My prince, mine. And nobody in the whole wide world is going to . . .

"Well, Fan," Court said gravely, "how do I look?"

"Beautiful," Fancy breathed.

"Beautiful?" Court said. "That's a funny word to use about a man."

"But you do," Fancy said; "you look beautiful, Court—just too beautiful for words. . . ."

Court looked at her. She was crying.

"Now what in hellfire ails you?" he said.

"I'm scared," she wept. "Oh, Court, honey, I'm scared stiff!"

"Don't be," Court said gently. "You've changed, Fan. Now you can hold your own with any of them. You can talk as nice, and you're a hell of a lot prettier and . . ."

"I'm not afraid of them," Fancy sobbed. "I'm scared of losing you!"

"Hell, baby, you couldn't give me away. Besides why are you scared of losing me all of a sudden?"

"You're so handsome. And all of those women are in love with you and you really don't love me, and besides you wanted a son instead of a daughter and . . ."

"Stop it!" Court roared. "You'll be a mess." He caught her by the shoulders, hard. "Fan," he said, "look at me."

She turned her face back toward him.

"There's time for a son. We're both young yet. So don't think about it now. And I'm not going to leave you—not ever."

Fancy looked at him. Her blue eyes were very clear.

"Not even—for Fern?" she said.

Court stood very still for a long, long time. Fancy could hear the clock on the mantel ticking. The sound of it filled the room.

"Not even for Fern," he said. Then he walked away from her to the door. "You come down as soon as you can," he said.

Fancy didn't remember a thing about the wedding afterwards. She seemed to be watching, but her eyes were shut off from her mind. After it was over, she told Court she had a headache, which was the truth, and went upstairs and lay down until it was nearly time for the reception.

Then she dressed again in another dress, all white, and came down the stairs. The big hall was crowded with people and snatches of talk came up to her.

"Yes sir! Cleveland's a good man! Honest as they come. I thought that scandal about the kid had finished him, but he came back fighting. Sure has made us one damned fine President—sure has. . . ."

"They say that Court's the power behind General Gordon. I wouldn't know, but . . ."

"And his wife, my dear—have you seen her? A nobody from Carolina! With all the nice, sweet girls we have here, you'd have thought he'd . . ."

"Laid the cornerstone two years ago under McDaniels; and believe it or not, Tom, the last time I was in Atlanta the building was damn near completed. It's the finest capitol building in the nation, sir—not even excluding Washington! I tell you the State of Georgia is progressing like nobody's business!"

"Well, now, John Gordon has been mixed up in a few shady deals—like that business of farming out convict labor. But on the other hand, who started the Georgia School of Technology, and the Georgia Normal and Industrial College? Got us a Federal grant for the Agricultural Experimental Station; those things aren't to be sneezed at, I say. . . ."

"Progress—that's what it is, boy—progress. Never will forget the day they turned on them newfangled electric lights atop of Big Steve on the corner of Greene and Jackson Streets. And the other day I talked to a man clear 'cross town—called him by telephone from Oertel's Drugstore. No sir, not even New York's going to outdo us down here in Augusta. . . ."

"Now it depends on how you look at it. Maybe education does make niggers uppity. But that there Paine Institute has been running all of four years now and a more quiet, orderly set of young niggers you'd never hope to see. . . ."

"And my dear, the minute Court got his hands on some money—these fellows rushed right in and married those two! If it hadn't been for Court, those two faded wrecks would be old maids today. . . ."

"There he is now! Oh, Sarah, isn't he the darlingest thing!"

Yes, Fancy thought, there he is. And he is the darlingest thing. But he's mine. Don't forget that. Don't any of you uppity females forget that.

Then she moved through the crowd and took Court's arm.

"So here you are," Court said. "I was getting worried about you, hon. Gentlemen, allow me to present my wife."

Fancy could hear the talk dying. All over the hall it died. And one by one they turned to look at her. Many of them had seen her before —at Court's trial. But many of them had not. And they, the ones who had never seen her before tonight, had the funniest expressions on their faces. Fancy thought that they looked stricken.

"Why," a whisper came over to her, "she *is* pretty! I'd heard she was, but I never would have believed it!"

And a man's snort, answering.

"Pretty, hell! That there girl is beautiful."

She could see the women looking at her dress, as if they were memorizing it. Tomorrow, she thought, they'll be telling each other what I had on, right down to my skin. But she made herself smile when Court introduced her to them and tried to remember their names. She couldn't, though. There were just too many of them.

Then Ernest, the butler, announced that dinner was served. Fancy and Court led the guests into the big dining salon. There was too much food, and too much wine, and too many people, so that Fancy couldn't eat anything. Besides, the men kept proposing toasts to the happy couples, so that even only sipping each one to be polite, she found that her head was spinning. She wasn't having a good time. She kept remembering a pile of ashes in the bedroom grate, and a half burned-out envelope postmarked Boston .Then she looked up and caught Saphira's eye. Saph was sitting next to her Joe, but when she looked at Fancy she winked her eye. Somehow, after that, Fancy felt better. She smiled at Saph, and looked at old Jeff Brantley, sound asleep over his half filled plate, his old fingers wrapped around his empty champagne glass.

Now the Negroes were coming with the desserts, chocolate layer cake and raisin cake and sweet potato pie, and coconut cake and huge bowls of ice cream. Behind them came more waiters with a big cut-glass bowl filled with sillabub, heavy cream whipped very stiffly with sugar, and dashed with sherry.

Fancy ate a dish of ice cream and that took care of the wine. On her left, a fat woman confessed that she was 'fair about to burst.' Fancy thought she looked it.

Then the dinner was over, and the Negroes took all the tables out of the hall and the dancing started. It came to Fancy that she seldom got a chance to dance with Court. Nothing in their life together had been normal or ordinary or usual enough for that. But, now, swinging through the first waltz with him, she remembered all the times they had danced during the five years they had lived at Melody. Those had been the good years. The best. It was fun dancing with Court. He danced beautifully. So, for that matter, did she. She could see that people were stopping to watch them.

Then he bowed to her and was gone. He had to dance with the other ladies; she knew that. But every time his partner happened to be young and pretty, Fancy stiffened and missed a step. I'm being a fool, she told herself, but I can't help it.

Then Court did a funny thing. He stopped dead in the middle of a dance and stood there staring at the door. He whispered something to his partner, one of the pretty young McQuinizy girls from Savannah, and walked toward the door. Fancy looked after him. Then she, too, stopped dancing.

For Jed Hawkins stood in the doorway, looking over the gathering with a mocking grin on his face.

"You'll excuse me, won't you?" she said to her partner, and started off after Court.

When she was close, she saw that Jed wasn't dressed for the evening, and she realized suddenly that it was strange that he wasn't. That business suit he had on meant only one thing: Court hadn't invited him.

Invitations had been sent to everybody of any importance in the State. That should have included Jed. He had been a State Senator twice now. In spite of his youth, people were mentioning him as a likely prospect for the governor's chair. . . .

Thinking about it now, Fancy remembered positively that his name hadn't been on that list. She had checked it over with Court herself. She should have noticed the omission then. But when she had left Savannah, she had pushed Jed Hawkins out of her mind. And so many things had happened afterwards: Lynne's being born,

Tyler dying like that, so terribly, the mill. She realized that the thought of Jed hadn't entered her head in nearly two years. That was a good thing. It meant that what had happened between them had had no real importance. She was glad of that.

Then she saw Court's face. He hadn't forgotten. He had left Jed's name off that list on purpose.

It made her feel good right down to the tips of her toes. Court cared enough about her to be a little afraid of Jed's boundless charm. Then she remembered that letter with the words, "My own darling—" still showing on the thick gray ash, and the envelope postmarked Boston, and what got into her then was a kind of meanness she hadn't known she had.

"Congratulations, Court," Jed said. "This is sure one fine turn-out. Yessir, mighty fine. . . ."

Fancy could see Court struggling with himself. But for all their faults the Brantleys had always been gentlemen.

"Come in and join us, won't you, Jed?" he said quietly.

"Don't reckon I'm dressed right for—"

"Oh, bother!" Fancy said. "You look a sight better than three-quarters of the men here. Come in, or I'm going to be mighty mad at you, Jed."

"That does it," Jed grinned. "What's the occasion, Court?"

"My sisters," Court said, "got married today—both of 'em."

"Well now, reckon that does call for a celebration. Happened to be down in Waynesboro on business; but I came the rest of the way up here to see you two—youall and the new addition. Is she like you, Fan?"

"Very much," Court said.

"Then I reckon I'll wait," Jed said, "till she grows up. Missed out with her maw, but me'n' little Lynne are going to come to an agreement right now."

Fancy took his hand.

"Come on," she said, "I'll show her to you."

Court looked at her.

"No, Fan," he said; "Jed hasn't even had a drink, and you can't leave your guests. It would be downright impolite."

"Oh, bother my guests!" Fancy said, but Jed shook his head.

"Court's right, honey," he grinned. "Besides which, if you were

244

to drag me upstairs, every woman in the house would start speculating on just what we were going to do up there. And the conclusions they'd arrive at would be mighty interesting; but they sure Lord wouldn't do you any good. Besides which," and that engaging grin of his widened, "when folks crowd Court here into shooting me, I aim to be guilty as hell. That would be worth dying for. So, honeychild, I'll just mosey up and see my little sweetie pie myself after a while. Her mammy's with her, isn't she? Good—then me'n' my future sweetheart can chat in private. . . ."

"Jed," Fancy said, "you're so blamed sensible that it hurts. And I think I mostly hate people anyhow. . . ."

"Why?" Jed said.

"They get things so mixed up. They interfere where they've got no business to. They—" she looked Court straight in the face, "write letters and say things they shouldn't, and try to steal what sure Lord doesn't belong to them. Yes, I hate 'em all right. Especially women."

Court's face was stony. He didn't say anything. Jed looked at him, then back at Fancy.

"I think I'll take that drink now, boy," he said.

Fancy waited until Jed had had his bourbon and branch water, and had chatted for a while with Court. Then she went up to where the two of them stood.

"Come on," she said, "you haven't danced with me yet."

Jed glanced uneasily at Court. The look on Court's face delighted Fancy to the bottom of her soul. What she was doing, what she was going to do, was foolishness and worse, but she didn't care. Court had hurt her too much and too often. Time she paid him back. With interest.

She danced with Jed. She tilted her head back and laughed. She was gay—too gay, so that the frown on Court's face got blacker by the minute. Then, seeing that he was dancing with one of the ladies present, at the other end of the hall, and couldn't see her, she tightened her grip on Jed's arm.

"Come on!" she whispered, "let's go out in the garden."

"No," Jed said; "'tain't safe. Court wouldn't like it. Wouldn't myself if I were in his shoes."

"Oh, bother Court and what he doesn't like!" Fancy said. It came to her then, that she meant it, and that was a funny thing. And right then she learned something—something that every honest woman knows but precious few will admit—that nobody on earth is capable of loving another person all the time, or even as much sometimes as she does at others. Any two people who live together have times when they're mighty close to hating each other, and that's a natural thing. Thinking about it, Fancy got a glimpse of something else: that the time could come, when after years of worshiping Court Brantley and getting only bits and scraps and cold leftovers of affection from him, she wouldn't care any more. One morning she would wake up and be free. Like that. It was an awful thing to think, so she pushed it from her mind.

She took Jed by the hand and led him out a side door into the garden where the fountains were. They were white in the moonlight, and the roses next to them were white, too, so that out there it was very pretty.

Jed stood by the pool and stared at her.

"You're lovely," he said. His voice sounded strange. Deep, kind of. Hoarse—a little strained. "God, but you're lovely!"

"Thanks, Jed," Fancy said.

"You didn't bring me out here," he said, "for a tête-à-tête. Now did you?"

She recognized that tone now. Jed was angry. With her.

"No," Fancy said.

"Court made you mad. Some young filly or another's been writing him letters. I gathered that much. So you thought you'd use me—to kind of even up the score. Not that you give one hoot up a hollow stump about me. . . ."

"Should I?" Fancy said.

"No. Not according to the rules. But I don't play according to rules. Neither do you. Found that out the last time we—went into a garden."

"I'm sorry, Jed," Fancy said.

"Don't be. Not now. Be sorry later. I'll do all the sorrowing necessary for tonight."

"Why?" Fancy whispered.

"Because the girl I love thinks I'm something to be used. Because she ain't above playing children's games. You kick my dog, I hit your cat. Hell, baby, what do you think I am?"

"A very nice man," Fancy said. "A man who ought to find himself some nice, sweet girl and . . ."

Jed snorted.

"While you're still alive and in the same world with me?" he growled. "Come on, Fan, let's go back in. . . ."

Fancy looked at him in wonder.

"Aren't you," she said, "even going to try to kiss me?"

"No. Reckon I do have rules after all. One of them is, I only kiss gals who want me to. Me, special. Meaning it—not for a lark. I don't play children's parlor games, Fan."

Fancy got up very slowly from the bench. It had all gone wrong. She felt like a fool. Feeling like that, mean-mad and ugly, she'd wanted only to hurt Court. And she had ended up by hurting Jed— and herself.

The worst of it was that when they came up the path, they saw Court coming toward them. He stopped and stood there, waiting.

"This," he said quietly, "sure doesn't look good, Jed."

"Damned right it doesn't," Jed said, "and the hell of it is it only looks that way. What kind of a fool do you think I am, Court Brantley?"

"Don't know," Court said. "What kind are you?"

"A mighty big one, I'll admit. But not the kind who plays a hand he ain't got a Chinaman's chance of winning. If I started something with this girl whose only fault is she's crazy enough to be in love with you, I'd take her so damn far away that you'd never find her. Not just out into your pretty garden, Court—halfway across the world."

"I see," Court said drily. "Then why did you come out here?"

"So she could cry on the shoulder of a friend she trusts over a man who ain't got any better sense than to try to keep up something he ought to have dropped years ago. Who don't know the difference between a blue diamond and polished glass. Hell, boy, I can't take Fan from you—though I wish to God I could. But you can throw her away. And you're doing it—damned fast."

"I think," Court said, "that you're wearing your welcome mighty thin, Jed."

"Consider it plumb wore out," Jed said. "Night, Fan. When you've had enough of this arrogant jackass, just sing out. I'll be waiting. . . ."

Then Court hit him. His left hand jabbed out very fast, the forearm stiff, traveling no more than eight inches, with all Court's weight behind it, pivoting off the ball of his left foot, without any warning, smooth-working, fast, and Jed Hawkins went down into the rose bushes.

He floundered there, breaking the stems so that the white blossoms showered petals. Like snow, Fancy thought, crazily, like snow. Then he was up again, swinging both arms like a windmill, clumsily, and Court Brantley laughing a little, boring in, hooking short rights and lefts to his middle until his hands came down, and then swinging very smoothly and very hard, so that Fancy thought sure the blow would tear his head off; but Jed Hawkins got up again, even after that.

She couldn't stand it. She loved Court, but this wasn't fair. Court was bigger and stronger, and ever so much better at this, and Jed's face was already bad to look at, bleeding from the nose and the corners of his mouth and his eyes closing.

"Stop it!" she screamed at Court. "Court Brantley, you stop it!"

Court didn't even look at her. He moved in on Jed, catlike, his face absolutely murderous. She could see that Jed was out on his feet. This time Court didn't try to knock him down. He just hooked Jed's head, back and forth, right, then left, each hook setting it up for the next so that it was getting to be a bloody mess and Fancy couldn't stand it.

She whirled between them, raking her long nails down Court's face, bringing blood. Court Brantley had been a gentleman all his life, but five minutes ago, he had stopped being one, had become something else, something very ugly that Fancy had no name for. He felt her nails dig in, and he brought his opened right hand up hard, the back of it smashing across her mouth, so that she went down into the thorny bushes, and lay there.

That stopped it.

"You bastard," Jed Hawkins whispered.

Court didn't say anything to him. He put out his hand to Fancy, but she refused it. As she got up, the rose bushes tore her dress, and there was mud on it and her face was a mess, with the red mark of his hand across it, the lips swollen and trembling.

"I'm sorry, Fan," Court said.

She didn't answer him. She got up and started back toward the house and then she saw it. Her guests, all her guests. At the windows. On the little veranda on the side of the house. And the moonlight so bright you could read a newspaper by it.

Court looked at Jed Hawkins.

"You," he said, "get out of here."

"Don't worry," Jed Hawkins said, "I'm going."

Fancy stopped on the path, looking at all those people. Her face felt like fire, and the rose thorns had scratched her arms. But she wasn't thinking about that. She was feeling cheapened, dirtied. Down deep. On the inside, where nothing would ever do it any good.

Like a street woman being fought over by a couple of drunken brutes. Like—like—like hill trash, the image came unbidden into her mind. They see through me now. I'm not nobody, just a thing my husband has to fight other men over and slap around to keep straight. Oh, God, oh Jesus, I—

Then she put her head up high and walked toward them. Very calmly. Straight. She looked at them all, one by one, straight in the face, coming toward them very slowly, so that they dropped their gaze and opened a way for her.

She went through the crowd without saying anything or looking at them until she came to the big stairway. That far, she carried it off. But she broke there. She covered her face with one arm, and ran up the stairs, blindly, trailing a glissando of broken sobs behind her.

Court came in, and turned to his guests.

"Mighty sorry, folks," he said. "Took on a spot too much, I reckon. Me'n' Jed had words, and Fan tried to separate us. . . . My apologies. . . ."

"It's all right, Court," Bob McCullen said. "Reckon we all get riled up, once in a while. . . ."

But it wasn't all right. And, looking up that stairway where Fancy had fled, Court had the feeling it never would be. . . .

15

IT WAS RAINING. It seemed to Fancy that all she had done that summer of 1888 was to quarrel with Court and listen to the rain. She hadn't quarreled with him about Fern or any other woman. Their arguments now were about the mill. They had started because Fancy wanted to learn something about a mill—how it was run and all. And now that Lynne was able to walk a little, Fancy didn't have too much to do. Matilda took care of the child, and that left Fancy with an awful lot of time for thinking.

One of the things that she thought was that although Court was young and strong, she'd be in an awful mess if anything ever happened to him. She knew a little about the mill, but not enough to run it if she had to. So she started in to learn. And that was one of the strange things about Fancy—whatever she set her mind on learning, she learned very thoroughly. She started going down to the mill, and getting the girls to teach her to run the light machinery. By the time that Court, who was busy in the office, found it out, she could run every piece of machinery in the plant that was operated by women.

She knew how the heavier machines worked too. She stood by

and watched the men operate them and asked dozens of questions. And when Court came home at night she asked him from whom he bought the cotton, and how much he paid for it, and how to tell good cotton from bad. Court answered her questions and also told her how he sold it, and to whom, and how much he got for it.

"Of course," he said, "there's the matter of freight rates, and wages to the hands, and doctor bills for the sick, and the salaries of the teachers in the mill school, and the preacher's salary, too. And you've got to figure in a certain amount of loss in lint, and repairs to broken-down machines and—say, why the devil do you want to know all this, Fan?"

"I just want to know, that's all," Fancy said.

But the next day he walked through the plant and found her doffing bobbins along with the bobbin boys. He stood there watching her.

"Learning the business from the ground up, eh, Fan?" he said. "What's the matter—planning to take over?"

"No, hon," Fancy said. "Just thought it would come in mighty handy to know how to run this place if you got sick or something. . . ."

"I'm not going to get sick," Court said. "And ladies in your position don't doff bobbins. I won't have my wife lowering herself so."

"Lowering myself? How can I do that any more? Appears to me you've done enough slapping me before all those people at your sisters' wedding," Fancy said. "Suppose you had an accident? Suppose you even got killed? Don't you see, Court, that I'd be helpless? Anybody could come in here and cheat my eyeballs out, and I wouldn't know the difference. That is, I wouldn't have known the difference. I do now."

"You," Court said, "could always call in your beloved Jed."

Fancy looked him in the face. Calmly.

"Jed doesn't know one blamed thing about a mill," she said.

"Then you could call in Wyche Weathers. He does. And he's just as ready as Jed to take you off my hands. Or perhaps any of half a dozen other men that I don't know about."

Fancy didn't say anything for a long while. She needed the time to get the shake out of her voice. But she didn't get it out. Not entirely.

"White trash from the Carolina hills, eh Court?" she said. "Still think I'm no good, don't you? All right. Wyche writes me. And not one of his letters ever started off, 'My own darling—' like that two-timing Fern wrote you! But you know that; you've seen every letter he's ever written me. There wasn't a thing in them that I couldn't have read to Lynne. And Jed doesn't write me at all."

"You didn't have to show me your mail," Court said stiffly. "I didn't ask. Anyhow, after this, you stay home where you belong!"

"Who's going to make me?"

"I am," Court said.

"I don't think so," Fancy said quietly; "I don't think you're man enough."

They made it up after a while, without ever saying, "I was wrong; I'm sorry." They made it up by letting the matter drop. But it came up again and there were more quarrels. And all that summer and into the fall, it rained.

Because of the rain, Court took some of the stronger men out of the mill and raised the level of the bluff between Dry Gully and the river, thus making a very effective levee out of it. There was some grumbling about that down in Augusta. Augusta didn't have a levee, and throughout its history from the time of the Yazoo Freshet right down to 1888 the town had been flooded many times.

"It'll raise the water level down here sure as shooting," the older citizens complained. "That upper valley used to be a natural spillway and kind of kept us from having bad floods down here. But with this here levee of Court's piling it up, we're sure to get washed out, come any kind of high water. . . ."

"They're right," Court admitted to Fancy when she asked him about it, "but without the mill, where would the town be? The Ellises have moved on. They've cut over, bled white, and ruined the woodlands for miles around. Nobody ever thinks of blaming them for the fact that they've tripled Augusta's flood danger by denuding the earth of its natural barriers, the trees. Besides, I've got sluice gates and spillways that I could open if it got too bad. And dangblast it, Fan, why the devil don't they build a levee to protect the city? They've been talking about it for a hundred years!"

252

He was smart, Fancy had to admit that. And the best thing about him was the way he handled his workers. He acts, she thought, like he's their father, and him only thirty-six. Everybody right down to old Maud thinks nothing of walking into Hiberion and telling him their troubles and asking him to help him. And he always does. Court's a good man. I guess I wasn't rightly cut out to make him the kind of wife he needs. Everybody in town, except children and the colored people, calls him by his first name. The colored people too, only they put Mister in front of it. And every man in the mill can stop work and come into the office and make a suggestion or a complaint. And he'll listen to them, too. If he can't do what they want, he'll explain why just like they were the president of the bank or the chairman of the board of directors.

The mill hands loved the ground he walked on. Fancy knew that, and she knew why. It was mighty hard to hate a man who would shut up shop any time he felt like it and give a picnic or a barbecue for all his hands. Many a time Fancy had heard him walking down the line and calling out:

"Ned, Tad, Lester—you boys go home and get your shotguns and meet me in my office in an hour. Heard there's a mighty heap of quail out by the old Brewster place. . . ."

The men swore he was the best shot in Richmond County.

"Yessir, you ought to of seen him! Ten miles we tramped and him not even breathing hard. Reckon he got twicet as many birds as the rest of us put together. And when ole Tad here come out with a jug of corn likker, he took his swig right along with the next man, not even wiping the bottle with his hand. Ain't many big men like ole Court, I'll tell you. . . ."

"When my Sal come down with the misery in the chest, he come over to the house and brung his wife with him, and her this big with child. Fair thought he was going to bust out crying when he looked at poor Sal. Had Doc Brewster over quicker'n a wink, and all the medicines that could be fetched up from Augusta. Course it didn't do no good, Sal ups and dies; but it sure Lord warn't because Court warn't in there a-trying. . . ."

The minister at Dry Gully Church called him a gallant gentleman. Fancy had heard him say that many times. She often went to church in Dry Gully, because the simple, forceful preaching was more to her liking than the dignified services of the Episcopal Church in Augusta. The teachers at Dry Gully School could never praise him enough. Court wouldn't have liked such praise, so Fancy didn't tell him about it. And his people thought it wasn't any more than the truth, so they didn't tell him either.

It was a funny thing, Fancy said, that everybody loves him and can get along with him except me. I love him, too; but I sure Lord can't get along with him—not longer than a week at a time. . . .

So things went smoothly for Court Brantley. When a union organizer showed up and tried to unionize the mill, the workers beat him up and threw him out. He made the mistake of calling Court an "oppressor of labor." Court didn't think of himself as an oppressor of labor. The little houses that he had built for his people were miserable shacks—even he knew that; but they were tight against the wind and the rain, and they were painted, a thing the mill people had never even hoped to see. His workers, called pine-barren crackers, white trash, rednecks, by the great and proud, were treated like men and women by him. Besides, they were so used to freezing in the damp Georgia winters, and roasting in the summer sun, that any degree of comfort seemed real luxury to them. And the houses he gave them, perched upon the Godforsaken ravines and red hillsides, were better houses than most of the small farmers of Georgia lived in, and were not even to be spoken of in the same breath with the miserable shanties in which the 'croppers shivered in half the year and baked the other half.

Even the wages Court paid, twenty-five cents a day to bobbin boys, forty to sixty cents a day for spinners, and seventy cents to one whole dollar for weavers, seemed like a lot of money to the poor whites he hired. The three-dollar-a-day man, the trained mechanics who kept the machinery running, became the big men of Dry. Gully. They ordered tailor-made suits from Augusta, and smoked nickel cigars.

So, if an entire family, from ten-year-old Willie, busy at doffing bobbins, to seventy-year-old Grandpaw, slowly sweeping up the lint while Maw twisted lint and Paw wove, had to work sixty-eight hours a week to meet even their simple wants, it must not be imagined that they thought of Court Brantley as a mighty mean man—since other mills not too far away paid less, and other workers had a seventy-two hour week.

254

Therefore, when Sal came down with a misery in her chest and lay there a-spittin' blood, Lester Watts didn't blame Court Brantley. When Ted Spink's kid was born a queer, still brat who would never be right in the head, Ted didn't even connect it with the mill. Not that, nor the pains in his back and the ringing in his ears. He never saw the sun any more from one week end to the next, but neither Ted nor Lester nor any of the others knew that sunlight had anything to do with health. Sow belly or fatback and greens and corn pone might and did riddle his family with pellagra, but what else had he eaten before he came to Dry Gully, and whenever before had he had so much?

These things, the preacher told him, were visitations from God for his sins. And if Ted sometimes wondered when he ever got the time or the energy to commit any sins, a little thinking could call to mind some mighty good substitutes: the time he got drunk down in Augusta and was thrown out of Riley's Saloon, that painted little daughter of joy he got mixed up with the Saturday night he managed to slip his block, because Lu wasn't feeling up to going into town, the crap game he got into in back of Riley's, that had his whole family eating stale cornbread for a week, washed down with water, which at least cost nothing. . . .

If Ted had asked Court, Court would have sworn at him and told him he was entitled to a couple of sins; but Ted was mightily afraid that Court might find out what he'd been up to. Like all the mill workers, Ted rated Court only a little way beneath God. How the devil did he know so much? Which member of the family was sick, and Sary Lou's marks in school, and old man Spink's rheumatism. Like the other day when he'd stopped by the creel, and said:

"Now look here, Ted, I know a man's a man; but if you keep on going down to Myrtie Torrence's place, like you did last Saturday night, you're going to catch something you don't want and bring it home to poor Lu. . . ."

Ted had stood there, staring at him in wonder.

It was very simple, really. It did something for a mill hand's pride to be on friendly terms with Court. They talked their heads off to him. If anybody in the mill, down to the smallest bobbin boy did something out of the ordinary, Court knew about it the first thing in the morning. And Court had a wonderful memory. Besides, he thought of them all as being his family, and was always asking after them, getting the details of their lives outside of the mill, which, being a Southerner, he never thought of as being none of his damned business. And he was always giving them advice.

"I know what I'm talking about," he said to a group of younger workers as they sat around the campfire after a 'possum hunt. "I made some damn bad mistakes myself not too long ago. I'm not setting myself up as a plaster saint. I couldn't; you fellows know my history much too well. But a man who can't profit by his own mistakes is a fool; and a man who's got sense enough to learn something from somebody else's is plumb, downright smart. That's all I'm trying to do—smarten you boys up a bit, that's all. . . ."

They nodded in sage agreement, chewing on their blades of grass.

And still it rained. Fancy thought if she heard the sound of it any more, dripping off the eaves of the house, she'd go fair out of her mind. It gave her much too much time for thinking and wondering and one of the things she wondered about was how Maw and Pap and Randy were making out, over there in Carolina. She remembered how bad those first years at Melody had been for her and Court, and Melody was a good plantation, rich, black bottom land. That hillside farm of Pap's was worse than bad—it was terrible.

So that morning, just before Court started out for Dry Gully, she spoke to him about it.

"I feel kind of ashamed," she told him, "that I haven't been back to see my folks. Wrote 'em once or twice, but they didn't answer. I really didn't expect them to—they're mighty poor hands at writing."

"Why don't you run over there?" Court said. "It's not too much of a drive. Take Thomas and the closed carriage. Spend a few days with them."

Fancy looked at him.

"Thanks, Court," she said. "Thought maybe you'd raise some objection, but I should have known better. You're glad enough to get me out from underfoot, aren't you?"

"I didn't say that," Court said.

"Know you didn't. Didn't need to—it's true enough, though. All right, it doesn't matter. I meant to go anyway. And, Court . . ."

256

"Yes, Fan?"

"I should take them something—something nice. . . ."

Court put his hand in his breast pocket and came out with his checkbook. Then he went into his study and scrawled his name at the bottom of a check. But he didn't write in any figures. He left that part blank.

"Here," he said. "From what you've told me about your folks, they're probably in damned bad shape financially. Straighten 'em out. Pay off their debts. Buy that brother of yours some decent stock, and some good farming equipment. A tract of better land, too—if you want to. Spend what you have to—it's yours anyhow. Never could have made it without you. . . ."

Fancy got up and kissed him, hard.

"Never will understand you," she said, winking back her tears. "Half the time I'd like to shoot you, then you go and do something like this. . . ."

"Don't mention it," Court grinned. "I always want to shoot you—in the daytime."

"Court Brantley!" Fancy laughed. "What a thing to say!"

She started out early that next morning. Thomas had a hard time getting through, because most of the Carolina lowlands were already flooded. A couple of times they had to be hauled out of the mud by the local farmers with their teams. But when they got up into the hills it was better. At least it was better at first but afterwards it got worse because the hill trails really weren't made for such a fine carriage.

But Thomas was a good driver and they made it, although it took them all day to go the twenty miles.

The first thing Fancy saw when she got home was that the house looked a little better. The porch and the steps had been repaired, and all the windows had oiled paper in them. A wisp of smoke curled up from the chimney and she could smell collard greens cooking. Thomas helped her down from the carriage, and she went up on the porch and knocked.

A young woman answered the door. She was skinny as a rail fence and had hair like wet straw. Her lower lip bulged over a wad of snuff. She had a baby in her arms.

This, Fancy thought, this is what I would have looked like—if I had stayed. . . .

The young woman stood there looking at her, her jaw dropping open, so that Fancy could see her bad, uneven teeth.

"Good evening," Fancy said. "Mister Williamson at home?"

"Yes'm," the girl said; then she turned back toward the room and called: "Ran—dee! Company!"

Randy got up and came to the door. Just looking at him, Fancy wanted to cry. He looked so—so beaten. Two other children came with him, clinging to his knees. Their clothes were made of sacking, and their feet were bare.

"Howdy, Ma'am," Randy said politely, but his eyes were puzzled. It was dusk, but there was light enough to see.

"Randy," Fancy whispered, "don't you know me?"

"No'm," Randy said. "Got a feeling I've seed you somewheres, Ma'am, but I can't rightly place you. . . ."

"May I come in, please?" Fancy said.

"Why, shore, Ma'am!" Randy said. "Our little shack ain't much, but we'd be mighty honored. . . ."

But the minute she was inside, where the lamp was, Randy stopped dead. His mouth worked several times before he got it out:

"Fan! Great, jumping Jehosiphats, Sal—this here's my sister, Fan!"

"Howdy, Ma'am," Sal said. "Mighty proud to make your acquaintance."

Fancy took the thin calloused hand. The children came up to her timidly.

"This here is Ted—and this is Lester," Randy said proudly. "The baby's a girl. We called her Lucy. Children, meet yore Aunt Fancy."

Fancy knelt on the well scrubbed floor and kissed them.

"I—I didn't bring them anything," she wailed; "I didn't even know about them." Then she got up, looking at Randy.

"Ran," she whispered, "what about Maw?"

Randy looked down at the floor.

"Gone," he said, "these six years, Fan. Didn't seem to have much heart for living—after you left. . . ."

"And, Pap?"

"The year after that. Took to drinking worse than ever after Maw died. Got liquored up one day whilst I was out in the fields and wandered off. Took me three days to find him. Never would of, I reckon, wasn't for the buzzards. . . ."

"Oh, Randy, no!"

"They hadn't got at him," Randy said quickly. "They was still up there—a-circling."

"Thank God for that," Fancy said.

"You shore do look fine," Randy said. "Married?"

"Yes. A fine man, Randy—didn't have much when I started with him, but now he's one of the richest men in the State. . . ."

"You always was lucky," Randy said.

"Ran—how's the farm?"

"We can eat," Randy said tiredly, "that's about all."

"Tell me something," Fancy said; "you know of any good land hereabouts—for sale?"

"You planning to farm, Fan? As I recollect, you never had much use for it."

"No, Ran," Fancy said, "I'm not going to farm—you are."

It took him a little while to get her meaning. When he did, lean, work-hardened man that he was, he cried a little. Sal cried a great deal.

"I'd sure admire to kiss you, Ma'am," she blubbered; "I surely would!"

Fancy kissed her.

They all sat up late that night, talking. Randy offered to fix a place for Thomas to sleep in the barn. But Thomas gave one look at the dirty straw and his broad nostrils flared.

"No, thank you, sah!" he said; "I'll bunk in the carriage." Thomas was a house Negro—and had been one all his life.

The next morning Fancy and Randy drove out to old man Wilkins' place. It was in a valley, and was the best farm in the entire county. But old man Wilkins had died five years ago, and left a young widow, younger than Fancy. Unable to farm the place herself, she had married again, but she had followed her heart instead of her head, and the man of her choice was a dreamy youth who liked to sit and watch the sun go down over the mountains. When, driven by his bride's tongue-lashing, he'd tried to work the place, he'd doubled up over the plow and started coughing—blood. So, the Wilkins place was for sale.

When Fancy got back into her carriage to drive home, Randy Williamson was the owner of the best farm in the county, the children had shoes and store-bought clothes for the first time in their lives, and Sal had three new dresses. And the stonecutter in the village was hard at work on a marble headstone to replace the simple wooden cross over Maw and Pap's grave. . . .

But it didn't stop raining, down in Augusta. By the tenth of September, the Savannah crept up over its banks and flooded the city. On the eleventh, it was thirty-eight feet high. Fancy lay awake all the first part of the night listening to the noise in the darkness. She could hear the water, and the people crying, and men shouting. People passed by on rafts and in boats.

Court was awake too, listening; but he didn't say anything to her. Along about eleven o'clock one of the Negroes came and knocked on the door and told them there was a man downstairs to see Court. Court slipped on his dressing gown and went downstairs. He stayed a long time, and when he came back, he started to get dressed without a word.

"What's the matter, Court?" Fancy said.

"Bunch of people up at the mill," Court said. "They want to open the sluice gates to relieve the pressure down here. I've got to go up there, quick!"

Fancy was already out of bed.

"I'm coming too," she said.

"Don't be a fool, Fan," Court said. "It's going to be a whole lot of trouble getting up there—and the mood those folks are in, it might be dangerous."

"I don't care," Fancy said; "I'm coming."

"All right," Court said; "on your head be it."

It was a lot of trouble getting up to Dry Gully. The water in the streets of Augusta was so deep by then that part of the time the horses had to swim. The canal banks were still holding. After they let go, not even a horse could have got through.

Fancy was wet and cold and miserable by the time they reached the mill. Court turned to Brayton, his assistant manager—the man who had brought the message.

"Where are they?" he said.

"Over there," Brayton said, and pointed.

Fancy could see the group of men standing in front of the mill. They had shotguns in their hands. She thought that something about some of them looked familiar, and when she got closer she saw what it was. Leading the group were Tom and Buck Ellis.

"All right, boys," Court said; "speak your piece."

A man named Ronald Raeburn stepped forward.

"It's this way, Mister Brantley," he said. "We're already under water down in Augusta. . . ."

"I know that," Court said.

"But now the city engineer says the canal banks are threatening to let go. If they do that, it'll be the worst disaster in the city's history —Lord knows how many people will get drowned. So we figgered—"

"You figgered?" Court said; "or Tom and Buck Ellis figgered—which?"

"Well now, Tom did say . . ."

"I don't give a damn what he said," Court said quietly. "I know what's on his mind. This looked like one damn fine chance of getting even with me by ruining my mill beyond repair. That business about relieving the pressure down below is just so much hogwash."

Then Joe Cummings stepped forward.

"No it isn't, Court," he said.

Court looked at him.

"You, too, Joe?" he said.

"No—not me, too. You'll notice I don't have a gun in my hands. I came with the others because I agree that there might be a chance to keep those banks from collapsing. Thought I could talk to you man to man—as a friend. I don't hold with using force. I don't even have a gun with me."

"All right," Court said. "Know what it'll cost me if I open those gates?"

"Yes. And I know what it'll cost the folks down in Augusta if you don't, Court. Their lives. Don't think Dry Gully Mill, important as it is, stacks up above that. What do you say, Court?"

"No," Court said.

"Then by God," Buck Ellis said, "we'll damned well see that you open them!"

"I'm outnumbered, Buck," Court said; "but somebody's going to get hurt if you try it. And given my choice, reckon you've got a pretty fair idea who that somebody'd be."

"Come on, boys," Buck Ellis said, "let's take him!"

Fancy put up her hand.

"Wait a minute, boys!" she said.

The men stopped, looking at her.

"Joe," she said, "is that the truth? Folks will get drowned if we don't open the gates?"

"Yes'm," Joe Cummings said.

"What guarantee," Court growled, "do I have that those banks won't let go even if I do open them?"

"None," Joe said honestly. "It's a chance you'd have to take. But it's a good chance, Court. It's the only decent choice."

"Standing there jawing," Tom Ellis said. "Let's get started!"

Court put his hand inside his coat and let it rest there.

"No, Court," Fancy said. "Don't pull a gun. Not for this. Not over a thing like this."

Court stared at her.

"You against me, too?" he said.

"No," Fancy whispered, "not ever against you, honey. I'm always for you. It's not being against you to tell you that you can't let people get drowned on account of buildings or machinery. Please, Court . . ."

Brayton looked at Court, helplessly.

The squareness went out of Court's shoulders. He slumped forward a little like a man who was very tired and very old.

"Open them, Brayton," he said.

"Yessir," Brayton said. "Right away, sir!"

Court looked at the group of men who stood before the gates of the mill.

"Now, if you—gentlemen will excuse me, I'm going home. Stay and amuse yourselves. I expect you'll find the spectacle mighty interesting. . . ."

He turned and rode away from the gates. Fancy turned her horse's head and rode after him.

"Court, wait!" she called.

Court pulled up his horse and waited.

"Court, I—" Fancy began; but Court didn't say anything. He just looked at her. He sat there like that a long time, looking at her. Then he flapped the reins over the Morgan's neck, and the two of them started off together toward the city.

But when they came down off the Sandhill, they couldn't go any further. The streets had been filled up with water before but now they were millraces, torrents. While they were sitting there, looking at the flood, a man came up to them.

"You folks better turn back," he said. "The canal banks gave way half an hour ago—God knows how many folks have drowned!"

Fancy turned toward Court, but he didn't even look at her. Then she started to cry.

But he still didn't say anything, no word of comfort—nothing at all. He just sat there listening to her cry and looking at the dark waters. Then, finally, he turned his horse away from the flood.

"Come on," he said, "we'll stay at the Lewises' tonight."

"Oh, Court," Fancy whispered; "I'm so sorry!"

"You're sorry," Court said. "That helps. That helps one hell of a lot. Come on. . . ."

Riding through the streets on the morning of September thirteenth, after the crest of the flood had passed and the waters had receded, Fancy knew that nothing would ever be the same or even right between them again. She kept looking at Court out of the corners of her eyes, seeing his face drawn, tired, grim. She reckoned he hadn't said five words to her in all of the two days that they had stayed at the house of their friends. Never, she thought bitterly, will he forgive me for this. . . . Still it was a chance, and as Joe Cummings had said, it was the only decent choice. Only it turned out to be a useless one, and we're right back where we started from with the mill ruined and us loaded down with debt. . . .

When she got back to Hiberion, she felt like crying all over again, seeing the furniture on the ground floor wrecked and six inches of stinking red mud all over everything. So more to help the way she felt than any other reason, she called the servants in and started to clean up. By mid-afternoon, Hiberion began to look a little better.

Court drank a cup of black coffee and headed back toward the mill. When he came home that night, his face was a little less grim and Fancy almost started to hope. Still he sat through dinner without saying anything until she couldn't stand it any longer.

"Court," she said, "is it—bad?"

"Not as bad as I expected," Court said. "Only four machines are ruined beyond repair. But they happen to be the biggest machines in the plant—and the most expensive. I'm going down to the bank to see about a loan tomorrow morning. If I get it, I'll have to go North —to New York, I reckon, and order some new ones. We've only been set back about five years by your generosity, Fan."

He stood up, looking at her.

"Incidentally," he said, "ten people drowned, in spite of our opened sluice gates. And the damage to the city is a little over a million dollars."

He stood up then and left the dining room without even saying good night.

A week later, he sat in the offices of Bryant and Sons, manufacturers of textile equipment in New York City.

"Sorry, Mr. Brantley," Fred Bryant said, "but that particular type of creel is made only by Satterlee of Boston. I think you'll find his roves and cards about the best, too. Wish I could help you, but we specialize in lighter machinery for smaller plants than yours. . . ."

Court got up.

"Reckon I'll have to go to Boston, then," he said.

"Yes," Fred Bryant said, "Boston's your best bet."

When he came out on the sidewalk, Court stood still, looking at the crowds.

Boston.

The one place on earth I shouldn't go to right now. Not now, not feeling like I do.

It's business. It's in Fan's interest. . . .

Boston.

I'll be there a day at the most. Then I'll catch a train and hightail it back to Augusta so fast that . . .

Boston.

He hailed a cab and went back to the hotel. He took a stiff drink of bourbon, and repacked his bag.

Why doesn't he come home? Fancy thought. It's been a month since I heard from him last. Said he couldn't find the machines in New York, and he'd have to look elsewhere. But where is elsewhere? She's up there. And Boston isn't far from New York. Surely it shouldn't take Court a whole month to buy four machines. . . .

I'd go looking for him, if I knew where to look. But New York's a big city, and Boston's a big city. . . .

Boston. Always Boston. God Almighty why doesn't he come?

He did come home two days later, looking so tired and sick that Fancy didn't have the heart to question him. The machines arrived almost the same time that he did, and thereafter Court was in the mill morning and night seeing that they were set up properly.

Once the mill was in working order again, he drove himself and his men almost to the breaking point. He did well, too, Fancy had to admit that. They were getting so many orders now that the mill had a hard time handling them all. And every time he got his hands on some money, Court paid it back to the bank.

When it was over, when things had eased a little, Fancy didn't ask Court whether he'd been to Boston or not. Many times she wanted to, but she didn't ask him. Court didn't tell her, either. And that was just as well.

16

I'T'S BEEN a long time," Wyche Weathers said.

"Seven or eight years," Court said. "Thought you'd scratched us off your list, Wyche."

Wyche grinned at him.

"Nothing like that, boy. Just had all I could do keeping my head above water last year. I'm going to remember '93. That was some panic—five hundred banks went down, eight thousand businesses—a heap of the big railroads. . . ."

Fancy came up and leaned against the back of Court's chair. "But you didn't," she said, "neither of you."

Wyche looked toward where eight-year-old Lynne was sitting on the floor, reading a book.

"She's lovely," he said. "Going to be prettier'n you, Fan."

"Thank you, Wyche," Fancy said.

They were sitting in the dining room of Hiberion. It was a spring day early in 1894, and Wyche had come down that morning from Spartanburg to visit them. Fancy was very happy over the way Court had received him. Court was behaving very well. Then it came to her that Court had never been actually jealous of Wyche. He knew he didn't have to be. I wonder, Fancy thought, how he'd act if this were Jed?

Jed was in town, too. She knew that, although she hadn't seen him. She very much didn't want to see him. She hoped he wouldn't come to Hiberion. It had been very peaceful lately, and she didn't want any trouble with Court. Right then, of course, to her disgust, Wyche had to go and mention it.

"Heard tell Jed Hawkins is in town," he said, "rallying himself around whooping up the niggers."

"Yes," Court said, "there's a move afoot to disenfranchise them. I'm for it. The poor bastards don't know what to do with a vote."

"I'm not," Wyche said. "Take it away and they'll never get it back. By the way, Court, how are your sisters?"

"Just fine," Court said. "They aren't here any more. Did you know that?"

"No," Wyche said, "I didn't."

"Those fellows, Wilson and Plainfield, didn't work out in the mill. For different reasons. Wilson was a mite too sharp. Wanted to cut too many corners. But Joe was a good sort. He quit because he got to thinking about things and decided that he oughtn't to be making his way on my bounty. So I helped them some more—in a way that was right smart business, Wyche. I set 'em up in a ready-to-wear clothing manufacturing business. They've a big store in Savannah, and a factory. Joe and Saph live out at Melody, now, and keep the old place in good repair. They don't do much planting, though. Joe's too busy for that."

"I see," Wyche said. "What about Agnes and Tom?"

"They live in town. A damned good arrangement, Wyche. Agnes wants to shine in society—and no two married women can live in the same house. Besides, an angel out of Glory couldn't get along with Agnes, anyhow."

"Court," Fancy said, "is that any way to talk about your sister?"

"It's the truth," Court said.

Wyche looked at Lynne.

"Funny you haven't had any more," he said.

"It is," Court said. "Damned if I can understand it. Fan and I both love kids. Given our choice, reckon we'd have half a dozen by now."

"I'd settle for one more," Fancy said; "just one—if it were a boy."

Wyche looked at her, thinking: How nice she talks. Poised, too—you'd think that she'd been born here in Hiberion instead of Court. Women are funny that way. Given a role to play and they play it to the hilt. Little Fan in the role of Grand Duchess—great lady. Only she's not acting any more. She's it. Last time I saw her, it was an act. Not now. It's the way she is, the way, maybe, she was born to be—given the chance. Funny how people like her can come from nowhere, out of the most unlikely surroundings, from a family that in ninety-nine generations produced nothing of note before. Then, on top of the dung heap—a rose. Among the quacking ducklings—a swan. . . .

"Give yourselves time," he said. "You're both young, yet."

"No, Wyche," Court said. "Leaseways I'm not. I'm forty-two."

"And I'm thirty-three," Fancy said. "It's getting to be too late, Wyche. It's got to be within the next three or four years or not at all. Doc Brewster says—that reminds me, I have to go see him. . . ."

"Why?" Court said.

"General checkup. Headaches, bad digestion—and I've been losing weight. He's been after me to come in for weeks, but I just haven't got around to it."

"What did he say," Wyche asked, "about women in general I mean? You were going to tell us, then you interrupted yourself."

"Oh, yes. Doc Brewster says that it's not good for a woman past thirty-five to have a child. Some do—in their forties even; but it's not good for them."

"It's worse for the child," Wyche said. "By the time he's in his teens, he has parents who are old enough to have been his grandparents. Too big a gap—it makes for bad relations. People that far apart just don't think alike. A woman that long out of her girlhood can't remember how she felt when a pimply boy took a shine to her."

He looked at Court, gravely.

"Too bad about your father," he said.

"No it wasn't," Court said. "Father died happy—roaring drunk and full of hell. Besides he lived to see Hiberion restored, and something like the old life come back again. And he was proud of me before he died. All in all, it was a good way to go, Wyche. We all did our best for him, and there are no regrets. . . ."

"Good," Wyche said. "What do you think of Atkinson, Court?"

"I don't know. They say he's a good man. But he's depending mighty heavily on the colored vote. Those all-night picnics are a scandal. He gets the niggers drunk, then buys their vote at a dollar a head. Hawkins is acting for him around here, which is enough to set me against him. I don't like Hawkins."

"Why?" Wyche said.

"He's a crook. And there are other reasons. Let's not talk about it. To hell with politics anyhow. . . ."

"Wyche," Fancy said, "did you go to the Columbian Exposition in Chicago?"

Lynne put down her book and jumped up.

"We did!" she said. "We went to the Egyptian village. Mama smoked a water pipe. It made her sick. But Daddy had the most fun of all. He stood around and watched the naked ladies wiggling their stomachs—like this."

Then she showed him.

Wyche threw back his head and roared.

"Lynne," Fancy said, "why don't you go and practice your piano lessons?"

"Because I don't want to," Lynne said. "I hate the piano. I hate lessons anyhow. I have to take too many of them. Music and singing and dancing and French—I hate French most of all."

"Who makes you do all that?" Wyche said.

"Mama. She's mean to me. She doesn't love me like Daddy does. He brings me candy and Mama takes it away. Says it isn't good for me."

"Well, now," Wyche said, "your mother knows best. Reckon she's just trying to make a lady out of you."

"Don't want to be a lady. I want to go West and be a cowgirl and shoot buffaloes—and Injuns."

"Lynne—" Fancy began.

"Oh, leave the child be, Fan," Court said.

Fancy didn't say anything. Wyche looked from one of them to the other, then he turned back to Lynne.

"What else did you see at the World's Fair?" he said.

"I rode on the ferris wheel," Lynne said. "So did Daddy and

Mama. They went with me. They were scared stiff, but they wouldn't admit it!"

"Reckon I'd have been scared, too," Wyche said. "Tell you what, honey. Let's go down in the parlor and you play the piano for me. I'd sure like some pretty music."

"That's a trick to get me to practice," Lynne said. "But I'll do it for you, Uncle Wy. . . ."

She didn't play badly, but she'd never make a pianist. Wyche could see that. She'd be able to entertain a drawing room full of friends and relatives who were not too critical. But nothing more.

Court sat there smiling. To him it was all right. Everything that Lynne did was going to be all right with Court. But Fancy frowned every time Lynne stumbled or missed a note.

She wants too much for that kid, Wyche thought. Not having had it herself, she wants Lynne to have it. Everything—the whole world. And it can't be done. It'll turn out badly—with the child hating her. Kids are a hell of a lot more like weeds than like flowers. Can't prune 'em too close. Got to let 'em grow.

"How's that, Uncle Wy?" Lynne said.

"Beautiful, baby—just beautiful. Now if your paw'll let me use the telephone, I'll send for what I brought you."

"Send for it?" Lynne said. "Couldn't you have brought it in your pocket, Uncle Wy? Or is it too big?"

"It's too big," Wyche said. "Where's the phone, Court?"

"Out in the hall," Court said. "Help yourself."

Wyche came back in a few minutes, and sat down, looking at Fancy.

She's better now, he thought. The years become her. And she'll keep on getting better and better. By the time she's old, she'll be a queen. A real queen—with grace and dignity. . . . Then he saw Court looking at him.

"She's something, boy," he said. "You ought to be mighty proud."

"I am," Court said. But Wyche didn't like the way he said it.

"Show Uncle Wyche how well you can read, darling," Fancy said.

"No," Lynne said, "I won't!"

"Lynne!" Fancy said.

"It's all right, Fan," Wyche said. "Some other time."

Fancy didn't say anything else, and after that the doorbell rang.

They still had the big knocker on the door, but now Court had had electric lights put in, and an electric doorbell that rang in two places at once—in the hall and in the pantry. Ernest came out of the pantry and went to the door. He came back into the parlor with his eyes opened wide.

"Marse Court!" he said. "Man out there with a pony! Say he was told to bring it here."

"A pony!" Lynne squealed. "Oh, Uncle Wy! You darling!" Then she threw both arms around his neck and kissed him.

"Come on," Wyche grinned, "let's go see him."

They all went out of the house together. There was a colored boy standing in front of the gate holding a Shetland pony. The pony was spotted and glossy. He was hitched to a little wicker cart.

"Oh, Wyche, you shouldn't have!" Fancy said.

"Why not?" Wyche said. "Nothing's too good for the little princess."

"Mighty handsome of you, Wyche," Court said. "Come on, let's have a look at that thing."

But just as he reached the gate the telegraph boy came riding up on a bicycle.

"Telegram for Mister Brantley," he said.

Court took the telegram, and tossed the boy a coin. Then he opened it.

Wyche saw him stiffen. The color went out of his face. Then he straightened up and looked at them.

"Court," Fancy said, "is something wrong?"

"Yes," Court said slowly. "There's some trouble in New York. I was kind of—depending upon getting the Mosher and Levine cotton goods contract. Means a hell of a lot to me. I'll have to go to New York tonight—and the bad part about that is that there isn't a train out of here before two-thirty in the morning. I'll have to put in another bid—see if I can't swing things my way."

He's lying, Wyche thought. He's on top of the heap now. He's doing better than I am, and I ain't doing bad. The state my mill's in, the loss of one contract or of ten wouldn't make any difference. We've both got more business than we can rightly handle. Besides, from all I've heard, he was cool as a cucumber last year right smack-dab in the midst of the worst panic in fifty years. Made himself a profit when everybody was losing the shirts off their backs. He wouldn't get that excited over business. No sir, it's something else.

"Court," Fancy whispered, "will you be long?"

Seeing her face, Wyche had to turn away. It wasn't good to see her look at Court like that. With her heart in her eyes. Breaking there.

Whatever this tall bastard's up to, Wyche decided, she knows—or at least suspects. God damn him to bitter hell, I'll . . .

"No, hon," Court said. "A week—at the most."

"I'll get your things together," Fancy said.

"All right," Court said. "Tell you what: you do it now, and we can all go out and have some fun tonight till train time. Go to one of your friend Jed Hawkins' nigger picnics. They tell me they're a sight to see."

"All right, Court," Fancy said.

"I have to run back out to the mill and give Brayton some last-minute instructions," Court said. "Want to come with me, Wyche?"

"Heck no! I'm on vacation. Don't want to see the inside of another blasted mill till I get back to Spartanburg."

"Suit yourself," Court said. "Wyche, stick around while I'm gone, won't you? I don't like leaving Fan alone. There's one certain party around who has given her trouble before. . . . What I mean is . . ."

"Don't say any more than you want to, Court," Wyche said. "I'll 'tend to things."

"Thanks," Court said.

In half an hour, after he had gone, Fancy came back down the stairs.

"All packed," she said. "Wyche . . ."

"Yes, baby?"

"You know what Court was talking about?"

"No."

"Jed Hawkins. Court thinks Jed's in love with me."

"Is he?"

"Yes. But the bad part about it is that Court thinks that I—"

"Do you?"

"No, Wyche. Tell you what—let's take a little ride. I want to talk

272

to you. Alone, I mean. The servants around here have mighty big ears, and they repeat everything they hear."

"All right, baby," Wyche said.

They started riding down Broad Street. When they got to McIntosh, Fancy turned the buggy into it.

"It's good to see you, Wyche."

"Thanks, Fan."

"You know, Wyche, sometimes I think I've been a fool."

"Why, Fan?"

"Letting you go for Court."

"You love him, Fan. Don't forget that. Don't ever forget that."

"I know. I love him. But is that enough? Love isn't everything. 'Specially not one-sided love."

"One-sided?" Wyche said.

"He doesn't love me. He pretends to, but he doesn't." Fancy thought suddenly, sharply about that time that Court had hit her, at Saph's and Agnes' wedding, before all those people. She started to tell Wyche about that. But she didn't. It wasn't a good thing to tell anybody. Especially not Wyche. . . . "For all I know," she whispered, "he might be carrying on with that Fern. He goes North every year and stays for the longest times. Wyche, how far is Boston from New York?"

"Far enough. Two—three hundred miles. Don't know exactly. Why?"

"His letters come from New York. He writes me once a week, sometimes twice. They're postmarked New York. They're written on the stationery of the hotel he says he stays at. . . ."

Wyche looked at her.

"Just what are you driving at, Fan?" he said.

"Trains go very fast, Wyche," Fancy said.

"Oh," Wyche said, "you think that he—"

"Goes up to Boston between times to see her. Or that she comes down to New York—and stays with him. There—I've said it! Oh, Wyche, how awful!"

"You mustn't think such things, Fan," Wyche said. "I don't believe anything like that's going on. You're just upsetting yourself like this for nothing. Forget it. Everything's going to be all right."

"All right, Wyche," Fancy said. "But there's another thing. . . ."

273

"What's that, baby?"

"He—he's turning Lynne against me."

"How?" Wyche said.

"He spoils her. Every time he comes into the house he brings a new toy—or some candy. Doc Brewster says candy is bad for her teeth—that she should have very little of it. So I have to take it away from her. Then she runs to Court and he takes her side. If she's bad, I have to punish her. Court won't. All the things she needs, I have to see that she gets—like her music and deportment and all the other things a young lady needs. Being a child, she doesn't want those things. She doesn't realize how important they are. So she throws tantrums. Then Court says, 'Come on, baby, let's go for a ride.' And he takes her down to Oertel's and fills her up on ice cream sodas. . . ."

"Fan, don't you think that maybe you're being a mite too strict?"

"You men!" Fancy said; then she smiled at him: "Reckon I am, Wyche," she said. "I missed so much when I was a child. There've been so many times when I didn't know what to do—or the right thing to say, and I was so afraid and ashamed I could have died. I've learned to get along with Court's kind of people. I know how to keep from embarrassing him now. But it came hard, Wyche. I had to get after I was grown, the training I should have had as a child. I had to learn proper grammar and which fork to use and how to greet people. Court and I have been married fourteen years and it's taken every one of them for me to learn the simple, ordinary things a girl in my position should have known already. . . ."

She smiled at him.

"Of course," she said, "in my case it wasn't anybody's fault. Mine, maybe, for aiming so high above me."

"Baby," Wyche said, "there ain't anything above you—except heaven, maybe, and God's own angels."

"Thanks, Wyche," Fancy said. "Reckon we'd better turn back now."

Back at the house, Court was waiting to take them to the political picnic Jed Hawkins was staging for the Negroes. They got into the buggy and drove down to the Terry. Court was right about that picnic.

In that election year of 1894, the white vote was so hopelessly divided that the blacks without knowing it, held the whip hand. But Jed Hawkins was taking care of that. He was running for state comptroller, and he didn't mean to let the colored brethren keep his fingers out of that rich pie.

He had a whole wagon-load of beer, and even a few hogsheads of corn liquor. There were torch-lights all around the picnic grounds, which were packed with a milling throng of black humanity.

They were, Fancy saw, feeling their oats. They were laughing, skylarking, pushing each other. They formed lines to the beer wagon, where a grinning cracker who, had it not been for the necessities of politics, would not have spat upon them, served them foaming glasses of beer.

There was a barbecue going on, too, and Jed, himself, was making a point of heaping the plates of his dark constituents.

Court frowned, looking at it.

"The bastard," he said. "I've been as good a friend to the colored folks as they've ever had in this State. But I don't believe in dropping the line like that. Any time a white man starts getting that damned friendly, it's time for those poor devils to look out. . . ."

"Damned right," Wyche said.

Fancy didn't say anything. She was too busy watching the show. A Negro with a banjo got up on the wagon and began to play. And right away, a crowd of youngsters started to shuffle, and do a buck and wing. They were very good at it, and Fancy enjoyed watching them. But then she saw young Dred standing on the edge of the crowd. His face was something to see. It was filled with disgust. If he could, Fancy realized, he would have killed every one of those dancing youngsters.

She felt afraid suddenly. She had talked to Belle many times, and she knew that Phil's illegitimate son was growing up a rebel, filled with hatred for the system that held him bound to a race for which he felt no kinship, and for the customs of a region that denied every outlet to the pride of manhood he instinctively felt.

"He's going to get hisself kilt!" Belle had wailed. "Oh, Miz Fancy, the whitefolks going to kill him sure!"

Fancy looked around the crowd. There were many whites pres-

275

ent, come, like Court and Wyche and herself, to see the show. She recognized the Ellis brothers. That was bad.

But the banjo playing was over now, and Jed Hawkins climbed up on the wagon. He was in fine form. He told them how important the ballot was. He urged them not to waste it. He cracked bad jokes that had them all roaring.

"I know the problems of you people," he cried; "I've summered and wintered with you! I had a good mother, rest her soul, and she done her best for me. But ever' living thing I know 'bout gitting along with folks—"

He can talk better than that, Fancy thought bitterly. What does he want to talk like a colored man for? Then she knew. It was a trick. Jed Hawkins was full of tricks.

"Ever' living thing, I tell you—I learnt at the knee of my good ole Mammy! Yessir, Aunt Hannah taught me to respect myself, and other people! She was just a little ole black woman with no book-larnin'—but inside her heart, folks, she was just as white as I be! I tell you, my old Mammy—"

He staggered back suddenly, and clapped a hand to his head. When he drew it away, Fancy saw the little stream of blood in the light of the lanterns.

Jed bent down and picked up the stone.

"Who threw this?" he roared. "Which one of you God-damned burr-headed black bastids . . ." Then he caught himself. "Sorry folks," he said; "I thought I was amongst friends. . . ."

"You is!" they called to him. "Here's the one, Mister Hawkins! This damfool little ole yaller nigger, here!"

Fancy saw Dred struggling in the clutches of two powerful blacks.

Court looked at Wyche and nodded. Wyche put his hand inside his coat.

"Come on," he said.

They walked without haste to where the two Negroes held Dred. But when they got there, the Ellises were before them.

"All right boys," Buck Ellis said, "give him to us. We'll learn him."

The Negroes thrust Dred forward. Then Court stepped between Dred and the Ellises.

"I'll take him," he said quietly.

"Now do tell!" Tom Ellis said. "How you Brantleys do stick to-

276

gether! Take up for your own, don't you, Court? Even when what's yourn is half nigger and a bastid."

"I said I'll take him," Court said.

"You'n' who else?" Buck Ellis snarled.

"And me, Buck," Wyche Weathers said. "We don't want no trouble—don't like to see nobody hurt. But if anybody gets hurt, I'll give you just one guess who that body's going to be."

The Ellises fell back, half a step.

"Come along, Dred," Court said.

They moved easily through the crowd. The Negroes opened to let them through. They could hear the white men muttering. But there were ten blacks to every white, and nobody knew exactly what to expect. When Court and Wyche got back to the buggy, Fancy was already in it, waiting.

Court half lifted, half threw Dred into the back of the buggy.

"Now what?" Wyche said. "Them Ellises are going to get themselves a mob together so damned fast that . . ."

"I know," Court said. "Hiberion, first, Wyche. I'm going to give you a horse. You take this fool boy up to the mill. Hide him in the shipping room. Stay there with him until almost train time. Then bring him to the depot by some roundabout way. . . ."

"They'll come to Hiberion," Wyche warned.

"I know," Court said. "I can handle them."

"Oh, Court, no!" Fancy said. "They'll wreck the house! They might even shoot . . ."

"I'm not going to fight them, Fan. I'm going to invite them in—let them search the place. Give them a cock and bull story about sending the boy away with one of the servants . . ."

"That makes sense," Wyche said. "But how are you going to take a niggerboy on the train with you? They'll make a fuss—send him to another car. . . ."

"The conductor won't know Dred," Court said. "Who's going to tell him the boy's colored?"

That was true, Fancy realized. Even with his dark olive complexion, Dred was much more white than black.

She looked at the boy. He was crying very softly.

"Dred," she whispered, "why did you do that?"

"Could of said my ole colored nurse, Miz Fancy!" Dred sobbed.

277

"Didn't have to call her his ole black Mammy. They always calls us names—Uncle, and Aunty and boy even when we's a hundred years old! Ole black Mammy, ole black Mammy! Bragging 'bout her heart being white. If having a white heart makes a body act like whitefolks do, I hope to Jesus that mine is black as night!"

"You shut your trap, boy," Court growled. "You've done enough harm."

"Yessir," Dred whispered; "I'm mighty sorry, Mister Court."

Fancy watched Wyche riding away fast on Court's big Morgan, the boy clinging to him, looking so small and pitiful. She couldn't have felt any worse if Dred had been her own child.

She was there beside Court when the Ellises came with the mob. She watched the yard filling up with lean, hard-eyed white men, shotguns slung over the crook of their arms. Buck Ellis had a mule-skinner's whip.

"Bring him out, Court Brantley!" they roared. "Bring out the little yaller bastid!"

Court stepped out on the veranda and faced them.

"He's not here," he said quietly. "I sent him away. Listen to me, men! He's only a child and—"

"He's lying!" Buck Ellis cried. "He ain't had time to!"

Court raised his hand.

"Gentlemen!" he said, "I invite you all to come in. Search the house if you like—and the outbuildings. I tell you the boy's not here."

They came into the house, looking a little sheepish.

"Get whiskey," Court said out of the side of his mouth to Fancy.

She went into the pantry and came back with her arms full of bottles.

"Don't drink it!" Tom Ellis said. "He's trying to give that little nigger time to git away!"

"Hell, Tom," one of the men said, "for a snort of that good bourbon, I'd let most any nigger git away. Some of you boys mosey 'round the place. We'll save your drinks till you come back."

Some of the men moved off. Fancy poured them tumblers full of bourbon.

"Thank you, Ma'am," they said politely. One of them whispered to her:

"We warn't going to kill him—jest tan his hide a little to teach him some sense."

Fancy didn't answer. Then the others came back.

"He ain't here, boys," one of them said.

"'Pears to me," Tom Ellis said, "that we ought to hold Court Brantley accountable for gitting him away!"

Court put his hand inside his coat.

"I invited you in peaceably," he said evenly. "I didn't aim to kill a white man over any nigger, not even one I've got some interest in. But this is my house. My wife's here, and my daughter. That's a different story. There's only one of me to a hundred of you. But I'm not going out of this house with you on my own hook. You can take me out feet first, but as God sits in Glory, some of you are going with me—the same damned way."

The men looked at him, indecisively. Then there was a little noise in the doorway. Fancy saw Jed Hawkins standing there, a little white bandage around his forehead.

"Look, men," he said, "as the injured party, 'pears to me I ought to be heard in this matter. . . ."

"Why shore, Jed," one of the men answered, "speak yore piece!"

He sounds relieved, Fancy thought.

"I got a little bump on my head. That ain't proper grounds for a lynching. I'm a Southern white man, and I believe in keeping the niggers in their place. But I ain't taking to heart what one fool kid did—'specially not that kid, 'cause that was his white blood talking. Proud white blood. The best. Let him go. And I won't look kindly on any of you raising a hand against Mister Brantley here. I admire and respect him. And I honor his wife, who is the finest, sweetest lady who ever drew breath! So I'm asking you, as a favor to me, to go home peacefully. Mister Brantley'll send that boy away, and keep him away—won't you, Court?"

"Yes," Court said, "I'll do that, Mister Hawkins."

"Hell, he's talking sense," one of the men said. "Let the little nigger go! I say. Who's with me?"

"Me!" they all cried at once, "I am! Let him go!"

All except the Ellises.

"Have a drink, Jed," Court said; "and thanks. That was mighty white of you."

"Don't mention it," Jed Hawkins said.

The men stayed a half hour longer until every drop of the bourbon was gone. Then Jed Hawkins went away and took them with him.

Wyche brought Dred to the depot through the back streets, but he didn't need to. He could have ridden down the middle of Broad Street itself.

After the train had gone, Fancy stood there with Wyche. She was crying.

"Wyche," she said, "does it have to be like this?"

"Reckon it does, babydoll," Wyche said. "Transplant the same number of Negroes to New York or Boston in proportion to their numbers as we have here and I wouldn't give a fig for their chances. Hell, during the draft riots in New York, in the Civil War, they killed more niggers in one night than we lynch in the South in ten years. Burned a colored orphanage with all the children in it . . ."

"How awful!" Fancy was horrified. "But you sound like you're defending the way we treat them down here."

"I'm not," Wyche said. "I'm just talking about human nature. What in hellfire would happen to those pine-barren crackers if they didn't have the blacks to look down on? They'd go crazy—or revolt; because even European serfs don't live any worse than they do. Having the Negro to feel superior to kind of makes it up to them. I don't hate any man. There're an awful lot of Negroes I'm damned fond of, who're really friends of mine. I'm fond of 'em like I'm fond of my white friends—in exactly the same way, not like these planter aristocrats who have pet Negroes like they have pet hounds. What I mean is I have black friends—like old Maud, for instance, who manage to like me in spite of the fact that my skin's the wrong color from their point of view. But I have to admit that blacks and whites can't really live together. Not now, not ever. A Negro is just too damned physically, visibly different from a white man. Notice I said physically. I've known black boys who were in the first rank intellectually, which makes life damned miserable for them, the poor bastards. . . ."

"Wyche," Fancy said, "you say the strangest things . . ."

"I know. But the main trouble is that the Negro in the mass is actually inferior to the white man in the mass, theories be damned."

"I don't know, Wyche," Fancy said.

"Don't get me wrong, Fan. I know how fond you are of Phil's yard children. I didn't say he was born that way. I sorrowfully and shamefully admit we made him that way. You can break the spirit of a horse. What do you think it does to a bright boy to know it would cost him his life if he ever reared up on his haunches and acted like a man? Being bought and sold like mules did something to them. And even after that was over, the system we worked out to bolster up our uncertain vanities kept up the dirty work. It's like Dred was saying: you don't ever call a black man, 'Mister.' Up to forty-five, he's 'boy'; and after that he's 'Uncle.' The ones you know, you call by their first names—no matter how slightly you know 'em. The women are Mary Jane while they're young, and after that they're 'Mammy' or 'Auntie.' We carry the thing even to such extremes of pure damned pettiness. We put them in places like the Terry—and keep them there. We deny them anything like comfort. Heck, we've got it fixed so they don't even get enough to eat. Then, when they rear up and act like the beasts we've made of them, we lynch them with a barbaric savagery that would disgrace a Sioux. I don't like it, Fan. Never did, never will. A man pulling off his cap and shuffling his feet, and getting off the sidewalk to let me pass doesn't make me feel good inside. Hell, he makes me feel sick."

"Wyche," Fancy said, "we'd better drive by and let his mother know he's safe. Reckon she's nearly out of her mind by now."

"All right," Wyche said.

It was a long time before they could get Belle calm enough to understand them. When they did, she started crying all over again—this time from joy.

Wyche looked at Angel and Delight, and then back at their mother. He didn't say anything for a long time, and when he did, all he said was:

"These kids getting any schooling, Belle?"

"I was sending 'em to Miss Lucy Laney's School on Gwinnett Street," Belle said, "but Mister Phil didn't like the idea. Said too much schooling was bad for 'em."

"You send 'em back."

"Mister Phil won't pay for it, Mister Wyche. Course Miss Laney would take 'em for nothing, but I ain't got the heart. . . ."

"Send 'em back," Wyche said. "I'll pay for it. After they finish there—send 'em somewhere else. Hampton, Tuskegee, Howard. I'll pay for that, too. Then we'll see."

Fancy stood up, and put both her arms around his neck. Then she kissed him, hard. On the mouth.

"Wyche," she said, "you're just about the best man in the world!"

"Do that again," Wyche said, "and I'll turn out to be the worst. Come on, let's get out of here."

He helped her up into the buggy.

"I feel like I've been torn to pieces inside," Fancy said. "Oh, Wyche, I don't think I'll ever be whole again."

"That," Wyche said, "is the South, Fan. That's part of its ancient charm."

When they got back to Hiberion, the house was dark. But when they came up on the big veranda, they heard a noise. Just a little noise—like the creak of one of the rocking chairs. Wyche put his hand inside his coat where his gun was. Then a man came out of the shadows and stood in front of them. Dark as it was, Fancy could see the white of the little bandage around his forehead.

"Fan," Jed Hawkins said.

Wyche took his hand out from under his coat.

"This is one hell of a time," he said grimly, "to pay a call, Jed."

"I know. But I had to see Fan—Mrs. Brantley. It's important, Wyche. Fan, could you spare me ten minutes—just ten—" he looked at Wyche, "alone?"

Fancy stared at him, trying to make out the expression on his face. But she couldn't. It was too dark.

"All right," she said, "come in, won't you?"

The three of them went into the big hall together.

"You'll excuse us, won't you, Wyche?" Fancy said.

"Sure, baby," Wyche said. "You see, I've got two advantages over Court. I ain't married to you. And I know for a fact you can be trusted. However, I can't say as much for this—politician. If you need me, Fan, just sing out."

"I won't need you," Fancy said. "I trust Jed. You go to bed, Wyche."

"In a little while," Wyche said. "After I hear you come up those stairs."

Jed looked at him as he went up the stairs.

"Thank you for what you did, Jed," Fancy said. "That was mighty fine of you."

Jed didn't answer her. He kept looking up the stairway. He looked worried.

"Fan," he said, "what's Wyche Weathers to you?"

"An old friend," Fancy said simply, "nothing more."

"Good!" Jed said. "Lord, but I was worried. Right when I'd found out I had a chance—he had to show up. . . ."

"A chance?" Fancy said. "What do you mean, Jed? You think because Court's out of town—by the way, how did you know that? You must have known, or you wouldn't have come here."

"I was in the depot when the train pulled out," Jed grinned. "Kind of thought he'd put that bastard of Phil's on it. But I was downright surprised when he got on it himself—with a valise."

"And you think that because he isn't here you can—"

"Oh, no," Jed said, "nothing like that, honey. Know you better than that. You wouldn't play that kind of a game. You're too smart."

"Not too good, eh Jed? Just too smart."

"Both, maybe. Fan, look at me. You think that if I needed a casual light o' love—a one-night-stand, I'd come to you?"

Fancy looked at him wonderingly.

"No," she said, "I don't think that, Jed."

"Hell, Fan, women like that are a dime a dozen. But you ain't a dime a dozen. Folks don't know how to count high enough to set a valuation on you."

"Thanks, Jed."

"Don't thank me. Thank God—He made you what you are. The first time I saw you all I could think was: Why in hellfire did that long-tall, no-good, overbred, mangy hound dog of a Brantley have to see her first!"

"Jed, it's awful late. Get to the point, won't you?"

"Just wanted to ask you something, honey. Fan—if something were to happen between you and Court—where would I stand?"

Fancy stared at him.

"But nothing is going to happen between Court and me," she said.

"I wouldn't be too sure of that," Jed Hawkins said.

Fancy took a step toward him so that she could see his face better.

"You know something," she whispered. "Something that I don't. All right, Jed, what is it? Tell me?"

Jed shook his head.

"No, Fan," he said.

"Why not?"

"Against the rules, honey. I don't play that way."

Fancy sighed.

"All right, then—don't tell me." She smiled at him. "Reckon you're something kind of special, Jed. This is the second time tonight you've proved that. First when you took up for that boy, and now when you've got something on Court—something that you think maybe would even break us up, and you won't use it. You're a bigger man than people think, Jed Hawkins."

Jed frowned.

"I ought to let it go at that," he said, "but you're the one person on earth I can't lie to. All right, I do know something. But the reason I ain't going to tell you is not because I'm too honorable. Hell, honeychild, I'd lie, steal, blaspheme, cheat, and abuse orphans to get you. But I'm not going to do this. I'm not because it just isn't smart."

"Why not?"

"I think you'll find out yourself. You're nobody's fool. And I know damn well that if I were the one who spilled it, you'd hate me. You'd think I took unfair advantage of the situation—and you'd be dead, damned right. Which is the only reason I don't take unfair advantage. Which is the reason I'm going to squat my hindquarters right down in a room at the Globe—near a telephone. . . ."

"You think I'd call you?"

"I hope you'll call me. I hope you'll remember that there's a red-headed, freckle-faced son of—of his mother, who loves you more than life, or fear of death or hope of heaven. Who'd never do to you what's being done to you now. Who asks only one thing—that he be given the privilege of spending the rest of his life worshiping you, the way you ought to be worshiped. . . ."

"Thanks, Jed," Fancy whispered; "you—you're mighty sweet. . . ."

"Then you'll call me?"

"I don't know, Jed."

"I'll be waiting," Jed said, and half turned toward the door. Then he turned back, his face working.

"I'd kill that long-tall son of a bitch," he said, "if I thought you'd forgive me for it. If I thought you'd understand. . . ."

"Understand what, Jed?"

"That I was doing it for your sake—not for mine."

"Jed," Fancy said, "I'd better tell you something."

"Speak your piece, honey," Jed said.

"It wouldn't make any difference why you did it—if you harmed Court. It doesn't even make any difference what he's doing. You see, Jed—I love him."

Jed looked at her a long time until it got so quiet that she could hear him breathing. Then he moved, breaking the silence.

"I'll still wait," he said. Then he turned very quickly and went through the doorway without saying anything else at all.

17

Fancy thought about what Jed Hawkins had said. But it wasn't the kind of thing that it did any good to think about. If she kept on brooding over it, she would have to do something: go to New York, maybe, and find out if Court really was at the hotel, and if he were, whether he was there alone. She didn't want to do that. She hadn't been very happy with Court, but she kept on hoping. Maybe things would change. Maybe he would forget Fern. Maybe . . .

But three weeks went by and she didn't hear from him. Not even a postcard. She almost made up her mind that she would go, that even finding out couldn't be any worse than this terrible wondering, but she kept changing her mind until the worry made her sick.

Nerves, she told herself, and dismissed the idea of calling Doc Brewster. But the headaches went on and the sleeplessness until she knew finally that she would have to call him, or she was going to get really sick, the bad kind of sickness—the kind that was inside her mind and heart and would kill her finally, taking a very long time in very bad ways, so she went downstairs into the hall where the tele-

286

phone was. She had even put her hand on the crank when the door-bell rang.

She answered it herself instead of waiting for Ernest to come from the back of the house. Saphira stood there with her husband, Joseph Plainfield. Joe looked so all-fired pleased with himself that Fancy felt like strangling him.

"What's the matter with you?" she said. "You're not becoming a papa at this late date, are you?"

"Nothing like that," Joe grinned. "It's business, Fan. Heck, honey, it's a gold mine, right here in Augusta all these years—right under our noses and we didn't see it!"

"What," Fancy said, "has been right here in Augusta under our noses that we didn't see?"

"The climate, honey! Remember that big old house Major Tully built for Mrs. Tully just before the War? Well, after the Major died, the old lady had to open the house to paying guests. Last time we were here, last February, remember? Me 'n' Saph happened to stop by there to sort of pay our respects. Do you know where most of her guests come from?"

"No, where?"

"New York. Boston. Philadelphia. Rich folks trying to get away from those terrible winters they have up there. One of Court's best friends—man by the name of Woodbury—Stanton Woodbury, is up there right now. Had a talk with him this morning. Of course he's only been there since March, and he's going to have to go back to Boston any day now, but he swears he's going to spend the entire winter down here next year. Didn't Court tell you?"

"No," Fancy said, "he didn't."

"Funny. Mister Woodbury says Court was up to see him a couple of days before he left for New York. They were classmates at Harvard. Appears to me that Court ought to have had him and his Missus out to the house. . . ."

"Well, he didn't," Saphira said, "so he must have some reason not to."

"I don't see your point," Fancy said. "The climate—rich people from the North, and Mrs. Tully's house on the Hill. What's it all about, Joe?"

"Fan, honey—don't you see? It would be doggoned easy to convert that house into a first-class resort hotel. I'm going to dicker with Mrs. Tully. Even if she won't sell, I'm going to ask her to let us put money into expanding it. Build a tennis court, bridle paths, more rooms, a decent lobby. We'd make a million!"

"I would like," Fancy said, "to meet Court's friend."

"That's easy," Joe said. "We're going up there tonight. Mrs. Tully is giving a party for her guests. No reason why you shouldn't come along."

"Think it would be all right, Saph?" Fancy said.

"Of course, darling. We've already felt Mrs. T. out on this proposition—that's why she invited us. As a relative of ours, you'll be more than welcome. So get out your best bib and tucker and come along."

I really don't feel up to it, Fancy thought, but there's something behind Court's not inviting them here. He's not that ashamed of me. I wonder if what Jed . . .

She dressed carefully that night. She put on her dress of rose silk with its bertha of Irish crochet lace. Her hat was trimmed with the same lace and had pink velvet bows. Her belt was made of pink velvet, too, and the dress had heavy pouch-shaped sleeves that the fashion designers called bishop sleeves. They fitted very tight about her wrists above her white gloves. The dress was tight about her hips, drawn in with a yoke made of scallops corded with the pink velvet, but it didn't have any bustle, because after 1890 fashionable ladies didn't wear them any more. The skirt came down to the ground and had deep, inverted box pleats. She looked very nice and she knew it.

Stanton Woodbury knew it too, the minute he saw her.

"Gad!" he said, forcing his bulk up out of the chair, "what a pretty woman! Who the devil is she, Mrs. Tully?"

"Why that's Mrs. Brantley," Mrs. Tully said. "My dear—come here a moment, please—I want you to meet Mister Woodbury."

Fancy came across the floor from where she had been standing with Joe and Saphira, and put out one gloved hand.

"I'm very glad to meet you, sir," she said. "My husband—"

She didn't finish what she had started to say. Stanton Woodbury didn't let her.

"Brantley?" he boomed; "you must be related to Court. Finest

288

chap I know. Friend of mine—has been for years. Often dine at his house on Beacon Hill. His wife's a charming girl."

"You must have the wrong Brantley," Mrs. Tully said. "This is—"

"No, I don't! Court Brantley. Classmate of mine at Harvard. Came from right here in Augusta. Has a textile mill down here—lives here part of the year. Right?"

"Right," Fancy whispered. "Now if you'll excuse me . . ."

"No you don't! I want you to meet my wife. Any relative of Court's is a friend of ours. Oh—Lizzie!"

"Yes, dear?" Elizabeth Woodbury said.

"Meet Miss Brantley—relative of Court's. Beauty, isn't she?"

"She is indeed," Elizabeth Woodbury said. "You're not his sister are you, dear?"

"No," Fancy said, "I'm not. Your husband is—a little mistaken. It's Mrs. Brantley—not Miss."

"Oh, then you must be his brother's wife?"

"No," Fancy said, "I'm not his brother's wife either. . . ."

Mrs. Woodbury looked uncertain. Fancy had answered her questions, but she didn't know anything.

"Just say," Fancy said quietly, "that I'm the wife—of—of a distant relative. But I'm terribly fond of Court. Would you mind giving me his address in Boston? I'm planning to go up there in a few days. . . ."

"Not at all," Stanton Woodbury said. "It's—here, I've got it right in this little book."

"May I copy it, please?" Fancy said.

"Sure thing—go right ahead."

Mrs. Tully didn't say anything. She couldn't. She was in a state close to apoplexy.

"What a strange girl," Mrs. Woodbury said, when Fancy had gone back to Saph and Joe. "Why I do believe she's leaving! And she just got here. . . . There was something odd in her manner, too. The way she answered me, why—"

Mrs. Tully recovered her voice.

"I reckon," she said, "I reckon you'd act odd too, Mrs. Woodbury, if you'd just been told that your husband had another wife in Boston!"

Stanton Woodbury's jaw dropped open.

"You don't mean—?" he said.

289

"That girl is Court Brantley's wife. His lawful wife—unless he married the other one first. But that's not likely, since he's been married to this one for fourteen years."

"The cad!" Stanton Woodbury boomed. "The bounder! And to think, Lizzie, we've entertained them in our home many's the time!"

But Elizabeth was looking toward the door.

"Poor little thing," she whispered. "Poor lost, hurt little thing. . . ."

"Fan, you're the limit!" Joe Plainfield said. "You knew how important this was to me, so what did you do? You got a headache, and have to leave."

"Hush, Joe," Saphira said.

"I lied about the headache," Fancy said. "Just take me to the trolley line, Joe. Then you two go on back."

Joe stared at her.

"If you don't have a headache," he said, "then what the devil ails you?"

"There isn't any word for it," Fancy said. "All I can tell you is how it feels."

"And how does it feel, Fan?" Saphira said.

"A little like dying. No. More than a little."

"Fan, you were talking to the Woodburys. What did they say to you? What did they tell you? Tell me, honey. Don't sit there looking like that. God, Fan, you frighten me."

"Don't be frightened, Saph," Fancy said. "Here's the trolley line now. Go on back to the party. Enjoy yourselves. I—I'll be all right. . . ."

"You're sure, Fan?" Joe said. Even he looked worried now.

"Quite sure," Fancy said.

But when they got back to the party, Saphira and Joe went straight to Mrs. Tully and she told them. Saph gripped Joe's arm, hard.

"We'd better get home, Joe," she said.

"Good God! You don't think that she'd—"

"I don't know. I don't know," Saph whispered. "All I know is that we'd better get moving—fast!"

When they got to Hiberion, they came up the stairs at once without saying anything to anybody. Fancy was in her room, packing.

"Fan, honey," Saphira said, "you're not—?"

"Going up there? Yes, Saph."

"But, darling, what good would it do?"

"No good, Saph. But I've just got to see for myself. I won't do anything wrong. I won't shoot her—though I feel like it."

"Court's the one who ought to be shot," Joe Plainfield said, "or at least horsewhipped."

"And tarred and feathered to boot," Saphira added bitterly. "Oh, Fan, baby, I'm so sorry!"

"Don't be. I'm all right. I'm going to be all right. It—it takes a little getting used to, that's all. . . ."

"But, honey—what are you going to do?"

"Nothing, everything. Leave him, I reckon. He doesn't want me. He never did. I'll get a divorce—so he can have her."

"A divorce!" Saphira said.

"Yes. Shocking, isn't it? They'll be calling me a gay divorcée in town, now, and whispering about me behind their fans. Shooing their men out of my way. And I won't have any friends."

"You," Joe said, "will always have friends, Fan."

"I don't care about that. That's the outside part. It's what's inside that's bad. The remembering. How glad I used to be to see him when he came home from—the North. How I used to fly into his arms. The same arms that had just—turned her loose. . . ."

"Fan, for the love of God . . ."

Fancy put out her hand and let it rest on Saphira's arm.

"You've been good to me, Saph. You always were—right from the first. Thank you for that; and try not to think too badly of me. . . ."

"Of you? It's that hound dog of a brother of mine I'm thinking about! And what I'm thinking would sure Lord curl his hair!"

"Want me to go up there with you, Fan?" Joe said. "In a case like this you need—"

"No, thank you, Joe. I won't need anybody. I'm not going to do anything. Just pay them a little social call. Very politely. We'll sit and chat, and maybe have tea. Then I'll come home—and afterwards I'll go away for a while."

"Away?" Joe said. "Why?"

"To get her divorce, silly," Saphira said. "She wouldn't want to get it here. Think of the scandal!"

"Well, that does it," Fancy said, and snapped the valise shut. "Mind driving me to the depot, Joe? There's a train at midnight."

"Not at all," Joe said.

"Fan," Saphira said, looking at her, "how can you be so calm!"

"Calm," Fancy whispered. "That's the wrong word, Saph. Killed is better."

"Oh, Fan!" Saphira wailed.

Later she looked at them, standing in the garish glow of the electric lights, under the big iron shed of the depot. There was the light, and there was the shadow, and there was nothing in between. Nothing between joy and disaster. Then the train started moving, and the lights jerked backward one by one. Fancy turned and waved at them.

She came up to the brownstone house on Beacon Street in the afternoon, and stood there looking at it. Then she went up to the door and rang the bell.

An Irish girl opened the door.

"Yes, Mum?" the girl said.

"Is Mr. Brantley at home?" Fancy said. Her own voice surprised her.

"No, Mum. Mrs. Brantley either. You want to leave your card, Mum?"

"No," Fancy said. "Have you any idea when they'll be back?"

"Not soon, Mum, you can depend on that. What with Mrs. Brantley being in the hospital, and Mr. Brantley attending the Textile Manufacturers Association meetings, and visiting her between times, there's no telling when he'll be home. . . ."

"In the hospital?" Fancy said. "Is she ill?"

"Oh, yes, Mum! Thought we were going to lose her, sure! And all account of that awful gas jet. She had the window open, and it blew out. Wouldn't have made much difference, only feeling cold, the poor thing, she got up and closed the window, not noticing about the jet. Of course, Bridget—she's our cook, does swear that it wasn't no accident; but, faith, Mum, when you're as old as Bridget, you get to taking queer notions, I do say. . . ."

"But she's better now?"

"Out of danger, the doctors say. 'Twere Terence, our coachman, who thought of sending the Master that telegram. That's Terence, for you, Mum, great presence of mind, I always did say. . . ."

The telegram. That telegram. God, how smoothly Court had lied! But there was one more thing she had to find out. It wouldn't do any good, but she had to know.

"Why," she said, "does Bridget say the—gas was no accident?"

"Because of the quarreling, Mum. But then, married couples always do have their differences, don't they? I'm not the one to put much importance on such goings on. 'Tis a sad life, she's had, though—the poor thing, what with Mr. Brantley being away so much, down there in Georgia among all those heathen Southerners. . . ."

"Yes," Fancy whispered, "I guess her life has been sad, come to think of it."

"Who'll I tell 'em was here, Mum?" the Irish girl said.

"Just—a woman they used to know. A woman called—Fancy. Tell them that. They'll understand." Then she turned and went back down the steps.

"Fancy," the Irish girl said to herself. "Bless me, but that's a funny name!"

On his way to the hospital, Court again had that feeling of being trapped. Fool, he told himself, this was what you wanted—remember? You went through hell when you heard she'd married Ty. Only Ty was the lucky one. He's dead and out of this. . . .

Or maybe I'm being unfair to Fern. Maybe she wouldn't have been like this if things had taken their normal course. This jealous shrew with a viperish tongue. All right—why shouldn't she be? What have you given her, Court Brantley? A precarious hold on the fringes of your life. Months of absence—then a little stolen time granted each year with ever greater reluctance.

All that time alone—no wonder she broods. That explains the imaginary ills, I reckon. My God, her medicine chest should supply a dispensary! She faded so fast, too. Five years older than Fancy—

and you'd swear the difference was fifteen—or twenty. Querulous—quarrelsome. And I can't leave her. Haven't the heart. What would she do now? She gave me her life on a silver platter. Pretty as she was, rich, she could have had almost any man even after Ty died. But now . . .

He shook his head, thinking of it, and went into the hospital. As he walked toward the desk, it came to him that the people who thought the world well lost for love never really reckoned the cost until afterwards. And afterwards was too late.

Fern was propped up on the pillows. She watched him out of the brown eyes that were always opaque now, that always hid something. She was so thin that it hurt to look at her, her skin drawn tight over cheekbones and jaw, the cheeks themselves hollow, and the little web of lines crawling away from the corners of her eyes. Court bent down to kiss her, thinking: Once she was beautiful—once, but she turned her face a little aside so that he only brushed the corner of her mouth.

"Did you bring my things?" Fern said. Her voice was high and harsh. It grated on his ear.

"Yes," he said tiredly.

"You don't seem to be a bit enthusiastic about taking me home," she said.

"I'm just tired, Fern," Court said. "I had a hard day."

"You're tired all right," she said, raising herself up a little, searching his face; "but it's me you're tired of, isn't it, Court? Answer me! Isn't it?"

Court stood there looking at her. But he didn't say anything. He just looked at her.

Then she started to cry.

But Court had seen her cry before. Too many times. That weapon was blunted from over-use.

"Oh, come off it," he said. "Here're your things—get into them. I'll wait outside." Then he turned and marched into the hall.

He could hear her in there, sniffling and sobbing a little, and he knew how her face was going to look afterwards, her eyes red, with puffy lids, and those lips he had wasted so many years dreaming of, would be sullen and moist and trembling. And he hated Fern suddenly with a hatred that was absolutely bottomless, that was equaled perhaps, only by the hatred and contempt he felt for himself.

I should go home to Fan now I should get down on my knees and kiss the hem of her skirt and rise and thank God for so blessing me I should never leave her again no never leave her always stay where she is where goodness is and sweetness and devotion and faith. . . . But I'm trapped. I'm saddled with these the wages of my sin these so heavy wages which are nothing so simple and final and acceptable as death. I loved her wanted her had to have her but it wasn't that easy. Didn't know I would become involved in this clinging endless suffocating battle of wills, this conflict that has no end and no victory. Well, I asked for it. Little Fern. A doll of Dresden china. Pink and white and golden. Lovely. Desirable. Where has she gone? By what alchemy, what metamorphosis did this weeping witch take her place?

Then Fern came out of the room and took his arm.

On the way home they didn't talk. But when they were almost there, Fern reached over and touched his arm.

"That drugstore," she said; "I've got a prescription—something for nerves that Doctor O'Brian gave me."

"Nothing—dangerous?" Court said.

"Oh, no. He took all those awful pills away from me. Besides, darling, I—I wouldn't do that again. . . ."

"You'd better not," Court said. Then he took the prescription and went into the drugstore.

When they got home, she was quiet. She lay back among the pillows, listening while Court read to her. She even achieved a certain wan beauty. Looking at her, he could even remember what she had been like—before. Her brown eyes had lost a little of that pleading, dog-like look that so infuriated him, and a little light showed in them. A little secret glow, as though she had mastered something finally—and was content.

"Court," she said, "ring for Mary, won't you? I'd like a cup of hot tea ever so much."

Court pulled the bell cord, and went back to the novel he was reading to her. It was sickening stuff, but she liked it. It described the last agonies of a woman dying for lost love. . . .

Then Mary came into the room.

"Yes, Mum?" she said.

"Bring me a cup of tea, Mary," Fern said, "like a good girl."

"Yes, Mum, right away, Mum," Mary said, and turned to go. But in the doorway she paused. "Oh, sir," she said, "there was a lady here asking after you and Madame. . . ."

"A lady?" Court said.

"Yes, sir. A very pretty lady. She didn't want to wait. So I asked her her name, and she said the funniest thing. . . ."

Fern looked at Court.

"What did she say, Mary?" Court said.

"She said to tell you she was the woman called Fancy. Said you'd understand. Oh, sir—do people really have names like that?"

"Reckon they do, Mary," Court said. "Now go get that tea, please."

He turned and looked at Fern. The big clock on the mantel ticked, filling the room with the sound. Then, very slowly, Court turned and started toward the door.

"You—you're going to her," Fern said. It wasn't a question.

"Yes," Court said, "I'm going to her. Now. I should have gone long ago."

"And you won't be back."

"No," Court said, "I won't be back."

Fern leaned forward and hugged her own knees. Then she laughed. It was a clear sound, surprisingly strong.

"You're wrong, Court," she laughed. "You're coming back. You're coming back and this time you'll never leave me."

Court shrugged.

" 'Bye, Fern," he said.

But she didn't answer him. She just sat there, laughing.

Fancy sat in the little parlor, watching the door. He's had time enough, now, she thought. Even if he didn't catch the train until the next day, he's had time enough. I could go now. I should go now. But I can't. Not till I've seen him. Not till he's told me why. . . .

Only he won't. The Brantleys never explain why they do the things they do. They don't even know why, maybe. And Court's too stiffnecked to try to explain. Wouldn't do any good anyhow. I wouldn't have him now. Not now—not knowing at last exactly where I stand with him. No. I'm going to walk out of his life as quietly as I came into it. I'm going to take with me precisely what I brought. My clothes, and myself. . . .

So many things I can't take. All the years. The way we felt— or at least the way I felt. Oh, God, oh Jesus—where is he? Why doesn't he walk through that door and . . .

But he didn't come.

Fancy got up and went to the telephone. She turned the crank and gave the operator a number.

"Jed?" she whispered.

"Fan! Fan, baby—you called me! You did call—"

"Yes, Jed—I called you. You were right—on all counts. I found out—and I called you."

"Fan, honey, darling—"

"Wait, Jed—let me talk. Let me say this before I lose my nerve. Jed—I—I'll meet you in Aiken—tomorrow. . . ."

There was a long silence. The wires crackled. When Jed spoke again, his voice was hoarse, and deep.

"For keeps, Fan?" he said.

"Yes, Jed—for keeps."

Then she hung up the phone.

She started to pack, but she couldn't finish it. She felt too sick— too hurt-sick to do anything. She went into Lynne's bedroom and looked at the child sleeping, one clenched fist over her eyes.

I'll miss you, darling, she thought. But you're his—and it's him you love, not me. I can't take anything of his with me when I go—not even the child he gave me. . . . I helped him get all those things, but he doesn't know that or believe it, and was always ashamed of me. He's taught you that, without even meaning to. . . . So, good-bye, my darling—try not to hate me—too much. . . .

She started to cry. Not wanting to wake the child, she went back to her own bedroom and lay down upon the bed and cried all night.

In the morning she was too ill to move, but she dragged herself up and went down and had breakfast with Lynne.

They were eating when Court walked into the dining room.

"Daddy!" Lynne squealed. "You're back!"

Court bent down and kissed her. Then he straightened up.

" 'Lo, Fan," he said.

" 'Lo, Court," Fancy said.

"Lynne, run upstairs for a while," Court said. "Your mother and I have things to talk about."

"All right, Daddy," Lynne said.

They went into the little drawing room.

"Well, Fan?" Court said.

Fancy just looked at him.

"Don't you have anything to say?" Court said.

"What's the good of talking now, Court? It's done. We're finished. We've been finished for a long time. I guess I knew it. But I kept hoping. Foolish of me, wasn't it?"

"No," Court said, "it wasn't foolish, Fan. I kept hoping, too."

"Only it isn't any good any more, is it?"

"I reckon not."

This idiotic conversation, Fancy thought. This solemn talk where we say everything but what we can't say. And what we can't say is sure Lord what we ought to. . . .

"Now what, Fan?" Court said. "What do we do now?"

"You don't do anything, Court. I'm leaving. Now—today. Go and get your Fern—put her in this house. This house I helped you rebuild. And I hope it will haunt her!"

"Fan," Court whispered, "don't go. . . ."

Fancy stood up, looking at him.

"Don't go? Stay here, you mean? Stay and remember—that to you I was always the woman you married by mistake—always the poor white trash you were ashamed of? The one you could slap in the face before all your friends? No thank you, Court. I'm taking nothing with me—except a few clothes. I'm leaving you everything—even the child you've taught to hate me—"

"Lynne doesn't," Court began; but the door flew open and Lynne came into the room.

"Let her go, Daddy!" she cried. "I do hate her! I do! I do!"

"Lynne—" Fancy said.

"I hate you! I hate you! You're wicked! You danced naked on a circus wagon! Tildy Mae says you're nothing but a wh—"

Then Court slapped her, hard across the mouth.

She fell back, looking at him. She stopped crying. She was too surprised to cry.

"You hit me!" she said. "Daddy—you—you hit me. . . ."

"I know. And I'll do it again if I ever hear tell of your speaking to your mother like that. Listen to me, Lynne. Maybe your mother has been strict with you; but right now it appears to me you needed it. Your mother is a good woman, Lynne—the best. Now tell her you're sorry!"

"I—I'm sorry, Mother," Lynne got out, then she ran, wailing, from the room.

Court walked over to the bell cord and pulled it. Ernest came into the room.

"Tell Tildy Mae to come here," Court said.

Then he leaned back against the wall, waiting.

Tildy came shuffling up from the kitchen, her face sullen.

"Yessir?" she said.

"Lynne just repeated some remarks," Court said, "that you made in reference to Mrs. Brantley . . ."

"Lord, Mister Court, I never . . ."

"Shut up! You get your things and get out of here, Tildy. And mighty damned quick, too, or so help me God, I'll take a buggy whip to your black hide. You heard me, get!"

Tildy got.

"Court," Fancy said. "I've been planning to do that for years."

She started toward the stairs.

"Where're you going, Fan?"

"To get my things," Fancy said.

"Fan," Court whispered, "please . . ."

"No, Court."

"Then go, damn you! I'm not going to get on my knees if that's what you want. . . ."

"No, Court—that's not what I want," Fancy said.

Sitting in the hack, on her way to the depot, Fancy thought about it. It had started off cool and quiet, and that was the way she had wanted it. But then it had become ugly. Loud and ugly. Cheap. Funny—marriage was a thing that you went into feeling almost holy about, something you meant to last, that had dignity about it. But when it was broken it always ended like this in very bad and ugly ways that afterwards you didn't like to think about or want to remember.

But she would remember this, she knew that. She would remember it all the rest of her life. It would leave a sickness in her. A hurt that she would one day die of.

When she got to Aiken, two hours later, she went into the lobby of the hotel and asked for Jed. He came down in two minutes and took her by the arm. They came out on the sidewalk together.

It was there that Court Brantley met them.

Fancy couldn't bear to look at his face. But she couldn't turn away. It was bad to look at. A man dying on the inside. Terribly.

He put his hand inside his coat, then Fancy spoke to him:

"Take your hand off that gun, Court," she said. "You have no right to—now."

Court looked at her. At Jed. Jed's face was white. He was shaking.

"How long has this been going on?" Court gritted.

The way Fancy answered him was wrong. She knew that. But Fancy was a woman.

"Wouldn't you like to know," she said.

"I—I haven't a weapon," Jed said. "Give me a chance, Court. You wouldn't . . ."

"Go get one," Court said. "I'll wait."

"No you won't, boy," the deep voice said.

They all turned then and saw Sheriff Bowen standing right behind them.

"Aren't you a little out of your jurisdiction?" Court growled. "This is Carolina, Sheriff—not Georgia."

"Yep, I know that. Can't even arrest you, Court. Hell, son, I don't want to. I didn't come to meddle in your private affairs—though it's a good thing I got here when I did. Warn't even in no hurry until I saw you riding away from the house hell for leather like that. Good horse you got—eighteen miles in a little over an hour and a half. . . ."

Court's face was puzzled.

"Then what did you come for?" he said.

Sheriff Bowen looked at Fancy.

"Hope you'll forgive me, Ma'am, but I got to lock your husband up for something mighty bad. Only I don't want to be the one who has to break the news to you. Court Brantley, you acted right honorable the last time you got in trouble. I'm going to ask you to act that way again. First I'm going to ask you for your gun—not as the sheriff, but as your friend. I got no authority over here, and you don't have to give it to me. But if you don't, I'll have to try to take it. . . ."

Court stared at him.

"Ain't as young as I was, and I reckon you're quicker on the draw than I be. Still, if you don't give me your weapon, I'm duty and honor bound to try to take it."

Slowly Court drew the pistol out and passed it over, butt first.

"Thanks, son. Now I'm going to ask you to step over there, and tell your wife—apart from me and this gentleman, just what you was up to in Boston. She's going to find out, remember. Just rather that you told her."

"I know, Sheriff," Fancy said.

"Mighty sorry, Ma'am. I was hoping you didn't—that even Court here didn't know."

"I don't," Court said, "at least not what you're arresting me for."

"I ain't. Got no right to here. All I'm doing is asking you to step over to the sheriff's office here, with me, and turn yourself in. And you don't have to do that. Only that'll put me to the trouble of going to get him and a posse to hunt you down."

"That won't be necessary," Court said. "But don't you think you ought to tell me what I'm supposed to turn myself in for?"

"On second thought," Sheriff Bowen said, "you could come back to Augusta with me and let me arrest you there. . . . Nope. Better here. Away from all the wagging tongues. . . ."

"Sheriff," Fancy said, "for the love of God!"

"Get to the point, man," Jed Hawkins said. "What for?"

"Murder," Sheriff Bowen said.

"Who?" Fancy breathed.

"Old Matt Vance's daughter. Got a wire from Boston yesterday asking me to apprehend Court, here. Only he hadn't got back yet. Figured there was some mistake so I wired back asking for details. Got 'em this morning—night letter. Yep, pore little Fern's gone all right. Poison. That's how come I knew Court didn't do it. A gun, yep. His big fist maybe—if she got him real riled up. But poison—no. Ain't a man's weapon. A woman. A little effeminate sneak. But not Court Brantley. Still I got to lock him up till this is cleared up. . . ."

Fancy turned to Jed and put out her hand.

" 'Bye, Jed," she said.

Jed took her hand and held it.

"'Bye, Fan," he said. "I could lick everything but this—everything but your God-damned decency . . ."

"Thanks, Jed," Fancy said. Then she put her arm through Court's. "Come on," she said, "let's go turn you in so I can get busy. I've got work to do."

Court looked at her.

"All right," he said.

18

Fancy stood outside the prison and looked at it. It was ugly. Prisons are always ugly, but the Boston jail was even uglier. It was dark, and massive and barred. It had the smell of a prison.

I won't cry, Fancy thought. I won't. But that took some doing. Up until this morning, she had had some hope. Surely, sooner or later, somebody—the judge, the jurors, the attorneys, would recognize the letter Fern had left for what it was: the product of a sick and vengeful brain.

"If anything happens to me, it will be foul play. Arrest my husband, Court Brantley. He has threatened my life several times, as he is in love with a woman in Georgia, and wants to get rid of me. . . ."

Such a flimsy thing. A few words scrawled on a piece of paper by a woman with death already in her. Surely nobody . . .

But they did.

Fancy had thought of everything. She had sent to Georgia for her wedding license, to prove that Fern had lied about that one thing at least. If they could be made to believe that she lied about that, then perhaps . . .

But Court wouldn't let her use it.

"It wouldn't change anything, Fan," he said tiredly. "A man is just as likely to kill his paramour as his wife. Why blacken her name? She's dead. . . ."

And this morning the district attorney had called the pharmacist to the stand. He had recognized Court as the man who bought the sleeping tablets. That did it.

Before now, there had been hope.

Standing there before the prison it hit Fancy, suddenly. She wasn't going to be able to free Court. They, presently, were going to take him out of this grim pile, and hang him by his neck until he was dead.

"Oh, no!" she wept. "No, God, no!"

She could hear the echoes her crying made.

She straightened up suddenly and walked into the prison, her face pale, still. She said the few necessary words to the desk sergeant, and then followed the turnkey down the corridor between the iron barred doors. The turnkey opened the cell door and let her in.

" 'Lo, Court," Fancy said.

" 'Lo, Fan."

He was thin. He hadn't shaved. There was gray in his hair now. A lot of it. Just looking at him was bad.

I won't cry. I won't!

"Fan—Fan, baby . . ."

She ran to him, put her arms around him, feeling his ribs standing out, even under the coarse stuff of the prison shirt.

"It's going to be all right," she said breathlessly. "We'll get some new evidence. We'll . . ."

"No, Fan."

"You mustn't give up, Court! Oh, darling you mustn't. . . . You're all I've got. You're all Lynne's got. Court, isn't there anything you may have forgot? Anything at all that would make them see . . ."

"No, Fan."

She did cry then. Terribly.

Court stroked her hair.

"It's all right, baby," he said. "I had it coming. I'm not guilty of killing Fern. But I'm guilty of worse things: hurting you, being blind, being a fool and a coward. . . ."

304

"You're not a coward—you were always brave and fine and . . ."

"I could shoot a man. I could even face a mob. I've that kind of guts. So does a savage—or an ape."

"Court, please!"

"That kind of courage has always wrecked men and nations, hon. What I needed was the quiet kind of guts—the kind that sticks to what's right in spite of all kinds of temptations. And I didn't have that. I didn't even have sense enough to look at you and to look at Fern and see which of you was real and true fine and which was mighty shoddy goods. Took me two months to find out. But after that, being a Brantley, I was trapped. By pride, by pity, by refusing to admit I'd been taken. . . ."

"That's over with, Court," Fancy whispered, her cheek against his face in spite of his coarse beard. "I only missed being as big a fool by an accident. Don't let's talk about that. Let's talk about the future. Let's think; let's plan. . . ."

"The future," Court said. "There isn't any future, Fan."

"Court, for God's sake . . ."

"Don't let them make Lynne ashamed of me, Fan. Take her away if you have to. Bring her up to be like you—just like you—so damned wonderful that the world will have to kneel at her feet. . . ."

"You mustn't say such things, Court. . . ."

"Oh, yes. I must. I should have said them long ago. Years ago—when I knew already that no man on earth from the beginning of time was ever so blessed. I fretted myself over the mill, over piling up money, while all the time I had a treasure beyond price in the crook of my arm. Took me a long time to see that. I was too concerned with things like where you were born and who your folks were and the way you talked. Tormented you into changing, into imitating the dress and airs and talk of women not fit to kiss your shoe soles. Even that didn't hurt you. It couldn't. What's inside you can never be hurt or broken or dirtied. I don't know what it is. A reflection of Glory, maybe. Some of that kind of fire that burns where God is—the kind that can't burn out. . . ."

"Court—"

"Yes, Fan?"

"It can go out, though. It will—if you let them do this to you. . . ."

Fancy put up her arms and pushed away from him.

"I can," she said. "I don't know what it is yet I'll have to do, but I can—and I will!"

Then she kissed him, hard, and ran to the door. The turnkey opened it and let her out.

She got a hack almost immediately. When she was inside, she gave the driver the address of the house on Beacon Street. Whatever it was that would free Court would have to be there. Something Fern had overlooked. Something she had forgotten.

"There isn't much," Court said wearily, "that I can do about that, hon."

She wasn't that smart, Fancy thought. She was never that smart. She can't win now. You can't let her, God. If You let her drag him down to death after her, what good are You, God? Tell me that. What good?

Mary Jane answered the door.

"Oh, Mum," she said, "ain't it just too awful! Her dead and them aiming to hang the Master, and he never did it. I tell you, Mum— he never!"

Fancy felt something inside her loosen. Here was hope. Mary Jane was on her side.

"Could you let me in?" she whispered, "I want to search the house. Maybe I could find something—anything. . . ."

"I'll do better than that, Mum. I'll help you."

Four hours later, they had to give it up. There was nothing. Fern had been thorough.

Mary Jane made tea for Fancy in the servants' quarters. Fancy was sipping it, without tasting it, without noticing what was around her, too hurt-sick to care when Terence, the coachman, came into the room.

"Good evening, Mum," he said.

"This is Terence," Mary Jane told her. "Terry, we've been trying to find something—anything to prove that the Master was innocent. Do you know, could you tell us . . ."

Terence did a funny thing. He looked quickly over his shoulder. Then he went to the door and looked out, up and down the hall. He came back into the room and bent over close to Fancy's ear.

"Ask Bridget," he whispered. Then he turned and walked out of the room.

306

"Bridget!" Fancy said, "where is she, Mary?"

"In the kitchen. She would know something all right. She and Madame was this close. All the rest of us worshiped the Master. But Bridget hated him. 'Twas her idea that he was unkind to Madame. And Bridget fair doted on Madame. . . ."

But Fancy was already racing toward the kitchen.

"Bridget," she said, "please—I've got to talk to you. . . ."

"I've nothing to say to the likes of you, Mum," Bridget snapped.

Fancy stared at her.

"But," she whispered, "they—they're going to hang him, Bridget! If there's anything you know—anything at all that would help . . ."

"I don't know anything," Bridget said.

She was lying. Fancy could see that.

"You—you'd let an innocent man—die?"

"He let her die—the poor, sweet little thing. And do you know where she died? In these two arms, Mum—while he was off running to your arms—to the arms of his kept woman! Faith, and I hope that they do hang him. 'Tis a pity that they can't hang you, too!"

Fancy knotted her fists so hard that her nails broke against her palms. But she spoke softly. Gently.

"Did he give her those pills?"

"I ain't a-saying," Bridget said. "That's for the law to decide."

They would finish it tomorrow. Tomorrow the defense would sum up its weak plea. Tomorrow the district attorney would be a tower of scorn. The jury would file out. And Bridget stood there with Court Brantley's life in her big, red hands.

Then Fancy had it. The way. It had been there all the time.

"You don't approve of kept women, do you Bridget?" she said.

"Approve! Faith and they should be horsewhipped—one and all!" Bridget said.

Fancy turned to Mary.

"Call Terence," she said.

Terence came.

"Can you drive me to the Vendome?" Fancy said. "I have something over there I want to show Bridget. Something I hope will change her mind. . . ."

"Certainly, Mum," Terence said.

They were back within the hour. Fancy walked straight up to Bridget and laid the scroll of parchment in her hands.

"Read it, Bridget," she said grimly. "Read it aloud."

"Know all men by these presents," Bridget read, "that this twelfth day of August A. D. Eighteen hundred and Eighty, I, Judge J. Lister Harris, hereby certify, that Courtland Brantley and Miss Fancy Williamson were joined in the Bonds of Holy Matrimony, to which fact, attested to by the hereunder signed witnesses, I hereby sign my name, and set my seal. . . ."

Bridget gave the certificate back. She was shaking.

" 'Tain't so," she whispered. "It's a fake, I don't believe . . ."

"Ever seen an official State Seal, Bridget?" Fancy said. "Were you ever married?"

"Yes, Mum. My poor Tim died years ago. . . ."

"Then you've seen a wedding certificate?"

"Yes'm." Bridget's voice was weaker now.

"All right. Court Brantley and I have been married these fourteen years. If necessary, I can bring to Boston these people who witnessed the ceremony. Fourteen years ago, Fern Vance was already married to—Court's brother. Have you ever seen *her* wedding certificate, Bridget? Have you?"

"No'm. . . ."

"You couldn't have, because she hadn't any. You don't approve of kept women, do you, Bridget? Well, who was the kept woman? Who tried to keep my husband away from me, after having tricked him into this ugly relationship that he didn't even want? Who was it that came to his hotel after him—knowing that he had a wife and a child? Who, Bridget? You were talking mighty big a little while ago —where's your brash tongue now?"

"I don't believe it!" Bridget cried. "Her so little and sweet, and doting on him so. . . ."

"Did he," Fancy said quietly, "kill her? Answer me, Bridget—did he?"

"Yes! Anyhow, 'twere the same thing!"

"Ah! The same thing. But it's never the same thing, Bridget. Did my husband give that cheap little cheat you were so fond of—those pills?"

"I ain't a-saying," Bridget said.

Fancy turned to Terence.

"Terence, go call me a policeman," she said.

"You can't!" Bridget said. "There ain't no law . . ."

"Oh, yes—there's a law all right. Material witness. As such you can be held until you decide to talk—to tell the truth. If you don't talk, you can be held for obstructing justice. If you lie—that's perjury —five to fifteen years. Well, Bridget?"

"He—he drove her to it!" Bridget sobbed. "Always a-threatening to leave her and niver come back! She—she asked me for some water—Mary wasn't here—and I saw her open the bottle. I never dreamed she was a-going to take them all. . . ."

"Terence," Fancy whispered, "get me some paper, and a pen. Now Bridget, tell me all about it—just like it happened. I'm going to write it down. Mary and Terence will have to sign it as witnesses. . . ."

"Will they," Bridget got out, "put me in jail?"

"Not if you tell the truth. You'll have to come to court tomorrow and testify there. That's all. . . . Thank you, Terence. Now Bridget, begin at the beginning. . . ."

"I didn't know about that note," Bridget wailed. "Faith and me sainted mother, if I knew that! I only read about it in the papers afterwards. . . ."

But you would have let him die, Fancy thought. She must have had something after all to win such loyalty.

"It's all right, Bridget," she said, "just start talking. . . ."

Afterwards, she was very tired. She was tired all over. The reaction had her. But she had no time to stop. She finally reached defense attorney O'Conner by telephone. Then she walked all the way to the jail, because it was too late to get a cab.

They wouldn't let her see him, of course. It was long after visiting hours. But the desk sergeant took her note in to him.

When she got back to the Vendome, she couldn't sleep. In a few hours now it was going to be tomorrow. There was going to be a tomorrow, now. The sun would come up. Life would go on. Her life.

For that was what Court Brantley was to her, anyhow. Her life— all of it.

END